It had to be a trick. . . . . ted silly standing with a feather duster in his hand, his back to the two brothers.

"Do it," Charlie mouthed.

Bob Ford's throat went dry. But he knew he would never get a chance like this again.

He drew the Smith & Wesson. Jesse heard the hammer click on Bob's gun. He stopped, then started to turn. . . .

No one tried to stop them. It seemed as if everyone was dazed, rattled.

Bob found the telegraph office and bolted inside. He spotted the top-box telephone on the wall. He worked the crank, heard the buzzing in the receiver and finally, above the static, a human voice.

"There's been a shooting," Bob said. "No, I shot him. . . . Yes, I *want* to surrender. . . . For the love of God, man, I've killed Jesse James!"

Praise for Johnny D. Boggs

"Boggs is a master. Every page brings surprises, every chapter crackles with action."

—Bruce H. Thorstad, author of
Deadwood Dick and the Code of the West

"An entertaining Western in the classic mold . . . with interesting stuff on the weaponry of the times." —*Booklist*

"A rib-tickling story filled with traditional Western action."
—*Roundup*

"Action from the first page to the last. . . . The reader has to decide which is the best: the action, the characters, or the setting. This combination is so winning that to make a choice is impossible. Just enjoy it all." —*Rendezvous*

ARM OF THE BANDIT

A GUNS AND GAVEL NOVEL

JOHNNY D. BOGGS

A SIGNET BOOK

SIGNET
Published by New American Library, a division of
Penguin Putnam Inc., 375 Hudson Street,
New York, New York 10014, U.S.A.
Penguin Books Ltd, 80 Strand,
London WC2R 0RL, England
Penguin Books Australia Ltd, Ringwood,
Victoria, Australia
Penguin Books Canada Ltd, 10 Alcorn Avenue,
Toronto, Ontario, Canada M4V 3B2
Penguin Books (N.Z.) Ltd, 182–190 Wairau Road,
Auckland 10, New Zealand

Penguin Books Ltd, Registered Offices:
Harmondsworth, Middlesex, England

First published by Signet, an imprint of New American Library,
a division of Penguin Putnam Inc.

First Printing, November 2002
10 9 8 7 6 5 4 3 2 1

The first thing we do, let's kill all the lawyers.
—William Shakespeare, *Henry VI, Part 2*, Act 4, Scene 2, 75

Prologue

*Our usually quiet city was startled last Tuesday by one
of the most cold-blooded murders, and heavy robberies
on record.*

—*Liberty Tribune,* February 16, 1866

January 28, 1866
Kearney, Missouri

Every time he drew a breath, it felt as if coal oil filled his
lungs. He lay on his back in the bitterly cold loft, grinding his
teeth against the biting pain, gripping a Navy Colt revolver in
his right hand, waiting, listening, perhaps dying.

Well, Jesse James thought, if he did die up here, his family
wouldn't have to dress him in his Sunday-go-to-meetings. In
his black woolen sack suit, best white shirt with paper collar
and black ribbon tie, he felt fit for a pine box. Only a few
hours earlier he had been baptized and accepted as a member
of the Kearney Baptist Church, so he was ready to see those
streets of gold. 'Course, that didn't mean he was willing to go
peacefully. No, the first Yankee to show his face would get a
.36-caliber ball between his eyes, and he would take as many
of those cowardly sons of bitches with him as he could. So
would Frank.

His older brother sat beside him, hunched over in the
cramped confines of the loft, working a quid of tobacco in his
mouth and silently spitting into an old Arbuckles coffee can.
His brother could chew anywhere, anytime, and never get sick.
Dressed in black broadcloth, Frank sat quietly, eyes focused on

the light shining through the cracks in the loft floor, index finger caressing the cylinder of the Remington .44 resting on his thigh.

Jesse could hear the commotion in the farmhouse below: bluebellies yelling that the James boys had been spotted in town this morning, so their mother, if she wanted no harm to come to her boys, had better turn the two guerrillas in . . . and old Ma giving them Yanks plenty of hell, saying that it was a pure-dee shame that a God-fearing woman such as herself had to worry over bluecoats tormenting her and her family on the Sabbath, that as far as she knew her oldest sons were down in Texas, living law-abiding lives, and that the Yanks had won the war, almost over a year now, so why must they and scum-sucking carpetbaggers keep pestering her, a weak, old woman?

Old maybe, but Ma had never been weak. Hell, if Captain Quantrill and Bloody Bill had fifty women with Ma's temperament, them abolitionist vermin and Kansas redlegs would have been the ones begging for quarter.

Listening to his mother's pleading above the squawking hens, Yankees cursing and younguns crying below, Jesse felt his hand tighten against the revolver. Just because he had ridden with Quantrill, those bluebellies would never let Frank and him live in peace. They'd hang them both, then laugh at Ma's tears. It wasn't enough that Jesse himself had taken that damned oath of allegiance; now he wished he had never taken the pledge. Back in May, after word came that William Clarke Quantrill had been mortally wounded by federal troops in Kentucky and Bobby Lee had surrendered over in Virginia, Jesse and some of the boys decided it was time to bow to the damnyankees. They mounted up and rode to Lexington, but a bunch of drunken bluecoats opened fire, leaving Jesse to die with a bullet in his lung.

He had spent the night in Taho Creek and crawled the next morning onto the road, where a farmer happened by and took him to a hotel. Lying in a bed there, waiting for Ma, he pledged his loyalty to the Union, just as Frank had done. Bluecoats had forced his mother and stepfather from their Clay County home to Nebraska during the War, but they came back to Missouri upon hearing word that Jesse was shot and dying.

Frank came, too, put Jesse on a steamboat in Harlem, just north of Kansas City, and took Jesse to Nebraska to die or get better.

That was where Jesse saw his cousin, Zerelda Amanda Mimms. She had the same name as Ma, so he started calling the pretty gal Zee. An angel was this Zee Mimms, nursing him, spoon-feeding him, even shaving him. Anybody else, and he would have felt embarrassed, would have raised holy hell at not being strong enough to tend himself, even needing help with the damned chamber pot. With Zee, however, he really didn't mind.

By the fall, Jesse knew he was in love with his cousin and could tell she loved him, too. Maybe that was why Ma decided it was time to take him back to Missouri. She kept telling him it was because he didn't want to die in some damnyankee state like Nebraska, but Jesse knew better. First cousins shouldn't ever feel that way about each other, but Jesse figured God would look after him and Zee, wouldn't mind if they got married.

Only, he thought as he shivered in the loft, where was God now? Since that Yankee ball had collapsed his lung, Jesse had read the Good Book cover to cover he didn't know how many times. Maybe God was testing him, or telling him something. Yeah, sending him a message. Jesse kept seeing himself on that dun horse he rode, kept thinking God was speaking to him with that verse in the Revelation of St. John the Divine:

> And I looked, and behold a pale horse: and his name that sat on him was Death, and Hell followed with him.

Well, if he lived, he would show those damnyankees hell.

February 3, 1866
Watkins Mill, Missouri

At first, Frank James thought his brother daft to suggest meeting Cole Younger and Arch Clements at a place as busy as the woolen mill on the first Saturday of the month. As he helped

Jesse off the dun gelding, however, he began to see the logic to it all. Gray-bearded Waltus L. Watkins himself had just passed the two James brothers on his way to the three-story brick factory he had built five years back, and the old man had grunted a barely inaudible "mornin'" without taking a second look. Folks from all over Clay County and across central Missouri had descended upon the mill like locusts to shop. With so many people coming to buy shawls and blankets, plus plenty more visiting Watkins's sawmill, gristmill and blacksmith shop, Frank, Jesse, Cole Younger and Little Arch Clements would be lost in the crowd.

The James brothers tethered their horses in front of the smithy's and took a seat on a makeshift bench against the wall, giving them a clear view of the road. Cole Younger and Arch Clements were already there, Cole nonchalantly whittling a stick and Clements cleaning wax out of his ears with a bony index finger.

They looked like a circus act, Frank thought as he opened his pocketknife and began carving the tobacco plug—Cole the giant, and Clements the midget. Cole Younger stood a good six feet tall, the same height as Frank, but while Frank was rail thin, Cole was built like a strapping mule. His face was sunburned, and his mustache and whiskers had a trace of red while a black slouch hat hid his dark hair. He wore a linen duster, high-topped black boots, blue overalls and a gold ring on his left pinky. At two hundred pounds, Cole looked strong enough to work hours upon hours at either the woolen mill or the blacksmith's. Blond-haired Arch Clements, on the other hand, was a short, wiry cuss apt to be blown all the way to Carthage by a stiff north wind. His blue eyes darted nervously, and ears now cleaned to his satisfaction, he kept fidgeting with his cheap satinet coat and Kentucky cloth breeches.

They were good men, though, and had proved themselves time and again against redlegs and Union trash in countless fights during the War.

"How's that beautiful mother of yourn?" Cole asked as Frank and Jesse settled in beside the two men.

Frank stifled a laugh lest it upset Jesse. Beautiful? Hell,

Frank James loved his ma but would be the first to admit she was a good inch taller, twenty or thirty pounds heavier and uglier than Cole Younger. "Fair to middling," he answered. "How you doing, Archie?"

Clements began a tirade against the Yankees, cursing them every which way and taking the Lord's name in vain, which didn't set well with Jesse since his baptism. Frank half expected his brother to try to thrash Clements—although he wouldn't stand a chance with his weak lung—or at least tell him that he could say *bastard* and *sumbitch* all he wanted but had best remember the third commandment with women and children present. Instead, Jesse's head bobbed as he said, "Yankees ain't a-gonna let us live in peace on this earth."

That got things down to business.

"What you got in mind, Dingus?" Cole asked.

Frank smiled at Jesse's moniker. During the War for Southern Independence, Jesse, no more than a boy, had been cleaning an old .44-caliber horse pistol when the heavy hammer accidentally slipped and slammed into his left hand, pinching off the tip of his middle finger. He flew into a rage, hurled the Dragoon across the guerrilla camp and swore, "That Colt's the dodd-dingus pistol I ever laid eyes on." Dingus stuck, even to the point that Bloody Bill Anderson had once blurted out, before most of his army, "Dingus, the hell's your real name, anyhow?" to the delight of the boys.

Jesse glanced over both shoulders, making sure no strangers were close before pulling a wadded-up newspaper from his coat pocket. Clements, sitting closest to Jesse, leaned forward as Jesse unfolded the *Liberty Tribune*, which wasn't much of a newspaper, but then Liberty wasn't much of a town. DEVOTED TO POLITICS AND GENERAL NEWS the *Tribune* masthead proudly proclaimed.

When Jesse tapped the top left-hand corner of advertisements, Arch Clements straightened and said, "Hell, Dingus, you want us to rob a boot-and-shoe manufactory?"

"Not the cobbler's advertisement, you idjit," Jesse shot back over Frank's and Cole's chuckles. "This one." He jabbed his finger at the first ad in the second column.

CLAY COUNTY SAVINGS ASSOCIATION.

Directors,

James M. Jones,   Alex J. Calmott,

Wm. Baining,   James Love,

ALEX J. CALHOUN, President.

G. Bird, Cashier.

THIS ASSOCIATION, Chartered with Banking privileges by the Legislature of Missouri, continues to do business with customers upon the most liberal terms.

Exchange upon St. Louis and the Eastern and Northern Cities, Bought and Sold.

Liberal prices paid for Government Vouchers, Clay County Rail Road Bonds, County and City Warrants and other public securities.

Uncurrent and mutilated Bank Notes purchased at fair prices.

Discounts, upon time, made upon undoubted collateral security, or mortgage upon unencumbered real estate.

Gold and Silver, Union Military Bonds and Defense Warrants bought and sold.

Revenue Stamps and Fractional Currency kept constantly on hand.

Deposits, general and special, received and secured by double fire- and burglar-proof vault and safe.

Deposits Received and Paid Out Without Charge.

Farmers, Mechanics, Merchants, Professional Men, Administrators, Guardians and business men generally, are invited to open accounts with the Association under the belief that they will be benefited thereby.

OFFICE—Banking House formerly occupied by Farmer's Bank, Northeast corner of the Public Square.

Business hours from 9 A.M. to 3 P.M.

Clements read the ad before passing the newspaper over to Cole, who had folded his pocketknife and pitched his whittling stick at his feet. "Why this particular bank?" he asked after a minute.

"Yankee money," Jesse answered, spitting. "'Sides, I ain't forgettin' what them high and mighty Liberty men said 'bout us and Cap'n Quantrill. Called us 'monsters of society,' they did."

Frank could tell Cole Younger was none too happy, so he decided it was time to pipe in. "It's far enough from our homes that we won't likely be recognized, Cole. We can slip in and light a shuck for home like nothing happened. The way Dingus has things figured out, we'll make ourselves seen away from Liberty and get a few alibis going in case we're ever suspected. And, Cole, there's a hell of a lot of money and bonds floating in that bank. You gotta admit, them damnyanks owe us something for all the misery they've put our families through."

Picking up the paper, Younger seemed engrossed in the account of the arrest of Confederate admiral Raphael Semmes. Frank deposited a mouthful of tobacco juice in front of his boots, wiped his mouth with the back of his hand and watched the latest arrivals: a rickety farm wagon hauling a balding farmer, tired wife and passel of kids. Frank had ridden into Liberty a few days ago, changed a ten-dollar bill and left. Jesse's plan would work, but he certainly wouldn't want to try it without Cole Younger at his side.

"'Deposits,'" Cole read, "'general and special, received and secured by double fire- and burglar-proof vault and safe.'" Lowering the paper, he asked, "If you got everything figgered, Dingus, how we gonna blow that safe open and light out of there before the whole town comes down on our heads?"

Jesse answered with a grin, "We ain't a-gonna have to blow that vault 'cause it'll be opened already. We'll just ride in all friendly-like early in the afternoon and make a withdrawal."

"In broad daylight!" Cole roared. Frank glanced around nervously, but no one paid them any attention. "Hell's bells, Jesse James, what kind of harebrained scheme you talkin' 'bout? You can't just rob a bank in the middle of the day. It ain't never been done."

"That's right. We'll be the first."

Cole shook his head, tossed the *Tribune* to Clements and stared at Frank. "You a party to this nonsense, Frank?"

"It'll work, Cole," Frank said calmly. "I scouted things myself. The Good Lord didn't shortchange Dingus when it come to brains, old friend. Yeah, it ain't never been done, not counting in the War, but that don't mean it can't be done."

Twisting his scraggly beard, Clements decided to join the debate. "It'll take an army," he said.

"Boys we can trust," Frank agreed. "Boys who know their way around this country."

"Bud and Donny Pence," Cole offered. Frank felt relieved; Cole was in. "Sure my brother-in-law will ride with us. He ain't never met fear's acquaintance. The Sheperds. Red Monkers maybe, and Joab Perry."

"Need fourteen or so, I'm a-thinkin'," Jesse said. "Now here's the way I got it worked out."

"And nobody dies," Frank said urgently. "We don't kill no one if we can help it."

February 13, 1866
Liberty, Missouri

Colder than a witch's teat.

Dingus hadn't figured a blizzard into his plan, but the way the snow was blowing and the wind howling, a major storm seemed imminent. Frank James and Cole Younger reined in their mounts, pulled up the collars of their Billy Yank greatcoats, dismounted in front of the brick building and loose-reined the well-trained horses.

The weather, however, might be a blessing. Liberty's streets were practically empty except for several men in slouch hats and light blue greatcoats, and Frank knew those men well. Plus, he had read about some sort of trial going on at the courthouse, and criminal cases always attracted a crowd in this neck of the woods. Around here, folks were likely to find more entertainment in *The State of Missouri vs. John Smith* than *A Midsummer Night's Dream*.

As Cole Younger reached for his pocket watch, Frank stamped his feet against the boardwalk to get the blood circulating again while finding familiar faces across the public square. The Sheperd brothers, Oll and one-eyed George, stood in front of the hitching post by the courthouse, smoking cigars and bouncing on the balls of their feet to stay warm while Frank Gregg checked the cinches. John Jarrette, Cole Younger's nervy in-law, had ridden in from the northwest, along with Red Monkers and Allen Parmer, and they were letting their horses drink from the water trough across the square. Little Arch Clements and Bud Pence walked toward the bank; Frank saw their mounts tethered at the corner. Donny Pence, Bill Wickerson and Ben Cooper waited just outside of town. Reinforcements, Dingus had explained. Everyone was in place.

Except Dingus.

He wasn't up to this, not yet anyway, not with his lung. He wouldn't have been able to stay in the saddle at a canter, let alone a gallop, so Frank had forced him to stay behind, back at Ma's farm, where she could look after him. He'd get his share of the spoils.

"Reckon it's 'bout that time," Cole Younger said. Frank nodded and followed his friend into the Clay County Savings Association.

They pulled off their gloves and warmed their hands over the stove in the lobby while studying the two bank officials—a short bespectacled gent in suspenders, puffed tie and sleeve garters and a teenager chewing on the end of a pencil—sitting at desks across the counter. The Regulator clock read one fifty-seven.

"Warm yourselves, friends," the older man said casually. "Let us know if we can help."

Cole Younger nodded, whether to Frank or the cashier, Frank couldn't tell. After stuffing his gloves inside his gunbelt, Frank walked to the counter, spurs jingling against the hardwood floors. He pulled a greenback from his vest pocket and announced, "Like to change this."

"Certainly," said the long-legged boy, rising and covering the distance from his desk to the counter in four strides. He had just stopped and was reaching for the bill when Frank drew his Remington and shoved the long barrel in the kid's face.

"What in—"

"Shut up," Frank said. "Do as we say and you might live through the day."

The older cashier shot up from his desk, started saying something about leaving his son alone, but Cole Younger hurdled the counter, cocked his revolver and pointed it at the man, who fell silent.

"You're gonna fill these bags with all the money in this establishment," Frank ordered, pulling two flour sacks from beneath the greatcoat and tossing one to his partner. The boy just stood there like an oaf, so Cole slammed the Colt's butt into the small of the boy's back.

"Damn your hides, be quick!"

The older cashier still stood, trembling. "What . . . what . . . what are we supposed to do?"

It struck Frank as downright comical. No one had ever tried robbing a bank in broad daylight, except during the war, so who knew what they were supposed to do? Frank wasn't certain himself. "Just be quiet," he said, holstering his pistol because the man and his son weren't likely threats. He began filling a flour sack with coins.

Cole used the gun barrel to gesture the teen over, and the two disappeared inside the green vault. Frank picked up a black tin box and waved it at the older cashier. "What's in this?" he demanded. When the man faltered, Frank swore, drew his Remington and said, "Damn it, mister, you tell me what I want to know or I'll blow your head off."

The wall clock chimed twice.

"Government bonds," the man said.

Grinning, Frank tossed the box in his sack. "How about bearable stamps?"

"No," the man said. "They're not . . . due in till . . . Thursday."

He was lying, but Frank didn't have time to force the matter. Cole was already shouting for the older cashier to come inside the vault. He obeyed, and Cole stepped out with his bloated sack and slammed the vault door, leaving the two men inside. Frank grimaced. The vault was on a time lock. He didn't know when it could be opened, but it would likely be tomorrow, which meant the man and his son might suffocate before they were freed.

They hurried outside, where the riders were waiting, already mounted. Frank handed his bag to George Sheperd while Cole gave his to John Jarrette, and pulled himself into his saddle. Frank was gathering the reins to his roan when the cashier cried from the window. "The bank's being robbed! Bushwhackers are robbing the bank!"

Arch Clements picked that moment to draw his revolver and fire over his head. Frank swore as his horse shied from the noise. The snow began falling harder, and he could make out new faces on the town square, faces of confused townsmen. He cursed his spinning horse, cursed Arch Clements for shooting, cursed his partner for not locking that damned vault.

"Get off the damned streets!" It was Cole Younger. "Get off the damned streets, you fools! Don't get yourselves kilt!"

Someone else fired, and another joined in.

"Stay where you are!" John Jarrette screamed, and Frank saw the two boys standing in front of the Green House just across the street. One of the kids, his face masked with bewilderment, stepped onto the street. Cursing, Little Arch Clements emptied his revolver at the boys.

"Son of a bitch!" Frank said, and gave up trying to put a boot in the stirrup. He gripped the horn tightly and swung into the saddle as his horse loped out of Liberty, followed by Cole and the rest of the gang. The last thing Frank saw was one of the boys Arch Clements had fired at, facedown in a patch of scarlet snow.

February 17, 1866
Kearney, Missouri

"'We hope to God,'" read Dingus, his face beaming, "'the villains may be overhauled, and brought to the end of a rope. Indeed we cannot believe they will escape.

"'The murderers and robbers are believed by many citizens, and the officers of the bank, to be a gang of old bushwhacking desperadoes who stay mostly in Jackson County. But it makes no difference who they are, or what they claim to be; they should be swung up in the most summary manner. . . .'" He broke out laughing, folded the *Tribune* and shook his head.

"They ain't got a clue," he said.

"Nope," Frank said, and thanked God.

"The bank's put up a five-thousand-dollar reward, and I see where the other bank in Liberty has offered another two thousand. Maybe we shoulda robbed both banks. How much did we get?"

"About twenty thousand in coin, fourteen thousand in greenbacks and yellowbacks and, by my count, forty-two thousand in U.S. negotiable bonds," answered Frank, still amazed at the take. Even with the fourteen-way split, it was a right smart amount of money, more than he had ever seen.

"No stamps, though, right?"

"No stamps."

"We can still cash some of 'em. Red knows this fella over in Ohio who'll pay for those bonds." Dingus laughed again. "Big brother, I told you it would work. Went off without a hitch."

"I wouldn't say without a hitch, Dingus. Arch shot that one boy dead. Jolly Wymore. Comes from good stock, I hear. He was going to William Jewell College. Dingus, Pa helped start that school."

The glory left his brother's face. "Yeah," he said somberly. "That was a shame. I'll write his folks, send our condolences. Not admittin' to nothin', just a-tellin' 'em how sorry we was to hear." He couldn't keep a sad face long before the ecstasy returned.

"The way I got things a-figgered, brother," he said, "is that we had too many boys. Half that number'll work. More money for ever'body. You think Cole'd be game for another job? I know Archie is. He was a-tellin' me so just last night."

"What the Sam Hill are you talking about, Dingus? Another robbery? Hell, we just stole seventy-six thousand dollars."

His brother had the look again, the one Frank had seen so many times in the eyes of Bloody Bill, Arch Clements and plenty of redlegs and Rebels alike. The look of death.

"We've just started the ball," Jesse said icily.

Part I

Chapter 1

*The rebellion had also given birth to a horde of
adventurers, who for years afterward infested the
country, and preyed with systematic rigor and success
upon the honest industry and frugal enterprise.*
    —Allan Pinkerton, *Thirty Years a Detective,* 1884

January 24, 1881
Kansas City, Missouri

William H. Wallace settled into the leather chair behind the cluttered desk in his Kansas City office. He preferred to work there rather than in his small room at the county courthouse in Independence. Duly-elected prosecuting attorney of Jackson County. He still found it hard to believe, because only five years ago he had been a struggling lawyer and former schoolteacher. Even more shocking was the fact that during his campaign he preached temperance and closing the Kansas City saloons on Sundays, and he promised not to cower before bushwhackers and guerrillas. "The time of the outlaw in Missouri has ended," he had said. "I will promise the James brothers a fair trial, but justice will meet them. Citizens cannot continue to live in abject fear of these bandits. I stand for law and order."

They voted him in, but he wondered if they really believed him.

After draining the last of his coffee, he opened the nearest, and thickest, folder, a collection of newspaper clippings, affidavits, police and Pinkerton reports titled SUSPECTED CRIMES OF THE JAMES-YOUNGER GANG.

February 13, 1866, Clay County Savings Association, Liberty, Missouri: They hadn't been suspected at first, but later it became clear that Frank and Jesse James, Cole Younger and a number of others had robbed the bank of between $50,000 and $80,000 and killed an innocent bystander. Bank officials paid customers sixty cents on the dollar before going out of business. Archie Clements, suspected in the robbery as well, was shot dead in Lexington on December 13 of that year when Major Bacon Montgomery and his soldiers tried to arrest Clements and his gang of cutthroats. Attempted arrest? Wallace laughed. Clements had been shot more than thirty times.

October 30, 1866, Alexander Mitchell and Company Bank, Lexington, Missouri: The take had been a mere $2,011, but no one could tell if the Jameses and Youngers had been involved in this robbery, or if it had been the act, as one newspaper claimed, of "Kansas redleg robbers."

March 20, 1868, Nimrod & Co. Bank, Russellville, Kentucky: The gang made off with $12,000, but Oliver Sheperd was killed resisting arrest and George Sheperd was caught, tried, convicted and sent to prison for three years. The James brothers and Cole Younger were likely in on the job, but this one was out of Wallace's jurisdiction.

December 7, 1869, Daviess County Savings Association, Gallatin, Missouri: After this bloody affair, the James brothers became suspects for the first time and would later be linked to the robberies in Russellville, Lexington and Liberty. The bank president, John W. Sheets, had been murdered, clerk William McDowell wounded, and the killers rode off with $700.

Wallace thumbed through the other documents. A bank in Corydon, Iowa, on June 3, 1871, with $40,000 taken . . . another bank in Columbia, Kentucky, on April 29, 1872, in which a cashier had been killed and $15,000 lost . . . $4,000 robbed from the Ste. Genevieve, Missouri, bank on May 27, 1873 before the outlaws turned to robbing trains.

WAYLAID BY KU-KLUX
DIABOLICAL ATTEMPT TO WRECK
A NIGHT EXPRESS TRAIN
ENGINEER KILLED, ENGINE DITCHED
AND TENDER AND BAGGAGE CARS CRUSHED

Wallace glanced at the cutout of the article in the July 23, 1873, edition of the *St. Louis Daily Globe* detailing the Iowa robbery of the Chicago, Rock Island and Pacific train. He sighed and read on about the train robberies at Gad's Hill, Missouri, and Muncie, Kansas, in 1874, a bank in Huntington, West Virginia, in 1875, and another train in Otterville, Missouri, on July 7, 1876. The James-Younger Gang had been so successful, they inspired a slew of copycats: a Richmond, Missouri, bank in 1867; the daring Kansas City Fair box office of seventy-two; a stagecoach in Hot Springs, Arkansas, and two omnibuses in Lexington, Missouri, in seventy-four; and a bank in Corinth, Mississippi, later that year. Or maybe it had been the Jameses and Youngers who robbed the fair and other outlaws had robbed the train at Gad's Hill. Who knew?

Pinkerton agents had been killed, and the law never caught a break until townsmen of Northfield, Minnesota, and outlaws got shot to pieces on September 7, 1876. The Youngers had been captured, Clell Miller, Bill Chadwell and Charley Pitts gunned down, but Frank and Jesse James escaped. Those taciturn Youngers, serving life sentences by pleading guilty to avoid the rope, wouldn't even admit that the James boys had been with them.

Things had quieted after Northfield, but now it seemed as if the James Gang was back in business. A Chicago & Alton train had been robbed near Glendale on October 7, 1879, and they'd strike again. Sighing, Wallace closed the folder, thinking maybe he shouldn't have made such bold promises. The James Gang had been roaming the country since 1866. Fifteen years. Not a bad career in their line of work. How could he think he could stop them?

Wallace removed his reading glasses and rubbed his tired eyes. When he looked up, a curly-haired girl in shirtwaist, bonnet and over-gaiters stood nervously in the doorway to his office. The freckle-faced redhead had to be in her early teens.

"May I help you?" he asked, rising, wondering how long she had been standing there.

She started to say something but stopped, squeezing the change purse in her tiny hands, licking her lips, trying to summon up enough courage to speak.

"I am William Wallace," he said. Nothing, so he tried another tactic. "Where are your parents?"

"Shoppin'," she said hesitantly. "Told 'em I'd meet 'em at the Empire Clothin' Comp'ny."

"That's across from Market Square, on Main Street. If you're lost, I can ask one of my—"

"I ain't lost, mister. I know my way round this city. Come to see you. My name's Lizzie Wymore of Liberty, Missouri."

"Well, Miss Lizzie Wymore of Liberty, Missouri, how old are you?"

"Turned sixteen on Christmas."

"A belated happy birthday. And how may I—"

The name struck him suddenly. Wymore. Freckle-faced Lizzie had to be the sister of the teenage boy killed in the streets of Liberty during that bank robbery in sixty-six. He rounded the desk and escorted his visitor to the couch, where he sat beside her.

"You would be George Wymore's sister?" he asked gently.

"Jolly. Ever'body called him Jolly. Only Mama an' Papa called him George." She sniffed, shook her head and the floodgates opened. "Leastways, that's what they always tells me. See, I was only a baby when Jolly got kilt. Jolly took the buckboard to town, to go to school. It was cold, snowing something fierce—leastways, again, that's what I always hear. My brother had on this coat he got for Christmas, cost Mama fifteen whole dollars. Can't tell you how many times I've spied on Mama an' seen her cryin' over that coat. They buried him in something else 'cause it was all covered in blood. You can put your finger through the hole of the bullet that kilt him. Here." She opened her purse and pulled out a button. "I took this offen Jolly's coat. Mama won't notice. She don't hardly notice nothin' no more. I want you to have it."

"Miss Wymore . . ." Wallace began as he fingered the big black button.

"I know, I know, you think I'm just a dumb girl, but I ain't. I come here to give you that button 'cause I wants you to carry it round with you. I wants you to remember what them outlaws did to my brother. I read in the newspapers 'bout your election, all 'bout you saying you'd bring them rowdies to justice. I'm holdin' you to it, mister. Ever' time you touch that there button, I want you to know what it means to my folks to see justice done. I got nine brothers an' sisters still livin', Mr. Wallace." Tears rolled across her freckles. "Would to God I had ten."

He slipped the button into his trouser pocket and smiled lamely. "Thank you, Miss Wymore, but I hate to inform you that the Liberty robbery is outside my jurisdiction. I am solicitor of Jackson County. Your hometown lies in Clay County."

"I know that. But the law back home ain't got no plans to even try to bring the James boys to justice. I figger you does."

He thanked Lizzie Wymore again before escorting her out of his office. "You jus' catch that Jesse James," she told him before disappearing on the crowded sidewalk. "You jus' do your job."

If I ever get a chance, he thought, absently feeling the button in his pocket, *I most certainly will.*

September 28, 1881
Independence, Missouri

When that imbecile of a jury foreman announced the unanimous verdict, Major John Newman Edwards groaned. He must not have been the only one, either, because the next thing Edwards heard was that uppity judge's gavel banging like the musketry of gallant Rebels fighting tyrants during the late War for Southern Independence at battlefields consecrated by Missouri blood such as Wilson's Creek. *Banging like the musketry of gallant Rebels* . . . He liked that a lot—it flowed, like much of his seamless prose—so he wrote it down next to the word his pencil had just scratched.

Guilty. Edwards couldn't believe it. Twelve men in Jackson County had found a member of the James Gang guilty. Bill Ryan had been well in his cups when he started raising hell in Nashville and found himself arrested. That hotshot attorney from Kansas City, William Wallace, did a little investigating, figured out who the drunken lout was, got Ryan extradited from Tennessee and put the man on trial here in Independence for the glorious—some James haters called it "nefarious"—Glendale train robbery of seventy-nine. Folks across the state, and Edwards was one of them, thought the lawyer mad. You couldn't convict a member of the James Gang for anything, and if you tried, you'd wind up deader than dirt. Besides, Mr. High-and-Mighty William Hockaday Wallace didn't have that much evidence.

It was all Tucker Bassham's fault. The blowhard was serving ten years in Jefferson City when Wallace and the governor managed to pardon the oaf in exchange for testimony against Ryan. Edwards swore he would never call that lout Tucker again; *Judas* Bassham seemed much more appropriate.

Ryan's lawyers informed the court of their attention to file a motion for a new trial, but no one cared. Wallace was too busy with the mandatory handshakes, and the deputies were escorting one pale-looking Bill Ryan to jail. Edwards stuffed his writing tablet and pencil inside his coat pocket before making his way out of the courtroom.

He wondered what Jesse and Frank James would think. Edwards knew the James boys, liked everything about them, their daring, their brand of justice. Some of those newfangled squirts who called themselves journalists said reporters should be impartial, but John Newman Edwards didn't cotton to such a falsity. Impartiality and fairness led to dull newspapers, and no one had ever accused John Newman Edwards of being dull. Folks called him "the Victor Hugo of the West," and had been doing so since shortly after the "lost cause."

Times were changing, he thought, for him as well as Missouri. Gone were his flowing beard and much of his hair, although he still sported a walrus mustache. He had put on some weight over the years, too, but hadn't forgotten how to make a statement with his wardrobe: striped breeches tucked in Coffeyville boots, red shirt, plaid scarf, green brocade vest and gray frock coat with velvet collar, topped with a high-crown black hat. He pulled a flask from a coat pocket and took three pulls, but once William Wallace exited the Independence courthouse, Edwards exchanged his flask for his writing tablet and pencil.

"An interview, Mr. Wallace?" he asked the solicitor.

Mr. High-and-Mighty almost laughed. "You, Major Edwards, would dare be seen with the likes of me? I thought you just made up your quotations."

"Sarcasm does not suit you, sir. Just a few questions. I'll buy you a celebratory drink, too." He nodded to the nearest saloon, which would serve another purpose as well, because he had just emptied his flask.

"Make it coffee," Wallace said and, to the surprise of John Newman Edwards, crossed the street. The journalist had to run to catch up with Mr. High-and-Mighty.

"Ah, yes, you are a temperance man, but tell me, sir, have you ever imbibed in intoxicating liquors?"

"Once."

"A lost case, I take it."

"Lost love," Wallace answered and entered the saloon.

The saloon was practically empty, but Edwards knew it would fill up soon. They stood at the bar, where true to form, Mr. High-and-Mighty ordered black coffee, and Edwards, always thirsty, asked for a tall tumbler of the house's best rye.

"I will not pry into your lost love, sir," Edwards said. "That is for those randy sensationalists whom I detest. My interest is the trial. Are you not fearful of retribution?"

"Not in the least. These men you label heroes, Major, are really cowards."

He bristled at the slander but held his tongue. You couldn't expect anything but trite comments from a damned fool. Edwards scribbled a few notes and continued. "You never felt threatened during the trial?"

"No, sir."

That made Edwards laugh so hard he almost spilled his rye. "Your left armpit has an unnatural bulge, sir," he said after regaining control. "Too large for a derringer. Perhaps a pocket revolver, although if I were to fathom a guess—"

"Colt Thunderer," Wallace cut him off. "Next question."

It felt good to catch Mr. High-and-Mighty in a lie. "Instead of a question, will you allow me to make an observation?" He didn't wait for a response. "All this trial proves is that noble citizens such as Jesse James cannot hope to get a fair trial in Missouri. You convicted Bill Ryan using testimony from a rat, a liar and a cheat, which is the perfect description of this fiend Bassham. Is this what our Founding Fathers had in mind a century ago?"

The prosecutor finished his coffee. "You tell your friend Jesse James that I will promise him a fair trial. Frank, too. Times have changed, Major Edwards. They cannot hide forever."

"With your methods, sir, you promise them prison or a rope." He motioned for the bartender to refill his tumbler.

"Beats a bullet," answered the prosecutor, reaching into his vest pocket for change.

"My treat, sir," Edwards told him.

"Thank you, but I insist on paying my own way."

"As you wish." He closed his writing tablet and sipped the rye. "A final question," he said a second later and lowered the tumbler. "Do you really think the Ryan conviction will be upheld?"

"I do."

Edwards's eyes gleamed. "Care to make a wager?"

He was surprised to find Mr. High-and-Mighty dipping into his vest pocket again. Would the temperance man dare gamble? Wallace held a coin in his fingers and said, "I'll bet you this." Edwards squinted. His eyesight was going. He couldn't make out the coin in the dark saloon, had to lean closer. Big, black . . . hell, that was no coin.

"A button!" he exclaimed.

Mr. High-and-Mighty William Hockaday Wallace was laughing, pocketing the button as he exited the saloon.

Chapter 2

But that dirty little coward that shot Mr. Howard,
he laid poor Jesse in his grave.

—"Jesse James," folk song

April 3, 1882
St. Joseph, Missouri

The bitch yelped like a Cheyenne, barking, snapping, snarling playfully as Jesse's snot-nosed imp taunted the puppy with a shoestring. Not that Bob Ford knew exactly what a yelping Cheyenne sounded like, but he seriously doubted if one could have played hell with his nerves the way Little Jesse and that damned mutt did.

Now the six-year-old's little sister joined the fracas, giggling in her diaper, her interest moving like a pendulum from brother to puppy, puppy to brother. Their father glanced once at the scene, looked up briefly at Bob and his nervous brother, and called from the parlor: "Zee, get these damned kids out of here so I can talk business with Charles and Robert."

Zee walked into the room, drying her hands on an apron and giving Jesse a stern look before telling the children to follow her into the kitchen. "Take the pup with you," Jesse told his son, and his wife closed the door behind them.

Jesse had been like this all day, ever since reading in the morning paper that Dick Liddil had surrendered. "Damned traitor," he had said. "Ought to be hung." His wife made no comment as she raked eggs scrambled in bacon grease onto the plates of Jesse, his friends and the children. No plate for herself. She typically ate while cooking, then cleaned while her family and guests wolfed down grub. Zee always fixed enough food to feed an army, Bob thought, and she was a good cook, but Jesse's mood spoiled his appetite. The outlaw's disposition and Bob's stomach soured even further when Charlie started asking about the job they were planning down in Platte City. Jesse calmly set his fork on the plate, wiped his mouth with a napkin and gave Bob's big brother an icy look. "I won't tell you again not to talk about those matters in front of my family." His voice chilled everyone.

Bob and Charlie knew all about Dick Liddil's surrender. The authorities were supposed to keep that out of the press, damn them. . . . Jesse would be on his guard now, expecting Liddil to talk about the jobs he had pulled with the gang in Glendale, Winston and Blue Cut. Liddil had plenty of reasons to sell Jesse James down the river because Jesse had made it known that he planned to kill Liddil himself after he shot dead Jesse's favorite cousin, Wood Hite, in some argument over a petticoat. Bob knew what had happened in Richmond four months ago. He had been there. In fact, when the shooting started, he joined in, siding with Liddil. They had buried Wood Hite that night. Jesse didn't know Bob's part in the matter, of course. If he had, Bob Ford knew he'd already be dead.

The killer would find out soon enough, though. You couldn't keep a secret from the man. He had friends, spies and kin as plentiful as cockroaches all across Missouri. That was why Bob had decided to meet secretly with Governor Thomas Crittenden back in January.

"You give me Jesse James, young man," the newly elected governor had told him in a storeroom at the St. James Hotel during a banquet, "and I'll see that you and your brother receive a full pardon, and split a ten-thousand-dollar reward."

Crittenden cautiously added, "Dead or alive."

Winter turned into spring, and Bob still didn't know how he could fulfill his end of the agreement. Jesse and the Fords had scouted a few towns before deciding to hit the National Bank in Riverton, Iowa. Bob wondered if Crittenden could arrange a pardon for that crime, as well. Probably not. Probably didn't matter. The only ones in on that deal had been Jesse, Charlie and Bob. If the Ford brothers murdered Jesse, no one could ever pin the robbery on them. Sure, some folks suspected the James Gang, but, hell, they had been blamed for half the crimes on both sides of the Mississippi since sixty-six. The Iowa take had been a mere pittance, though, so the outlaws rode hard to Clay County to see Jesse's mother and let their trail cool down a mite.

Jesse's mom, that one-armed catamount, couldn't stand Bob or Charlie, telling Jesse—not caring if Bob heard—that the Fords were nothing but trash, couldn't carry a Younger's saddle and had the look of damnyanks. "They'll betray you, my angel," she said with a mouthful of snuff. "You ain't careful, them two snakes'll shoot down my little angel."

"Ma," Jesse reassured her with a laugh, "you know I can take care of myself." Shortly before he rode out, however, he whispered to his ugly half sister Sallie, "Iffen you don't hear from me in six months, I'll be gone to Glory."

When Bob and Charlie finally rode off with Jesse, the killer was carrying a puppy underneath his coat to give to his son.

"We'll hit the bank in Platte City tomorrow," Jesse said now, creating a makeshift map of the town using pieces from a checkerboard. "There's a big trial goin' on there so I'm a-bettin' everyone in town'll be at the courthouse here, listenin' to them speeches, like they was at Liberty in sixty-six. We go in fast and light a shuck out of there. Fools won't know nothin' till it's too late."

"Just the three of us?" Charlie asked.

"Naw. Got a few other boys meetin' here this evenin'. We'll ride out tonight."

Bob didn't like that one bit. Charlie shot him a nervous look, but Bob ignored him. His older brother wasn't cut out for this sort of thing, the lies, the spying, the waiting. Damn, the waiting. It pricked one's nerves like fingernails on a chalkboard. Charlie had never been much of an owlhoot, and he certainly wasn't cut out to ride with the legendary Jesse James. Nor was Bob. Only twenty years old, he had never done much more than steal a few horses before Charlie introduced him to Jesse. When sober, that is. In his cups, Bob Ford could be just as wicked as the rest—but that didn't count.

"Let's check on the horses," Jesse said, and walked out the front door. Bob and Charlie cautiously followed.

As they curried the animals in the rickety plank corral next to the house, Jesse whispered that this would be his last job if all went well. Pretty soon he'd be able to get a fair trial in Missouri and put the owlhoot trail behind him, live peacefully with Zee and the younguns, maybe see Frank again. He hadn't been with his older brother in months now, wouldn't even tell Bob or Charlie where he was hiding out. Jesse mentioned again the quarter section up in Nebraska that he planned to buy as soon as he got his cut from the Platte City job. He and Zee would move up there and take it easy.

Horseshit, Bob thought. Jesse James would never quit robbing banks and trains. Forty times in the past year or so Bob had heard Jesse's dreams. Waiting on a chance to get a fair trial, waiting to pull one job that could buy his way to freedom. Quit? Not Jesse. He did this because he liked it, liked everything about it, including the killing. Hell, that was probably why Frank had cut loose, figuring if he stayed with his kid brother he'd wind up dead. Fair trial? A fair trial would only put Jesse James on the gallows, and most likely, the Ford brothers right beside him.

That was why Bob had met with Crittenden. That was why he knew he had to kill Jesse.

Soon.

"That damned Dick Liddil," Jesse murmured as he worked the currycomb. "I should have killed the yellow bastard a long time ago."

"Yeah, Jesse," Charlie agreed just to say something.

He said the wrong thing. Jesse dropped the comb and stepped toward the imbecile. "You stupid peckerwood," Jesse said through clenched teeth, fists balled, body trembling. "You call me Mr. Howard when we're in public. Thomas Howard."

Those hard, bitter eyes . . . the black mustache and beard . . . he looked like one of Satan's disciples. Probably was.

"But . . ." Charlie started to plead that no one was around, no one could hear them, then thought better of it. You never

argued when Jesse was in one of his moods. Do that and you'd
likely wind up like Ed Miller.

Ed, they said, had ridden with Jesse for a spell, but the two
men never liked one another. The stories went that they had
taken off after some job, gotten into an argument, and Ed
Miller never came back. Some guessed Ed tried to shoot Jesse
but missed, and Jesse returned fire with better aim and results.
Others say Jesse shot Miller in the back. Or maybe Ed just
rode off, figured to hell with Jesse James, and left the gang.
Bob didn't think so, though. His palm rested on the butt of the
.44-caliber Smith & Wesson New Model Number 3 holstered
on his right hip, hidden by his tan sack coat. Jesse had given
Bob that revolver shortly after he joined the gang. Scratched
into the backstrap were the initials E.M.

"Sorry . . . Thomas," Charlie said.

Jesse nodded before going back to work.

An hour later, the three men returned to the little frame
house on the hilltop overlooking the bustling World's Hotel.
"Leave the door open," Jesse said as he took off his coat and
tossed it on the sofa. "Get us a draft a-goin'." He wiped his
damp forehead. "I'm a mite warm, boys, after that chore."

Bob could hear the children still playing with that puppy—
they'd wear the thing to death if they didn't stop soon—and
Zee slaving in the kitchen, maybe fixing another meal. "The
boys should be here soon," Jesse said, "and we can light out
after supper." Bob glanced at Charlie, saw him twitching his
paper collar and sweating worse than Jesse. His nerves would
give them both away if he didn't watch it.

Jesse peered through the open door, scratched his thick
beard and said, "Might be suspicious if someone sees me
a-wearin' my guns in my own house."

Bob held his breath as Jesse unbuckled the heavy rig around
his waist. No wonder he had worked up a sweat, choring with
a damned arsenal around his waist. He half expected the killer
to whip out one of the three revolvers—open-top Merwin &
Hulbert, Colt Peacemaker or the .45 Schofield he called
"Baby"—and shoot him and his brother dead. Only nothing
happened. Jesse dropped the heavy gunbelt on top of his coat

and turned, hollow blue eyes suddenly focused on a sampler hanging on the wall. It read:

IN GOD WE TRUST

"Dusty," Jesse said. He found a feather duster in the far corner of the parlor, dragged a straight-back chair underneath the wall hanging and climbed up. Charlie glanced at Bob as Jesse went to work with the duster.

It had to be a trick.

Jesse never took off his guns. He looked silly standing there with a feather duster in his hand, his back to the two brothers. "Do it," Charlie mouthed.

Bob's throat went dry. He could hear the children and Jesse's wife clearly, the jingling of trace chains as a wagon went down Lafayette Street, a hotel employee scolding a drunken beggar to stop hounding the World's customers, his own heart pounding, Jesse humming "I'm a Good Old Rebel." He could smell the scent of horses on his clothes, the black shoe polish Jesse used to dye his hair and beard, his own nervous sweat.

It had to be a trick.

But he knew he would never get a chance like this again.

Bob threw back his coat, drew the Smith & Wesson. In the corner of his eye, he saw Charlie pulling his own revolver. Jesse heard the hammer click on Bob's gun. He stopped, started to turn. . . .

The gunshot exploded, thick smoke stinging Bob's eyes. Yet he still saw it all: Jesse's head slamming forward . . . blood splattering the sampler . . . feather duster sailing across the parlor . . . Jesse crashing to the floor. . . . Bob stared at his smoking gun and quickly holstered it as Zee and the children ran into the room.

Zee screamed.

The puppy darted around, nipping at little Mary's heels. She began to cry. Little Jesse just stood dumbstruck.

Zee cradled Jesse's bloody head in her arms, tears streaming down her face, rocking him gently. Bob focused on the dark hole in Jesse's temple. He couldn't believe it.

"Mama," the boy asked, "what's wrong with Papa?"

Zee just rocked.

"A gun . . ." Charlie licked his lips. He had shoved his Colt, unfired, into his holster. Charlie took a tentative step toward Jesse's wife, now widow, and said, "It was a gun, Zee. It accidentally went off."

"Yes." She looked up at the brothers with tear- and hate-filled eyes and choked out the remaining words. "I guess it went off on purpose."

The puppy barked.

Bob and Charlie Ford ran.

Through the wooden gate and down the street, ignoring the crowd starting to gather in front of the home of Mr. and Mrs. Thomas Howard and family. For some reason, no one tried to stop the two fleeing men. It seemed everyone was dazed, confused, and they didn't know the half of it. Bob found the telegraph office and bolted inside, his brother right behind him.

"Frank'll kill us, Bob," Charlie said between sobs. "He's gonna kill us for shore. Oh, my God, Bob, what have we done?"

"Shut up. Shut up, damn you." Bob scratched out a note on the paper and handed it to the bald clerk behind the booth. "I want you to send this to Governor Crittenden and Clay County sheriff Timberlake. Now."

The little man took the note, glanced at it and said, "Is this some sort of—"

"Just send the damned thing!" Bob whirled around. Charlie was utterly useless, which Bob should have expected. He spotted the top-box telephone on the wall. "How do you work that thing?" he practically screamed at the telegraph operator.

"Costs a nickel. Who you plan on calling?" the clerk said.

"The city marshal's office, you dunce."

He took in the instructions, worked the crank, heard the buzzing in the black long-pole receiver and finally, above the static, a human voice.

"I need the city marshal," he said excitedly into the mahogany contraption underneath the twin shiny bells. "It's an emergency."

More static. Eventually, another voice, a man this time.

"Marshal Craig, please," Bob said. He waited. "There's been a shooting. . . . Thirteen-eighteen Lafayette Street . . . Thirteen-eighteen . . . That's right. . . . No, I did it. I shot him. Robert Ford . . . Yes, I'll surrender. I *want* to surrender. . . . Hurry. . . . For the love of God, man, I've killed Jesse James!"

Chapter 3

There is a rumor that Frank James has been seen and recognized in St. Joseph during the past two days. Frank is believed to be not far away, and the gentle racket of his little pistol is liable to be heard in the camp of the traitors who entrapped his brother.
—*St. Joseph Daily Herald,* April 6, 1882

April 8, 1882
Lynchburg, Virginia

It always happened this way. Every time she saw him, her heart seemed to flutter, even after almost eight years of marriage. My, how dashing he looked in his new clothes: gray morning coat trimmed in red with a matching velvet collar, double-breasted vest, cravat, woolen trousers and Congress gaiters, all in black. His full beard and sandy hair had been neatly trimmed. He must have stopped off at the barbershop on his morning walk. She wished he would shave the beard—it hid his handsome face—but she understood his reasons. Frank tipped his gray derby and smiled as he passed the Oakleys, their neighbors, stopping a block from their home for idle chat.

"Good mornin', Mr. Warren," Mae said in her rich Virginia accent, her voice carrying clearly in the crisp air.

Warren. Annie still hadn't grown used to that alias, because they had been using Woodson for so long. Mr. and Mrs. James Warren and their son, Robert. Previously, Ben J. Woodson; wife, Annie; son, Robert. How many other names had they used? One of these days, Robert, now four, would get his own surname wrong and arouse suspicion. The family would then be forced to take to the mountains and live like wild animals until Frank could find a new hideout, probably a new family name.

"A beautiful day," Frank told Mae Oakley.

"Quite," Rudolph Oakley said and started talking about a racehorse he had won money on recently, which, naturally, piqued Frank's interest. He could talk for hours about horses.

Sighing, Annie glanced toward the pretty frame house they had been renting from C. V. Winfree for a few months now. She had been working in the flower garden by the porch, getting it ready for spring planting—if spring ever came. It remained a little nippy mornings and nights here in the Blue Ridge country. Robert sat in the flower bed, digging, dirtying his clothes and grinding mud into his face, utterly enjoying himself. She laughed at the sight before remembering the newspaper in her left hand.

Mr. Winfree had brought by a New York newspaper shortly after breakfast when he came to collect the rent. "I know how James likes to read the papers," he had said after Annie handed him the envelope Frank had left. "My brother-in-law read it on the train coming down here."

"Thank you, Mr. Winfree. You'll find two months' rent there, sir." Frank had been lucky at the racetrack last week.

"You folks . . . you're the best tenants I ever had. Sure hope you don't ever leave."

"We love it here, sir."

They'd soon leave, though, because of what had happened. After Winfree left, Annie sat down to polish off the coffee and read the paper. The headline screamed at her. At first, she didn't believe it. She had read those stories before, even read that her own husband had been shot dead, yet this one was different. It didn't come across like some dime novelist's fanciful tale. In her heart, she knew it was true.

"I'll certainly remember that horse's name, Rudolph," she heard Frank saying. "Thanks for the tip."

"You and Annie must come over for supper this week," Mae told him. "And bring that darlin' boy of yours."

"A delightful proposition." His eyes traveled down Wise

Street and detected Annie. "'Parting is such sweet sorrow,'" he told Mae with a bow, "but I see my wife waiting, and do not wish to keep you from your errands. Good day, my friends."

His smile radiated as he carried his tall, lean form toward her, but tears began to well in her eyes, and Frank's smile faded. He hurried to her.

"What is it?" he asked.

The newspaper shook in her hand. Mouth trembling, she started to hand it to him. A screen door slammed, startling her. Tim Collins gave them a hearty, "Hallo, neighbor," as he bolted to the sidewalk and headed downtown, most likely for his eye-opener over at Shannsey's. He stopped beside them when he saw the paper.

"Y'all heard the news?" he asked excitedly.

Frank looked bewildered. Annie couldn't hold it in any-more. "Jesse James has been killed," she said. She wanted him to hear it from her, not that blowhard who beat his wife.

It had to stagger Frank, but he kept up his act. Tim Collins nodded enthusiastically. "Heard 'bout it last night at Shannsey's."

"My God," Frank said. "How did it happen?"

"Shot dead," Collins said. "Reckon they'll be after that scoundrel Frank now. His time's numbered. Yep, they'll plant him alongside his brother, I'm bettin', 'fore summer. High time, too. Well, folks, be seein' y'all."

When Collins had passed, Frank took the newspaper from Annie's small hand. She opened the gate to let him through. "Who killed him?" he asked numbly.

"Robert Ford."

He nodded, climbed the steps up the porch and opened the door to their home.

"Papa!" their filthy son exclaimed.

Frank James didn't hear him.

He was still sitting on the large mahogany and satin divan in the parlor after she had bathed Robert and put him down for his nap. The *Daily Herald* lay at his feet. "Paper says Dingus put his guns on the bed, and when he went to wash his face in a basin, Ford blew his brains out," Frank said, his voice quavering.

Annie never cared much for Jesse's nickname, just about the only thing Frank ever called his younger brother. So had Cole and the other Youngers, at least when Cole had been on friendly terms with Jesse. Most of the time, Cole despised Jesse. The feeling was mutual, and Frank often played the role of peacekeeper. Dingus. What a stupid name.

"I know," Annie told Frank softly and reached for him. "Come on, let me make you some coffee."

He left the paper on the floor, shed his coat, vest and tie and moved to the kitchen, where Annie made a fresh pot. "Paper says the funeral was nice," Frank spoke, his voice toneless. "They sang 'What a Friend We Have in Jesus.' That was Dingus's favorite." He sighed. "Poor Ma."

"I know." She couldn't think of anything else to say.

She wanted to help him out of his melancholy. She wanted the old Frank James back: the slim, good-looking man of six feet who could spout out Shakespeare and poetry as well as she reckoned Edwin Booth could. The dashing outlaw who had wooed her with his charm and smile and talked her into eloping with him in June of seventy-four when she was twenty-one and he ten years older. Not that Frank needed to charm and smile too much. She had been smitten the moment she saw him.

More important, though, she wanted a life—a real life—for her husband and son. Not the running, the hiding, the torment and heartbreak. She could never have this while Jesse was alive, although there had been some semblance of this since winter. That drunken lout Collins had been right about one thing, though. They'd be coming after Frank now—Pinkertons, marshals, bounty hunters, railroad swine. She could not bear to see Frank James murdered by some coward. Poor Zee. Poor Little Jesse and Mary. She felt for them. Yet she also felt thankful it was Zee in mourning, not herself.

Frank had put his outlaw days behind him, something Jesse never could. Her husband wasn't the cold-blooded killer the Yankee papers said he was. He had taken the owlhoot trail after the War because of Northern tyranny. The law had practically forced the followers of Quantrill and Anderson to become outlaws. Frank had never shot down a man in cold blood. She knew she couldn't make the same claim of Jesse. Her husband killed only to protect the lives of his own family, his pals, himself.

She placed the mug in front of him, but Frank didn't notice. He sat, elbows resting on the table, head bowed, massaging his temples. He sat like that most of the night, and Annie left him alone, letting him grieve in his own way for his kid brother.

Annie felt no grief for Jesse. In a lot of ways, she thought, she and Cole Younger had much in common.

April 17, 1882
St. Joseph, Missouri

Never, *never*, had Bob Ford imagined all this. Western Missouri seemed to be speeding along like a runaway locomotive. The St. Joseph police had arrested Bob and Charlie. That much he had expected—that much he *wanted*, if only to get off the streets and into protection. Jesse had too many friends in this part of the country, and Charlie had been right about one thing: Frank James most certainly would be gunning for the Fords.

Police and neighbors had found Mrs. Zee Howard cradling her dead husband, just as she had been doing when Bob and Charlie got spooked and fled. At first, she insisted her man was Thomas Howard, gentleman gambler, but the weight became too much for her, and she broke down and cried out that yes, this was Jesse James. Telegraph operators and gossips quickly spread the news across town, Missouri and the nation.

An assistant county coroner moved Jesse's body to Sidenfaden's funeral parlor. Jesse's mother was escorted into town from Clay County, and the old hag broke down when she saw her boy in his coffin. "Is that him?" Marshal Enos Craig had asked, and she collapsed, wailing, "Would to God that it weren't." They brought in Sheriff Timberlake and that prosecutor from Jackson County, Wallace was his name. As soon as the law positively identified the corpse, some photographer was there to make a few plates of Jesse James in a pine box. Within a day, the James W. Porch Studio was selling prints of the dead man for ten bits apiece. The line stretched two city blocks.

People poured off trains, riverboats and stagecoaches. You couldn't get a room in the World's Hotel for a week, even with management putting three or four tourists in one bed and still charging full rate. The police had to post guards at 1318 Lafayette Street to keep the gawkers from walking off with anything Jesse James had owned, even planks from the house and corral. 'Course, those lawdogs were only a step above brigands themselves. They quickly moved Zee and the kids out of the house and stole—confiscated, they called it—anything that wasn't nailed down.

It wasn't even suppertime the day of the shooting when the coroner's inquest was finished, the jury ruling that Jesse James had been shot dead by one Robert Ford.

At the governor's request, Jesse's body was finally released to the killer's family, and a train carried corpse and clan to Kearney, where Jesse lay in state like a damned president in the Kearney Hotel so brainless passersby would be able to say, "I seen Jesse James." To hell with them. Bob Ford could always claim, "I shot Jesse James."

He shot him, however, from behind. Shot him when he wasn't even armed. Even the newspapers that hated Jesse James scolded Bob for what they called cowardice. Hell, none of those ink spillers would have had nerve enough to shoot Jesse.

Among the journalists who praised Jesse James, John Newman Edwards had been the most vehement in his diatribes against the Ford brothers. Then again, the fire-breathing old sot had always made Jesse to be some sort of hero, had even penned some book glorifying Quantrill and his raiders, Jesse included, back in seventy-seven, so his stance surprised nobody. He had compared Jesse, Frank and the Youngers to the Knights of the Round Table. " 'There never was a more cowardly and unnecessary murder committed in all of America than this murder of Jesse James,' " he wrote in *Sedalia Democrat*. Bob had gotten a good chuckle out of that.

The Pinkertons, of course, hailed Bob Ford. So did a few

newspapers, but most couldn't just come to terms with the fact that Robert Ford shot Jesse James down like a mangy dog.

They planted Jesse on April 6. Four days later, poor Zee was auctioning off everything she had left. Didn't even clear a hundred and twenty-five dollars for her troubles.

By then, someone had reckoned that maybe Wood Hite's body might bring some money. Word seeped out of where Dick Liddil and Bob had planted the scalawag, and a bunch of cretins dug up Hite's corpse and turned it over to the law. Dumb oafs. There was no reward for that rotten carcass. All that did was lead to another inquest and get Bob Ford indicted on a second murder charge.

So here he stood in the county courthouse in St. Joseph, beside his shaking big brother, listening as the clerk read the indictment of first-degree murder for the shooting of Jesse James.

"How do the defendants plead?" the stiff-backed judge asked from his bench.

"Guilty," Bob said easily. His older brother, Charlie, had a tougher time getting the word out.

"Robert Ford," the judge said. "For this cold and callous crime, it is my duty to pronounce sentence. On the nineteenth of May, you are to be taken to some convenient place and hanged by the neck until you are dead, dead, dead. May God have mercy on your soul."

His eyes turned to Charlie. "Charles Ford, for this cold and callous crime, it is my duty to pronounce the same sentence. On the nineteenth of May, you are to be taken to some convenient place and hanged by the neck until you are dead, dead, dead. May God have mercy on your soul."

The gavel fell.

Back in their cell, Charlie fell to his knees and wailed, prayed for forgiveness, swore that, if he could do it again, he wouldn't take no part in killing Jesse. Bob just shook his head. Charlie would come to his senses eventually, realize that his baby brother had everything worked out.

Late that afternoon, Marshal Craig came by and unlocked the cell. Charlie cowered, eyes wide, and pleaded, "You ain't gonna lynch us. Please, God, don't let 'em lynch us."

The city lawman eyed both men with contempt. "You Fords are free to go. Governor's pardoned the both of you."

Bob smiled. Sure, he still had to face trial for the shooting of Wood Hite in Ray County, but he'd get off. Hell, that was self-defense. Wood had a gun in his hand, even put a bullet in Dick Liddil's leg. Bob had simply been defending himself. No jury would convict him of that.

Frank James worried him, though. Still, there was talk of Frank giving himself up. That would please Bob. Maybe the law would finally hang that sumbitch.

Chapter 4

*Beautiful, glorious, consecrated old Missouri soil! Let
others defame thee as they will—thank heaven, in life, in
death, you are good enough for me.*

—William H. Wallace

April 21, 1882
Lynchburg, Virginia

Lord, how he missed his home. Home before the War, before
the redlegs, Jim Lane, General Order Number Eleven . . . be-
fore the railroads and those damned Pinkerton bushwhackers.
Frank had liked Nashville, and he knew Annie really loved
Lynchburg, but this wasn't home for either of them. That was
Missouri.

He had accepted Dingus's death. It proved easy to do. Frank
always knew it would end like this—Jesse shot from behind—
yet he always thought it would come from some Pinkerton
man's hand, though, not one of the gang's own members. The
Fords, however, were nothing more than white trash. It had
been different right after the surrender, with Cole and his
brothers, Jim Cummins, John Jarrette, those men. They had
been carrying on the War. That changed with Northfield, one
of Jesse's harebrained ideas. Bloody massacre that had turned
out to be, the Youngers shot to pieces, Clell Miller and Bill
Chadwell dead on the streets.

Leaving Cole behind in that damnyankee state had been the
hardest thing Frank ever had to do.

"I hate doing this," Frank had said.

"No choice," Cole shot back. "Get out of here now, Frank, or you'll die with us."

They didn't shake hands. Didn't need to. Their eyes bid their good-byes, their regrets. But Cole said in a whisper as Dingus went to fetch a horse they'd have to ride double, "You'd do best to keep ridin', Frank, leave your brother behind. He'll wind up gettin' you kilt, too. And I don't wanna see that."

Cole and his brothers hadn't died, though. Pleaded guilty and got life sentences.

That had been up in Minnesota. Frank wondered if he could get similar treatment in Missouri. Life in prison? He'd be better off dead.

"'What's past is prologue,'" he said, not really knowing why.

"What, dear?" Annie asked.

He smiled at her. "Nothing," he said and turned pensive again. After a while he looked up. She sat on the divan, reading a copy of *Harper's Bazaar* while little Robert played with a locomotive Frank had carved himself and blackened with shoe polish. They deserved a chance.

"I was thinking," he began, and waited for Annie to look up. God, how he would miss her if . . . Well, best not think about that. He'd have plenty of time for thinking, he figured, plenty of time for compunction.

"I was thinking maybe I'd write a letter to Major Edwards." Her eyes danced, and Frank knew he had made the right decision. "Maybe see if he could act as an intermediary between me and Crittenden."

"I'll stand by you, Frank," she said. "And I'll help you any way I can."

"I know." He forced a laugh. "Might have to take you up on that offer."

May 31, 1882
Jefferson City, Missouri

William H. Wallace had put on his best suit for the train trip from Kansas City down to the capital, where he hailed a hansom cab to take him to the governor's mansion. Somehow, however, dust collected on the black broadcloth between the depot and 100 Madison Avenue, where he recognized an ornate Renaissance Revival brick building, three stories high, surrounded by a towering wrought-iron fence. He stood slapping his coat with gloves at the bottom of the doorsteps when someone called his name. A fair-skinned man with thinning sandy hair and a meticulously groomed mustache strolled up the walkway from the street and offered his hand.

"You are William Hockaday Wallace?" the stranger said.

"I am." He thought about adding, *But you can leave out the Hockaday, sir,* decided against it and gripped the man's flaccid hand. It wasn't much of a handshake.

"I thought so."

Obviously. Wallace waited for the well-dressed, well-groomed stranger to make his point.

"I am William Decatur Hamilton, prosecuting attorney for Daviess County. I trust you are here on the same business as I." His voice dropped to a hush. "Shall we?"

Wallace decided quickly that he did not like William Decatur Hamilton but followed the blowhard up the steps and pulled the door chime. A gaunt, white-haired Negro butler answered the door and showed them into an exquisite double parlor, asking them to please wait as it would be ten minutes or so before the governor could see them. William Decatur Hamilton became quite indignant that he had to wait. Wallace, having given up on his dusty coat, simply got comfortable in a lounge chair and picked up a copy of the *Daily Tribune.*

Their voices echoed throughout the drafty room. Hamilton's voice, that is. He did all the talking. Wallace just listened with one ear, his mind focused more on the newspaper and the walnut parlor organ sitting in the corner than his Daviess County colleague's banter.

Wallace didn't know what Governor Crittenden wanted, but he could guess. On the other hand, that cock of the walk William Decatur Hamilton spouted off reasons loud enough for Crittenden's entire house staff or some snooping reporter with an ear to the window to hear, forgetting that Crittenden's invitation had cautioned diplomacy and secrecy, that the visit was of a most highly sensitive nature.

"Frank James," Hamilton said. "Papers are full of news and speculation. Have you heard what the *New York Times* is reporting?" The attorney didn't wait for Wallace's response. "They say that the deal's already done, that that scoundrel will turn himself in, plead guilty and Tom will pardon him the way he did the Ford brothers. I'd have a lot more guts than Tom's showing right now if I were governor. Much rather see a trial by jury. Then hang the rapscallion."

Wallace gave up on the newspaper. "Jury trials are far from resolute." He was surprised he got that much in, even more so when he managed to add, "Frank James could easily be acquitted in this part of the country, in this day and age."

"Balderdash. I'll hang Frank James. You can bet on that, sir."

Straight-nosed, heavyset Thomas T. Crittenden offered each man a cigar and a chair before settling his ample frame behind his cherry desk and tugging on the ends of his mustache. He tried to sum up the two men while they got comfortable in the leather chairs in his library. Hamilton, the Daviess County attorney, ran the cigar under his nose, savoring the smell but careful not to upset the appearance of his upturned mustache. Wallace simply stuck his in his coat pocket. The Jackson County prosecutor could use a better wardrobe, Crittenden thought.

Wallace sported a prominent Roman nose, dark hair with a widow's peak, a thick mustache and intelligent brown eyes. He could be just about anything: Presbyterian minister, schoolteacher, newspaper hack or lawyer. The governor glanced at the file flat on his desk. Well, Wallace's father had been a preacher, and William Hockaday Wallace had practiced the three other vocations, proving to be more than a fair hand as schoolman, journalist and lawyer. Two years ago, he had been elected Jackson County's prosecutor and become one zealous attorney. Acted more like the son of a Baptist fire-breather, in a courtroom at least, than a Presbyterian Bible-thumper.

Hamilton, on the other hand, had a delicate appearance, and

he looked like the kind of man who wanted Thomas Crittenden's job, and would stab anyone in the back to get here. Hell,
for five dollars and a train ticket to St. Louis, Hamilton could
have the damned position.

"I like the way you handled the Bill Ryan case, Mr. Wallace," Crittenden said at last, more to irk the Daviess County
barrister than to compliment the Jackson County lawyer.

"Thank you, Governor." Polite. To the point. Crittenden
liked that. Hamilton, he figured, would have bored him for
twenty minutes on the aspects of the case. Everyone from
politicians and pundits to farmers and whores had predicted
Bill Ryan would never be convicted, but Wallace had done it.
Got the rapscallion sentenced to twenty-five years despite not
much in the way of evidence. Folks also predicted William H.
Wallace would be shot dead for daring to send one of the
James Gang to prison, but the Jackson County solicitor was
still breathing fresh Missouri air.

"Gentlemen, I've asked you up here because I'd like you to
start preparing cases for trial against Frank James." No need
for silly chatter. Lawyers should be smart enough to know why
they had been invited to the governor's home.

"Then it's true!" Hamilton almost leaped out of his chair.

"What's true?" Crittenden asked.

"That you've made a deal with Frank James."

"Bosh. I have not heard from Frank James personally." A
half-truth. He had been corresponding with John Newman Edwards, but no deal had been made. "Don't believe everything
you read in the newspapers. I have not talked to Frank James,
nobody has tried to gun me down on my way home because of
the assassination of Jesse James and I never, ever told Robert
Ford that he could bring in Jesse James dead." He emphasized
the last part, which was an outright lie. He had told the kid
"dead or alive" earlier this year, but let the Ford boy prove that
one.

"Frank James, though, will be brought to justice. And I
would like a conviction." Another political exaggeration.
Frank James had a lot of support in Missouri, Democratic support, and Crittenden, once a blue-blooded Republican, had
won the governor's job running as a Democrat. "We just need

to find our strongest evidence against the bandit. So I would like you solicitors to be prepared just in case this matter does come to trial." He stood, didn't bother to offer a handshake, just opened the door leading to the massive hall, where Jonathan, the butler, stood waiting to escort the visitors out. "I trust you two can keep this matter between us. No need to give the newspapers more to write about." He directed this to Wallace. A good lawyer, maybe, but he had too much contact with the newspapers, and that Thomas Crittenden didn't like.

June 12, 1882
Kansas City, Missouri

William Wallace pulled off his reading spectacles and pinched his nose. All this reading gave him a headache. He reached for his mug and realized the coffee had turned cold. He started to rise to see if someone had brewed a fresh pot on the potbellied stove downstairs. Likely not. Nobody would want to stoke a fire as hot as the afternoon had turned. Most of his colleagues thought him quite muddled anyway for wanting coffee available in the Jackson County solicitor's office.

He lowered the mug as his assistant opened the door to his office and escorted two women inside. "These two ladies have requested an interview with you, sir," the young attorney said. "Say it is of the utmost importance."

I'm sure it is, Wallace thought. "Thank you, Darius. Close the door behind you. Ladies?" He gestured to the couch on the far wall. When they were seated, Wallace sat down.

One of the women looked to be in her late fifties, maybe even older. She was dressed entirely in black with her right sleeve pinned up. He tried not to stare, but he had never seen a one-armed lady. She had to be the roughest, meanest woman he had ever seen: bitter eyes, hard frown, callused left hand, shabby dress, weathered face, plump body. Probably hadn't cracked a smile in twenty years. Had to be six feet tall, too, and would likely kick Wallace's ass in a fight. The other woman was much younger, buxom though petite, slim, maybe an inch over five feet tall—dwarfed by the one-armed hag—her face hidden by a black veil.

She lifted the veil. "Do you remember me, Mr. Wallace?" she asked.

"Could I ever forget?" Wallace leaned forward, smiling and forgetting his stepmother's constant scolding to keep his elbows off tables and desks. "You used to race that blue roan gelding of yours up and down the streets of Independence, your father screaming at you to start acting like a lady, your mother worried sick you'd fall off."

"And I challenged you to a shooting contest when you came to a picnic at Little Santa Fe when I was teaching school there." She was a striking woman, blond hair neatly curled, perfect lips, dark blue eyes, hypnotic smile.

"You beat me, too," Wallace added.

"You let me win."

He shook his head with a laugh. "Not hardly . . . Annie Ralston. It has been much too long." He meant that sincerely. He had been quite captivated by her—to the point that he would sometimes make a habit of riding by the fine white farmhouse outside the city limits—strange how he could remember that—or by the Independence Female School when she was studying there on the chance he might catch a glimpse of her. He could also remember his heart sinking when Annie's father, Samuel, told him the news, said he had disowned her for shaming him so. Wallace had gone into a saloon and gotten drunk that day.

"It's Annie James now," she said.

"I know." His voice and eyes revealed his feelings.

"This is Frank's mother, Zerelda Samuel."

He had suspected that because of the missing arm. The Pinkertons had raided the Clay County farm a few years back trying to catch the James boys. Allan Pinkerton never wavered from his stance that his operatives had thrown in a smoke device to force the family outside. Jameses, Youngers, Samuels and just about everyone else cried it had been a bomb. On a late January night in seventy-five, Mrs. Samuel, her husband, Reuben—Frank and Jesse's stepdad—and eight-year-old Archie woke up to the noise of glass breaking and the smell of smoke. Mr. Samuel saw the burning thing on the floor, scooped it up with a shovel and tossed it toward the fireplace. Smoke bomb or explosive, the device detonated, blowing off Zerelda's arm and killing poor Archie, Jesse and Frank's innocent stepbrother. Missouri itself almost went up in flames after that incident.

"How can I be of assistance?" Wallace asked.

"Mr. Wallace—" Annie began.

"It's William."

"Thank you. William, I want you to know that in my heart I know you had nothing to do with Jesse's death."

"I didn't. It was a cowardly act."

"Frank would like to turn himself in. But he . . . well, it's me, really. I'm frightened that someone will assassinate him while he's trying to give up."

"Mrs. James, if your husband surrenders to me, if he is harmed it will be over my dead body."

She seemed relieved. "It's Annie."

Wallace smiled again.

"Annie. Tell your husband to turn himself in. It's his only chance. But he'll have to trust other officers of the court. I don't believe any constable, marshal or attorney had anything to do with Jesse's death. That was just the Ford brothers and their wickedness." He intentionally omitted Crittenden.

"You don't know what it's like, William. Frank's in agony. He cannot even cut a stick of wood without looking around to see if someone's slipping up behind him to collect that ten-thousand-dollar reward."

"Judas money!" Zerelda Samuel snapped. "You don't know what it's like, young man. You a Kentuckian, ain't you? Them Ford snakes killed my angel. My Jesse and my Buck never were no bad boys."

Buck? Wallace figured it was Mrs. Samuel's pet name for Frank.

"It was the War that done it," the old woman railed. "The railroads. Them damnyankees. And those Pinkerton shootists. You seed what they done to my arm! God help me, I already losted two of my dear boys. Murdered! If someone was to cut down me darlin' Buck, I'd just die." She was crying, not for herself, Wallace realized, but for Jesse, for Frank, for little Archie. It must be hard being a mother of outlaws.

That woman had been through so much, but Jesse's death seemed to have broken her. Annie put her arm around the woman's shoulder, letting her grieve. Wallace waited in silence.

He wanted to correct Mrs. Samuel. Yes, he had been born in Clark County, Kentucky, but had moved to Missouri when he was eight. His family settled on a farm here in Jackson County. He knew what it was like to grow up in Western Missouri during the Border Wars. His father supported the Confederacy, and Wallace still dreamed of the burning homes, lynchings, murdered men—both Northern and Southern—the raids, black flags, William Quantrill and Bloody Bill Anderson, Odon Guitar and Jim Lane.

Nor could he ever forget August 23, 1863, and Union General Thomas Ewing's General Order Number Eleven:

All persons living in Cass, Jackson and Bates Counties, Missouri . . . are hereby ordered to remove from their present places of residence within fifteen days of the date hereof. Those who, within that time, establish their loyalty to the satisfaction of the commanding officer of the military station nearest their present places of residence, will receive from him certificates stating the fact of their loyalty. . . .

Forever etched in his memory were the heavily loaded wagon, the tiring journey across Missouri to Columbia and, eventually, Fulton . . . neither his father, stepmother nor brothers talking much . . . passing the already abandoned homes of neighbors in the hot, still summer day, the eerie silence broken by the pitiful howls of a coonhound left behind at the Jennison's farm. Every time he had heard a dog howl since then, he remembered that terrible day, those trying times.

He hadn't, however, become a bandit, a killer.

"What kind of terms would you be agreeable to?" Annie asked after several minutes.

Wallace took a deep breath and slowly exhaled. "I'd have to

wire the governor. I don't think your husband can go unpunished, but I'm sure a short stay in prison would be satisfactory to all parties involved."

"Could you let us know?"

"Of course."

He wired Crittenden that day, got a reply within an hour saying he could name the terms. That stunned Wallace until he realized the move had been entirely political. The governor was simply washing his hands of the matter and would let Wallace take the criticism—or some vindictive son of a bitch's bullet. He wrote a note outlining the terms and had it delivered to Annie at the hotel where she said she could be reached. Her reply came two days later.

> *William:*
>
> *After careful consideration, Frank has decided to reject your kind offer. Prison would kill him. He is holding out for a full pardon.*
>
> *Thank you for your kindness. I hope you understand, and that this will not come between us.*
>
> > *Sincerely,*
> > *Ann R. James*

The quick reply meant Frank had to be nearby. He didn't think Annie would risk sending a wire. Not that it mattered. The law hadn't been able to catch Frank James in sixteen years. Full pardon? Crittenden would never agree to that—or would he? Frowning, Wallace wadded up the stationery and tossed it in his wastebasket.

Chapter 5

She was a society favorite, and loved gayety, but after her marriage she was ostracized by those among whom she had been a favorite.
—*Washington Post,* on Ann Ralston James, December 14, 1914

September 10, 1882
Independence, Missouri

Of all people, Ezra Hickman had to open the door. The last time Annie James had seen her brother-in-law had been at the Kansas City depot back in seventy-four when she had duped him—indeed, she had hoodwinked her entire family—to elope with Frank. Eight years hadn't changed him much, she thought, as he just stood there gaping, bits of black pepper stuck in his teeth—proof that he had been sampling her mother's cooking before dinner was served. She could smell roast beef and her stomach began to moan, but the hunger passed once she heard the laughter of children—Ezra's, no doubt—and her mother begging Annie's sister to please get those terrors from underneath her feet so she could finish setting the table.

Annie thought she might cry. She remembered those sounds from her own childhood, at Rock Creek, Omaha, and later here at the farmhouse just outside of town: screaming to get out of her Sunday dress after church while her mother served up enough food to feed the state militia; big brother, John, picking at her relentlessly; her father rushing to the rescue of his wife and favorite daughter, whisking Annie away to his study, where she would peel out of the itchy dress and pull on a riding skirt and calico blouse while her father poured three fingers of Jameson's and clipped a cigar. Sometimes, when the mood struck him, he would offer Annie a sip of Irish whiskey, but after a sniff she would shake her head, saying it burned her nose, and he would laugh so hard he trembled and tears welled in his eyes.

"Father," her brother-in-law called out, "you'd best come to the door."

Ezra Hickman retreated, still holding the door open—"Letting in flies," Annie's parents would have scolded—but leaving Annie on the porch like some unwelcome lightning-rod salesman, not daring to invite her in, waiting for Samuel Ralston to solve this dilemma, but she knew this time her father wouldn't be coming to her rescue.

Unlike Ezra Hickman, the past eight years had aged Samuel Ralston considerably. He had always seemed like an old man to Annie, but now, at seventy-two, he resembled Methuselah, with gray hair thinning, thick lenses in his eyeglasses and a cane helping him to maneuver his way around the house.

He had been named after his uncle, and often bragged about his namesake, who in 1798 had dared rebel against British rule in Ireland and wound up being exiled to America. Her father, however, had never been much of an iconoclast; indeed, during the recent unpleasantness, he had been first and foremost a Mason, as always, and then a Unionist, all of which made her elopement with Alexander Franklin James, Confederate guerrilla and bushwhacker, that much harder on him.

He had settled in Jackson County, Missouri, before the war, but after General Order Number Eleven, even though he had pledged his loyalty to the Union, he moved the family west, out of harm's way, or so he thought, to Nebraska. They had first settled on a farm outside Rock Creek, but once her father took a load of birdshot in his arm during some little row, they moved to Omaha, where he and John, then in his early twenties, started a freighting company to keep the Ralston family fed and clothed. After Order Number Eleven was rescinded, they moved back to Jackson County, Missouri.

The war had taken its toll on Sam Ralston's fortune, but he recovered. Annie could not remember ever being in want. Her father had given her, and the rest of her siblings, everything they needed. He had put her through the Independence Female College, promised her anything, yet she had denied him, shamed him, hurt him.

Even as he stood in the doorway, however, even as her lips began to quiver, she knew she would not have done anything different. She loved Frank. She wouldn't defend him, or her own feelings, to her parents in an argument neither side could ever hope to win. If Samuel Ralston still wanted to disown her, so be it, but she hoped, even prayed, that not be the case. Now she waited.

Their eyes met and held. Waiting for her husband to return from some robbery or raid had been excruciating, yet the few seconds that passed on that porch lasted an eternity. She didn't know how long she could stand this.

"Tell Mama," her father told Ezra, "to set another place for dinner."

Annie couldn't hold back any longer. She rushed the short distance separating them and buried her face in his chest. The aromas of a freshly clipped cigar stuck in his vest pocket and Sunday whiskey on his breath comforted her. The cedar walking cane clattered against the hardwood floor, and Samuel Ralston wrapped his arms around his daughter's tiny waist, pulled her tighter, and cried himself.

"You're still nothing but skin and bones," her mother said in the parlor after they finished eating. "I could squeeze your waist with one hand."

An exaggeration, but Annie had always prided herself on her eighteen-inch corseted waist. She stood five feet high, weighed between one hundred and one hundred ten pounds, and expected her mother, who had always chided her daughters and daughters-in-law that men liked women with a little meat on their hips, to blame her thinness on the worried life of being an outlaw's wife, so she quickly changed the subject.

Annie pointed to the sewing machine, a bolt of cardinal silk at its side. She remembered seeing the high-arm machine with oak woodwork in a window in some Nashville store and casually mentioning how her mother would love it, and Frank had surprised her by buying it shortly before they had left Tennessee for Missouri in the spring of eighty-one, Annie staying with General Shelby in Page City while Frank met up with Jesse for one of his deals. It had been shipped to Page City, and from there to her mother.

"I see you got the sewing machine," she said absently.

"Yes, though I don't use it as often as I want, just to mend things. I'm getting old, Annie."

"I wasn't sure—" She stopped herself, but her mother finished the sentence.

"That your father would allow it in our house?" She did not bother to answer her own question. "He's failing, dear. Now don't get that look on your face. Samuel Ralston will wind up burying us all, but he felt ashamed, threatening to disown you and all. But I guess when the sewing machine arrived, when we realized it was from you, he thought it might be as close to you as he'd ever get."

"Frank came to see you."

"Yes," said her mother, nodding. "He and your father had a terrible fight."

Remembering, Annie pursed her lips and closed her eyes. Her memory had become her curse; she couldn't forget anything. In June of seventy-four she had told her parents she was going to visit her sister, and took the train to Kansas City. Ezra greeted her at the depot, but she let the cad believe that she had met one of her friends from college on the train and wanted to visit a tad longer, said she would take a buggy to the Hickmans' home in an hour, no more than two, and Ezra had nodded his stupid nod and left, head down, dragging his feet, like some spurned suitor. Once he had disappeared, Annie grabbed her bags and took the next train to Omaha, where Frank would be waiting. They had married on June 6, honeymooned briefly, and soon fled, lest someone recognize her outlaw husband. She sent a brief note home before leaving Nebraska, using her middle name.

Dear Mother:

I am married and am going west.

> *Love,*
> *Annie Reynolds*

Frank visited the Ralstons in seventy-six, after the Northfield indiscretion. He told her parents she was fine, but her father exploded. "You," Frank had recalled his in-law yelling, once safely back in Tennessee, "are a damned rascal. You stole my precious Annie, and I want her back." Frank spat out his own venom. "By God, she is my wife now. She shan't come back home, and you, sir, shan't see her ever again!"

Two more years passed before she wrote her parents, and that had been in February of seventy-eight, after she had given birth to Robert. Two years later, she began writing them again, posting the letters to General Jo Shelby or some other trusted go-between, who would take them to Independence. Finally, she had sent them the Acme High Arm.

"Does Frank plan on surrendering?" her mother blurted out.

"If he can work out some sort of deal," she answered, "if the governor will promise him a fair trial."

"He'll need a good lawyer, Annie. Why, the stories I hear told are enough to make my skin crawl."

"Don't believe all of those stories, Mama. They are mostly falsehoods spread by the Pinkertons. And Frank was never as spiteful as Jesse."

She smelled the cigar before her father stepped into the parlor. "Does he have a lawyer?" he asked.

"Not yet." She felt herself trembling.

"Is that why you have come home, daughter? Is that why you sent us the sewing machine?"

"No."

"And by the saints, where is our grandson? Are you that ashamed of us?"

"Of course not." Not sure how her meeting would turn out, she had left Robert with Frank. "Maybe I can come back next Sunday, and bring Robert. He's growing like a weed, will turn five in February."

Samuel Ralston hobbled to the sofa and eased himself beside his wife. "If your husband is man enough to place himself in the hands of the law," he said at last, "I will write a letter to my old friend Colonel John Finis Philips. Your old man still has some connections, Annie."

Smiling, she looked down and noticed she had been wringing her hands. Eight years after she had run away from home, Samuel Ralston still refused to deny his daughter anything.

September 21, 1882
St. Louis, Missouri

Such clandestine matters never agreed with John Finis Philips, yet he had expected things would come to this after Samuel Ralston's unannounced visit to Philips's Kansas City office. Ralston was a moderate Unionist, and Philips, Missouri-born Democrat, thought most Republicans ill-bred dunces even though Philips had abhorred slavery and secession. Besides, not only was Sam Ralston a friend, he carried much weight in Jackson County, and Philips had designs on hanging his shingle on a higher loft than his second-story downtown office.

Philips would turn forty-eight on New Year's Eve. He had been educated at Center College in Kentucky and the University of Missouri. He had been admitted to the bar in 1857 and since then had served in the state convention of 1861, National Convention of 1868, had campaigned, and lost, for Congress in sixty-eight and campaigned again, winning this time, in seventy-four. He had also served in the glorious state militia's Seventh Cavalry during the War, commanded the Missouri's Central District, and folks still called him by his rank. Right now, he had his eyes focused on a position in the Supreme Court Commission, and after that . . . who knew? He had kept his glee hidden beneath his thick mustache and beard when Ralston came to him, but he would have paid good money to represent Frank James in a criminal trial. Frank James had a lot more clout in Missouri than Sam Ralston.

Still, it annoyed him to have to travel across the state by train and wander in the gloaming along the Mississippi River waterfront looking for some wayfarer's establishment called Donovan's. St. Louis boasted some of the finest hotels in the West, but he found himself soiling his boots with mud, piss and vomit as he climbed the rickety steps that led to the saloon.

Smoke hung in the frame building like fog, and more sots drank and cursed in this one ramshackle hut on a dreary Thursday night than a drummer would find in every Kansas City saloon combined on any Saturday, or so it seemed, but Philips had no difficulty in finding John Newman Edwards. In brick-colored pants, yellow brocade vest and green coat, the latter some thirty years out of fashion, the nincompoop stood out like a leper.

"Thank you for joining me, sir," the newspaperman said with whiskey-soaked breath.

Philips didn't answer. Nor did he wait for Edwards to fill an extra shot glass from the half-empty bottle of King Bee whiskey sitting on the table. The lawyer took a drink, refilled his glass, and corked the bottle.

"Shall we get down to business, sir?" he asked.

"Excellent," the journalist replied, topped his whiskey, took a sip and asked, "What chance has Frank James of receiving a fair trial under the current political dominion in our fair state?"

"His trial will be just—"

"You don't believe Crittenden would have the good man murdered, to prevent this honorable Missourian from testifying against the nefarious deeds of such brigands as the Pinkertons, Federal tyrants and Jim Lane? What happened to Frank's brother portends more treachery for any stalwart soldier who had enough courage to wear the gray. Why, after the end of the hostilities, Frank and Jesse strove only to support their poor mother, a pleasant, God-fearing woman who had lost her arm to the most foul, most wicked vermin ever to draw a breath of fresh air."

"Save it for your newspapers," Philips interjected when Edwards paused for breath and King Bee whiskey. Zerelda Samuel had lost her arm a decade after the surrender, but Edwards had always been a little loose with his facts. "Since Jesse's death, Frank James is guaranteed a fair trial, and the

press alone will ensure impartiality. There will be more journalists than you have ever seen, more than attended the trial of
Charles Guiteau. Guiteau only assassinated President Garfield,
but Frank James is, well, Frank James. The rest will be up to
the judge and jury—and lawyers, of course. On both sides. It
is my understanding that Governor Crittenden has asked
William Wallace of Kansas City and the Daviess County solicitor, I disremember his name, to start preparing a case or cases
against James."

Edwards leaned back in his chair, soaking in Philips's comments, before reaching for his whiskey, killing it and asking,
"But you, sir, wore the blue. Why should Frank James trust
you, a former enemy?"

"I am a lawyer, so it is my solemn duty to defend my clients
with the utmost zeal. I have befriended many men who served
in the Confederacy as well, General Jo Shelby for one, and
even some raiders who rode with Anderson and Quantrill. The
War is over, and has been for seventeen years. More important,
sir, I am a Democrat."

The journalist poured another drink for both men. "How
would you approach the case?"

"Cases," Philips corrected. "We can only assume Crittenden's prosecutors are sorting through facts and evidence, trying to build their strongest case, the Blue Cut or Glendale train
robberies, maybe even something older. What has he been indicted for already? Blue Cut and the Pinkerton detective's
murder?"

"Balderdash, the both of them—" Edwards began, but
Philips held up his hand in protest, and to his surprise, the
reprobate shut up and let him continue.

"And if Frank is acquitted, he is most likely to face another
trial, and not only in Missouri. Alabama, Kentucky, Minnesota, Iowa . . . the James boys threw a wide loop. This could
be a long, most arduous process."

"One that could make you quite wealthy, I suppose, and
Frank James destitute."

"Unlikely, sir. My rates are reasonable, even more so in this
matter."

"Yours perhaps, but there will be other lawyers on our team.

You must be aware of that. This great legal clash will not be like some dime novel's showdown, *mano a mano*. It will be a baseball game, one lawyer pitching evidence, another batting, others in the field, on the bases. Even a barrister with your capable talents could not fight this fight alone. It requires a team, which is why I have also been in contact with Lieutenant Governor Charles Johnson, Colonel Christopher Garner of Richmond and the gallant Henry Clay Dean, the Sage of Rebel Cove."

A dejected Colonel Philips reached for his whiskey. "Oh," he said.

September 24, 1882
Kansas City, Missouri

"Care for some coffee, Mr. Hamilton?" William Wallace asked.

"No," the attorney said, rubbing his eyes. "What I'd like is a glass of rye at a gentleman's establishment."

Smiling, Wallace topped his mug and said, "Well, you'll not get that in this town, I'm afraid. Not on a Sunday."

"Thanks to you," Hamilton said. The Daviess County solicitor tried to make his comment sound like a joke, but a humorless man like William Hamilton would always fail in comedy. Besides, Wallace understood that his colleague meant it. Everything was his fault: the fact they couldn't build an airtight case against Frank James in any crime, the fact that the window was swollen shut in Wallace's office so that they couldn't get any fresh air or breeze and now the fact that Hamilton wanted a drink and couldn't get one because Wallace had managed to close every saloon in Kansas City in observation of the Sabbath.

Well, the hell with him.

Wallace took his cup back to his desk and stared at the file. A bank in Independence had been robbed in 1878, and a few people had originally suspected the James Gang was back in action after the Northfield fiasco left the gang shot to pieces up in Minnesota in 1876. Eyewitness accounts seemed far from conclusive, though, and for every person Wallace or his associates could find who agreed to testify that the James brothers had committed the crime, three more would say, "Nah, it wasn't Frank and Jesse but some border trash who wanted to plant suspicion on the Jameses." Wallace eventually found himself agreeing with the naysayers, and even if he believed the James Gang had been involved, he would never bring such a shoddy case to court for certain acquittal.

"How's the Whicher case looking?" he asked Hamilton.

J. H. Whicher was a twenty-six-year-old Pinkerton operative who showed up at the James farm on March 10, 1874. He told Mrs. Samuel that he was a lowly traveler and asked to work for food and found at the farm. Apparently, the lunatic detective thought Mrs. Samuel would be daft enough to hire him on the spot, so that he would soon know the whereabouts of the James brothers and the Pinkertons would get their men. J. H. Whicher thought he was a great detective but proved to be one dumb bastard. His body was found shot to pieces on March 11 at the Liberty-Independence-Lexington crossroads.

"I've seen stronger cases. The only person who saw Whicher and his murderers," Hamilton said, "was John Brickley. Three men came to the Blue Mills Ferry early that morning, said they were lawmen and had captured this horse thief. Brickley said the fourth man was bound and gagged. He ferried them over and never saw them again. He identified the alleged horse thief as Whicher, and described the three men. The deputy sheriff was John Thomason, and he thought, from the descriptions, that the three killers were Jesse James, Arthur McCoy and Jim Anderson."

Wallace shook his head. "That's about as weak as the Independence robbery. No Frank James. No eyewitnesses."

"Well, we could argue—"

"We'd lose. Even if Brickley could put Frank James on the ferry, he didn't witness the murder. Certainly, we could draw a pretty good line between Blue Mills and the crossroads where they dumped Whicher's body, but it's just not that strong of a case."

Hamilton relented. "As I said, it's not strong, but it's a murder charge. By the grace of God, we could put Frank James on the gallows. That's why I like the Gallatin bank robbery back in sixty-nine. Those assassins murdered John Sheets, shot the clerk, stole seven hundred dollars. There were witnesses, too. I would present a strong case. The jury would have no choice but to convict, and Frank James would be hanged. . . ."

And William Hamilton would run for governor, Wallace said to himself. *Maybe even the United States Senate.* William Decatur Hamilton wanted to try Frank James in Daviess County, where he would be the lead prosecutor. Of course, Wallace wanted to see Frank James behind bars, maybe with a noose around his neck, but he wasn't certain trying the outlaw for a bank robbery thirteen years ago would do that. Yet the evidence had to be stronger than what they had for the Independence robbery or the Whicher murder.

He lifted his cup, found the coffee cold and sighed.

Chapter 6

The Jesse James band of outlaws is no more; the desperadoes are totally scattered, death has claimed many and the prison guards many more, and the few at large are cautioned to depart from their wickedness and lead law-abiding lives.

—J.W. Buel, *The Border Bandits: Jesse and Frank James,* undated

October 1, 1882
St. Louis, Missouri

To Honorable T. T. Crittenden, Governor

Your Excellency:

Time has demonstrated that however careful a man may follow the path of good citizenship, and however successful I may be in gaining the confidence and respect of those who associate with me daily and hourly in every act, the work of heaping infamy on the name my children are to bear goes steadily on and on. As it began so many years ago, the greater the crime which startles the people of our Western states, the greater the certainty that it will be attributed to my act or instigation. However strange it may seem that a man of the reputation I have, should assume to possess either pride or sensibility, I have the hardihood to lay claim to some degree of both.

For years, the one desire of my life has been to regain

the citizenship which I lost in the dark days when, in Western Missouri, every man's hand was against his neighbor's, and to have an opportunity of proving, by submission to the most rigorous test, that I am not unworthy. Logically, it is said, that where there's so much smoke, there must be the fire; that although some of the charges made against me may be unjust, all are not without foundation, and that the evasion of the officers of the law is not the course of an innocent man. May I bow to their logic and reply that the man who is now making this appeal does not do so from the standpoint of a martyr.

He comes to you, their representative, to say that though his suffering has been a hundredfold greater than they have any knowledge of, unmeasurably greater than the course which he evaded would have attached to his acts, he recognizes that he has no right to complain of his lot. He comes as a man who, conscious of an honest purpose, asks to be permitted to do what an earnest, law-abiding citizen may to remove from Missouri the odium for which, in part, he is responsible. He comes as a man who, outlaw though he has been, has innocent ones who call him father and husband, and who possesses a love as strong and devoted as was ever found in men whose lives are blameless before the world, and one who is anxious to remove from their closet the skeleton which has so long been its hideous occupant.

If it were not for the fear of the responsibility for that which I did not do, rather than for that which I did, Governor Crittenden, you should never have had to put a price upon my head; but an excited and justly indignant public is not discriminative, and when a man is stripped of the safeguard of that presumptive innocence with which the law theoretically surrounds him, as I would be, he is put to the dangerous necessity of proving a negative. That fear is still with me, and as I write, it prompts me to abandon my present purposes, and having for nearly twenty years proved my ability to

*evade an attempt to capture me, to take my little family
and go to some remote section where I can live a quiet
life, free from apprehension. That I refuse to obey such
an impulse; that I prefer to go back to my boyhood home
and face my disgrace, in order to live it down; that I am
willing to place myself under a surveillance to which no
man in Missouri has ever yet been subjected, as must
naturally be the case, should I return; that I choose this
rough course when some other ones offer, I humbly
submit, is a proof that I am not so bad as I have been
painted, and that the elements of manhood have not
been omitted from my nature.*

*Right terribly, Governor Crittenden, have the offenses
against society which have been charged against the
James family been avenged. God knows enough blood
has been spilled, enough hearts broken, enough lives
blighted. God knows that if it is the purpose of the law
to prevent crime by making its punishment awful to
contemplate, that purpose has been served in a large
degree in the ten years of terror and tragedy. Is its
demand for vengeance insatiable? Is "justice tempered
with mercy" a mere poetical nothing? Must the great
State of Missouri indulge a spirit of revenge, until it has
recovered its last ounce of flesh, or laying all
considerations of mercy aside, cannot your state, would
to God I could say "my state," better afford now that it
has vindicated its laws as no state ever did before, to say
to its supplicants, "Yes, come in. We will convert your
very notoriety into a proper instrument of good order;
we will purely, as an unsentimental investment, restore
you to citizenship, and give you an opportunity to prove
your contrition and further purpose. We will call upon
you to utilize your experience and knowledge of
wrongdoing in the enforcement of the laws which you
have in the past been charged with violating. You have
won the confidence of all who now condemn you. We
point to it all as a proof of our wisdom."*

*If I were certain that I would not be made a
scapegoat, I would never have troubled you with this*

petition, but would have long ago faced your courts and met your charges; but being once in the toils, I would have had to accept all the chances; and where none would have been interested in my innocence of what might be alleged, many might find it to their advantage to assist in convicting me. Put yourself in my place for one moment, and then judge of my course in keeping out of the law's clutches. There is another consideration, other than already mentioned, which has weighed heavier in favor of my taking my present step. For five months I have been in constant dread that some rash friend of mine or Jesse's, or some silly person seeking notoriety, might carry out the threats of assassination which have, according to published reports, poured in upon you. Suppose for one moment that that had occurred, is there a man living who would not have held me responsible for it? And yet, not only were the threats not mine, as you will discover by comparing them to my writing, but the thought of revenge was never for one moment entertained by me.

I have now stated my case, and have, I trust, avoided savor of mawkishness, and I ask, if you cannot give me some hope for amnesty under the conditions I have specified? It may strike you that modesty is not the prominent characteristic of this request, but it should be remembered that it comes from a man who is still at large, although it need not be the cause of a deal of apprehension. I do not appeal as a man who, having followed the wrong course until his head is whitening and he is tottering on the verge of the grave, is taught repentance by his incapacity for further iniquity, but as one who is yet young and vigorous and who has reasonable ground to believe that there are many years left him for active service within the pale of society, than those which he has spent outside of it. I submit that is it not a proper question for your consideration, whether it would not be better to have Frank James a hunter of fugitives than a fugitive? Whether Frank James, humbled, repented and reformed before all the world,

will not be an example more fraught with good to the
rising generation than Frank James, a mysterious
wanderer, or the occupant of a felon's cell, or grave?

This appeal, though anomalous and possibly without
a complete precedent, is not the result of a sudden whim,
but is born of a determination which has been forming
for years, and which has already stood the test of four
years of a sober, industrious farm life, as I will have no
difficulty in satisfying you. I am prouder of the nerve
which has enabled me to take this step in behalf of my
better nature, than any courageous act of all my past
life. I write this letter from St. Louis and leave it here to
be mailed. An answer addressed in care of my wife at
Independence, Mo., will reach me. I will not say how
fervently I pray that it will not be the answer of a
Nemesis.

"Yours contritely and hopefully," Major John Newman Edwards dictated. "Frank James."

After scratching his signature, Frank James rubbed his wrist
and suddenly chortled.

"What strikes you as humorous, my good man?" asked Edwards, peering over the outlaw's shoulder at the final page of
the draft, checking penmanship and spelling although, after
half a bottle of whiskey, Frank James wasn't sure the journalist
could see anything but a blur.

"Well," he answered, "that's the longest letter I ever wrote,
and I didn't say one thing about the weather."

"And undoubtedly, old comrade, it is the best letter you
have ever penned. Now come, let us check out of this dismal
hotel and ride the rails. I shall disembark at Sedalia, while you
should continue on to Independence and await word from your
lovely wife regarding the governor's reply. I also shall arrange
an interview with a reporter I know, a good man, Frank
O'Neil, political editor for the *Republican* in St. Louis. We
shall sit in different cars. Pretend you do not know me. It is
imperative. . . ."

While Edwards continued lecturing on stealth, Frank James
blew on the paper to dry the ink, folded the letter and stuffed it

in an envelope. "Major Edwards," he said, handing the letter to his friend, "I do have a little experience in evading capture."

October 4, 1882
Independence, Missouri

Harry Bolingbroke, Duke of Hereford, was marching to the castle with the Duke of York and Earl of Northumberland when someone tapped on the door. Frank James closed his copy of *Richard II*, swung his long legs over the bed, and drew the Remington revolver from the holster on his right hip. He crossed the hotel room, thumbing back the hammer as he walked, and kept the muzzle pointed at the floor until he reached the door. As his left hand gripped the knob, he stepped away from the door and raised the barrel.

"Yeah?" he said huskily.

"It's Annie." Recognizing her voice, he exhaled, carefully lowered the hammer and holstered the long-barreled .44. He slid the bolt and stepped back, inviting his wife inside.

She wasn't smiling as she pulled a letter from her purse.

> *Executive Department*
> *Jefferson City, Mo.*
> *October 3, 1882*
> *Frank James*
> *c/o Mrs. Ann Ralston James*
> *Independence, Mo.*
>
> *Sir:*
>
> *Your letter, dated St. Louis, 1 October 1882, has been received in which you apply to me for amnesty or a pardon. Under the constitution of the state I cannot grant a pardon, even if agreed to, before conviction of some crime. Whether you can be convicted of any violation of the law is not for me to say; that the courts of the state will determine in the proper way when you are before them.*
>
> *I think it was wise in you to abandon the life you are*

charged with leading, and in surrendering to the legal authorities of the state you will have an opportunity to prove it to the world; if guilty, the law decrees the punishment. If you surrender, you, as any other man charged with crime, shall and will have a fair and impartial trial.

The intelligence and character of the courts of this state are ample guarantees of such a trial without any prejudice or sympathy of the people but under the judicial form of justice and well-established laws. As determined as I am to see the laws enforced against all grades of crime, I am nonetheless convinced of the importance to society of having every man within the grasp of the law protected in his rights, however lawless he may have been, when he yields voluntarily and submissively to that law and appeals to that and me for justice and mercy.

You may be innocent or you may be guilty of the heinous crimes charged to you. That, the court will determine, as before said, and after the voice of the court is heard, then if it becomes necessary, I will decide what my action will be.

> *Yours truly,*
> *Thomas T. Crittenden*
> *Governor of Missouri*

"Well," he said, "I guess it's what I expected. Where's Robert?"

"With his grandparents. I told Mother I'd probably stay the night."

He raised his eyebrows. "Why, ma'am, that is rather forward of you."

"Don't joke." There was an urgency in her voice, and he immediately felt shamed. "Not now," she added softly, and he realized she had been crying. She found a chair and collapsed in it.

A hell of a life he had given her. Eight years of misery, of worry, of assumed names and lies. He had greeted his beloved spouse with a cocked revolver in his hand. He couldn't even remember the last time he hadn't been heeled. Even during their lovemaking, he had made sure a pistol had been within reach, under a pillow or holstered on the bedpost. He unbuckled the shell belt—now about a size too small for his expanding waistline, anyway—and draped it on a coatrack.

"I'll need to send a wire to Major Edwards," he told her as he pulled on his frock coat. "As soon as I get a reply, I'll be back. You'll wait?"

"Of course."

He felt better, but still pulled the Remington from the holster and slid it into a coat pocket. This close to ending his life on the run, he didn't want to get shot dead now.

Edwards's reply—WILL MEET YOU AT INDEPENDENCE DEPOT 7TH INST STOP MAJOR EDWARDS—came quickly, and Frank James understood the code. Instead of rendezvousing with the major at the Independence train station on the seventh, he would join him in Sedalia tomorrow. He didn't know what Edwards had planned, but he wasn't about to stop trusting him. Edwards had gotten him this far.

He walked, shoulders slumped, head down, back to the Merchants' Hotel. He had been running since the war, and now everything would change. His life would no longer be in his own hands, or Cole's or Dingus's, but in those of some lawyers he didn't even know. He could be hanged or spend the rest of his life in prison, never to see Annie or his son again. It would have been so easy, he thought, to buy a ticket and board a train for California.

Maybe he could find his daddy's grave this time. His pa hadn't had much luck, either, lighting out to strike it rich in the spring of 1850 only to come down with camp fever and get planted in an unmarked grave in Hangtown. He imagined what would have happened if the Reverend Robert James had found his fortune instead of his death in California. He would have moved the family west, and Dingus and Frank would have avoided the War for Southern Independence, the murders, Bloody Bill and William Quantrill, would have never heard of General Order Number Eleven or Northfield, Minnesota.

Frank James would be a different man now, but he wouldn't be married to Annie.

He opened the door to his room and saw her. She had ordered a hot bath and sat soaking in the tub, humming "Silver Threads Among the Gold." He quickly closed the door, worked the bolt, shoved his .44 in the holster and hung his coat and hat. "Bring me a towel," she called out and stood, and Frank James stood transfixed, staring at her small, wet back, mesmerized as he had been on their wedding night at her peachy skin and that perfectly shaped . . . He caught himself, cleared his throat and found the towel.

She giggled as he handed it to her, almost stepping into the tub himself. "Help me out," she asked, and he put his hands over her thin waist and lifted her onto the floor. She dropped the towel, and he leaned forward and kissed her, moving his hands up her waist. She responded hungrily, knowing this might be their last night together, and began pushing him back toward the bed. He slipped off his suspenders, fell back onto the mattress, small, delicate, beautiful Annie climbing on top of him, her kisses growing harder. He cupped her breasts, heard himself groaning as she began working on his trouser buttons.

She stopped suddenly, cursing, and whispered, "Frank, I can't undo these buttons. Help me, please."

His wife didn't have to ask twice.

October 5, 1882
Jefferson City, Missouri

The sleepy-eyed little troll examined the signatures in the registration book and said not too enthusiastically, "Welcome to the McCarty House, Major Edwards, Mr. Winfrey," before cutting loose with a massive yawn. "Can I help with your bags?"

"We'll manage," Edwards said testily, taking the key and ascending the stairs with Frank James, alias B. F. Winfrey of Marshall, Missouri, where they entered the third room on the left. Both men immediately opened their carpetbags, the journalist rooting for his whiskey and Frank James, who had shaved his beard but kept his mustache, reaching for shell belt and revolver.

Edwards uncorked the bottle, took a pull and stared at the gunbelt the outlaw was hanging over a bedpost. "Why don't you carry a derringer or a smaller pistol, my good man? Something less unseemly, easily hidden?"

"Never took much stock in hideaway guns," Frank answered. "I prefer firepower. So did Dingus, Cole, all the boys." He thumbed open the chamber gate, pulled the hammer to half-cock and rotated the cylinder on his forearm. Satisfied, he shut the gate, lowered the hammer and slid the Remington into the holster. "And I don't keep the hammer on an empty chamber, either. There are six beans in the wheel, sir. Figured five bullets might get me killed. Six might keep me alive. Ain't blowed my foot off yet."

Absorbing this, the journalist passed the bottle to his companion with a quick nod. "That gives me an idea. You shall hand over your gunbelt personally to the governor tomorrow afternoon."

Frank James seemed skeptical, drank, and returned the bottle of rye. "Major, if I walk up to the governor wearing this, I'll likely be shot dead in two seconds. No offense, but—"

"No, no, no, no, Frank, you must trust me. I shall arrange everything. You'll even remove your cartridges, and Crittenden will know everything is safe. We'll make sure a few reporters and politicians are on hand for your surrender. You'll tell Crittenden . . ." He took a drink for inspiration, which didn't help, so he had another, and his eyes gleamed with immense satisfaction. "You'll tell him, 'I want to hand over to you that which no living man except myself has been permitted to touch since 1861.' Yes, that is extraordinary."

"Extraordinary is the word," Frank agreed, reaching for the bottle. "This model didn't even come out till seventy-five, and I've worn it only six years."

"It doesn't matter, Frank. My fellow scribes will love it, and it will be in every newspaper across the nation. You must quit thinking of yourself as a soldier or outlaw and see yourself as an entrepreneur and hero, the most famous man in America today. Publicity, my friend, is everything."

Chapter 7

Frank was at the McCarthy House this evening and many prominent citizens were there seeking the honor of shaking hands with him.
   —*Topeka* (Kansas) *Daily Capital*, October 6, 1882

October 5, 1882
Jefferson City, Missouri

They dined on biscuits and gravy that morning in the hotel, retired to the veranda, where each smoked a cigar and read a newspaper, Frank James digesting the *Jefferson City Examiner* and Major Edwards critiquing the previous afternoon's *Kansas City Evening Star*. The hotel manager, who had been asleep when the two checked in, came outside and warmly greeted the Sedalia journalist, who in turn introduced Frank James as B. F. Winfrey, an old friend from Marshall. The manager insisted on bringing each man another cup of coffee and an oatmeal cookie, which the guests enjoyed before exchanging newspapers.

Afterward, Edwards suggested a stroll about town, and Frank James agreed. He didn't feel nervous at all, which surprised him. This was undoubtedly his last day of freedom, at least for a while, and he had bowed to Edwards's insistence that he not tote his Remington .44 around town. No sense in risking being arrested for carrying a concealed weapon. That would ruin the surrender the major had coordinated. He couldn't remember the last time he had gone anywhere without a weapon, not even church, or when he had walked along a Missouri boardwalk without grinding his teeth and wiping clammy palms against his trousers. Despite any anxiousness, he remained wary and alert, scouting possible ambush sites behind rain barrels and atop brick facades, a habit that had kept him alive for twenty years, while sizing up passersby with quick glances, looking for bulges in their coats, nervousness in their eyes, anything that might reveal them as a Pinkerton operative or bounty hunter.

The streets throughout Missouri's capital city, however, seemed filled only with businessmen and fair women on this day, and at least a half dozen men stopped Edwards to shake his hand, compliment him on his latest editorial, and offer to buy him a whiskey, which, to the surprise of Frank James, the major declined.

They window-shopped, tipped their hats to passing women and, after a wagon loaded with whiskey barrels drove by, reminding Edwards of his thirst, ducked inside a saloon across from the *Examiner* offices for the major's eye-opener. Shortly after noon, they returned to the McCarthy House for scalloped oysters, carrots, fresh bread and a bottle of red wine. They spent the rest of the afternoon in the lobby, discussing the stock market, railroads, a yellow fever outbreak in New Orleans and various newspaper topics with other hotel guests and polished off two more cigars and a late-afternoon brandy. They retired upstairs at four thirty.

Frank unloaded the Remington and pushed the cartridges into the loops on his shell belt, only to discover he had room for just five bullets, so he tossed the last shell to Edwards. "A souvenir," he said as he buckled on the belt and found his long linen duster. The duster might look conspicuous along the capital city boardwalks, but it was long and loose enough to hide the gunbelt. Besides, Edwards commented, the James-Younger Gang had been known for wearing dusters, so the wardrobe would please the waiting journalists and politicians.

Dressed in a conservative gray herringbone sack suit, Major Edwards had shunned his usual gaudy colors and clashing fabrics—at least, that was what Annie told him; Frank James didn't see anything wrong with wearing striped breeches and a plaid shirt—and looked as drab as the autumn sky.

"Shall we?" Edwards asked as he slipped a flask into an inside coat pocket.

He wished the major would have offered him a drink first. After running a long finger underneath the tight collar of his boiled shirt, he bobbed his head slightly, buttoned the duster about his waist and said, "Let's start the ball."

The note he had been delivered said to expect them shortly before five o'clock today, and had suggested inviting a few members of the press and men of authority—not that Governor Thomas T. Crittenden needed any advice from a clod like John Newman Edwards. Crittenden glanced at the Waterbury clock on his office wall before considering the bored men he had invited to witness this momentous occasion. None of them had any clue as to why he had invited them here, although State Supreme Court Justice John Ward Henry was no dunce, and the Frank James interview that ran in the *St. Louis Republican* two days earlier should have been a clue. Shaking his left foot and squirming in a chair, state treasurer Phil E. Chappel looked in dire need of a privy, while the state auditor and adjutant general sat chattering about nothing, undoubtedly expecting food or spirits to arrive shortly. Crittenden had also invited a few journalists—writers for the *Globe-Democrat* and *Republican* in St. Louis, the *Kansas City Times* and *Topeka Daily Capital*, the scribes who hadn't tormented him recently—but they probably expected him to reveal the latest threats he had received since Jesse James's assassination. As far as those newspaper editors who had gotten his Irish up, he snickered in spite of himself, enjoying the fact that they'd have to get the biggest story since Jesse James's death off the wires.

Five minutes till five. Had Edwards played him for a fool? Crittenden began grinding his teeth, cursing his gullibility, but relaxed when footsteps echoed in the rotunda. A moment later came the hushed voice of his secretary, Finis R. Farr, and the unmistakable hyperbole of John Edwards. Farr stuck his head in the office and announced, "Governor, Major Edwards and a guest are here to see you."

Crittenden rose, nodded at the journalists to start taking notes and said, "Show them in." Only a couple writers took interest, however, and most guests greeted the newcomers with polite nods and fake smiles before continuing their own dull babble. The rest simply shook their feet or twiddled their thumbs.

Frank James was taller than Crittenden had expected, slender, with thinning hair and a thick mustache. Nothing about the man really stood out except his blazing blue eyes and that ridiculous duster he wore. Crittenden almost didn't recognize Edwards in his somber suit. "Governor Crittenden," said the journalist, and the rye-soaked breath assured the governor that this indeed was the Victor Hugo of the West. "I desire to introduce you to my friend, Frank James."

That commanded everyone's attention. Even Finis Farr left his desk to stand in the doorway and gawk. Frank James stepped forward, unbuttoned his duster and worked on the buckle of a well-oiled gunbelt. Someone—Crittenden thought it was the *Globe-Democrat* hack—swore, probably thinking the outlaw was about to splatter the Missouri flag behind the governor's desk with Crittenden's brains, and for an instant Crittenden felt fear. It would be easy, he realized, for Frank James to avenge his brother's death. Hell, he'd probably get away with it, and those damned ink spillers, including that varmint John Edwards, would have an even bigger story. The apprehension faded immediately, though, as the humble-looking outlaw wrapped the belt around the holster and held out leather and iron.

"Governor Crittenden," Frank James said mechanically, "I want to hand over to you that which no living man except myself has been permitted to touch since 1861, and to say that I am your prisoner." When the governor hesitated, the outlaw offered, "I have taken all the cartridges out of the weapon. You can handle it in safety."

He almost laughed as he took the heavy weapon and rig. This had all the earmarks of Major Edwards. Crittenden wasn't a fool, and he had more than a passing knowledge of firearms. The revolver was a Remington New Army model 1875.

"Not since 1861?" he asked with a wink.

The outlaw blinked, hadn't expected this, but recovered like a well-trained actor to ad lib, "The cartridge belt has been mine for only seventeen years."

Crittenden placed the Remington and gun leather on his desk, gestured at the other men and said what he had rehearsed all morning, "You shall have every protection afforded by the laws of your country, and as fair a trial as though you were the son of a president." Turning to his guests, he announced, "Gentlemen, may I present to you, Frank James."

While handshakes and introductions were being delivered, Crittenden asked Farr for another chair, which was quickly brought in. Frank James sat down, crossed his long legs, and answered questions from the reporters, sometimes addressing the journalists with his answers, sometimes speaking directly to Crittenden.

"What about the death threats mailed to the governor?" the *Times* reporter asked.

Frank James shot Crittenden a glance. "Over the past few days, I have received threats from several men in several states," Crittenden explained. The outlaw shook his head, turned to the reporters and gave his speech about all those crimes being blamed on poor Frank James, how he was guiltless, how he was painted as a blackheart but had been a law-abiding citizen who just wanted to do well for his wife and son, basically rehashing what he had written in that rambling appeal mailed from St. Louis. Turning back to the governor, he said, "I am in your hands to do with me as you see best."

This man is a born thespian, or even a politician. Crittenden patted James's shoulder and approached his secretary. "Send an aide out for a bottle of Scotch, better make it two, and a box of cigars."

"Yes, sir," Farr said. "But what are we going to do with him?"

"There are indictments against James in Jackson County, so tonight you'll escort our prisoner there. Wire William Wallace and the sheriff. Tell them to meet you at Independence with an arrest warrant. Also telegraph Hamilton, the prosecutor in Gallatin. We'll discard our celebrity into their hands."

The secretary simply stared, so the governor said, "Don't

worry, Finis. He just surrendered. I don't think he's planning an escape."

"Yes, sir," Farr said, but he didn't look altogether relieved as he hurried to find an aide.

Crittenden turned, found himself shaking hands with Justice Henry and heard the jurist saying, "He has won my sympathy already. If I were governor, I would pardon him right away, sir."

He gave John Henry Ward his biggest grin and slapped the self-proclaimed great legal mind on his back, telling the justice, "Yes, I know, I know," instead of what he wanted to say.

Frank James wasn't going anywhere, John Newman Edwards thought with a laugh, not tonight anyway. The distinguished guerrilla sat in the lobby of the McCarthy House, conversing with the same men who had engaged him in stimulating colloquy earlier this epic day. Only now, instead of yellow fever and the stock exchange, the discussions concerned Quantrill and Anderson, Wilson's Creek and Lawrence, the Youngers and Pinkertons and, naturally, Jesse James. As the hour approached ten o'clock, scores of men, plus one or two women and quite a few schoolboys, filled the lobby while others stood on the veranda, on windowsills, in the streets, trying to get as close as they could to the world's greatest border bandit, anything so they could brag to their grandchildren about how close they stood next to Alexander Franklin James, the greatest of the border bandits. By jingo, Edwards would bet his flask that the fabric would be ripped off the chair where Frank James now sat and sold as mementos.

The good men of Callaway County stood in front of their hero, congratulating him, pumping his hand, saying how they would free him on the spot if they could and generally offering to do just about everything but empty his cuspidor or slop bucket, and Edwards reckoned they would have gladly done either. All Frank James had to do was ask.

This was how things should be, he thought, the triumphant return home of Ulysses after so many adventures and trials . . . Romans cheering, hailing, bowing to Julius Caesar. Frank James made some crack, and the crowd's response almost knocked the shutters off the McCarthy House. Frank James seemed to be enjoying himself. Edwards had never realized just how gracious, how much an entertainer the man really was. He had always considered Frank the shy one, reticent, not a man for crowds or fame. Jesse had been the one to write the newspapers or leave witty notes for the posses they had escaped. Maybe Frank was coming out of hibernation now that he no longer found himself hidden in his younger brother's shadow.

Poor Jesse. He should have lived to see this. Jesse James should be here now, be the one onstage, sharing the glory with his big brother. But alas, such things were not meant to be. God works in mysterious ways. Perhaps Jesse had to die for Frank to live the life of . . . Edwards drew a blank, couldn't think of an appropriate name, but no matter—he wasn't on deadline.

"Sir?"

The peevish little secretary from the governor's office stood at his side.

"Yes, Farr?"

"There has been a change in plans," he began, but Frank James had the crowd guffawing once more, so Edwards told the imp to speak up.

"Governor Crittenden says you and Frank James should spend the night in town!" he shouted above the din, which didn't appear to be lessening anytime soon. "A group of Jackson County officials is taking a train here this night. I will accompany you and them to Independence on the seven-ten after breakfast. If there are any problems obtaining a room here at the McCarthy House, the governor says he will take care—"

Edwards stopped the secretary with a chortle. "Farr," he said. "I don't think anyone will sleep in Jefferson City tonight."

October 6, 1882
Cass County, Missouri

As soon as the journalist left after his ten-minute interview aboard the rocking train, William Wallace propped his feet on the seat across from him, tucked the copy of the *Republican* (the one with the Frank James story that ran on the third) beneath the seat, removed his hat and ran his fingers through his hair, watching Frank James stare at the farmsteads and patches of woods speeding past them. Wallace hadn't had a moment alone with his prisoner until now, and he tried to think of something to say, but nothing came to him.

In the row behind Frank James's seat were Marshal John Murphy, Sheriff James Timberlake and a reporter from Topeka, Kansas. Behind Wallace sat Police Commissioner Henry Craig, Finis Farr and two other hangers-on from Jefferson City. Major Edwards sat toward the back, concentrating on the story he was writing. People filled the aisle every minute, just passing from car to car so they could see Frank James. Maybe, if they were lucky, the killer would say hello or give them a friendly nod.

The outlaw opened the window as the train began to slow. He looked intently at the scenery and smiled. "That's mighty good bushwhacking country," he said to no one in particular. "I know every foot of that ground." Reporters' pencils began scratching. "Many a time have I watched from these hills and seen the soldiers pass up and down at all the stations all the way from Jefferson City."

Shaking his head at his fond recollections, Frank James turned from the window and looked at Wallace curiously. "Lose a button off your coat?"

Wallace met the question with bewilderment. Frank James pointed a long finger. "That button in your hand. I was going to say my wife's meeting us at Independence. She's a darned good seamstress."

He stared at the black button he had been twirling between his fingers. He hadn't realized he had been fooling with the reminder Lizzie Wymore had given him a year and a half ago, didn't even recall pulling it out. He slid the item into a pocket and said, "It's not from my coat." The outlaw's head bobbed as the two stared at each other in silence.

The conductor fought his way through the crowded aisle, informing passengers that they would be arriving at Pleasant Hill shortly.

"Won't be long now," Wallace said just to break the silence.

"Nope," the outlaw agreed.

Wallace relaxed, decided to push the conversation forward. "So Annie will be meeting us at Independence?"

"Meeting *me,* sir," he said, eyes blazing. He grinned to show his jealousy was an act. "How long have you known my wife?"

Longer than you, he thought, but answered, "I knew her in passing for several years, and saw her from time to time when she was teaching at Little Santa Fe." Frank James knew all of this already, and Wallace didn't feel comfortable talking about the man's wife. Wallace wanted to steer the conversation in another direction, somewhere that would help him in a courtroom.

"When were you last in Kansas City?"

"Don't rightly recall."

"Zerelda, your brother's widow, says you hid in her garret for two weeks after the Blue Cut robbery."

Frank James looked out the window. Wallace hadn't expected the outlaw to say anything damning, but it had been worth a shot. "I think she is mistaken," the outlaw said, and the locomotive's whistle gave a long toot as the train approached Pleasant Hill. Wallace could smell the engine's smoke, knew the conversation was over for now. The Topeka reporter asked a follow-up question about the Blue Cut robbery, but Frank James pretended he couldn't hear above the squealing wheels and brakes as the train slowed.

"Criminy," Finis Farr said, and Wallace looked out the window to see what had prompted the secretary's remark. At least forty people crowded the depot. One bearded man in homespun shirt and ducking trousers stuck a meaty paw through the open window and yelled, "Frank! Is it you?"

Cautiously, Frank James stood to shake the man's hand. "It's me, Bill Baldwin. Matt's brother. You don't remember me?"

The outlaw grinned widely. "Sure, Bill, of course I remember you. It's been too long. How is Matt?"

"Fair to middlin'." The man matched Frank James's grin. "Gawd A'mighty, Frank, it shore is good to see you again. You need anythin', jus' let me or Matt know. You know we're here for you 'cause you always was there for us Baldwins, you and Jesse."

"Hell, Bill, I know that. You take care of yourself, and don't you and Matt fret none over me." He gripped the man's hand again before falling back in his seat, smile widening even more, shaking his head.

Another man moved in to greet Frank James, but Sheriff Timberlake shoved his way between James and Wallace and pushed up the window with an oath. The crowd hissed and hooted, but Timberlake growled back and gave Frank James a withering stare before returning to his seat and barking at the conductor to get the damned train moving.

As the train pulled out of Pleasant Hill, Wallace asked, "Did that Bill Baldwin ride with you and Quantrill?"

"Not sure," the bandit answered. "To tell you the truth, Mr. Wallace, I don't have a notion who Bill Baldwin is, nor his brother, Matt."

Chapter 8

Louisville, Sept. 18—Charlie and Bob Ford, slayers of Jesse James, appeared . . . in this city last night, and were hissed and hooted at by the audience in the scene where Bob Ford shoots James. They say they will not come to Kentucky again.
—*Liberty Tribune*, September 21, 1883

October 6, 1882
Independence, Missouri

"How do you feel about your husband surrendering?"

The reporter reeked. His breath smelled of cigarettes and whiskey, and Annie James would not care to fathom a guess as to the last time he had bathed. He repeated the question and moved closer to hear her answer, smiling, as if his rotting teeth would make her feel comfortable, talkative.

"It's a good thing," she told him, pulling her son nearer while trying to back away from this wretched little man, only to find herself hemmed in by scores of Missourians who had descended upon the depot. She had known Frank and Jesse were popular among former Confederates, farmers and many Missouri Democrats—anyone who wasn't a banker, railroader or robber baron, some claimed—but never expected this. Years ago, she had enjoyed parties and crowds, but now she felt suffocated. Masses were to be avoided when you were Frank James's wife, and she shied away from the men carrying pencils and writing tablets, yet couldn't escape this malodorous scoundrel in front of her. The train was due at ten thirty, and it had to be close to that by now.

"What do you want for your husband and kid?"

"To farm," she said, hoping he would work his way through the mob to find some other soul to torment. "To live peacefully."

"What was it like to be married to Frank James, lady?"

A cry of "Smoke!" caused the mob to sway. "Here he comes!" a woman shouted before the reporter repeated his question. Someone jammed an elbow in her back and didn't even apologize. Another man shoved her aside, jarring little Robert, to get closer to the tracks. "Please," she began, almost bursting into tears, directing her plea at the reporter as well as the raucous gathering.

"Lady, just answer my questions. I got a job to do."

"Do it somewhere else," another woman said.

The reporter whirled to see one-armed Zerelda Samuel and Annie's father forcing their way to her rescue. Her mother-in-law scowled at the reporter and repeated her demand, but the miscreant turned his attack on the newcomers. "Why, you're Jesse James's mother. I'm Dan Steele with the *Daily Champion.* Are you relieved or scared that your son is surrendering? I mean, which is worse, to be shot dead like Jesse or risk hanging?"

Zerelda James Samuel leaned closer to the reporter, glanced at his tablet and sprayed it with snuff. Annie smiled, her father leaned on his cane to chuckle, and the reporter took the hint and his leave.

"Come on," said Mrs. Samuel, taking Annie by the hand and leading her into the throng. "Train's a-comin'." Strong as a steady mule, her mother-in-law plowed through men and women like an Acme Disc Cultivator, lowering her head and shoulders to push them aside, Annie, her father and Robert in tow. Zerelda Samuel's stern countenance, not to mention her hulking size, immediately stopped any complaints. When they reached the depot's edge, a sheriff's deputy told the crowd to make room for Frank James's family, and the assembly parted like some scene from the Old Testament.

"Look, Mommy," Robert said, pointing at the thick black smoke. The crowd's loud banter fell into a hushed whisper as the hissing, belching locomotive pulled into sight, smoke and cinders tearing their eyes. Annie's heart quickened, and she lowered her son onto the wooden platform. By the time the train pulled to a stop, everyone had fallen silent.

A pint-sized runt in bowler and sack suit stepped from the passenger car first, followed by Frank James. The silence ended with deafening cheers, and her husband simpered, tipping his straw hat and stepping toward his family.

"Buck!" his mother screamed, and Frank stooped to hug her. "My dear, dear son," she said, tears streaming down her cheeks. "Oh, my precious son." He pulled away from her, shook Annie's father's hand, ran his fingers through Robert's hair and embraced Annie, kissing her fiercely. She blushed. In her younger days, when suitors were lining at the door to see her, or when she was outshooting the men at Little Santa Fe, she would have been the one to cause others to blush, but she had changed since her marriage. She wanted nothing but privacy, for her family as well as herself.

He pulled away, wrapped an arm around her waist and gazed at the gathering. "It's been like this every place we stopped, Annie," he whispered. "Kinda feel like I'm running for public office." Lifting his head in recognition, he raised his voice, "Hello, Jim. It's been a spell. How's the wife and children?"

"Doin' great, Frank," a red-bearded man answered warmly. "By Gawd, it's good t' see ya ag'in."

"Frank!" a shorter man on the opposite end of the depot called. "Frank, it's me, David Tracey. Remember me?"

Frank's head spun in the direction of the new voice. "David Tracey, I'm not likely to forget you." He lowered his voice to tell Annie. "Rode with us at Lawrence. Meanest rapscallion ever to ride with Quantrill, and didn't give two hoots about me twenty years back." The voice raised again as he addressed the guerrilla. "Nobody's hanged you yet, Tracey?"

"Not hardly, my friend. And they'll dang sure never hang you!"

The crowd laughed and applauded, and Frank stepped forward to shake a few hands. Annie became aware of the men surrounding him, the little fellow who had stepped off the train first and others she recognized as Sheriff Timberlake, Major Edwards and Commissioner Craig.

"Hello, Annie."

She turned, pleased to see William Wallace, hat in hand. He smiled back, pulled on his hat and shook her hand. "Quite a turnout," she said.

"Yeah."

"I'm sorry, William. I'm sorry we couldn't agree to your terms earlier. I guess we should have. Crittenden wouldn't promise a pardon, either."

"It all worked out," he said. "I'm glad."

The crowd roared with laughter again. Frank was enjoying himself. Wallace looked behind her at the assembly and sighed in amazement. Her father walked up to shake Wallace's hand, and they spoke briefly before Wallace's gaze returned to Annie. "We have a carriage to take Frank into town," he said. "You and Robert can ride with us if you like, and your father and Mrs. Samuel can follow."

To jail. Her happiness vanished. She wondered if they had made a horrible mistake. Cole Younger and his two brothers were serving life sentences in Stillwater, Minnesota. What if Frank were locked up for the rest of his life? That would kill him, and her, as well.

Wallace offered his arm, and she took it, grabbing hold of her son's hand as they made their way to the steps.

If a hundred people had gathered at the depot, three times as many flocked to the courthouse. The judge hammered his gavel, officers called for order, but they were all shouted down. Court was adjourned, and the James entourage disembarked for the Merchants' Hotel, where the outlaw would be placed under temporary house arrest before being moved to jail after the excitement died down.

Frank James, wife and child.

He looked at his signature in the guest register and laughed. "That's the first time since sixty-six that I've signed my own name," he told the clerk, and the droves in the lobby cackled.

"I'll take Robert," Mrs. Samuel said. "Y'all get some rest."

Annie thanked her mother-in-law and followed Frank up the stairs, turning at the balcony at the sudden uproar below.

"Twenty-five dollars!" a man shouted at the clerk, who retreated until his back pressed against the mailboxes, clutching the heavy register against his chest.

"Thirty!"

"Fifty dollars. Fifty dollars, mister, for Frank James's signature."

"Seventy-five!"

She sighed, her husband laughed, and both entered the room, shaking their heads at the carnival downstairs.

October 10, 1882
New York, New York

His brother was in his cups when Bob Ford joined him behind the curtain at Bunnell's Dime Museum on Broadway and Ninth. 'Course, Charlie Ford had been roostered for most of the past six months, and the five hundred dollars they were getting paid a week kept Charlie well-fortified with courage.

How I Killed Jesse James kept bringing in the crowds, in Chicago, Cincinnati and now Manhattan. Bob Ford didn't care much for this venue, though. The promoters had rented out opera halls in the first two cities, but Bunnell's housed a bunch of circus freaks. Bob had buckled on his gunbelt in the dressing room he and his brother shared with a pale bald guy who had to weigh five hundred pounds, and Charlie had shared his flask with Galina Prokhor, who had a brownish-red beard and spoke in some sharp accent. Bob didn't care at all for these arrangements. The man who killed Jesse James shouldn't be performing in a damned freak show alongside some monstrosity with hands that belonged on a giant lobster, plus three-eyed dogs, a two-headed calf and skeletons purported to have been brought in from Egypt.

Those skeletons were about as authentic as the two horses on display. Dupes paid ten cents just to see—not even touch, mind you—a roan and bay Bob and Charlie swore were ridden by Jesse and Frank after the Winston robbery. Hell, those nags had been rented from a livery over on Lexington and likely hadn't been west of the Hudson.

"Ladies and gentlemen," slick-haired Gene Jefferson called out from the stage, "it is my honor and pleasure to introduce the illustrious Ford brothers of Missouri."

Bob shoved Charlie, who slipped his flask into a pocket and wobbled onto the stage. Puny kids filled most of the seats, although Bob noticed a couple of women in the back rows. They stared at him as they would while watching Lobster Larry roll his cigarettes with his deformed hands. Jefferson, his long, greasy hair smelling of perfume, continued with his introductions, telling how Robert Ford had risked his life and shot down the notorious desperado Jesse James.

The children clapped—a few whistled—but Bob could make out hisses and boos from some adults. Drunks, he figured. Vagrants and tramps who couldn't hold a job, else they wouldn't be at Bunnell's on a Tuesday afternoon. One dolt in a bell-crown hat and yellow brocade vest stood up, cupped his hands over his mouth and yelled, "Shot him in the back, you damned coward. We'll see how well you shoot against a man facing you after Frank's acquitted and comes gunning for you—"

His heckles were drowned out by others, those who had paid two nickels to see this act and didn't want some drunk to spoil it for them. Bob figured he'd silence him with his exhibition, anyway. Once the crowd quieted, Jefferson blabbered on another minute before bowing to the man who killed Jesse James.

He pushed his coattail back, turned to face the target twenty-five feet away and palmed the Navy Colt revolver that had been converted to take brass cartridges, lightly charged for the theater. Bob cocked and fired, cocked and fired . . . hitting the bull's-eye with all five shots. The crowd cheered, the drunk in the yellow vest sat slack-jawed and Bob holstered the revolver and followed Charlie off the stage.

This was his stage career. They wouldn't even let him talk, although his shooting spoke with much magnitude. The behemoth fat buffoon had left the dressing room when they returned, which suited Bob just fine. He unbuckled the gunbelt, tossed it on a table and asked his brother for a drink of whiskey.

"You homesick, Bob?" Charlie asked.

The liquor burned like acid and rocked his stomach. Charlie wasn't one to buy decent scamper juice, even when his pockets bulged with cash. "What makes you ask that?" he said, passing back the flask.

"'Cause I am. You reckon we can go back home, Bob? After we finish our tour?"

"You can, Charlie. I can't. Jesse's friends would shoot me dead the day I set foot in Missouri again." They'd likely shoot Charlie, too, but Bob didn't care. Hell, they'd be doing Charlie Ford a favor, ending his suffering. The simpleton felt guilty, and he hadn't even pulled the trigger.

Charlie held out the rotgut like a statue, and Bob decided he didn't mind the liquor's taste after all, so he grabbed the flask, unscrewed the top, and drained it. The drunken heckler's words bothered him like a rash. What if Frank James got off? What if he came gunning for his brother's killers? Frank James wouldn't be that stupid, would he? Wouldn't risk another arrest, would he?

"If you want to go home, Charlie, just let me know," he said suddenly. "'Cause if Frank goes to trial, I'd like you to be there."

"What for?" Charlie cried out.

"To keep an eye on things for me, brother. Don't fret none. You didn't kill Jesse. I did."

October 12, 1882
Kansas City, Missouri

Slamming the door would get everyone's attention, so that was just what Governor Thomas Crittenden did before assaulting his two lead prosecutors with a well-rehearsed cannonade. "Gentleman, I just came from the Independence jail, where I saw Frank James!" he shouted, making sure the lawyers and secretaries in the anteroom, as well as passersby on the street below, could hear.

"Did you have an appointment?" Wallace asked dryly.

Damn that impertinent jackass. Wallace had broken his concentration. The Jackson County solicitor looked up from his desk, coffee cup in one hand, spectacles in the other. "Don't get smart with me, Wallace," Crittenden said, shooting a withering glare at William Hamilton, too. "I've stayed in hotel rooms in our nation's capital that aren't as nicely furnished as Frank James's jail cell. He has a library, photographs hanging on the walls, steaks brought in for supper. Hell, he even has Brussels carpet on the floor. This man is under indictment, isn't he?"

"Without bail," Wallace said, "although Major Edwards approached me last week and informed me that if I would agree to bail, I would be even more popular in Missouri than Frank James. Edwards even said he would back my campaign for governor."

Blinking, Crittenden sank into the couch. His act had accomplished what he wanted—he had gotten some attention. Wallace's and Hamilton's assistants would be telling wives, friends and mothers that the governor was madder than a hornet, so he settled down. "What did you say?"

"I told him I'd like to be governor, but not for his price. I am under oath."

Crittenden reached into his breast pocket and withdrew a cigar, thought about offering one to Wallace and Hamilton but decided against it. After all, he was supposed to be angry at the solicitors. "The governor of Minnesota asked me to extradite Frank James so he can stand trial for the Northfield affair. I told him I would not until James has answered all of the charges he faces in Missouri. I came here to see how your cases are progressing."

The Jackson County prosecutor put on his glasses and set his mug on the desk. "The Independence robbery is all hearsay. I'm of a mind to dismiss that charge and concentrate on Blue Cut, but that case is weak as well. We haven't been able to place Frank at the scene of the Pinkerton detective's murder, either. Actually, I think our strongest cases are in the realm of my distinguished colleague." He bowed slightly at

the Daviess County attorney, and Crittenden turned to face that
blowhard while searching for a match in his vest pockets.

"As I told Prosecutor Wallace," Hamilton began, "I think
our best course is to try James for the bank robbery of sixty-
nine or the train robbery near Winston two years ago. Those
are not only foul robberies, but murder. We could hang Frank
James with a conviction."

Not likely, Crittenden thought. If Frank James were sentenced to death, Crittenden would have to commute the sentence to life in prison, or pardon the rascal outright. If he let
the bandit swing, well, Crittenden's life would be worthless.

"You'd be trail boss, I take it," he said, pausing to strike a
match against the office wall, "if we tried James in Gallatin."

"Naturally." Hamilton failed to hide his smirk.

"All right, gentleman," Crittenden said. He hated to leave—
the couch was damned comfortable—but he had to get back to
Independence to make an appearance so all of those Democrats would see how friendly he was to the border outlaw.
They would believe he supported Frank James, while the
lawyers and Republicans would think, after such an outburst in
Wallace's office, that he wanted Frank James behind bars or
six feet under. Crittenden, however, wasn't sure what he really
wanted, or what would be a political embarrassment. "Continue your investigations. I don't care how long it takes."

"What if his lawyers come in shouting habeas corpus?"
Wallace asked.

"They won't," Crittenden answered honestly. "He isn't
likely to be assassinated by some bounty hunter while in jail.
Mind you, I have rescinded the state's reward, but he's also
wanted in half the country. Besides, I don't think Frank James
is uncomfortable in the Independence jail."

"I can assure you of that, Governor," Hamilton said. "I
attended *Romeo and Juliet* at Wilson's Opera House in
Independence two nights ago. Frank James had a balcony seat—
escorted by two deputies, mind you—and when the actor playing Romeo saw him, he stopped his monologue and asked the
killer to stand and take a bow. The crowd gave him a standing
ovation."

Crittenden's mood improved. He might not have to worry

about signing some executive order that would pardon, reprieve, or hang Frank James. With any luck, the jury would acquit. He stood, tapped his ashes over a cuspidor and gave both lawyers a cigar.

"Like I said, gentlemen," he said, "take as long as needed. Just make sure you have a strong case before you go to trial."

Chapter 9

*I am willing to stand trial, sir. Every great crime and
robbery that has been committed in this western country
in the last twenty years has been laid at my door. The
courts will find that I am innocent.*

—Frank James

January 23, 1883
Kansas City, Missouri

Staring at the red strands reflecting in the mirror, William Wallace tried to remember: slightly longer end over . . . under . . . then what? He had been tying ribbon ties for years now, but maneuvering the thin silk this morning seemed as foreign to him as wrapping the coils in an executioner's noose. Nerves. A hell of a thing. He whispered directions as he fingered the ends of the tie, under, through the loop, pull to tighten and . . .

"Damn." The left side hung two inches longer, and he considered opting for an ascot or puffed tie but doubted if he could find one in the chest of drawers or armoire. He had been spending so much time at his office and on the road the past few months, trying to build a case against Frank James, that he had been lucky to find a shirt and tie that didn't need pressing, so he undid the knot and tried a third time. Two attempts later, the tie hung snugly and evenly. Relieved, Wallace slipped over his shoulder holster, checked the loads in the Colt Thunderer, pulled on his coat, grabbed his hat, greatcoat and woolen scarf and headed out the door.

He hailed a hack a block from Sue Boddington's Boarding-

house and rode to the courthouse, arriving just behind Frank
James, John Edwards, four guards and an army of lawyers.
They had come by train from Independence, trailed by dozens
of spectators—men, women and children—who didn't mind
the freezing temperature and biting wind. The Kansas City
court session was shaping up to resemble the zoo back in October in Independence when the defendant was first arraigned.
He hurried up the steps, shedding scarf and coat, and contorted
his body to slip through the door blocked by overmatched
bailiffs and spectators wanting a good seat.

In the courtroom sat sallow-looking Hamilton, sorting
through mountains of papers rising from the prosecution's
table. The cocksure attorney still believed Missouri's best
chance of convicting Frank James lay in the Winston or Gallatin robberies, but Jackson County had first crack at the desperado. The Independence or Blue Cut robberies, or the
Whicher slaying. Three months of investigations had not
helped any of those cases, and Wallace still thought Hamilton
was right. The only drawback to trying Frank James in Gallatin worked in the Daviess County solicitor's office. There
was a big difference between the two prosecutors; William
Wallace had always sought justice, while pompous, vindictive
William Hamilton wanted glory.

Wallace chanced a glance across the room. Frank James wore
a somber gray business suit—of a better cut than Wallace's or
Hamilton's wardrobe, for certain—and sat slouched, looking
comfortable and confident. Surrounded by Edwards, Colonel
John F. Philips, James Slover of Independence, John M. Glover
of St. Louis and Colonel Christopher Trigg Garner of Richmond,
the outlaw certainly had reason to look assured. His attorneys
were among the most respected in Missouri, and the brood
would likely grow before any trial date was set. Wallace jotted a
note to begin hiring other lawyers for the state's team.

The only problem was, heck, he wasn't certain for what
crime he planned on first trying Frank James—but he'd have
to make a decision soon.

"All rise."

His mind racing, he barely heard the preliminary proceedings and introductions. Hamilton had to nudge him after the

judge asked him to make his opening statements. He stood, chewed on his lower lip briefly and stepped around the table. Frank James was a rock, and everyone in the packed courtroom trained their eyes on the Jackson County prosecutor.

"Your Honor," Wallace began, focusing on the defendant, "after a lengthy investigation, I have decided that the State of Missouri does not have enough evidence to prove that Frank James was involved in the murder of Pinkerton detective Joseph Whicher or in the bank robbery in Independence. Therefore, we reluctantly dismiss both cases against the defendant."

Gasps filled the room, and the outlaw's lawyers stared dumbly. They hadn't expected this at all. Eyes glimmering in triumph, Frank James straightened in his seat and nodded. A thin man directly behind the defense table reached over the banister to pat James's back and whisper congratulatory remarks. Wallace cleared his throat and continued. "However, we will present an indictment against the defendant for robbery of the Blue Cut train on the seventh of September, 1881. With the court's permission, I will explain the charge."

Muffled complaints began rising in the chamber as Wallace walked back to the table. The gavel hammered for order, the defense attorneys rifled through their documents and Frank James no longer looked so content. As Wallace gathered his papers, William Hamilton leaned forward and whispered, "What are you doing, man? We don't have enough evidence to take to court on that one, either."

"I don't intend to, sir," he said with a slight grin. "While his showboating attorneys are trying to put together a defense for Blue Cut, we'll be gathering evidence for Winston and Gallatin. I'm letting you cut in on my dance, Mr. Hamilton. You'll try Frank James for murder."

He wasn't certain if the look on William Decatur Hamilton's face expressed sheer glee or total fear.

February 18, 1883
Missouri State Penitentiary, Jefferson City, Missouri

William Decatur Hamilton reluctantly caught up with Clarence Hite after Sunday Mass. He loathed his assignment and feared

for his safety, despite being chaperoned by two brick-faced go-
liaths carrying nightsticks that looked like toothpicks in their
hands. He had lost count of the number of criminals he had
sent behind the towering thirty-foot-high limestone walls.

Built on a bluff overlooking the Missouri River in 1836, the
prison housed the vilest men ever to draw a breath—simply
because Missouri seemed to breed such an ill lot. Some of
those evildoers, Hamilton figured, would love to rip out his
throat. After all, he had convicted many of them.

Not Clarence Hite, though, but only because the gyp hadn't
given Hamilton a chance. Arrested in Kentucky in February
1882, Hite had been extradited to Missouri and charged with
the Winston train robbery but pleaded guilty and was given
twenty-five years in this hellhole. Hamilton cursed the memory. If Hite had been man enough to stand trail, William Decatur Hamilton would have become the second prosecutor to
send a member of the James Gang to prison. Hite had turned
yellow, allowing William Hockaday Wallace to keep all that
glory for himself. It galled Hamilton that he had to interrogate
a swine like Hite while Wallace stood at the other end of
prison interviewing his claim to fame, Bill Ryan.

"That's him, boss." The guard on his left pointed the stick at
a pale man in stripes leaning against the limestone wall and
trying to roll a smoke in trembling hands.

"That's Clarence Hite?"

A year ago, Clarence Hite had been a strapping, big-
mouthed Kentuckian in his early twenties, full of brass, ever
the protector of his cousins, Jesse and Frank James, as a couple of missing teeth revealed. Now he resembled a cadaver,
spilling most of the Bull Durham tobacco onto the dewy
prison grounds. A sudden outburst of hacking coughs folded
his rail-thin body like a jackknife and destroyed the remnants
of his cigarette. When Hite straightened, he wiped specs of
blood off his lips.

"He's a lunger?" Hamilton said softly, instinctively retriev-
ing a handkerchief from an inside coat pocket to protect his
own mouth and nose.

"Yeah," the second guard replied. "He won't be needin' all

those twenty-five years. Young Hite's got hisself a death sentence."

"How long?"

The first guard answered. "Boss, if ya wants him to testify agin' Frank James, unless ya goes to trial in a month or so, ya best find yerself another witness. Warden be talkin' 'bout parolin' him in a week or two so he can go home to Kaintuck an' die."

"Go to hell," Bill Ryan told William Wallace, which was what he expected the prisoner to say.

Ryan's eyes hardened and his fists clenched. He would have gladly plucked out his right eye just for the chance to stain the stone walls with Wallace's brains, but the four guards standing behind the attorney kept slapping their clubs against their own ham-sized palms as a safeguard.

Wallace stepped inside the cramped cell and leaned against the iron bars. Ryan turned his back, unbuttoned his fly and pissed into the foul-smelling slop bucket by his bunk. "This is what I think of you and your damned offer," he said. It surprised Wallace that the convict didn't try to soil the trousers of the attorney who had confined him to this wretched existence. Wallace looked around the miserable quarters, breathing as little of the rancid air as possible. No wonder so many Jefferson City prisoners came down with consumption, although Ryan looked as strong and mean as he had after his extradition from Tennessee back in eighty-one.

"Ryan," Wallace said easily once the prisoner had turned around and buttoned his pants, "I figured you were a smart man." That was an outright lie. Bill Ryan was dumber than a fence post. "I thought just maybe you'd like to get out of prison before the twentieth century."

The convict laughed and spit in front of Wallace's boots. "Figger I'll get paroled, Wallace. I'm one cooperative prisoner."

"Then cooperate with me."

"No." The word came out like a gunshot. "You just talkin' in the wind, Wallace. I ain't hearin' you."

He had expected Ryan to be a hardcase. Testifying against Frank James would be tantamount to committing suicide, but they needed someone to put the outlaw at the scene. He hoped Hamilton was having better luck with Clarence Hite. "I can get you out quicker than any chance at parole. I'm talking about a full pardon from the governor."

Ryan answered with another curse before sitting on his bunk and adding, "I ain't no Tuck Bassham."

"Tucker Bassham isn't in this pigsty for twenty-five years."

"Twenty-four now. Not long till it's only twenty-three." He stretched his arms, muscles bulging against the striped shirt, and abruptly laughed, but his eyes held no humor. Once the laughter stopped, Ryan began a tirade. "That son of a bitch Bassham. He'd sell out his own mother, but I ain't like that, Wallace. No, sir. Hell, the only reason you put me in here was because of that Judas bastard. I could whup you and Bassham both, one hand tied behind my back, and nobody could stop me. Hell, if I had a mind to, I'd break your neck and all them guards could do was soil their breeches."

One guard stepped into the cell, but Wallace waved him back. Ryan had always struck him as a blowhard. Besides, the warden said Ryan had been a model prisoner since his arrival at Jefferson City. He wouldn't try anything that would risk pardon or parole.

"And Tuck Bassham's life ain't worth a piece of dried dung," the convict concluded. "Jesse'll see to that."

"Jesse's dead, Ryan, in case you've forgotten."

"That don't make no nevermind. Livin' or dead, Jesse James ain't one to trifle with. Frank ain't, neither. Ain't no way in hell I'm takin' the stand against Frank James, and I don't give a damn what you offer me. The James boys got friends." His smile returned, and this time he seemed genuinely happy. "Truth of the matter is, I don't think you'll live long enough to see Frank acquitted. Your life's as worthless as Bob Ford's."

February 19, 1883
Cole County, Missouri

A tired man with bags under his eyes looked back at him from the reflection in the window as the train sped through the black

Missouri night. William Wallace couldn't remember the last time he had gotten a good night's sleep, and he wouldn't be ending the trend tonight. He never could sleep on trains. He straightened in his seat, turned from the window and patted his coat pockets for a cigar and match.

The trip to the state prison had been fruitless. Bill Ryan refused to testify, and Clarence Hite would be dead of consumption before they'd ever bring Frank James to trial. Wallace found two cigars, put one in his mouth and offered the other to Hamilton, sitting across from him. They bit off the ends, which they spit into a cuspidor, and fired up the cigars.

"We could use Hite's confession," Hamilton said for the third time since leaving the penitentiary.

Shortly after arriving in the Jefferson City hoosegow, Clarence Hite had given a confession of his own free will, before Governor Crittenden, Commissioner Craig, Sheriff Timberlake and the warden, in which he implicated Jesse and Frank James in both the Winston and Blue Cut robberies. He also confirmed the widespread rumor that Jesse had killed Ed Miller in March of 1880.

Hite's confession, Hamilton argued, had been given before Jesse James's death, without promises of pardon or reward. It was a simple but detailed statement, an act to relieve a guilt-ridden soul, and could not be squashed by some mealy-mouthed defense counselor.

Wallace leaned back in the seat, blew a cloud of smoke toward the ceiling and shook his head. "It's no good," he said, growing tired of the same argument. He'd bet Jolly Wymore's button that Hamilton had been relieved to learn that Clarence Hite was dying and wouldn't be alive to testify. Defense attorneys, his colleague seemed to think, couldn't cross-examine a notarized confession. He hadn't seen Missouri's best lawyers at work. Men like John Philips and Chris Garner could shred paper evidence before a prosecutor could blink. Nor did Hamilton seem to be able to fathom that the most important aspect of any trial wasn't evidence, but the jury.

"You can't expect to find twelve men in Daviess County, or Jackson County, or anywhere in Western Missouri for that matter, who would be willing to convict Frank James on a piece of paper. We have to find someone other than the victims on the train who are willing to say, under oath, 'Yes, I swear to God, Frank James was there.'"

Hamilton dropped his cigar in the spittoon. It must have left a bitter taste in his mouth. "Well, just because it worked for you against Ryan—"

"Damn it, you may be a great prosecutor, but you've never tried a member of the James Gang, let alone a James brother. If we lose this case, everyone loses except Frank James, and I don't care how many times we bring him to trial. The man's a damned hero. The good men of Daviess County will be looking for just one reason to acquit. We can't give them that. That's why Hite's confession is worthless."

His colleague crossed his legs and shook his head in some sort of childlike pout. "Well, sir," he said, "that leaves us with Dick Liddil . . . if we can get him. And just getting him into a Missouri court will take some legal doing."

Wallace chortled. "Yeah, I know." His cigar tasted bitter, as well. Dick Liddil was as much of a bastard as Clarence Hite, Tucker Bassham or Bill Ryan.

"When I first became a lawyer," he said, his anger subsiding, "I was naive enough to think you dealt with a bunch of good people to send the bad ones to prison. But I've learned that you have to work with killers and robbers just as despicable as the ones we're trying to put away."

He sent his own cigar into the spittoon.

Chapter 10

*There now remains the agreeable task of speaking of Mr.
Johnson as a lawyer. He has made a specialty of
criminal practice, and stands unquestionably at the
head of that branch of the profession in Missouri.*
                                    —J. Thomas Scharf, *History of
                                        St. Louis City and County,* 1883

March 2, 1883
Independence, Missouri

His esteemed colleague of the bar, former lieutenant governor
of Missouri, Liberal Republican, commissioner of the state
supreme court, had mighty big ears. As Major Edwards introduced Charles Johnson, it took all of John F. Philips's concentration to keep his eyes trained on the St. Louis lawyer's slate
eyes and not those giant pieces of cauliflower shaped like the
ends of London Hearing Horns.

"Colonel Philips," Johnson said with a quick handshake, "it
shall be a pleasure to have you on my team."

My team! So Edwards—that drunken sot—had sold Philips
down the river, giving the first chair on Frank James's defense
team to this thin-lipped gent with the high forehead, Roman
nose and gabardine frock coat. "Thank you, sir," he replied
with a forced smile. Though deflated, he couldn't remain bitter
or show any disappointment. He—no, *they* had a job to do,
and that was to set Frank James free. No matter how much the
demotion hurt his pride, Philips couldn't fault Edwards, James
or the tall man smiling back at him.

At forty-seven, Charles P. Johnson looked thirty-seven. He was a well-cultivated man with powerful friends across the continent. Born in Illinois, he had published a newspaper in Sparta for three years before furthering his education and eventually moving to St. Louis, where he was admitted to the bar in 1857. Two years later, he had been elected city attorney. A Unionist and abolitionist, he served in the Third and Eighth Missouri regiments and carried dispatches between President Lincoln and General Lyon. After the war, he became a strong advocate of reenfranchising former Confederates, served in the legislature as well as St. Louis city and county attorney and spent 1873 to 1875 as lieutenant governor. When addressing him, though, everyone dropped the "lieutenant."

After introducing Johnson to the other attorneys, who had gathered in the vacant Merchants' Hotel dining room, Edwards broke out cigars and brandy. Cordialities finished, the lawyers sat around a table while the good major closed the dining hall's door for privacy.

"Governor," James Slover began, "don't you think you'll catch hell by taking this case?"

"We all shall, Mr. Slover, but we shall also garner much praise from those who have supported Frank James."

The Independence attorney shook his head. "What I mean, Governor, is that you are commissioner of the Missouri supreme court. Colonel Philips has already been hammered for his position on the court. Wallace and Hamilton are sure to be—"

"Overmatched," Johnson said, and nervous laughter filled the room. The question about Johnson's obvious conflict of interest and misplaced loyalties hung over the table, but no one dared bring it up again, which relieved Philips. As Slover had mentioned, Philips had secured a spot on the supreme court commission earlier this year and had suffered his share of criticism upon taking the Frank James case, but Missourians had short memories. Philips smoothed his mustache, watching Johnson in awe. Everything he had heard about the most brilliant legal mind in St. Louis had been true. This man was good. If he could take control of a table of established attorneys with such ease, imagine what he could do with twelve peasants sitting in a jury box.

"I met with Frank James last night," Johnson said. "He impresses me. He is a man loyal to his family, especially his mother, and I appreciate that immensely. My own mother saw that I was well-educated, well-read. I think he should most definitely take the stand in his own defense."

No one disagreed, and Colonel Christopher Trigg Garner added, "The state doesn't have much of a case in the Blue Cut matter."

"William Wallace has no intention of trying Frank James for the Blue Cut robbery," Johnson said, which jolted everyone. "We need to be preparing a defense for the Gallatin robberies, the bank robbery of sixty-nine or the Winston train robbery. Blue Cut is simply a stall for time."

"How do you know this?" a stunned Garner asked.

Smiling, Johnson picked up his cigar from the ashtray and puffed twice before responding. "Gentlemen, I hear things."

Staring again at those elephant ears, Philips couldn't help but chuckle. "I guess so," he said.

March 15, 1883
Jefferson City, Missouri

Thomas Crittenden leaned back in his leather chair in the executive office and absently tapped a gold-plated Fairchild pen on his desktop, dissecting the proposal Hamilton and Wallace had just laid before him. The two prosecutors waited, Hamilton looking paler than usual and Wallace self-assured and steady. Crittenden returned the pen to its holder and offered his guests a seat.

"Dick Liddil," the governor said, watching the Daviess County attorney squirm, "is a horse thief, a liar, a cheat, a robber, a fiend and a most disagreeable man."

"I'm well aware of that, sir," Wallace said, "but we'll need his testimony to convict James of the Winston train robbery."

Crittenden nodded. "So you are pursuing Winston?"

"Yes, sir." The answer came from Hamilton. "For now. It's our strongest case, and because of the two murders involved, we have a chance to send Frank James to the gallows or at least to prison for an indeterminable period."

"Why Liddil?"

Hamilton looked to Wallace for help, and the Jackson County solicitor cleared his throat before explaining. "He has turned state's evidence before. He speaks freely about his involvement with the James Gang from the Glendale robbery of seventy-nine and afterward. I've communicated with authorities in Alabama, and he's willing to cooperate if we can get him to Missouri."

The governor let out a sigh. Dick Liddil was in Alabama awaiting sentence for taking part in the robbery of the federal paymaster in Muscle Shoals on May 11, 1881, with the James boys and Bill Ryan. The men had made off with five thousand dollars. According to Liddil's testimony in Huntsville, he had been up in Kentucky during the Alabama robbery, but the jury hadn't believed a word and convicted him. Crittenden also had a letter from Alabama's governor requesting the extradition of Frank James to stand trial for his part in the Muscle Shoals crime, but Alabama, like Minnesota, and other jurisdictions, would have to wait.

"Bill Ryan refuses to testify," Wallace continued. "Clarence Hite died of consumption a few days ago in Kentucky. Liddil took part in the Winston robbery and will testify for us."

"But," Crittenden added, lifting a finger, "Dick Liddil is awaiting sentence in Alabama."

"Yes, sir. That's why we want you to write President Arthur."

"For a pardon?" Crittenden shook his head. He probably could have worked something out with the Alabama governor, but Dick Liddil had been convicted of a federal charge, so it was up to Chester A. Arthur to grant a reprieve.

"You pardoned Tucker Bassham," Wallace said, "and put Ryan where he belongs."

"Yes, I did pardon Bassham, and it was a most unpopular decision. Would you like to read the letters I received from our federal district attorney? How about the one from U.S. attorney general Benjamin Brewster."

"I know this is much to ask, but it's in the best interest of justice," Hamilton said nervously. "We've asked Senator Cockrell for help, and he's agreed to pressure Brewster in Washington, but we'd like you to petition President Arthur for a federal pardon," he added, prompting Crittenden to laugh.

"What's the name of the Alabama judge again?" he asked.

Hamilton gave him a blank look, but Wallace answered immediately, "Henry Bruce."

"I don't like our methods, gentlemen," Crittenden said after a while. "I dislike freeing felons to put felons behind bars. I didn't like it with Tucker Bassham, although I relented, and I don't like it in this matter. It will give the defense attorneys much to bandy in higher courts."

"I'm not fond of this either, Governor," Wallace said, "but the Ryan conviction has held up. So will Frank James's."

Silence filled another pause. At length, Crittenden's head bobbed slightly. "I'll write Attorney General Brewster and the president, but I think we are out of luck."

"Thank you, your excellency," said Hamilton, the first to shake his hand. Crittenden didn't care much for the lawyer's grip. He wondered if it would be a mistake to let this pale, politicking, spineless weasel handle the James trial. Wallace's handshake was solid, but the lawyer's eyes told the governor that he knew the powers in Washington, D.C., would never pardon a man like Liddil. Crittenden couldn't blame them.

"Tell me something, Mr. Wallace," Crittenden said in a hushed voice. "Who would you rather meet on the streets? Dick Liddil or Frank James?"

Frank James was a murderer, a man who had terrorized Missouri and surrounding states for twenty years. He had robbed railroads, banks and heaven only knew what else. Dick Liddil was a miserable horse thief and inept robber, but Crittenden would trust a man like Frank James, perhaps with his life, and wouldn't trust Dick Liddil with his ten-bit Fairchild ink pen.

The governor smiled knowingly when William Wallace didn't answer.

April 12, 1883
St. Louis, Missouri

A proper, God-fearing gentleman like Charles P. Johnson seldom swore, but he let out a muffled oath after John Glover read the telegram aloud in Johnson's opulent office. The for-

mer lieutenant governor and the St. Louis attorney were working out of Johnson's office while Colonel Philips and James
Slover handled matters around Kansas City and Independence,
and Colonel Garner interviewed potential witnesses in Daviess
and nearby counties.

The leaders of the anti–Frank James faction—Wallace,
Hamilton, Crittenden, Clay County sheriff James Timberlake,
Kansas City police commissioner Henry Craig and U.S. sena-
tor Francis Cockrell—had been spending a small fortune on
telegraphs and postage, pleading with Attorney General Ben
Brewster and President Arthur to pardon Dick Liddil down in
Alabama. They needed the scamp to testify against Frank
James, which meant Johnson's sources had been right and
Wallace and Hamilton planned on trying James for the Win-
ston train robbery. Brewster had declined to recommend a pardon and the president said he would not grant one, two
decisions that pleased Johnson.

Liddil would be rotting away in a federal prison while Frank
James was being tried in Missouri. At least, that was what
Johnson had figured until Slover brought in a telegram from
Colonel Philips in Kansas City.

Two days ago, Judge Henry Bruce, who had presided over
Liddil's trial in northern Alabama, released Dick Liddil on his
own recognizance. The judge had not even sentenced Liddil.
He would catch hell in the Alabama papers, not to mention
from Brewster and the president, but it didn't matter. Yesterday, according to Philips's telegraph, Craig and Timberlake
had posted bond on Liddil's behalf, and the convicted horse
thief and robber was likely on a train bound for Missouri.

Johnson held out his palm, signaling Slover to hand him the
telegram. He read it, balled the paper in his fist and tossed it
into the trash can behind his desk.

"All right," he said. "It's a setback, but a minor one. We can
crucify Dick Liddil on cross-examination. But let's start
preparing briefs and motions to have his testimony thrown out
before Liddil even takes the stand. Have Philips coax Major
Edwards, if he's sober, into writing a scathing article con-
demning the improprieties of this matter. Blast Craig and Timberlake. Give the governor a good dosage, as well."

Johnson ran his fingers over his bottom lip. If they indicted Frank James for the Winston robbery, he would likely be tried in Gallatin. "Also, ask Colonel Garner to find out who are the best defense attorneys in Gallatin. And instead of interviewing potential witnesses, tell the colonel to look into what it will take for us to seat a good jury. I want names of Democrats, God help me, men who have always been sympathetic to the James Gang and none too fond of railroads and banks. Farmers mainly. Tell him to use whatever methods are necessary."

"Sir, if you are suggesting bribery, I want no part—"

"I did not use the word *bribery,* Mr. Slover." Johnson's eyes hardened. "If you don't care for my methods and would like to leave our team, that, sir, can be arranged."

April 22, 1883
Independence, Missouri

"My husband has gone to town with Annie," said Mrs. Samuel Ralston, glancing at the name on the business card she had been handed before looking up to add, "Mr. Hamilton." She was younger than William Hamilton had expected, so he assumed she was Ralston's second wife. Her smile seemed genuine, downright infectious, and she went on to say that her husband and daughter should be home shortly, so if he would care to wait in the parlor she would gladly fix him a cup of tea.

Hamilton bowed slightly, accepting the invitation, and removed his bowler before crossing the threshold. Somewhere down the hall came harsh, repetitive notes of someone pounding the keys on a piano. Mrs. Ralston grimaced, lifted her skirt and hurried across the hardwood floor, ducking into the parlor and scolding, "Robert! Robert, you stop that this instant."

When Hamilton entered the room, he saw Mrs. Ralston lifting a young boy from a bench in front of the piano. "That's not the way you play, Robert," she admonished him gently, shaking her head and rolling her eyes at Hamilton. "Goodness," she told the boy again. "You are much too heavy for me to hold." She lowered him to the floor, told him to run outside and play and sat on the bench while gesturing to a sofa for her visitor.

"Your grandson?" asked Hamilton, his eyes following the boy as he disappeared in the hallway. Moments later came the slamming of a screen door.

"Yes. Annie and Frank's child. He's sweet, but a handful."

"Learning to play the piano?"

"Hardly, but at least he wasn't trying to become a seamstress," she said with a laugh and gestured to the sewing machine in the opposite corner. "I caught him there yesterday after he ruined a dress I was making for Annie."

"I'm sorry for the intrusion."

"It's no intrusion. Let me make you some tea, or would you prefer coffee?"

"Tea is fine, ma'am."

Sam Ralston and his daughter were visiting Frank James at the Independence jail. Hamilton knew this, figured they would not return home for a half hour, and had planned his visit accordingly. Annie Ralston James could not tell him anything that could be used against her husband in a court of law, and wouldn't even if she could, and Hamilton doubted if the outlaw's father-in-law would be cooperative with state prosecutors—maybe he would have been willing to testify against the bandit a few years ago, but not now. Not after he had made amends with his daughter and had a grandson to spoil.

Mrs. Samuel Ralston, however, was said to be a kind, gracious woman, talkative and, above all, trusting. She returned with a tray, set it on a nearby table and poured steaming tea into a china cup. "Sugar?" she asked, and Hamilton told her two cubes, please. She handed him his cup, poured another for herself and returned to the piano, picking up the sheet music young Robert James had knocked over during his sonata allegro. She moved to the sewing machine, collecting spools, patterns and cloth. Just like his mother, Hamilton thought, always cleaning up.

"This tea is excellent," Hamilton said, and noted his hostess's pleased smile. They sipped in silence until he set his empty cup on the table.

"Mrs. Samuel," he said, "that was most delicious." He struggled to think how he could lure her into a conversation. His palms suddenly felt sweaty, and the only thing he could say was, "My mother was a seamstress. I bought her a cabinet machine for Christmas two years ago."

"How nice of you, young man," she answered joyously. "My daughter sent me this machine as a birthday gift a couple of years ago."

His eyes suddenly shot to the machine, and he rose, walked over to it and rubbed his fingers across the oak woodwork.

"Don't tell me you sew, too," Mrs. Ralston said excitedly.

"Not at all." It was an Acme High Arm, built in Rockford, Illinois, with an automatic bobbin winder and self-threading vibrating shuttle and needle, seven drawers, cover and drop leaf.

"That's quite a daughter you have, ma'am, to have this shipped to you all the way from . . . Where was she then, Texas?"

"Oh, who knows, Mr. . . ."

"Hamilton."

"I'm sorry. My mind isn't as sharp as I grow older."

"It's quite all right. Frank James says he was down in Texas two years ago. I just assumed that's from where she would have freighted you the sewing machine."

"They were running around all over," she said. "You know how things were. Anyway, this was sent from Page City. I'm sure you know General Shelby."

Everyone in Missouri knew of Jo Shelby, the Confederate general and friend of the James boys. "Yes, ma'am," he answered, "though by reputation only."

"Well, he's a dear friend of Frank and Annie's, and he had it delivered to us with a note from her. She can tell you all the details. My mind isn't what it used to be."

"It's nothing of import," he told her with another smile as he returned to the sofa. "You got this last year?"

She shook her head. "No, it was late spring, I do believe, maybe the first of summer, in eighty-one. It didn't arrive on my birthday. You know how things are."

"Certainly." He pulled an open-faced watch from his vest pocket. "I'm sorry, ma'am, but I think I should be on my way. Could you tell your husband I shall seek to interview him another time?"

"Of course. I'm so sorry you came all this way for nothing."

He squeezed her hand, told Mrs. Ralston that her tea made the trip from Kansas City worthwhile, grabbed his bowler and walked down the hall with Mrs. Ralston. Frank James had told reporters, lawmen and lawyers he had been down in Texas at the time of the Winston train robbery, but this Acme High Arm might hang him—if Hamilton could find the missing pieces, if he could prove that the outlaw had had the sewing machine freighted to Page City, where he and his brother were planning a train robbery.

He stood on the porch after telling Mrs. Ralston good-bye, sorting out his thoughts, trying to figure out his next step. How did one trace the origins of a mass-produced sewing machine? Jo Shelby wouldn't cooperate; he treated the James boys, and anyone who had worn the gray, like blood kin. Frank James said he had lived in Nashville before heading to Texas with his family—only he hadn't gone to Texas. He had traveled to Missouri, shipped the Acme to his friend in Page City, who in turn had it carted to Independence. Frank James then took part in the Winston and Blue Cut robberies before lighting a shuck east. It was a good theory, he thought, and guessed that even Mr. Naysayer himself, William Hockaday Wallace, would agree.

Chapter 11

For murder, though it have no tongue, will speak
With most miraculous organ.
                    —*Hamlet*, Act 2, Scene 2, 605–606

June 6, 1883
Edgefield, Tennessee

The quaint, one-story frame house at 814 Fatherland Street made William Wallace a little jealous. Not that it towered like some mansion, but with an inviting side porch, three large rooms, a nice yard and a gravel walkway leading to the street, it definitely had more to offer than Wallace's spartan lodgings at Sue Boddington's Boardinghouse.

"Frank James," repeated John Trimble Jr., shaking his head in amazement. "Him and Jesse. Here. Never would have believed it."

Wallace had met with the landlord—one of a slew of potential witnesses he had been interviewing in Nashville—and driven out to the rental property. When Wallace had shown Trimble a photograph of Frank James and another one of Jesse James lying packed in ice in his coffin at Sidenfaden's Funeral Parlor, the man had almost fainted. Those were the renters, he said, who lit a shuck out of Tennessee in the spring of eighty-one.

Last month in Kansas City, Wallace had been in court again, asking for Frank James to be indicted for the murder of stonemason Frank McMillan and accessory to the murder of conductor William Westfall, both committed while participating in the Winston train robbery of 1881, and for the murder of cashier John W. Sheets during the robbery of the Gallatin bank in 1869. The State of Missouri, he had noted, was temporarily dropping the Blue Cut robbery charge against the defendant.

Frank James had entered a not-guilty plea, and a trial date had been set for May 21 in Gallatin. Indictments had been returned by a Daviess County grand jury, and a trial was continued to August 21. The bushwhacker could be tried for the murder of McMillan, and if the state lost that case, Frank James could rot in jail during trials for the murder of Sheets in 1869, accessory to the murder of Westfall during the Winston robbery and a score of other crimes, even the Blue Cut incident if it came to that. Wallace hoped one trial would do the job.

"So Jesse rented a house a block from here?"

"Yes, sir, only I knew him as J. B. Howard, and the one you say is Frank was B. J. Woodson. Howard—Jesse, that is—had a two-story over at 711. I can show you that one, if you'd like. 'Course, I don't own either property now. Sold them."

"Who bought this one?"

"A pressman named James May. He works in Nashville. That's where he probably is now. Anyway, I sold him this house in March of eighty-one, and he's the one who told me the Woodsons—again, that's what I knew them as—had gone. He wanted to see if they wished to continue renting the house, but he moved in instead once he found he didn't have any tenants."

"So they were only here for a couple of months?"

"Right. As I told you in my office, I rented it out in February of eighty-one. He paid eight dollars in advance, and he paid his rent for March. Mr. May moved in in April."

After leaving his card in the door with a note scribbled on the back requesting an interview with May, Wallace decided he would like to see the house at 711 Fatherland after all. According to Dick Liddil, the Jameses had fled to Kentucky after Bill Ryan had been arrested in Nashville. Trimble, perhaps May and other witnesses in the area would confirm this at trial, and Wallace could draw a map showing how Frank James had gone from Tennessee to Kentucky and on to Missouri—not Texas, as he claimed—to rob a couple of trains.

"Mr. Trimble, would you be willing to travel to Missouri to testify?"

The landlord shuffled his feet. "Well, sir, that's a far piece to go and . . ."

"The state will take care of your expenses, travel and board, maybe some for meals." That changed Trimble's attitude; the landlord's head bobbed vigorously and he said he would most certainly do his duty to put Frank James behind bars.

"You know, Mr. Wallace, you should really talk to Silas Norris's daughter," Trimble said after they climbed into the landlord's buggy. "They live over in Mechanicsville. She says she knew the James boys well, said they stayed with her in Kentucky, and she isn't fond of them at all, nor her ex-husband and his relatives."

Wallace pulled out paper and pencil, although he didn't think this woman would be of much use to him. He could find hundreds of people who said they knew the James brothers yet couldn't even identify them in a photograph. "I knew Jesse James" had become about as popular as "George Washington slept here." Still, he had to investigate every lead.

"What's the daughter's name?"

"Sarah Hite."

"Hite!" Struck dumb, he heard the pencil tip break. "As in Clarence or Wood Hite?"

"Well, she was married to George Hite, but, yeah, they were kin."

Wallace couldn't believe his luck.

June 11, 1883
Nashville, Tennessee

It was such a beautiful morning, William Wallace decided to walk from his hotel to the railroad depot. In a little more than a week, he had interviewed dozens of witnesses, people who could testify to Frank James's whereabouts in the events leading up to the Winston train robbery. He would bring James

May, John Trimble, Bill Earthman and James Moffatt to Gallatin to identify Frank James as the man, known to them as B. J. Woodson, who associated with Jesse James, alias J. B. Howard, Bill Ryan and the Hites. Not only that, but Sarah Norris Peck Hite and her father, Silas Norris, would gladly discuss the James Gang's stay in Kentucky. All he had to do was follow through on his promise to pay for their transportation and lodging. Crittenden might come through, or maybe he could work something out with Hamilton from the county budgets. Justice did have a price.

He glanced at the window display in a cobbler's shop, passed a hardware store, grocer and mercantile, and considered ducking inside a small café for a cup of coffee when he abruptly stopped. Wallace straightened, cocked his head in contemplation and spun around, no longer thirsty for black coffee. He hurried to the mercantile, momentarily peered through the window and pushed open the door, causing a bell to chime.

"Can I help you, sir?" asked a balding man in scuffed gaiters and dusty sleeve garters.

"That," Wallace said dryly, pointing at the sewing machines lined against the wall.

"Certainly." The clerk, or maybe he was the owner, led Wallace to the item, commenting, "You won't find a better price in all of Nashville, sir." Wallace could read the brand, ACME, and licked his lips. "You won't find a finer sewing machine for your . . . wife, I take it?" When Wallace didn't respond, the man kept on talking. "It's the lightest-running sewing machine on the market. Look at that cabinet work. Solid black walnut."

Walnut? That was wrong. "Does it come in oak?"

"Yes, sir," he said, and pointed to another machine. "This is oak." But it was wrong, too. What had Hamilton said about the sewing machine at the Ralston home? Seven drawers. He asked the salesman about that.

"Two drawers, five or seven," he said. "We don't have any seven-drawer models, though, but I could order one for you. It would take a couple of weeks to get one in from Illinois. Does that work for you, sir? That would cost you twenty-one dollars."

"Actually, I'm not interested in buying. I'm not married and I don't sew."

"Oh," the man said in defeat as Wallace handed him a card.

"Why don't you have any seven-drawer models?"

The man brightened at Wallace's name. "Hey, you're the attorney in town. I read about you in the *Daily American.* You're the one prosecuting Frank James."

"Yes, sir. Now about the seven-drawer models?"

"We don't sell that many. Only sold two or three in the seven years I've been here."

"I'm interested in one you would have sold in the spring of 1881."

The clerk rubbed his shining head. "Well, I'd have to look at my ledger books."

"I have time." He could catch another train.

July 2, 1883
Jefferson City, Missouri

"I'm not sure I follow where you're going with this Acme sewing machine," Thomas Crittenden said in the parlor of his mansion. "You say the James boys had sent guns and a sewing machine to Missouri?"

Asking for a progress report, the governor had invited Wallace and Hamilton to Jefferson City, and both men seemed genuinely excited, although Crittenden knew that would not be the case in a few minutes, once they heard his order.

"The guns I discovered by accident," Wallace explained, "after I started tracking down the sewing machine Annie James sent to her mother. Of course, we wouldn't know about the sewing machine if it weren't for Mr. Hamilton." Wallace nodded politely at his colleague, who smiled at the acknowledgment while sniffing the cigar Crittenden had given him. *Enjoy it now,* thought the governor.

"Anyway, the guns were shipped to John Ford in Lexington. That's Bob and Charlie Ford's brother, and from there to Richmond."

Crittenden contemplated the .44 Remington, gunbelt and

holster locked in his office safe. He certainly hoped the prosecutors didn't expect Frank James's revolver to be introduced as evidence. That gun, he fully expected, would earn him a small fortune one day, and it wasn't leaving his possession.

"Express agents in Lexington and Richmond will testify to this," Wallace continued. "The Jameses sent a hundred-forty-pound box to Missouri from Nashville."

"A lot of artillery," Crittenden said. "So you plan to prove that those were the guns in the Winston robbery?" He was skeptical. Most men west of the Mississippi carried rifles and revolvers, and no one with a gun in his face during a holdup would remember a serial number.

"No, sir. I think I can lead the jury to believe that Frank and Jesse wouldn't be far from their guns. If the guns were in Missouri, then Frank James wasn't in Texas like he says."

"And the sewing machine?"

"We believe his wife met with Jo Shelby. They bought the Acme in Nashville, shipped it to Page City and from there to Independence. Again, if I can show that Annie James was in Missouri, the jury will know her husband wasn't far away. These are just a couple of links, Governor. Combine them together with Liddil's testimony, eyewitnesses on the train and our other witnesses, and it's a solid case."

Most murder trials lasted a day or two. The prosecutor called a couple of witnesses, the defense attorney did the same, they gave their arguments, the judge instructed the jury and the verdict came back in a few hours, a day at the most. Crittenden shook his head with a wry grin. This one was shaping up to cost a pretty penny. A thorough man, William Wallace was not about to let Frank James slip from his grasp. He'd hammer every detail into the jury's heads. William Hamilton, on the other hand, had not said more than a dozen words today, which reaffirmed the decision Crittenden had already made.

"Once Mr. Hamilton presents all this to the jury," Wallace said, "I think we'll have a conviction."

Now's the time, Crittenden decided. "You're mistaken there. I'm sorry, Mr. Hamilton, but you'll be second chair."

"What?" The Daviess County solicitor's pale face suddenly reddened. If he had shown that kind of emotion during the past ten months, Crittenden might have let him handle the case, but he had waited too long.

"You shall invite Mr. Wallace to try the case in Daviess County," Crittenden said evenly, turning to the Jackson County attorney to add, "and you, sir, shall accept."

"But it's my case. Governor, I must protest!" Utterly livid, Hamilton shook in his fancy dress shoes.

"You shall not protest, sir!" Crittenden's voice thundered. "I'm doing this for the good of Missouri. You will respect my wishes or I'll see that you never hold any office again."

Wallace stood numbly. Silence seemed best in this matter, and Wallace was a smart man. A rabid dog, Hamilton looked mad enough to spit, but Crittenden's rebuke left him speechless.

"You'll authorize Mr. Wallace to take charge of the case," he ordered.

"This is highly improper," said Hamilton, having found his voice again.

"But quite legal," Crittenden added.

At length, Wallace cleared his throat. "There shall be some ink spilled over this in the papers. Both of us will be targets of criticism."

"That, too, shall pass." Crittenden crossed the room to open the parlor door and show his guests out. "This is in the best interest of justice, gentlemen. Wallace, you have experience going after the James Gang, and you're one hell of an attorney. Hamilton, I'm not taking you off the case. Second chair is a key position. You know the details of the crime, and, more importantly, you know Daviess County and the men who will comprise the jury. Carry on, both of you. You're running out of time."

As he watched the two men head to the front door, Crittenden couldn't help but smile. If he were Wallace, he'd damn sure watch his back.

July 22, 1883
Page City, Missouri

Brigadier General Joseph Orville Shelby sat on his front porch in his threadbare Confederate frock coat, fanning himself with a plantation-style straw hat, and lifted a glass containing clear liquid to salute his visitors.

John F. Philips assumed the Rebel hero was drinking water until the good general spoke, and his breath revealed the clear drink to be quite potent corn liquor.

"Gentlemen, a good day to you all. Forgive me for not risin', but this ol' man is tuckered out this mornin'." His slurred voice revealed traces of Kentucky aristocracy and his bright eyes beamed, but Philips knew Jo Shelby all too well. He wasn't tuckered out, just too drunk to climb out of his rocker. Philips checked his pocket watch as Major Edwards, former Lieutenant Governor Johnson and Colonel Garner shook hands with the thin, triangular-faced warrior with waxed mustache, flowing chin whiskers and dark locks streaked with gray that touched his shoulders. It was half past eight.

John Newman Edwards lifted the pitcher of spirits resting next to a massive French-made LeMat's revolver, and refreshed the general's drink before pouring himself half a tumbler.

Before the War of the Rebellion tore Missouri asunder, Jo Shelby had been a wealthy, slave-owning, thirty-year-old planter with other business interests. He had been courted with a Federal commission, but shunned it to wear the gray, leading Confederate cavalry at Wilson's Creek, Prairie Grove and throughout Missouri and Kansas. Despite taking a Yankee ball at Helena, Arkansas, in the summer of sixty-three, he ignored the wound to command a 1,500-mile raid across Missouri that fall, which earned his promotion to general. After the surrender, Price led hundreds of unreconstructed Rebels to Mexico, where the gallant general offered their services to Emperor Maximilian. Maybe if the French leader had accepted Shelby's generous proposition, the Missourians would have squashed the Mexican uprising and the emperor might have kept his head. Maximilian declined, however, giving the expatriates land instead, and Shelby and his boys took up farming until Maximilian's defeat and execution. He returned to Missouri in 1867.

"General," Edwards said after downing his morning hooch,

"as I informed you, Colonels Philips and Garner and Governor Johnson are leading the defense of Frank James."

"Frank James, Frank James, Frank James," Shelby said, nodding at each mention of the name. "I daresay a finer soldier never rode. Fought beside me, he did, while servin' under the noble George Todd. Poor Todd, shot down by a damned snake in the grass near Independence, but Frank James, by God, I would have given my right arm for a dozen more men of his darin'. You do yourselves proud, gentlemen. I know we were enemies in the past—y'all wore the blue and Major Edwards, Private James and myself the gray—but that is behind us. We must set Frank James free, and I shall do anything that will help in this matter, be it tell you all that I know—" He picked up the LeMat, thumbed back the hammer; Philips's throat turned to sand.

The LeMat held a nine-shot, .40-caliber cylinder plus a single 18-gauge grapeshot load underneath the main barrel, making it the world's wickedest piece of one-handed firepower. With Shelby in his cups, his aim was far from steady, and the cannon waved in the faces of his paling guests. Jo Shelby could have wiped out the leaders of Frank James's cause with one drunken jerk of the trigger.

"Or, by God, I shall break him out of jail myself!" Once the general slammed the LeMat, still cocked, onto the table, Philips heard Johnson and Garner sigh with relief.

"Thank you, General," Johnson said, but had to pause to collect his thoughts and nerves. "We'd like to talk to you about what we'll need from you once the trial begins."

"A pleasure, sir." Shelby downed his drink, and refilled his and Edwards's glasses.

What we need, Philips said to himself, *is you two to either join the temperance movement or go back to Mexico.*

Chapter 12

This is an old-fashioned Southern town, which means that its people are chiefly distinguished for their hospitality. The hotels are more than crowded, but the people show their characteristic liberality by providing lodging places for any who have claim to respectability.
—St. Joseph Weekly Gazette, August 23, 1883

August 4, 1883
Gallatin, Missouri

"Frank," Major Edwards said, "allow me to present to you the gallant William M. Rush Jr. and Joshua W. Alexander, both of Gallatin. They are the latest worthy barristers who hang their shingles in this gregarious burg and have flocked to your defense."

Both lawyers wore bowlers and herringbone suits, so Frank James guessed they did their shopping at Khauer's, whose proprietor had measured Frank in the cell for a suit and promised to have it ready before the trial date. Alexander gave him a nervous smile while Rush simply bobbed his head twice. Neither man really impressed him, although he recalled that Rush had served a term or two as the county prosecutor.

"What will you be doing for me, sir?" he asked.

"Jury selection," Rush answered. "It's my job to see you get twelve good men to hear your case."

He pursed his lips, decided Rush would be all right and did not bother interrogating Alexander. A sudden outburst of coughing sent him to his bunk. He gestured at his visitors to excuse him and find a place comfortable to sit. The Gallatin jail wasn't as capacious as his temporary home had been in Independence. Oh, he had his library—in fact he was currently rereading *Macbeth*—and a tintype of Annie and Robert beside his bunk, but the good jailers of Gallatin had no intention of escorting him to see *Romeo and Juliet* or padding his floor with carpet. Breathing damp jail air had brought about this cold and persistent cough, and he had probably dropped fifteen pounds since October. These days, he figured, a twelve-year-old boy could give him a right smart in a go at fisticuffs.

"Pardon me," he said after wiping his mouth with a handkerchief. "I look forward to the day when I can breathe free air and get my health back."

"That'll be soon, Frank," Alexander blurted.

Frank? He glared at the young attorney. *Mister, I don't know you from Adam's house cat, so don't go getting friendly with me.* The lawyer's face turned ashen, and Edwards started babbling on about how Annie and Robert would be up soon, how he had secured accommodations for her at one of the finer hotels, and that, God willing, this team of defense lawyers would free the noble Confederate once and for all.

He glanced at the two newcomers while considering his attorneys: Governor Johnson, Colonels Philips and Garner, Slover and Glover—Slover and Glover, that sounded like something out of a Mark Twain story—and these two gents. Seven lawyers for one man. He had never heard of such decadence, and wondered if those men truly believed in his innocence—after all, most had been his sworn enemies during the War—or if they only hoped to get their hands on the hidden loot the James Gang had stolen after tendering their bills. Hidden loot? Fanciful nonsense like most of the James-Younger stories.

"How about Henry Clay Dean?" he asked. "Is he coming?"

Edwards fell into awkward silence, which never happened, and stammered, vainly looking to Alexander and Rush for help before forming an apology. "Governor Johnson and Colonel Philips believe there is no place for Mr. Dean on the defense, Frank. My God, son, he's an old man. Time has passed by the noted Sage of Rebel Cove."

The three men stared at him with a look he had seen count-less times on faces of bank clerks, express agents, conductors and captured Kansas redlegs. It amused him, their fear, and he toyed with the idea of reenacting one of Dingus's tantrums, maybe getting Joshua W. Alexander to stain his trousers, but instead he shrugged. He didn't know Henry Clay Dean person-ally, but just about everyone in Missouri had once called him the Midwest's most brilliant legal mind. That had been years ago, though, so perhaps Major Edwards was right. Early in October, Dean had written a letter, volunteering his services, and he had passed it on to the major. What made Dean appeal-ing was his promise to work without charge, unlike these other carpetbaggers, but he let it go. Seven attorneys should be enough for one man.

"Where do we stand?" he asked.

"General Shelby promises to testify, and what that gallant soul says will carry much weight with a jury," Edwards an-swered. "The state will try to prove that you were in Missouri at the time of the Winston robbery, but we have another theory. Would you care to hear it?"

He shrugged again.

"Jim Cummins." The major clapped his hands and paced back and forth in the cramped cell. "By jingo, Jim Cummins was the fifth man on the Winston train, and Frank James was down in Texas living a law-abiding life."

Jim Cummins. Now there was a name worth a chuckle. Cole Younger had said it best about the sniveling runt. Like most of Quantrill's raiders, Cummins had been only a kid when he joined the cause, but couldn't do a damn thing right except when it came to horses. He spoke in such a god-awful drawl, it took him a day to finish one sentence, and he was so shy he wouldn't even take a piss in front of the other boys. That was what prompted Cole Younger to say, "He probably don't want us to see him squat." Although Cummins took the brunt of jokes from the boys—those who would speak to him, any-how—Dingus stood up for him every now and then, even let him ride with the gang after the surrender. Only Cummins had been such a restless sort, you couldn't count on him to show up for a deal. The last he heard, Cummins had tried to surren-

der a few times since October, but his luck and nervous man-
nerisms were such that no one really believed he was the guerrilla, so he had drifted west, maybe south. Wherever he was, it
wasn't Missouri.

"Interesting," he said.

"But we need to iron out our Texas defense," Alexander
said. "With your permission, I'd like to ask a few questions."

Grinning, Frank James swung his long legs onto his bunk.
So that was why Alexander had been hired.

"Ask me anything," he told him. "Guess we're getting a
mite pressed for time."

August 19, 1883
Gallatin, Missouri

Valise in hand and son in tow, Annie James stepped down on
the platform and stood there amazed until a man behind her
growled at her to get the hell out of his way. People swarmed
around the depot, shouting, pushing, scurrying around like a
battalion of ants. She remembered a similar scene from Frank
James's arrival at Independence back in October, only her husband was already here and these folks had not come to greet
Robert and her. She waited five minutes before she could ask a
harried express agent for directions to the Alpine Palace Hotel,
and he curtly told her to take the omnibus before hurrying to
aid another customer.

Placards wallpapered the agent's office, advertising rooms
at homes throughout town. When she overheard a man complain that even the wagon yards were full, she decided she had
better get to the hotel quickly. Major Edwards said everything
had been arranged, but she wouldn't be able to rest until she
had checked in. A kindly man in duckin trousers and dirty can-
vas suspenders helped carry the rest of her luggage to a single-
deck wagon, with M. P. CLOUDAS OMNIBUS painted on the side
in large white-block letters, pulled by four large mules.

"This lady and her son desire transportation to the Alpine
Palace," her Good Samaritan told the driver.

"We're full up, laddie," the man snapped in an Irish brogue.

He wore a gray herringbone cap and pained expression as he changed a silver dollar for another passenger. "She'll have to wait till I can get back here."

The stranger hooked his thumbs in his waistband, between an Army Colt she had not noticed till then, and stepped closer to the Irishman. "You have plenty of room on the roof of this contraption," he said icily.

"It's against company regulations."

Leaning closer, the man whispered something in the driver's ear, and his face paled and his eyes widened. "All right," he announced, "I can fit ten more folks on the roof, and I need a couple of gentlemen to give up their seats inside for this young lady and her son." When no one budged, he raised his voice another octave. "Come on, by the saints, you're Missourians. The roof won't kill you."

Robert tugged her arm. "I wanna ride on the roof, too," he told her when she looked down.

"No," she said sternly as two businessmen stepped off the omnibus, tipped their hats and climbed onto the bus's top.

"Thank you," she said blankly, although she doubted if the two gentlemen could hear her above the pandemonium.

Several others had formed a line, talking excitedly, paying their fares before scrambling onto the roof, shouting destinations and hauling carpetbags with them. Annie asked the driver how much she owed.

"No charge, Mrs. James," the driver said hurriedly and took another dime from a new passenger.

She turned quickly, trying to find her Good Samaritan, but he had disappeared in the horde. Stunned, Annie slowly took her seat in the omnibus and wrapped a protective arm around her son.

Twenty minutes later, the wagon stopped at the town square in front of the hotel. The driver helped carry her luggage inside, tipped his cap and hurried outside. Annie and Robert stood in line another ten minutes before a flushed clerk said grumpily, "Yeah, what can I do for you?"

"My name is Ann Ralston James. I believe you have a room for my son and me."

He looked up from the registration book with malevolent

dark eyes. "You're mistaken," he said harshly, then stared past her. "Next?"

"But"—Annie had to gather herself—"but Major Edwards told me—"

"Look, lady, I don't give a tinker's damn what anyone told you. It's just me working tonight, and this place has turned into Dodge City on a Saturday night. Now get out of here. Try another place, so I can—"

"Do you have a room?"

"Not for you. Skedaddle."

A man in a nice blue suit cut in front of her. Annie felt her ears and neck redden, temper boiling. She reached out to grab the man's collar and jerk him out of her way. She wasn't finished with this rude clerk yet. Major Edwards had promised her a room at the Palace Hotel and she planned on getting it. The man's voice, however, stopped her as he addressed the clerk. She knew that voice.

"Do you know who I am?" he asked the clerk.

"I do."

"Did John Edwards have a room held for Mrs. James?"

The clerk hesitated, shot a nervous glance at Annie and leaned over the counter. He didn't bother lowering his voice. "Listen, Captain Sheets was a good friend of my father's. Maybe Frank James is a hero to some, but not me. And I can't believe you'd be sticking up for the likes of—"

Annie blinked at the light pop. The clerk had straightened in stunned silence, rubbing the pink spot on his left check. Tears began welling, and his lips quivered.

"You planned on letting her room to someone else for a little profit, mister," her second helper of the evening told the clerk. "If I told Oscar about this, you'd be looking for another job."

"Please," said the trembling clerk. "I ain't lying to you about Captain Sheets and my pa."

The man wasn't moved to pity. He pointed to a sign hanging over the letter and key box.

NO PAINS SPARED
TO MAKE GUESTS
COMFORTABLE.

"You better live up to your credo," he said as he turned, bowing to Annie and Robert. "Hello, Annie. Good evening, Robert."

She smiled back. "Hello, William."

"Most folks really aren't as rude as the clerk," William Wallace told her in the Palace dining room. After she had registered, Wallace had carried her luggage to her room and offered to treat Annie and Robert to supper. They had to wait twenty minutes before they could be seated.

"The hotels are full," Wallace continued. "So folks are letting journalists, visitors, anyone in town really stay in their own homes."

"I don't blame him," she said. "If a friend of my father's had been killed in a bank robbery, I might feel the same." As she wiped a piece of cornbread from her mouth, she realized Wallace suddenly looked uncomfortable and recognized her mistake. Her husband had been charged with John W. Sheets's murder during the 1869 robbery of the Daviess County Savings Association, and he couldn't discuss any aspects of the case with Frank James's wife and son. She decided to change the subject.

"I never imagined this," she said, pointing out the window at the lively square. Robert slurped his milk, and she scolded him.

"The sheriff didn't expect this, either," Wallace said. "He's hired an army of special deputies." He finished his coffee and grinned at Robert. "Y'all must be exhausted."

"Far from it, William," Annie said and suddenly giggled. "All this energy . . . I might take Robert for a walk around town before retiring."

"Well," he said as he opened a change purse and dropped a few coins on the table, "if you'd care to have an old friend for your chaperon, I know something that your son might enjoy."

"What?" the boy shouted.

"Robert, where are your manners?"

"What, sir?" he corrected himself.

"A traveling show featuring men called Arizona Jack and Wild Harry, plus an Indian maiden, has set up in town."

Robert sat up excitedly. "A real Indian?"

Wallace smiled as he stood. "Let's find out."

Part II

Part II

Chapter 13

*The trial of Frank James, which we here give in full, will
show to the reader how terrible, how daring and how
powerful this band of outlaws had become, and how
they were shielded and protected by some who were
called among the best citizens in the country.*
       —*The Life and Trial of Frank James,*
        The Wide Awake Library, September 28, 1883

August 20, 1883
Gallatin, Missouri

He stared at his pocket watch briefly before slipping it into his
vest pocket. The silver-plated Waltham rattled against something and, curious, William Wallace stuck two fingers into the
pocket and withdrew Jolly Wymore's coat button.

"What's that?" asked the attorney sitting next to him,
Colonel John H. Shanklin. Wallace had hired Shanklin and his
partners, Marcus A. Low and Henry C. McDougal, to help the
prosecution. They had law offices in Gallatin and Trenton, and
Hamilton had also brought aboard Judge Joshua F. Hicklin, a
Gallatin attorney who had served as the Daviess County solicitor.

"A reminder," Wallace answered. He returned the button
and began pulling papers from his satchel. It was eight fifty-
two a.m.

Across the room, Charles Johnson, John Philips and a company of lawyers huddled around the defense table. Annie
James sat on a long bench in the defense box, highly irregular,

for she should have been seated in the first pew behind the banister, although Wallace wouldn't complain. The courtroom was already packed, and through the open windows he could hear the din of excitement on the streets. In fact, men and women stood outside the windows six or seven deep.

The trial of the century, some were calling it, and Wallace didn't doubt it.

He didn't hear Hamilton until his associate dropped into a chair next to him and asked, "When did you decide to add Charles Ford to our witness list?" His voice carried a well-honed edge.

"What are you talking about?"

"Ford's in town with his father. Damn it, you put a Ford on the stand, and not only will we lose the case, this courthouse will burn to the ground. Now when—"

"I don't know a thing about Charlie Ford, mister," he said, noticing the testiness in his own voice.

"Well, a reporter from the *Argus* came up to me—"

"Don't believe everything you hear from a reporter. Charlie Ford's likely touring with his brother five hundred miles from here, enjoying his stage career."

"Nope," Colonel Shanklin said cheerfully. "Charles Ford is in town. Saw him this morning at breakfast." Wallace and Hamilton fixed the colonel with hard looks, but nothing fazed the old Gallatin counselor. "Charlie got himself arrested in Plattsburg for carrying a concealed weapon. He came here to pay his fine, maybe catch the show." The white-haired gentleman laughed and spit his snuff into an airtight tin labeled PEACHES.

Wallace jerked around to scan the courtroom. "I don't want him in here," he said. The last thing he needed was Charles Ford to shift focus from the trial of Frank James to the murder of Jesse James. "God help us if Bob Ford's here."

The bailiff's announcement ended his search. "All rise!"

Judge Charles H. S. Goodman sported a mustache and beard as black as his robe. His dark eyes swept across the chamber before he moved forward while the bailiff began announcing the legal proceedings. A middle-aged native of Ohio, Goodman had moved to Missouri to practice law, made a name for himself among the bar and now rode circuit over Gentry County. Governor Crittenden, the stories went, had personally asked him to preside over the Frank James case because of Goodman's sterling reputation and harsh demeanor. He took sass from neither criminals nor lawyers, and his head was as thick and tough as a tome of Blackstone's *Commentaries*.

"Where do we stand, gentlemen?" Goodman asked.

Hamilton's voice quavered. "Your Honor, the prosecution at this time will not pursue the indictment against the defendant for the murder of John Sheets during the robbery of the Daviess County Savings Association in 1869." He raised his voice above the excited whispers while Goodman slammed the gavel and called for order. "The state will, however, prosecute Frank James on the second indictment at this time, for the murder of Frank McMillan during the Winston train robbery." A few shouts led to a stern warning from the judge. "Not all of the state's witnesses have arrived," Hamilton continued after order had been restored, "so we humbly request a recess."

"Is the defense ready for trial?"

"No, Your Honor." Charles Johnson spoke on behalf of the defense team. "The defense finds itself in the same predicament as the state. All of our witnesses have not arrived, so we, too, would like a recess." He added with a grin, "Getting to Gallatin is no easy task."

Goodman's voice rang louder than his gavel. "Take a look out these windows, Mr. Johnson. I don't think anyone is having trouble getting to Gallatin. Still, we will adjourn until two o'clock this afternoon." The gavel cracked again.

Charlie Ford found himself surrounded the moment he stepped out of Bostaph's Apothecary. They'd come to kill him, come to gun down the man who killed Jesse James, and he wanted to tell them, no, it weren't him, it was Robert. Robert done it. Ask anyone who ever rode with him and they'd tell you that Charles Ford wouldn't never harm Jesse. They shouted at him, and he braced for the bullets. When no bullets struck him, he longed for a sip of whiskey, something to steady his nerves, or at least take one or two of them pills the druggist had just sold him. He retreated until his back pressed against the glass window, twisting his sack of pills, eyes darting from face to face, trying to recognize someone, a friend maybe, or at least his pa. They continued yelling, all these strangers, waving tablets and pencils in his twitching face. He never should have listened to his kid brother, never should have come to Missouri, and especially not here. Where was his pa?

"Are you going to testify against Frank James?"

His head cleared. Why, these weren't friends of Jesse seeking revenge. Realizing he was surrounded by reporters, he stopped twisting the sack and gave them a nice grin. He had been confronted by scribes all across the continent. Well, mostly they wanted to interview Robert, but they'd talk to Charlie in a pinch. He straightened, took a deep breath and relaxed, although he still wanted that drink of scamper juice.

"Ain't been asked," he answered. Thinking of something better, he lied, "Sure. I'm here to help."

"Where's your brother?"

"Dick Liddil's here," he blurted. "I seen him. He's gonna testify."

All the reporters fired questions simultaneously: "What about Robert . . . ?" "Do you think Frank will be convicted or acquitted . . . ?" "Discuss your arrest in Plattsburg. . . ." "Dick Liddil? Is he to testify for or against Frank James . . . ?" "What has life been like since you murdered Jesse James . . . ?"

These men, and one woman—he'd never seen a woman reporter before—blasted questions quicker than Bob Ford could empty his revolver at some paper target on some stage at some theater in some big city. He'd try to think of an answer when another person shouted something. It damn sure confused him. God, he wanted a drink, something so he could swallow one of them horse pills in his sack.

"Dick Liddil. Don't know what he'll say," he finally answered. "But he's here."

"How long will you be in Gallatin . . . ?" "Are you staying for the entire trial . . . ?" "Tell us about Robert, your brother. . . ." "Aren't you scared of being shot down . . . ?" "Will you or will you not testify against Frank James . . . ?" "Did you take part in the bank robbery here in sixty-nine . . . ?" "Good God, Joe, he was just a kid then. But what about Winston . . . ?"

The county sheriff came to his rescue, pushing reporters aside, cursing them, telling them to quit blocking entrances to businesses. He waved a finger in Charlie Ford's face, saying if he wanted to give interviews he had better not do it in the middle of the town square or, by jingo, he'd be charged with disturbing the peace.

After the lawman's rebuke, Charlie jerked his head repeatedly and shot through an opening in the crowd. Half of the reporters followed him, while the rest stayed behind to hammer Sheriff Crozier with questions. A few townsfolk and drifters joined the parade. Maybe if he led them to one of the town's saloons, somebody might buy him a drink.

"Bring in Frank James," Judge Goodman announced after the case, *The State of Missouri v. Frank James,* had been called to start the two o'clock session. A murmur began to swell as two deputies escorted the defendant, wearing a confident look and Prince Albert coat, into the courtroom. Frank James led his son by the hand, nodded at his attorneys and settled into the bench beside his wife. He scooped up his son and started bouncing the five-year-old on his knee.

The boom of Goodman's gavel silenced the spectators, and the judge glanced at the prosecution table. "Is the state ready?" he asked.

Hamilton rose. "Yes, Your Honor."

"And the defense?"

This time, William Rush stood. "Your Honor," he said, "a few attachment processes have failed. We do, however, request that the jury be summoned so we can proceed with the case, but with the court's understanding that if some of our important witnesses—for whom attachments have been issued, I must make this clear—do not appear, the court will grant us a reasonable continuance so that we can secure their attendance."

Hamilton stood again, shaking his head while staring at the defense lawyers and speaking to the judge. "Your Honor, I must object. The defense has had ten months to secure any witnesses. The state is ready for trial. I see no reason for you to grant any continuance."

"You may not see," Goodman said, "but I do."

"Thank you, Your Honor," Rush said. "Your wisdom—"

"Be quiet, Mr. Rush," the judge barked. "I haven't finished. You have until tomorrow morning to get your witnesses together, but we shall not dillydally in this matter. I am issuing a venire facias to Sheriff Crozier for a panel of one hundred jurors. Furthermore, I take it upon myself now to announce a few rules that will be followed during this trial.

"Ladies and gentlemen, I am fully aware that this quaint little courthouse does not have a suitable gallery for witnesses, reporters and spectators. Therefore, beginning tomorrow court will convene in the opera house. Spectators will be admitted by ticket only, and I am ordering Sheriff Crozier to issue no more than four hundred tickets each day.

"Furthermore, order and dignity will be preserved at all costs. A man's life is on trial here, and I will not let the case become some sort of circus like the medicine and puppet shows being staged in Gallatin. I will tolerate no disorderly conduct. Lastly, any person detected in the courtroom with weapons on will be surely, swiftly and to the full extent of the law punished. That includes you, Colonel Garner. I had better not see such a bulge in your hip pocket tomorrow, sir."

The defense attorney, sitting between Slover and Alexander, slid a couple of inches and tried to smile, although the color drained from his face. Across the room, the .41-caliber Thunderer felt much heavier under William Wallace's left armpit.

"That is all," Goodman said. "Court will reconvene at the opera house at nine o'clock tomorrow morning."

Chapter 14

The idea seems to be rapidly gaining ground that liberty in America either does, or ought to, mean license. The impression with many appears to be that the great experiment being made by the American people is, as to whether or not a nation may exist without any laws whatever.

—William H. Wallace

August 20, 1883
Gallatin, Missouri

The Charles Ford entourage followed the weaving little would-be assassin inside Mann's Grocery, and William Wallace wondered which attraction would wind up drawing the biggest following—second biggest, that is, behind the Frank James trial—Charlie Ford, Arizona Jack's Indian Medicine Show or the puppet show being staged near Henry Orcutt's lumberyard. Wallace drew on his cigar and continued to stare out the window.

Joshua Hicklin asked something about Ford, and Wallace turned to listen. The prosecutors had gathered inside William Hamilton's second-story courthouse office to go over jury selection. After pitching the cigar into a cuspidor, Wallace apologized and asked Hicklin to repeat his question.

"I said reporters are interviewing Charles Ford as though he's privy to our decisions," Hicklin repeated. "Can't we do something about this? He already told those worms that Liddil's in town."

As a former journalist, Wallace resented "worms," but before he could answer, Hamilton chimed in, "It's not so bad, having Ford spread rumors. He might even give the defense pause, make them go off on some wild-goose chase."

"Liddil's no goose chase," Henry McDougal said stiffly.

"It will pass," Wallace said. "The reporters will soon forget about Charlie Ford. Right now, they're just following him around to be there in case he gets killed."

"Which could very well happen," said Marcus Low.

Wallace shook his head. "Sheriff Crozier's got two or three of his men following Ford. Let the reporters question him all they want. He'll keep them out of our hair. Meanwhile, tell Dick Liddil to stay in his room."

"He'll want a bottle," McDougal said.

"Give him one, but he stays sober the night before he testifies. Marcus, I want you to baby-sit him. I don't want him to leave that hotel room. I don't think anyone will try to kill Charlie Ford, but Gallatin's full of Frank James's friends who'd damn sure like to murder Dick Liddil before he testifies."

The attorneys resumed their singsong chatter again, talking about the jury and the selection process. Wallace turned his attention to the bedlam below. He thought about last night, letting Robert sit on his shoulders so he could see over the crowd attending the Indian medicine show, and how lovely Annie had looked. Last night had been a mistake. The lead prosecutor gallivanting across town with the wife and son of the accused! He should have known better, yet he couldn't get Annie Ralston James out of his mind.

On the street below, Sheriff George Crozier stopped in front of a group of men passing around a newspaper in front of a cobbler's store. The lawman pulled a piece of paper from his vest pocket, glanced at it, then began talking to a fellow in a sack suit and bell crown hat. The conversation grew agitated, but Crozier shook a finger in the man's face and pointed toward the opera house.

Charlie Ford had emerged from the grocery with a mouthful of jerky, pulling his train of reporters, deputies and hangers-on toward the lumberyard, but Wallace followed Crozier. The lawman studied his slip of paper again, stuck it in his vest and headed across the square, calling out someone's name. A tall man with gray dundrearies and a clay pipe stopped on the boardwalk and waited for Crozier. They talked briefly, and the tall man sighed, nodded and tapped his pipe on a hitching post.

"Shit," Wallace said, louder than he had intended, and hurried to the stairwell.

He caught up with Crozier on the west side of the square in front of McDonald & Frey's Blacksmith and had to shout to be heard above the clamor of a smithy at work with hammer, horseshoes and anvil.

"What's the meaning of this list?" Wallace asked, pointing at the paper protruding from the sheriff's vest pocket.

"Impanelin' a jury," Crozier snapped back. "That's what Judge Goodman tol' me to do."

"Let me see that list."

The sheriff straightened. "That ain't ethical. You got no call—"

Wallace had to restrain himself from grabbing the lapels of the man's broadcloth vest. "You're supposed to impanel one hundred jurors from Daviess County, not just Gallatin." He had reason to be upset. Low, Shanklin, Hicklin and Hamilton said most people in town these days would likely look on Frank James with favor, but you could seat an impartial jury by bringing in men from the county.

"I'll get you a good jury, Wallace, but I ain't a-gonna ride all over this county, in this heat, summonin' a bunch of farmers who ain't a-gonna show up nohow. An' I don't blame 'em, dry as it is. Cisterns ain't but half-full, and them farmers is a-hurtin' more'n most. You'll get your jury, a good one. Now leave me be so I can do my job."

Hamilton jumped when Wallace slammed the door, and he bit his lower lip when the Jackson County attorney kicked over a trash can. His colleague cursed, pacing back and forth, and Hamilton looked nervously at the other attorneys in the office, wondering if they knew what had sparked Wallace's outrage.

"That son of a bitch," Wallace said, whipped off his hat and sent it sailing across the rim toward the window. "Crozier's out there with a list for his jury, grabbing people in town. He refuses to go into the county."

Hamilton straightened in his chair.

"Did you see the list?" Shanklin asked as he spit out his snuff into the stained can he carried everywhere. Why he didn't just use a spittoon like everyone else in town baffled Hamilton. "I mean, was it Crozier's handwriting?"

Wallace gave Shanklin a how-in-hell-would-I-recognize-Crozier's-handwriting look before picking up his hat, dusting it off on his thigh and settling into a jury chair near the window. He apologized for his tirade and loosened his ribbon tie.

"What I mean, gentlemen," Shanklin said calmly, "is the list is grounds of impropriety. I know that the *honorable* William Rush has been hired to seat a jury sympathetic to Frank James. Should have mentioned it before, but, well I didn't believe that Rush would use any method to achieve this result."

This suggestion staggered Hamilton. "You think William Rush bribed Crozier, gave him a list of potential jurors?"

The old man sighed. "C. W. Middleton, John Wood and a couple others said they had heard rumors to that effect. I thought it was horse apples. But now . . ."

"It doesn't matter," Hicklin said. "We need a good jury, and Crozier isn't getting us one. This list gives us grounds to file an affidavit."

"Right," Wallace said with a nod, his tantrum over, focused again on his job. "We charge him with improper conduct. Take this before Judge Goodman, ask him to remove Crozier and replace him with . . ."

Joshua Hicklin finished the statement. "The county coroner. It's the law. The coroner can summon a jury in such cases."

It had all moved too fast for Hamilton. He felt dizzy as he tried to catch up with the discussion, to understand everything that was happening. "That's Claggett," Marcus Low said, and the name registered with Hamilton. D. M. Claggett lived over in Winston and was due to testify for the prosecution. He was quiet, unassuming and . . .

"Damn it," Hamilton heard himself shouting, "Claggett

served in the Confederacy. Do you truly think he would do us better than Crozier?"

The room fell silent. Wallace smoothed his mustache before asking, "Is he honest?"

"Honest, certainly," Shanklin replied with a shrug, and the other attorneys concurred.

"Listen," Wallace was saying, "all we desire is honesty. My family was loyal to the Southern cause. Police Commissioner Craig is a Southerner. Sheriff Timberlake served in the Confederate Army. I can give you a list of men who fought to bring the James Gang to justice, and many of them had Southern sympathies. We'll play this up during our arguments and, most likely, Governor Johnson and Colonel Philips will point out that they fought for the Union. I don't think a person's loyalties in a war over for nearly twenty years is a valid argument. Let's draw up this affidavit and get it to Judge Goodman forthwith."

With a sigh, Hamilton pulled papers from his top drawer. He wondered how things had gotten so out of hand. A year ago he had been dreaming how he would be the prosecutor to send Frank James to prison or the gallows, how he would ride his victory to the governor's mansion. He hadn't thought much of William Wallace when he first met the man in Jefferson City way back in May of eighty-two, and now Mr. William Hockaday Wallace was running the show while William Decatur Hamilton took dictation like some legal secretary.

"Let me get this straight," Charles Goodman said in his hotel room as he filled a tumbler with bourbon. "You are asking me to believe that Sheriff Crozier is impaneling a juror from a list provided him by William Rush of the defense?"

"I know it's hard to believe, Your Honor," Wallace said, "but a number of citizens approached Colonel Shanklin and said they had heard Rush planned to fix the jury."

"Hearsay," Goodman said and took a swallow.

"It's a damned lie, Judge!" Crozier bellowed. "Ain't nobody accusin' me—"

"Hold your temper, Sheriff, and your tongue," the judge

scolded, then gestured at Colonel John Philips with his tumbler.

"It's highly improper, Judge," the defense attorney said smoothly. "Crozier has a good reputation in this town, and Mr. Rush has twice served Daviess County as prosecutor. We shouldn't let these unnamed citizens besmirch the reputations of civil servants."

"We can name names if you like," Wallace said.

Time for another sip of bourbon. Goodman set the drink on the chest of drawers. "Why did Colonel Shanklin wait so long to bring this to our attention?"

"It was mere rumor," Wallace said, "till I noticed Crozier consorting his list."

The sheriff waved his fist in Wallace's face. "You try to swear me off, Wallace, and you'll play hell. Ain't—"

"Crozier, get out of here!" Goodman shouted. "Go have a drink and cool off. I'll see you in court tomorrow morning."

After Crozier slammed the door shut, Goodman refreshed his bourbon and opened the window. He looked down at the streets, listening to the commotion below, and asked Philips and Hamilton to leave. He wanted a private word with Wallace.

Hamilton, who hadn't said a word since entering the hotel room, started to protest, but Wallace asked him to wait in his office. Ever the gentleman, Philips just bowed slightly and held open the door for the Daviess County prosecutor.

"Look at the fireflies," the judge said absently, still staring outside, "dancing over by the courthouse." The air outside felt hot and humid, with no breeze to cool the second-story room. "Care for a drink?" Goodman asked as he turned around.

"No, thank you, sir."

"That's right," Goodman said as a smile brightened his hairy face. "You're a temperance man." He drained the tumbler and commented, "Well, George Crozier has certainly managed to bollix things up."

"Yes, sir."

"What's the weather been like this summer in Jackson County?"

"Hot. Dry. Same as here."

"Same in Gentry County, too," he said, leaning against the windowsill and returning to the subject. "Do you really believe Rush gave a list of potential jurors to Crozier?"

"I don't know, but I do know it is grounds for Crozier's removal. The mere suggestion of impropriety demands his replacement. Justice, sir, is being cheated."

"Everything I've heard about you, Mr. Wallace, is true," Goodman said heartily. "You are one stubborn son of a bitch."

Wallace returned the smile. "Yes, sir, when I'm in the right."

"Well, you may be in the right now. I appreciate the way you handled this matter, bringing it to my attention in front of Crozier and Colonel Philips. Not ex parte, but not in front of a roomful of reporters. But look outside, sir." He stepped away from the window. "There must be close to a thousand people in Gallatin for the trial, and more are yet to arrive. This isn't a town—it's a powder keg. That loudmouth dunderhead of a sheriff has already told the patrons in the nearest saloon what you want to do, and I daresay many of those drunks want Frank James acquitted. Don't talk, Mr. Wallace. Let me finish. Frank James is not the only person on trial in Gallatin. You are. The State of Missouri is. The defense attorneys are. So am I. I want you to know that despite my edict this afternoon, as long as you carry whatever you're carrying in that shoulder holster, as long as I can't tell you're loaded down with iron, feel free to bring your equalizer to the opera house. I wouldn't want you to be shot down on your way to the hotel. And if I relieved Sheriff Crozier and replaced him with Claggett, you would be shot dead and the streets of Gallatin would run red with blood. That's not how I desire to go down in history.

"It is not my habit to announce my decision beforehand, Mr. Wallace, but if you file this motion I will certainly overrule it in order to prevent bloodshed. We will begin seating a jury tomorrow. If your case is strong enough, the jury will have no choice but to convict. Good night."

Wallace kicked open the door to Hamilton's office for the second time this day and dropped his valise on the floor. "He turned us down," he snapped. "This is a damned burlesque. We can find more justice at that puppet show in town, and I'm finished."

The valise suddenly commanded Hamilton's attention. Colonel Shanklin, the only one who had remained in the solicitor's office at such a late hour, started to say something, but Hamilton couldn't comprehend the words. Wallace went about with his raving, picked up his bag and slammed the door shut behind him.

"What was that all about?" Hamilton asked as he reached for his glass of whiskey.

His eyes twinkling, the old colonel lifted his spit tin in salute before emptying his mouth of snuff. "You got your wish, my boy," Shanklin said. "The case is all yours now. Wallace just resigned."

Chapter 15

*There is no heroism in outlawry, and the fate of each
outlaw in his turn should be an everlasting lesson to the
young of the land.*
                                        —Cole Younger,
                        The Story of Cole Younger by Himself, 1903

August 21, 1883
Gallatin, Missouri

Once she recognized him in front of the depot's ticket window,
Annie James hesitated. She thought about fleeing back to the
safety of her hotel room, knowing her errand could wait, but
he turned at that instant, luggage in hand, and spotted her. Seeing her at the train station must have surprised him as much as
finding him had stunned her. He walked toward her, lowered
his valise and satchel and stuck a ticket inside his coat pocket.

"You're leaving?" she asked timidly.

He answered with a nod, and his Adam's apple bobbed as he
tried to explain. He finally just shrugged and said, "I quit,
Annie. The judge made a ruling I couldn't abide with, so I'm
heading back to Kansas City. Hamilton and the others can try
this case without me."

Her feelings were confused: glad he wouldn't be the one
trying to condemn her husband; sad that he wouldn't be here.
For some time, she had known Wallace was an honorable
lawyer, one she would gladly have trusted with her husband's
life had he not been a county prosecutor. On the other hand,
she did not like William Hamilton or his methods. He had

been the one to discover the sewing machine she gave her mother and would scheme to turn that into some kind of damning evidence, although, try as she might, she couldn't figure out just how he planned on doing this.

"What brings you here?" he asked.

"Frank's mother arrives today," she said. "I was just checking the schedule."

He accompanied her to the chalkboard on the wall, still decorated with flyers announcing rooms for let, and found the schedule. "Two thirty," she said absently. "When do you leave?"

"Nine, if it's on time."

"Well, I guess this is good-bye." She continued to stare at the board. "I was going to take Robert to the puppet show this evening. I was hoping . . ." Slowly she turned, and their eyes met. He could have kissed her then. She felt weak, maybe would have let him, but she was glad he didn't. Ever the gentleman, Wallace stammered that he had work waiting in Jackson County, that he would love to spend more time with Robert and her but . . . He couldn't finish, didn't really have to. Annie knew letting Wallace escort her and her son the other night had been a mistake—on her part as well as his. Letting him kiss her would have been a mistake, too. She was married and loved her husband, yet Wallace had always been a friend, a true friend, and she sometimes dreamed how her life might have turned out had she chosen another path.

"I know," she told him when he had finished his apology. She reached out and took his hand. "You're a good man, William. A kind man. I'm glad you're leaving. I can't bear to think of you as an enemy."

"We're not enemies," he said. "But you should know that I believe your husband is guilty. I would not prosecute him if I didn't think that." He wavered, but his feelings burst from him like a flash flood. "Damn it, Annie! He's a killer. How could—"

"Don't," she snapped. "Not now. You don't know him."

The argument had been building inside both of them. She had sensed it since she met with him in Kansas City, trying to negotiate Frank's surrender. Well, he would learn she was no novice when it came to these quarrels. She had defended Frank James to reporters, to her parents, to her friends and family.

"I know what he did," he went on. "I've kept my feelings bottled up inside me every time I've been with you. I care about you, Annie. I always have, but duty comes first. Your husband robbed the Winston train with Jesse, Dick Liddil and the Hite brothers. They killed two men."

"My husband," she seethed, "was in Texas at the time of the robbery, and he only killed when he had to, sir. He never shot anyone in cold blood. Never."

They stared at each other, faces flushed, silent. Annie had made the right choice after all. Wallace was bound by duty, but the man she married was bound by blood. Family had always come first with Frank, and he would never murder anyone. She looked at Wallace once more, felt a tear roll down her cheek, then spun around, hurrying back to the hotel, almost knocking over a man in a gray suit as she bounded down the depot's steps.

William Hamilton brushed off his coat while watching the small young woman run toward town. He had heard the raised voices, and thought some husband and wife were having a lit-tle row at the depot. It wouldn't have been the first time. The escaping woman, however, he placed as Annie James, and her husband was locked up tight in the calaboose, soon to be es-corted to the opera house. That meant she had been arguing with Wallace. With a sigh, he climbed up the steps and found his colleague picking up his luggage before heading to a bench in the shade.

He sat down beside Wallace, who ignored him, and crossed his legs. "I need to know one thing," said Hamilton, staring at a tinder and old freight car on a side track. "She's not the rea-son you resigned, is she?"

"Who?" Wallace snapped after an angry pause.

"Don't play me for a fool," he shot back, now facing Wal-lace. "I'm not blind, and I'm not stupid."

After a grunt, Wallace spoke in a dry whisper. "It has noth-ing to do with her. I quit because of Judge Goodman's deci-sion. I meant what I said last night. This is a damned farce."

"You took her and her son to the Indian medicine show the other night?"

Glaring bitterly, Wallace shifted position and growled, "Don't you have a case to try? Doesn't voir dire begin today?"

"Answer my question."

"The hell I will. I'm not on trial here."

"The hell you aren't." Hamilton jumped to his feet and had to restrain himself from slapping the insolent dullard. "The lead prosecutor escorts the defendant's wife and son about town, and afterward quits the case. If any reporter finds out about this, you can say good-bye to your career. You accuse Crozier of impropriety, perhaps corruption—well, how do you think this would go over with Judge Goodman?"

Wallace raised his right hand. "Wave that fist in my face once more, you conniving bastard, and I'll rip your arm off."

If Wallace thought Hamilton would retreat, he was in for a shock. Truth was, Hamilton's anger surprised himself, but he was in the right, and he had to know about Wallace and Ann James. "What was she doing here at the depot at eight in the morning?"

Wallace stood, inched closer to Hamilton and said, "She came to check the schedule. Mrs. Samuel arrives today and she wanted to find out what time the train arrives. That's all there was to it. You better get to the courthouse, Hamilton."

"Opera house," he corrected. "So there's nothing between you and Annie James?"

"No. You ask me one more question and they'll be picking up pieces of you all over this depot. You wanted to ramrod this prosecution, so go grab your glory."

He didn't remember shoving Wallace, but the next thing he knew, the Jackson County solicitor was tripping over his luggage. The ticket agent shouted something—the two men had forgotten all about him—but Hamilton couldn't hear. He charged, kicking at the lawyer's face. The heel of his right shoe caught a glancing blow off Wallace's forehead, sending his hat rolling on its brim across the platform. Hamilton tried to regain his balance, but Wallace wrapped his arms around Hamilton's legs, felling the counselor like a pine. Sharp pain sliced across his shoulders as he landed with a thud. Wallace was on top of him. He didn't know how that had happened, either.

Hamilton grabbed the lapels of Wallace's vest, and the two men rolled over, separating, and scrambled to their feet. Hamilton threw one punch, missed, and ducked another before Wallace locked him in a bear hug. Hamilton brought his knee up, heard Wallace grunt and relax, and he knew he had accomplished his goal. He pulled away, tried to swing, but found both arms pinned. Someone had grabbed him from behind. He looked up, struggling, laboring for breath. A black man in a railroad cap had taken hold of Wallace's arms, and another man was hissing in Hamilton's ear.

"Fools," the express agent said. Hamilton tried to free himself, but the agent's grip never faltered, and he surrendered, having never been cut out for such fisticuffs. "Y'all should know better. Jed, let Mr. Wallace go. Now I'm going to turn you loose, too, Mr. Hamilton, but if either of you try anything like this again, by thunder, I'll fetch Sheriff Crozier. Shake hands. Shake hands, I say."

Hamilton stepped toward Wallace, floundered, but extended his right hand at last. Their hands gripped, slightly at first, then tightening. Suddenly Wallace was smiling, soon laughing, and Hamilton joined in.

"That felt good," he heard himself saying as they returned to the bench.

"Yeah," Wallace agreed as both men sat down to catch their breath.

"I had to know about you and Mrs. James before you left," Hamilton said a few minutes later.

"There's nothing between us," Wallace said. "But you were right. I shouldn't have bought her supper, taken her and Robert to the show. That was stupid. My brain usually works better."

"She's a right handsome woman," he said. "I don't blame you."

"Well, it's over and done with. It's your case. Good luck."

"Wallace." Hamilton breathed the name in a heavy sigh. This came harder than he had expected. He still couldn't believe he had actually walked to the depot to do this. "William, you know this case better than anyone. We can't win it without you. I came here to ask you to reconsider, to stay with us, to see Frank James brought to justice." Wallace looked stunned. "I . . ." Hamilton shook his head. *Get it over with,* he told himself. "I'm not good enough. You're a better prosecutor than I am. If you leave, we've already lost."

He didn't know how long Wallace stared at him, but it seemingly lasted hours before he broke the silence. "I thought you wanted this case."

Nodding, Hamilton said, "I did." He cocked his head and continued. "At least, I thought I did. I am conniving." He forced a smile. "I'm not sure about the 'bastard' part. I cut my teeth here in Gallatin pursuing collections, trivial lawsuits. I'm a politician, but you, William, are a lawyer."

Wallace paused to rub the red spot where Hamilton's shoe had grazed his forehead. He looked away, saw his hat resting near the edge of the depot and walked over to pick it up, dust it off and pull it on his head, likely doing this to give himself time to think. When he returned, he held out his hand and helped Hamilton to his feet.

"You found the sewing machine connection," Wallace said. "You're a good lawyer, a good detective. You could put Frank James behind bars."

"I only overheard part of what you told Mrs. James," Hamilton said, shaking his head. "I heard you say 'duty comes first.' This is your duty, sir. Help me. Help Missouri."

Help Missouri. Hamilton regretted that part. It certainly sounded like something from the mouth of a politicking, conniving bastard.

Wallace grinned weakly and pulled his pocket watch from his vest pocket. "I've probably lost my room at the Palace," he said.

"Not yet," Hamilton said easily. "I told the clerk to hold it for you until he heard from me. I'll help carry your luggage. We still have time for you to wash your face and dust off your suit before court is called to order."

They shook hands again.

Reporters, Frank James had learned, were highly impressionable. Recite a few passages from the Bard, give them one or two good quotes and they'd believe anything you told them. He sat in the jail cell in the early evening talking to Mr. Noble Prentiss, a pretty good fellow from the *Atchison Daily Globe*, who had already penned some rather impressive, and complimentary, prose about Missouri's most famous jailbird. Not that Frank would ever admit it, but Prentiss could write a whole lot prettier than Major Edwards.

"You think you'll be acquitted?" Prentiss asked.

"I should be," he answered. "I'm innocent of these charges."

"What about the other charges?"

Frank laughed before answering. "If Jesse and I were guilty of half the crimes they say we committed, I'd be so rich I'd be a rival of many a railroad baron."

"You never robbed anyone? Never killed anyone?"

"I fought in the War, sir. Surely I have killed. Would to God I hadn't, but that's war. As Ben Franklin once said, 'There never was a good war or a bad peace.' But I never killed anyone who wasn't trying to kill me. Certainly no stonemason or train conductor."

"What about it, ma'am?" Prentiss asked, spinning toward Annie. She sat in a rocking chair in the corner of the cell, concentrating on her knitting, and looked up, a bit dazed. Frank James felt his temper rising. Had he known Prentiss would stoop to cheap journalism, he would never have granted an interview.

"Excuse me?" Annie said with a sad smile.

"Do you believe your husband never killed anyone in cold blood?"

"Certainly," she answered, and returned to her knitting.

Frank James settled back on his bunk, coughed and reached for a book. The reporter started to ask another question, but Colonel Philips arrived with a few deputies, ending the interview. Prentiss collected his notes, pulled on his hat and left the cell as Philips entered.

"Good evening, Mrs. James," he said with a grand bow. "We missed you in court today."

Annie looked up again and explained that Governor Johnson had told her she need not come for jury selection as it would be most boring. That it had been, Frank agreed, and listened as Philips rehashed the proceedings of the day. Fifty-two Democrats, forty-six Republicans and two Greenbackers—those fools who had been proposing the use of inconvertible paper money since seventy-four—had filled Crozier's venire. They would be thinned to forty and then to twelve. William Rush was doing a fine job, Philips said, then asked if Frank needed anything.

"I'm fit as a fiddle," he lied. "Thanks, Colonel."

"We have a long row to hoe yet, Frank," Philips said. "We'll continue voir dire tomorrow, maybe into Thursday." He told Annie, "I see no reason you should endure that hot opera house all day tomorrow, ma'am. It'll be more of the same. Stay in the hotel with Robert and your mother-in-law. Relax. This trial will be most arduous."

"Thank you," she said without looking up. "I shall."

Something was bothering her. He knew she had been crying, could tell by her eyes, how she kept on knitting. She had barely spoken to him all afternoon, and his first thoughts raced to solicitor Wallace. Annie said they had been together two nights ago, but he trusted her. Always had. So it must be something else. He waited until Colonel Philips and the deputies left before questioning her.

"What's the matter?" he asked firmly, swinging his legs over the bunk and suppressing a cough as he sat up.

"It's just the trial," she said to her knitting.

"That ain't what's bothering you," he said, and his words echoed in the cell, only they weren't being spoken by him—Dingus was speaking—and he knew exactly what had caused his wife's misery and worry.

He could picture his brother so clearly, hear him as well, even though his memories were seven years old. Somehow, they had gotten out of Minnesota, abandoning Cole, Jim and Bob Younger and Charley Pitts near some marsh called Hanksa Slough, leaving them to die after barely getting out of Northfield with their lives. Bill Chadwell and Clell Miller had been rubbed out in town, Cole and the others shot to pieces. Even Dingus had caught a ball, but God looked after the two James boys. That was what he remembered so vividly now, his kid brother quoting Scripture as they hid in a loft in Salina, Kansas.

"What are you a-frettin' over, Buck?" Dingus had asked through the pain caused by a the bullet in his thigh.

Frank had exploded. "Fretting over? By God, Dingus, we left Cole and his brothers to die up there in that damnyankee state." Dingus had never cared much for Cole, and the feeling had been mutual, but had befriended the other Youngers, especially young Bob. He expected that to shame his brother. After all, his stupid idea had done what neither Pinkertons nor anyone else could accomplish: wipe out the James-Younger Gang.

That look on Dingus's face had been chiseled into Frank's brain. The smirk, the beaming eyes, the way he had laughed when he said, "That ain't what's a-botherin' you, Buck. That ain't it a'tall."

Frank James swallowed and tried to shake off the nightmare. "Come here," he said, and Annie slowly pushed herself from the rocker, lowered her knitting and sat beside him, leaning her head on his shoulder. He put his arm around her small waist, pulled her closer.

"If things don't work out, Annie," he began, "if they hang me, or send me to prison for life, I figure that Wallace fellow will take care of you and Robert—"

"Frank . . ." she began, but he only pulled her closer.

"Hush, now," he said and kissed her forehead. "You always been a believer in me. I never will forget that."

"You're a good man," she said softly, and he heard her muffled sobs.

"Sometimes," he said. "You never asked me anything, just took my word. Sometimes I feel I've trapped your spirit, Annie girl, turned you into a recluse like me. Remember how you used to be, always ready to ride, racing boys down the streets of Independence? You were something. You still are. God, Annie, I'd hate to lose you. That'd be worse than prison, worse than dying."

"You're not going to lose me, Frank," she said.

"Maybe." His voice sounded far away. "I need to tell you about something I did."

Chapter 16

*But there are things done for money and for revenge of
which the daring of the act is the picture and the crime
the frame that it be set in. Crime of which daring is
simply an ingredient that has no palliation on earth or
forgiveness anywhere. But a feat of stupendous nerve
and fearlessness that makes one's hair rise to think of it,
with a condiment of crime to season it, become
chivalric; poetic; superb.*
                                        —John Newman Edwards, *Kansas City Times,*
                                        September 29, 1872

September 7, 1876
Northfield, Missouri

We sat on some crates stacked in front of Lee & Hitchcock's
Dry Goods, Dingus, Bob Younger and me, idling about, letting
the ham and eggs we had for lunch settle in our stomachs. Bob
had picked up a bottle of rye at one of the saloons, and me and
him shared it. Dingus never thought much of drinking before a
job, but with Bob being more than a tad jittery, he didn't say a
thing. Reckon I was mighty uncertain, too, which is why I par-
took.

    Guess I should tell you the whole story, from the beginning,
how we come to Northfield . . . Well, Dingus had liked the
idea of robbing a bank in Minnesota since he first heard about
it from Charley Pitts and Bill Chadwell. Cole and me never
rightly took with it—I told you that before—but Bob was
champing at the bit. You recollect that sweet little girl he was

nesting with? Anyhow, he figured if his share was big enough, he'd be finished with the robbing and would take to farming. God Almighty, how many times did Dingus say the very same thing? And I'm just as bad, Annie. I know that for certain. The only reason Jim Younger rode the rails up north with us is 'cause Cole had asked him to come back from Californy, figured if anybody could talk sense into Bob it would be Jim— only Bob wouldn't have none of it, said he was going with Dingus and the rest of us could go with them or go to hell. You know Cole. He'd stick with his brother, and Jim done the same. Guess I always stuck with Dingus, too, though after this one I tried to get as far away from him as I could. But he'd lure me back. I'm awful sorry about that.

Anyway, pretty soon, we all figured the plan might just work. Bill Chadwell—think his real name was Stiles—hailed from that neck of the woods, so he knew the lay of the land, and would steer us around the towns and on trails not many a body knew about so we'd get back home safely. Clell Miller and Charley Pitts had rode with us before, and we knew they could handle themselves in a pinch. Charley'd stick with Cole like a sand burr, and Clell thought the world of Dingus. So we up and robbed the Missouri Pacific Express at Rocky Cut for some operating cash and left Missouri.

Well, once we got to Yankee country, we drifted a mite— Red Wing, St. Paul . . . I've forgotten the names of most of them burgs—played some poker, posing as railroad inspectors, real estate investors, cattle buyers. The original plan was to hit the First National Bank in Mankato. Me and Dingus went inside, and I changed a fifty-dollar bill. Then we left, the idea being that if we liked the setup, we'd signal Cole and he'd bring the boys down the street, and me and Dingus would go back inside and do our business. Only Dingus said no, said it didn't feel right, so we rode out. Later, Cole asked him what had been the problem. I figured he didn't like there being so many folks in town that day, but he said someone recognized him.

Right. The Good Lord didn't shortchange my brother when it come to vainglory. Cole said so to Dingus's face, and it's a wonder they didn't shoot each other—you recall how them two got along. Anyway, that's when Charley Pitts and Bill Chadwell suggested we raid Northfield. It being the only bank in town, all them damnyankee farmers, millers and businessmen would have their savings in it. Plus, Chadwell told us, them good-for-nothing carpetbaggers Ben Butler and Adelbert Ames likely kept their stolen fortunes in the First National Bank of Northfield. You remember Ames, don't you? No matter. He got himself impeached as Mississippi's governor during the Reconstruction. And Butler did his share of pillaging under the damnyankee rule. That lit a fire in Dingus's belly, Bob's, too, and we split up again to meet just outside of Northfield.

We got there that Tuesday morning. It was kinda warm, right pretty day. Too nice of a day for what happened. Dingus, me and Bob, it was decided, would be the inside men. That was our first mistake. I always liked Cole being inside with me. Anyway, if we liked the looks of things, we'd go inside, and Cole and Clell would drift on down the street and keep folks out of the bank. Charley, Chadwell and Jim was to keep an eye on things down the other end of the street. They'd stay on this little bridge that crossed the Cannon River unless things got hot. Then they'd ride up shooting and we'd buffalo them timid souls. That's how we usually done things. Shoot in the sky, give lots of Johnny Reb yells, scare the devil out of everyone before heading out of town at a high lope, cut the telegraph wires and skedaddle. Last thing I told 'em at the Bridge Square, before we split up, was that nobody was to get killed. We weren't going to shoot civilians.

Anyhow, that's how we come to Northfield. After filling our bellies at a place called Jeft's, we lounged about. It was about two o'clock when Dingus stood up. To be honest, I expected him to mount up and we'd call the damned thing off. Town was getting full of folks, but he just walked toward the bank, leading his horse and saying, "'Who is this King of glory? The Lord strong and mighty, the Lord mighty in battle. Lift up your heads, O ye gates; even lift them up, ye everlasting doors; and the King of glory shall come in.'" That's from Psalms. He always liked to recite Scripture before hitting a bank or train.

Bob and me followed, wrapped our reins over the hitching post and went inside.

Things looked pretty good at first. Weren't no customers inside, only three bankers, so Dingus pushed back his duster and pulled out Baby—that's what he called his new Schofield revolver. Bob and me also had on dusters, and we done the same, cocked our pieces. "Throw up your hands!" Dingus hollers. "We're a-gonna rob this bank. If anyone halloos, we'll blow your damned brains out. We got forty men outside."

I climbed over the counter and stuck the barrel of my Remington under a gent's nose. He had dark hair, mustache and beard—don't rightly think I'll ever get that face out of my mind—and I took him for the cashier . . . only he said he wasn't. I called him a damned liar—he was sitting at the cashier's desk, for heaven's sake—said I'd blow his head off if he lied to me once more. You try to scare 'em, Annie, make 'em think you'd shake hands with old Beelzebub if he walked in. Cuss and shout, put a gun in a man's face, and he'll likely be too fearful to do nothing but obey, but this guy had plenty of sand. He stuck to his story, so I tapped the side of his noggin with my Remington, jerked him to his feet and shoved him toward the vault.

Dingus, all this time, he's shouting for someone to open the safe, but everyone is telling him that they don't know the combination, that the damned thing's on a time lock anyhow. We knew that for certain. Chadwell had tore out a story in one of the newspapers and had carried it in his vest pocket. It said the Northfield bank had a steel burglar-proof safe with a chronometer lock. I remember that sure as certain because Chadwell kept asking Dingus or Cole to tell him just what in hell a chronometer lock was. 'Course, I figured the safe could be opened now, it being so late in the day, and stuck my head in the vault to give it a look-see, when that damned cashier tried to slam the vault door shut. Son of a bitch nearly crushed my arm, but Bob kicked the fool in his *huevos,* doubled him over. It riled Dingus something fierce, and he unfolded his knife, put the blade under the man's chin and said, "Let's cut his damn throat." Might have done it, but I said let it lie, and about that time Bob saw one of them other bankers easing toward a teller's window, real Injun-like, so Bob goes over, shoves the fellow aside and picks up this little Smith & Wesson popgun. Later, he gave it to Charley Pitts. Bob, he's just laughing—maybe it was the whiskey—and says, "You couldn't do nothing with that little thang, anyway."

'Bout that time, the shooting started outside.

Best we ever got it figured, Cole and Clell had stationed themselves in front of the bank door, and when this gent come strolling down the boardwalk, Clell drew his gun and stuck it in the man's belly, tells him he can't go inside the bank just yet and to be still and keep his gullet shut. Only the fool turns and runs, starts screaming that the bank's being robbed. Well, Clell knew how I felt about not shooting nobody, so he didn't gun that man down, and Jim, Chadwell and Charley Pitts come galloping down the street, shooting and hollering, just like we had it figured. Cole's yelling, "Get off the damn street!" He's like me. Don't want to kill nobody if it can be helped.

Now, as Bob's teasing one of them bankers, and Dingus is pistol-whipping the one that tried to lock me in the vault, the third guy turns to run out the back door. I yell at Bob to stop, but he's got his pistol aimed and pulls the trigger before I can shout twice. The bullet hit the fellow in his shoulder, and he grunts but keeps on going, runs right through the double blind they got hanging over the back door. Bob takes off after him, shoots again, then comes back inside and says he got away.

Outside, it sounds like there's a damn full-pitch battle going on, and I guess that's what was happening. I heard Cole's voice, and he's crying out, "The game's up, boys! Get your asses out of there. We're gettin' all cut up here."

'Course, Dingus ain't having none of that. We figured there would be maybe seventy thousand dollars in that bank, and we ain't found nothing so far but some change and bills. He's dragging that cashier toward the vault, tells him to open that vault, but the fool just shakes his head, says he ain't gonna do it. Dingus fires a shot in the floor, just by the guy's head, but he still won't help. I can hear bullets thumping the walls outside, our boys giving them hell, screaming. Then Cole, he's pounding on the door and yelling at us, "They're killin' our men! Get out here!"

"Come on!" I shout at Dingus, and me and Bob head to the door. Bob runs out first, and his horse is dead. That was our first sight at Division Street, and it was quite a shock. I see Cole in the street, trying to help Clell Miller up, and Jim Younger's right beside him. Chadwell comes galloping by, there's a shot and he drops from his horse, deader than dirt. Charley Pitts is shooting, too—it's mighty hot now—and Bob steps onto the street, trying to catch the reins to one of our horses. Bob gets hit in his arm—I mean blood's everywhere—and Jim's screaming at Cole to forget Clell, that he's dead, and he had to be—poor man bled like a stuck pig—and Cole sees that Bob's been shot, and he gets up and runs to his brother. He shoves Bob up on his horse, tries to get on himself and takes a blast in his hip.

Dingus rushes past me—see, I'm standing in the doorway, shooting at the windows, still trying not to kill nobody—and he grunts and cusses, and I see he's caught a bullet in the leg. That's when I turned back to look inside the bank and I see that cashier standing up. Anyway, I think he's got a gun, so I fire a shot at him, missed him clearly, but he falls into his chair and topples over onto the floor.

God as my witness, I don't know why I did what I did next. Maybe it was watching my brother and best friend get shot. Hadn't seen that since the War. Clell Miller and Bill Chadwell dead in the streets. Bullet in Dingus's thigh and he's just laughing at me, at us maybe, at this hole damn enfilade we'd gotten ourselves into. Jesus forgive me, but I just ran back into the bank, jumped over the counter, put my barrel right on that cashier's head and pulled the trigger. It was almost like I was watching someone else kill that fella, but it was me doing it, and I couldn't stop myself. Blew his brains out. He didn't have no gun at all. I just stared at the poor guy for a second, all this time hearing Dingus laughing. . . . I could hear that laugh over all that gunfire outside.

Then Cole's screaming, telling me to get out now, so I run outside, help Dingus into his saddle, mount that dun I bought a while back in Red Wing and we ride like hell. Jim catches a bullet in the shoulder, but he stays in the saddle. Didn't have time to do nothing much but retreat. Certainly didn't have time to cut the telegraph lines, and with Bill Chadwell lying dead in the dust back in town, we didn't have a notion as to where we should hide.

You've read and heard the rest of the story, but I'll tell it true. We run our horses till they couldn't carry us no more, and the rains started. Cole had been hit three times, but Bob fared the worst. We stole some more horses, not much, though—I remember one being blind in one eye and another blind in both eyes—kept moving, dodging posses, half-starved. Rain probably helped keep the law off our trail, but it didn't do us no favors. Bob must have been hurting like blazes, and he had taken a fever. We were all sick with misery and aches, and it finally got to the point where Bob couldn't ride no more, not that we had enough horses for all of us no how, so Dingus comes up to me one night and tells me, "Bob's just a-slowin' us down. He ain't a-gonna make it, Buck, so I reckon one of us should finish him off and let's ride on."

I stared at him like I didn't even know him, and I sure as hell didn't know him right then. "Good God," I told him. "Bob Younger's your best friend. He stuck with you all this time and you want to kill him?" I felt like slapping him, felt like shooting him, my own brother. Maybe I should have.

But it didn't come to nothing. Dingus went away to sulk and later that night Cole limps up to me and tells us that it's time we parted company, says Bob's arm ain't getting any better, it was getting worse for sure and we should split up.

"I hate doing this," I told him.

"No choice," he says. "Get out of here now, Frank, or you'll die with us."

Charley Pitts wouldn't go with us. He'd always been partial to Cole, so he said he'd stay with them. Always will admire Charley for that. His loyalty got himself killed. Then Cole told me, after Dingus left to saddle one of them nags, he tells me, "You'd do best to keep ridin', Frank. Leave your brother behind. He'll wind up gettin' yourself kilt, too. And I don't wanna see that."

So we left 'em, Annie. The posse caught up with them in that swamp, shot 'em to pieces, killed Charley Pitts and stuck the Youngers in prison for life. Cole and his brothers been true to us all this time, never told the law that we was in on it with them, though I guess everyone knows it was me and Dingus. All that, and you want to know how much money we got from Northfield? Twenty-six dollars and seventy cents.

I'm the only one who got out of Minnesota with nary a scratch, and I'm the one who should have gotten killed. I know one other citizen got killed, but I can't say who shot him. For all I know he could have gotten hit by one of them Northfield men trying to kill us. But I murdered that cashier. It was me, Annie. It was me that killed him. Killed him for nothing more than spite, I reckon. Really don't know the whys and what-fors, but I killed him.

You stuck by me all this time, Annie girl. I know you never cared for the life I led, riding with Dingus, and after Northfield I tried, tried hard, to live the good life for you and, after Robert was born, my boy. Dingus always pulled me back, though. Never could shuck my brother till he was dead. I failed you, Annie. God help me, I'm sorry for that. Maybe it would have been better if I stayed with Cole and got myself killed. 'Cause all this time you believed that I never had no part in the killings, that was all Dingus's doing, but that was a lie, honey.

Ain't no better than my damned brother.

Chapter 17

*Prominent witnesses on the part of the state are
constantly receiving letters warning them to be careful
in their testimony against the prisoner. . . . The counsel
for the defense pretend to believe that these letters are
written by enemies of their client with a view of
prejudicing his case; but it is clearly more probably that
they have their source in the lawless element of which
the Jameses were such shining lights.*
—*Idaho Tri-Weekly Statesman*, August 28, 1883

*August 22, 1883
Gallatin, Missouri*

Would Annie ever come back? She hadn't shown up for jury
selection that morning, but Colonel Philips had told her not to
bother. Still, the strain on her face after he admitted murdering
that cashier in Northfield would torment Frank James for eternity. Well, it was his own damned fault. Nobody made him
shoot that gent, and no one made him confess his sins. After
finishing his story, she hadn't said anything, just looked hurt,
betrayed and calmly picked up her knitting, called for the jailer
in her soft voice, said she had finished her visit. She didn't
look back, and he figured he had lost her forever.

When the door opened that afternoon, he hoped, prayed
Annie was coming back. He couldn't hide his disappointment
when one of Crozier's deputies escorted a fat old man into the
cell and announced, "Visitor."

No fooling. Frank James closed his collection of Milton and

said, "What can I do for you?" He assumed he was talking to some reporter, a new gent, maybe one from some East Coast paper, but this guy spoke in pure Missouri twang.

"It's not a question, sir," he said, "of what you can do for me, but rather one of what I shall do for you. I am Henry Clay Dean."

A few years back, folks called Henry Clay Dean the greatest orator in these United States. He had been a fire-and-brimstone Methodist preacher, in fact had even been appointed chaplain of the Senate in fifty-five, before coming to the conclusion that lawyer-palavering paid a great deal better than sermon-preaching. Abolitionists and damnyanks didn't think too highly of Dean, but a right smart of Missourians still guessed the old man could walk across the Missouri River, if not the Mississippi.

Only he didn't look like much now. His gray hair fell long and shaggy. His mustache and beard were unkempt, eyes rheumy. He wore a black ribbon tie loosely over a stained paper collar, and the sleeves of his herringbone suit coat were frayed. The coat looked a couple of sizes too small for the lawyer's expanding paunch, and the buttons had pulled out the threads so much they were about to fall off.

"Do you remember the first time I laid eyes on you, sir?" Dean asked as he settled his ample frame into Annie's rocker and pulled out a plug of tobacco and pocketknife. He carved himself a fair-sized piece before passing both quid and blade to the prisoner. Dean certainly knew the way to get on Frank James's good side. The outlaw tore off a mouthful of tobacco and began working it with his teeth while returning the knife and remnants of Dean's plug.

"Don't rightly recollect us ever meeting, Mr. Dean," he told the lawyer once he had softened the quid.

"Corydon, Iowa, back in June of seventy-two," Dean said, laughed and spit. "No, make that seventy-one. I was speaking at the Methodist church that afternoon, discoursing the coming of the iron horse to that fair town, and had a good turnout." He winked and added, "I'm sure the free beer we offered had as much to do with the crowd as my stimulating oration. Anyway, as I was being introduced, you, sir, knocked on the door, stuck your head inside and said, 'Y'all might be interested in knowing that four men just robbed your bank.' You smiled, spit into a nearby spittoon and took your leave, as many of the patrons hounded you as some heckler. Personally, I thought nothing of this at the time, but a few good citizens decided perhaps they should check the situation, so they departed for the Ocobock Brothers' Bank to find the cashier hog-tied and gagged. I am told you took the bank for ten thousand dollars." He cackled like a hen. "I love a man with a sense of humor, sir, even a bandit."

Grinning at the memory, Frank James wiped his mouth with the back of his hand. Interrupting the speech had been Dingus's idea, but Frank had played the part, just like Dean had remembered. In good humor, ol' Jesse James loved a gum game, leaving notes for posses, once even handing the engineer an account of the train robbery the gang had just pulled off, telling him to make sure Silas Hutchings of the *St. Louis Dispatch* got it. After Frank left Corydon's Methodist meeting house, Dingus flipped a two-bit piece to some boy idling about and told him, "We've just robbed the bank. Go tell everyone." The James boys, Clell Miller and Cole Younger rode out of town laughing, seven thousand dollars—not ten—richer.

He wanted to tell Dean something like, "Well, had we known you were serving free suds, we would have stayed a mite." Of course, what he told his visitor was, "I'm afraid you're mistaken, Mr. Dean. I've never been to Corydon, Iowa."

"Pardon my mistake," Dean said with a knowing wink. "Let us get down to the matters at hand. I am here, sir, to help you. I have a great speech already written for your trial. I'm not one for witnesses, sir. You may have heard that about me. Interrogations of witnesses are simply dull. The jury barely listens. No, the key to winning a case is having a great closing argument, and that is what I shall give you. I will inspire those twelve men, show them that they must acquit. I will turn your trial into a case against the Pinkertons, the railroads, the filth from the bowels of humanity. I am sixty-one years of age, sir, but the fire burns hot, and I am here to help, to win. Free of charge."

Governor Johnson and Colonel Philips were running this
show, and they hadn't seen fit to bring in Dean after Major Edwards gave them the letter the great orator had written a while
back, but Rebel Cove lay up in Putnam County, near the Iowa
border, and it would be a shame for a gentleman like Henry
Clay Dean to make that trip for nothing. So Frank James held
out his hand and said, "Glad to have you with us, Mr. Dean."
The great orator let out a deep breath, which surprised the outlaw. The old man had been nervous, afraid he was about to be
sent packing. They shook hands, and Dean asked, "So how are
things going with the jury selection?"

"Couldn't be better," Frank answered, spitting again.

*   *   *

*You better be careful about your evidence against Frank
James.*

                                                A FRIEND

Frowning, William Wallace reread the letter before folding
it and handing it back to William Hamilton, who gave him another note. This first letter had been addressed to a Gallatin
businessman named Harfield Davis and had been posted here
in Gallatin. The second note, written in the same sloping
script, repeated the message and had been mailed to Alec Irving, another local merchant. Wallace shook his head and returned the second letter to Hamilton, sighed and faced the two
businessmen.

After the Gallatin bank robbery in sixty-nine, Harfield
Davis and Alec Irving had joined the posse that chased the
James-Younger Gang but lost the trail near Kearney. Davis had
even put up a hefty sum of reward money for the capture and
conviction of the robbers and murderers. They were well-re-
spected throughout Daviess County by everyone . . . well,
most everyone.

"You just received the letters?" Wallace asked.

"Yes, sir," Irving answered. "Picked up my mail this afternoon at Mann's Grocery." Davis nodded in confirmation.

"Mann didn't remember the letters? They were posted
today."

"No, sir," Hamilton answered. "I asked him. The post office has been busy with all the visitors in for the trial."

"What should we do?" Davis blurted out. "I've got my wife and family to think of."

Something like this was bound to happen, Wallace thought with a grimace, and would give the newspaper scribes something to chew on other than jury selection. "Shouldn't we take the matter before Judge Goodman and Sheriff Crozier?" Hamilton asked, and after Wallace agreed, they escorted the two men out of the office. Davis and Irving probably didn't have a thing to fear. They wouldn't even take the stand in the Winston trial, and you had to question the intelligence of a man who would write threatening notes to two witnesses scheduled to testify against Frank James, not for the Winston train robbery, but for the Gallatin bank robbery, an indictment put on hold. Still, threats had to be taken seriously.

While Hamilton led the businessmen to the sheriff's office, Wallace ducked inside Rottmann's Bakery and Restaurant and informed Charles Johnson and John Philips, who were having their supper, of the letters. By the time Wallace left the sheriff's office, the two lead defense attorneys were holding their own court in the lobby of the Alpine Palace Hotel, telling reporters the letters were part of a nefarious conspiracy.

"These two letters were undoubtedly mailed by enemies of Frank James," Johnson said, "in an attempt to turn popular opinion against him. Well, I tell you, these acts will surely fail!"

He was rambling on as Wallace bid good night to Hamilton and headed upstairs. He wondered where Annie James had been, wondered if she were still angry at him for his harsh words at the depot. She probably had him pegged as a liar and scoundrel, not that he could fault such a line of reasoning. After all, when she left him at the station, he was on his way back to Jackson County, had resigned from the prosecution team. Now, one day later, he was back on the case. He hadn't seen her all day, but he shouldn't be thinking about her now. Tomorrow morning, he had forty jurors to interview and challenge.

*   *   *

August 23, 1883
Gallatin, Missouri

It had been a good call moving the trial from the dilapidated courthouse to the opera house. Judge Goodman's bench sat at the front of the stage, and church pews lined several rows behind him, accommodating the stenographer, special guests (most of them women), bailiffs, deputies and members of the press. The sheriff had roped off a section in front of the main gallery for the defense, prosecutors and jury. Crozier must have been pleased with himself, because a wide grin stretched across the lawman's face.

Two newcomers sat on the defense bench. William Hamilton recognized the Reverend Henry Clay Dean, sitting quietly on the far end, but didn't know the mustached behemoth on John Philips's left. Sour-faced Mrs. Zerelda Samuel sat behind her son, a black armband around her one arm. Mrs. James and her boy weren't here for the second consecutive day.

"Gentlemen," Judge Goodman said with a nod after court had been called into session at ten o'clock. "I'm glad everyone was on time today. Before we get down to business, I notice the defense has grown a couple of new heads overnight."

"Yes, Your Honor," John Philips said with a bow. "May it please the court, I wish to introduce Henry Clay Dean, a new member to our defense."

Philips didn't look pleased at all. No one did on that side of the opera house, Hamilton thought, grinning at the idea of the unwelcome Sage of Rebel Cove commanding much thunder from high-minded lead defense attorneys. It served them right.

"Henry Clay Dean needs no introduction to this court," Goodman said, and the old fire-and-brimstone speaker beamed graciously. "But the man on your left does."

"Your Honor, this is Mr. Raymond B. Sloan of the Nashville bar. We ask the court to extend its courtesies to our most distinguished colleague from the volunteer state of Tennessee."

"Objections?" Goodman asked.

Hamilton shot a quick glance at Wallace, who looked as bewildered as everyone else on the prosecution. Who was Sloan? Another lawyer? A witness? Back in Tennessee, Wallace had said, rumors floated around that Frank James's friends in Nashville planned on hiring an attorney to attend the Missouri trial, although Sloan looked more like a man who wrestled bulls than read law books.

"I'm waiting, gentlemen," Goodman said sternly.

"No objections," Hamilton replied hesitantly, looking to Wallace for approval. He simply shrugged.

"All right then. Any motions?"

Colonel Garner rose and began, "Your Honor, the defense objects once more to the prosecution's withholding of the names of its witnesses. This mystery is confounding, sir, and we have a right to know who they plan to call. . . ."

Goodman's gavel silenced the Richmond counselor. "Sir, I overruled your pretrial motion once. Once we have a jury, we'll swear in witnesses for both you and the state, and you'll solve your mystery by learning the prosecution's witnesses. Now stop wasting the court's time."

"Well, Judge," Garner continued, "then there is the matter of these so-called death threats allegedly received by Alexander Irving and Harfield Davis. I—"

The gavel boomed again. "It's not relevant to the case at hand, Colonel." He looked annoyed, and the lawyers for both state and defense had already learned Judge Goodman demanded punctuality and disliked dragging things out with legal nonsense. "Don't we have a jury to seat?"

As he buttered his biscuit, Wallace listened to Hamilton read the list of the jurors one more time. "Lorenzo Gilreath, James Snyder, Oscar Chamberlain, Jason Winburn, Abisha Shellman, Joseph Smith, James Boggs, Charles Nance, Benjamin Feurt, William Richardson, William Merritt, Richard Hale. Every one of them a Democrat, farmers mostly, though Shellman also runs a sawmill near Winston. Well, I can't say I'm happy. We could have used a few Republicans."

Wallace bit into his biscuit and washed it down with black coffee. "We knew the jury wouldn't be to our liking as soon as Goodman rejected our motion. That's behind us, so let's concentrate on the case."

"Jo Shelby arrived last night."

"I saw him. He's staying at the Palace. He and Major Edwards seriously drained the restaurant's supply of whiskey. Probably why they weren't in court today."

They talked business over supper, and afterward Hamilton headed for his office and Wallace walked to the hotel to polish his opening statement for tomorrow morning. A crowd had gathered in front of the hotel, and he shook his head upon recognizing Henry Clay Dean's voice. Philips and Johnson hadn't let the old man speak at all today, and likely wouldn't during the length of the trial, so the noted orator was airing out his lungs tonight.

He spotted Annie then, dressed in a dazzling plaited cashmere walking suit trimmed with velvet. Robert wasn't with her, likely with his grandmother, and she stopped to listen to Dean. She hadn't noticed him, so he stuck the cigar he was about to light into his vest pocket and slowly headed down the boardwalk. Dean's voice was rising to its crescendo. People were already clapping, shouting amens and lifting their glasses of beer in salute. No one noticed the three riders tearing down the road, except Wallace, and he almost didn't discern the danger. Guns and knives in hand, two men in buckskins and a skinny woman with braided dark hair galloped toward the crowd.

"Annie!" Wallace screamed and broke into a sprint.

He heard Dean's "What in blazes—", the pounding of hooves, shouts, curses, a pistol shot, and reached the crowd, and Annie, as the riders drove into the assembly, horses rearing, snorting. Annie was so small, the screaming people fleeing into the hotel would have trampled her, but Wallace scooped her into his arms, half-stumbling down the boardwalk before tripping and spilling into the dusty alley that ran alongside the Alpine Palace.

"Are you all right?" he asked.

She nodded, still stunned, and he spun around, realized he held the Thunderer in his right hand, although he couldn't remember when he had managed to jerk it from his shoulder holster. Another shot echoed, and he charged back into the fray, not really knowing what he planned on doing. Someone screamed, "They're trying to kill Reverend Dean!" Another:

"Indians!" From the corner of his eye, he detected Sheriff Crozier leading a company of deputies into the melee. Wallace slammed the butt of his Colt against the side of the long-haired woman's head as she slashed away with her knife. She fell into a heap just as another man caught him in a bear hug. His attacker sported a blond mustache and goatee—Wallace remembered him vaguely from somewhere as they staggered back against the hotel wall. They weren't fighting much—it felt more like a drunken waltz—and the man's breath smelled more potent than the copper pipes of a still. Crozier drove the stock of his shotgun into the man's skull, and he dropped at Wallace's feet.

"Damned assassins!" someone shouted, and Crozier whirled to find the third raider.

"It's the James Gang!" a woman shrieked.

Wallace caught his breath, realized the assault, or whatever this had been, was ending. Annie still sat in the alley, so he stepped over the body of the man Crozier had cold-cocked, holstered his revolver and helped Annie to her feet. She collapsed into his arms, crying.

"Come on," he said, looking down the alley. "I'll take you to your room."

Chapter 18

*The general impression is that the defense has won half
the fight in seating the jury. The prosecution, however,
expresses itself as confident. Many anticipate
disagreement of jury.*
         —*Topeka* (Kansas) *Daily Capital*, August 24, 1883

August 24, 1883
Gallatin, Missouri

"What?"

He hadn't seen William Hamilton smile often, but the grin
on the solicitor's face kept widening. Shaking his head, still
not believing last night's action himself, Wallace related what
Sheriff Crozier had told him earlier that morning.

"Arizona Jack, Wild Harry and the Indian Princess. They
were all drunk, upset that puppet show kept drawing more
people than their Indian medicine show, so they rode their
horses into the crowd in front of the Alpine Palace."

Now Hamilton laughed, drawing attention in the packed
opera house. "Why not attack the puppeteers?"

"They were probably so drunk they couldn't find them."

"So you knocked out the Indian Princess? You hit a woman?
With a revolver's butt?"

Wallace began to regret ever telling his partner what had happened. "Well, she wasn't fighting like a princess, and it's a wonder she didn't hurt anyone with that Bowie knife of hers. And for
the record, she is no Indian princess, just an unemployed actress
Arizona Jack and Wild Harry picked up in Kansas City."

"What's Crozier going to do with them?"

"They're still sleeping it off. He'll fine them for disturbing the peace and run them out of town."

Hamilton started giggling again, about to say something, but Wallace felt a reprieve when the bailiff stepped inside and announced, "All rise."

What he hadn't revealed to Hamilton was Annie James's presence. No one had seen him take Annie by her arm and lead her up the back staircase and into her room. Robert, she said, was spending the night in his grandmother's room. They hadn't said much; he just let her cry on his shoulder while running his fingers through her silky hair, knowing he was a damn fool, knowing that if anyone caught him here it not only would ruin his career, but it would leave Annie Ralston James open to scandal and shame. Then again, she had to be used to that by now.

At first, he thought she had been crying over the incident in front of the hotel, but that wasn't it. She said she had been coming from church—at that hour? He made no judgment, no comments, simply kissed her forehead after the sobs had run their course, and she thanked him for his kindness, apologized for the little spat at the railroad depot and started to say something else, something about her husband, but stopped herself. He hadn't pushed the matter. "I should go now," he had told her, though he really wanted to stay, picked up his hat and cracked open the door, making sure no one could see him, before leaving for his own room down the hall.

"Gentlemen," Goodman said, "you have one hour each for your opening statements. That's one hour for the state and one hour for the defense, not one hour for every attorney in this courtroom. I don't wish to drag this trial on into the next year." That drew muffled laughter from the audience. "Also, during examinations of witnesses, only one attorney on each side will be allowed interrogations. I want to keep things as orderly as possible. Those are the rules. Now let us proceed to the matter at hand. Mr. Hamilton, will you or one of your colleagues make the opening statement?"

"Mr. Wallace has that honor, Judge," Hamilton said, and Wallace stood.

"Gentlemen of the jury," he began, "the State of Missouri will simply reveal the facts so that you twelve good men can draw your own conclusions." He looked directly at Frank James, saw his mother behind him, but not Annie. "I am well aware that at times the defendant was chivalrous and brave, but you twelve men are sworn to do your duty and not let your admiration influence good judgment. The evidence we shall present will show that Frank James was at Winston, and he was there to commit robbery."

It didn't take him an hour to reveal the prosecution's case, even though he spelled everything out in great detail. He tried to read the jury, but years on the bar had told him no one could ever predict how a jury would react. This morning over breakfast, he had heard rumors that Sheriff Crozier spent the night, after arresting Arizona Jack and his crew, with the jury members, drinking, eating and playing cards, but he didn't bother mentioning this to Judge Goodman. Crozier would have replied that he was doing his job, sequestering the jury, and Goodman had made it plain that he wanted no more dillydallying in this case. It was time to start the ball.

He thought he was doing pretty good with his speech. John Philips only objected once, claiming the state had introduced matters not in the indictment and that any evidence on those matters would be irrelevant and inadmissible. Goodman, however, overruled the objection, noted Philips's exception, and told Wallace to proceed.

Walking around, arms folded behind his back, he talked about Bill Ryan, about the gang's activities in Tennessee. He told of Clarence Hite's joining the gang, and he mentioned a crate of guns and a sewing machine that had been shipped from Tennessee to Missouri. Everything, he promised, would be linked together and prove beyond a shadow of a doubt that Frank James had taken part in the robbery that left two men, two good men, two family men, dead.

"Because," he went on, pacing back and forth in front of the jurors, "on the fifteenth of July, 1881, Frank James, his brother Jesse, the Hite brothers and Dick Liddil did rob the train at

Winston. Conductor Westfall was murdered by Jesse James in cold blood. You will learn the reason for this cold, callous act during this trial. And Frank McMillan, a stonemason who had never harmed anyone, was shot in the head, brutally murdered, while looking through the smoking car's window during the crime." He stopped and pointed dramatically—at least he hoped the jurors would find it dramatic—at the defendant. "It was Frank James who fired that fatal shot. This is all you need to consider, for the defendant is not on trial for anything but the murder of Frank McMillan. And he is guilty!" He began walking again, summing up the case, until he stood behind his chair forty minutes after beginning his summary. "Gentlemen, you must render a verdict of guilty, a verdict free from all personal or sentimental bias."

Goodman took a drink of water before telling the defense team to get on with it.

"May it please the court," Charles Johnson said, "the defense reserves the right to belay its opening statement until after the state has rested its case."

"Objection," Hamilton barked out.

Twisting the ends of his mustache, Goodman shook his head. "No, Mr. Hamilton, it is the defense's right. So be it, Governor. Is the state ready?"

"Yes, Your Honor," Hamilton said.

"And the defense."

"Ready and eager," Johnson said.

"Very well. Call your first witness."

Hamilton checked his notes. "The state calls John L. Penn."

Most of the witnesses, including John Penn, had been sworn in yesterday afternoon, so the Iowan walked directly to the witness stand, actually a jury chair with leather padding on the back. A short man with thinning sandy hair, he looked too little to be a stonemason, but he had large, callused hands and a deeply tanned face. Penn wore an ill-fitting plaid sack suit, sweated profusely and smelled of pipe tobacco and shaving powder. Hamilton rose slowly, straightened his coat and stepped around the prosecution's table. Wallace had given him the honor of examining the first witness.

"State your name and place of residence."

"John L. Penn. I live in Colfax, Iowa."

"Mr. Penn, what is your occupation?"

"Stonemason."

Nervous, Penn kept running a finger through his tight paper collar. Having butterflies flapping around in his own stomach, Hamilton couldn't blame the man. John Penn happened to be the first witness in the trial of the century. Hamilton would lead him through some easy questions first, get him to relax, then move into the crime.

"Did you know Frank McMillan?"

"Yes, sir. We was part of the stonemason gang."

"Where were you on the night of the fifteenth of July, 1881?"

"Workin' on a job in Winston. That's Winston, Missouri."

"Doing what?"

"Workin' in a quarry. Helpin' build a trestle for the railroad."

"Who was working with you?"

"Several men. Let's see, there was W. P. Elmer, R. W.—that's my brother—Mr. Doran, Frank and Old Man McMillan."

"Old Man McMillan meaning Frank's father, Thomas?"

"Yes, sir."

"By the fifteenth of July, had you finished your job?"

"No, sir, but it was Friday, so we was goin' home. Takin' the train to Davenport. Davenport, Iowa. We'd spend the weekend with our family, then catch a train Monday morning for Winston."

"Was Frank McMillan with you?"

"Yes, sir."

"You were friends, correct?"

"Yes, sir. Frank was friends with just about everyone."

"You took the Chicago, Rock Island and Pacific railroad at the Winston station?"

"That's right, sir."

"What time did you board the train?"

"Round nine o'clock."

"Frank McMillan boarded with you?"

"Yes, sir. He got on right behind me."

"What happened next, Mr. Penn? And take your time. Just tell us the story in your own words, how you remember it."

Penn swallowed and asked for a drink of water. A deputy brought it over, poured a glass, and the stonemason gulped it down. He wiped his sweaty brow, let out a breath and began.

Chapter 19

Cole says Frank James was always quiet and gentlemanly, while Jesse was inclined to be quarrelsome.
—*St. Louis Globe-Democrat,* October 11, 1883

July 15, 1881
Winston, Missouri

'Twas one of them nights when the sun went down but it didn't get no cooler, almost suffocatin' the heat was, and that crowd of people at the depot didn't help none. Lots of folks was gettin' on the eastbound that night, and we was all packed together on that sidin' just waitin' for the Express to arrive. Still, I do recollect seein' these five strangers. Guess why I noticed 'em was 'cause they was all wearin' these long linen dusters. Now dusters are good garments if you be ridin' horseback, but it don't seem practical to wear 'em on a train, but I didn't really pay that much attention to 'em. Just figured they was cowboys or somethin' headin' up the tracks.

Anyways, after the Express pulled up, me and Frank and Old Man McMillan got on the smokin' car. Figured it wouldn't be as crowded, but we guessed wrong. Must have been thirty or forty men inside, but we found us a seat and started rollin' our smokes. Folks was chattin', talkin' 'bout the weather, the heat, their jobs and such. Ever'body seemed eager to get home. Know Frank and me was. So we just sat there smokin' our cigarettes and talkin' 'bout nothin' much hardly. Well, the train left the station, and I see conductor Westfall come into

the smokin' car and start checkin' tickets. You know how that
goes if you ridden a train here and there. He'd take the ticket,
make shore it was the right one, keep the railroad's copy and
put the stub, checks they call 'em, in the hatbands. They been
doin' that since I been ridin' the rails. So folks started standin'
up to get their checks.

'Long 'bout that time, I hear some glass breakin' and when I
look up I see that the windows at the front of the car's been
smashed, and in walk these three men. They was all wearin'
them long dusters, had the collars pulled up, bandanas round
their necks and slouch hats pulled down real low. Each of 'em
gots a revolver in both hands, and they is all screamin' at us,
tellin' us to put our hands up. Two of 'em, that is. One of 'em
ain't sayin' nothin', just standin' in the front of the car.

I was pretty fearful. I mean, ever'body in that smokin' car
was scared, and we done like they tol' us, put our hands up.
One of the bandits stayed near the front door, the one that ain't
doin' no hollerin' at us, but two others suddenly run toward us.
Least, I thought they was comin' to me and Frank, but it was
Westfall, the conductor, they was after. Right a-fore they come
runnin', they said somethin', just what I don't know, and then
they started shootin' Westfall. Shootin' him right in front of
me. He got hit twice, first time in the arm, and he started stag-
gerin' toward the rear door, tryin' to get away from, I swear,
them two bandits just chasin' him and shootin', runnin' down
the aisle like demons, they was. I didn't see where the other
bullet hit him, but later learned it just drilled him in the head.
Seen it, I did. Saw where that bullet had just 'bout tore off the
side of his skull. He was dead, I mean to tell you. That wound
was mortal, but he kept on goin', don't ask me how, and them
two outlaws—the ones doin' the chasin'—they was plumb
possessed to kill him. Somehow, Westfall got to the platform
outside, and one of 'em—one of the outlaws—caught him
under his arms and just tossed him off the train like he was
nothin' more'n a sack of trash.

Horrible thing to see, I swear, and then them two men come
back to the front of the car, and I guess I'm thinkin' they was
gonna kill ever' last one of us. The first man, the one who
stayed at the front of the car durin' this shootin', he says some-

thin' to one of 'em who had just killed poor old Westfall, but again, I couldn't tell you what was said. My ears was ringin' from all that shootin'. Couldn't hardly see nothin' neither, the smoke's so thick, chokin' us, burnin' my eyes somethin' fierce. One of the bandits shoots in the ceilin'. Then they's talkin' 'mongst 'emselves. Like I said, it was confusin'. We was all huddled behind the seats, some of us even under the seats, almost scared to get religion. W. P. Elmer, he be sobbin' like a baby, and he weren't the only one. We wasn't shore what was gonna happen next. Anyways, for a spell, the outlaws walk out the front door, so me and Frank decided we'd go on out back in case they come back inside, which they later done.

Right a-fore we got outside, them bandits had come back inside, two of 'em at least, and they musta seen us 'cause one fired a couple of shots at us. A bullet shivered the glass in the door, cut my hand and face a mite, and Frank and me ducked down, just huggin' the railin' on that platform. That was why we didn't run no further. Feared we'd get shot. Who knows? Maybe if we'd kept on runnin', made it to the next car . . . I dunno. Might have gotten us both kilt. Well, I heard some talkin' 'mongst the bandits, but couldn't hear what was said, and Frank and me didn't say nothin', just sat there. I reckon one of the outlaws left the smokin' car, leavin' just one inside, and he stayed up front, just watchin', yellin' for them passengers to stay down, and he'd shoot through the car ever' few minutes.

So Frank and me was huddlin' together, scareder than a fox treed by coonhounds, 'cause even in the darkness, I could see the blood. Westfall's blood. I wasn't bleedin' too much. See, the lanterns was still shinin' through the smokin' car, so we could see a mite. Anyhows, Frank heard a man halloo in the car, and four shots sang out right after that. Frank, he heard the man call out, and he says, "It is Father!" You see, Old Man McMillan had stayed inside when Frank and me lit a shuck for the platform. So Frank hears his pa, and he jumps up to get a look-see. Frank was just peepin' in the window, and a bullet hit him, shot him right above the eye. He fell back, hard, and rolled over. I tried to catch him, but couldn't and he dropped off the platform. Disappeared in the night.

I sat there a spell, shocked, couldn't believe what had just happened, then got scared again, so I peeked once more and saw the man who had done the shootin', the one who had just killed poor Frank. It was probably stupid of me to look up—I mean, Frank had just gotten kilt lookin' through that window—but I was scared that robber might be comin' outside to shoot me. He wasn't. He was a big man, I could see that, and think he was the same one that had killed conductor Westfall, but can't say for shore. By that I mean I think he was one of the two who had chased Westfall down the aisle, shootin' and screamin' like a bunch of Injuns. Maybe not. Ain't certain 'bout that part, but he was a big fella.

The train was goin' slow long 'bout this time. See, them trains, they run fast once leavin' Winston, but they slacked up about twenty rods east of the switch, and that's where we was. Anyhows, the train slowed. Then I heard a man cry out to move on, and the train pulled out real slow, say, three-quarters of a mile, a-fore it stopped. I saw three men jump off from the front of the smokin' car. They jumped off on the south side and made their way to the baggage car. We figured things was over then, so I stood up, watched them men disappear in a hollow, while a bunch of other folks in the smokin' car was startin' to stand, too, talkin' 'mongst 'emselves, still all jittery. Then I heard some shootin', reckon several shots was fired, and the folks in the smokin' car dropped to the floor again, scurryin' about, hidin' behind and under the seats. The shootin' was comin' from the baggage car, up in front of us. That went on a spell.

We was all scared again. Then we waited till ever'thing had gotten real quiet. Finally, I went inside the smokin' car, and I tell you the glass in the back door was pretty much shattered.

Smoke from them pistols still hung thick, stung my eyes and made 'em cry. Anyways, we waited, not shore if the robbers was comin' back. Pretty soon we determined that the bandits had abandoned the train, so I tol' Old Man McMillan what had happened to Frank. He acted like I had knocked the breath out of him, practically doubled over, but pretty soon pulled hisself together, said we'd best go look for him, said maybe he was still alive. 'Course, I took Frank for dead. I mean, I shore wished we'd find him alive, just wounded, but that bullet nailed him right in the forehead, and I didn't see no way in God's name he could be alive. But Old Man McMillan, my brother—R. W. we call him; he had gotten on with us at Winston, like I done said—figured we'd best go lookin', so we grabbed some lanterns and took off afoot back toward Winston. Couple of other gents come with us.

Wasn't too far down the tracks when this handcar come up on us. Had 'bout twelve men, just darkies and Chinamen, but once we tol' 'em that the express had been robbed and two men shot, they acted like white folks and said they'd help us. They was railroad workers, and we asked 'em if they had seen anything, but they hadn't. Wouldn't have been lookin' for nothin' on the sides of the tracks, and it was mighty dark, but they helped us. So we all scattered about and kept on walkin', shinin' the lanterns, and Old Man McMillan kept callin' out his son's name.

We found Frank first, reckon it was 'bout a mile from the depot. You'da thought we had gone a lot farther than that afore he got kilt, shore felt like it, but that's where we found him. He was dead. Old Man McMillan just broke down, sobbin', and a couple of them darkies and my brother volunteered to stay there till we got back or the law come, so the rest of us went on lookin' for that conductor Westfall. Not too far from the section house we found him, just layin' peaceful-like, looked to be sleepin', on the north side of the track. But he was dead, too. Like I said, one of them bullets practically blowed his brains out.

Anyhows, them railroad workers took that handcar and went on back to Winston and reported the robbery. We all walked back yonder, too, and later tol' the sheriff and railroad folks what had happened, talked to that coroner, too, and then most of us took the next mornin' train to Davenport. Old Man McMillan come, too. So did Frank, only he was in a pine box.

That's 'bout it. Least, that's the way I remember it, Mr. Hamilton. Them bandits shot down Westfall like he was nothin' more than a mangy ol' cur dog, and they kilt Frank, too, broke his old man's heart, they did.

Damn shame.

Chapter 20

*The loyalty and devotion of Mrs. Frank James stamp her
as a true woman, especially when considered in
connection with the fact that she was once the beautiful,
accomplished and wealthy Annie Ralston.*
　　　　　　—St. Joseph Daily Gazette, August 24, 1883

August 24, 1883
Gallatin, Missouri

As soon as Hamilton had finished his examination, Charles
Johnson smiled evenly before rising. "Mr. Penn, you have a
pretty good memory for an event that happened so long ago,"
he said, folding his hands behind his back.

"I reckon so," the stonemason said.

"All of this gunplay, though. You had to be scared."

"I guaran-damn-tee you," he answered, and Johnson waited
for the laughter to die down.

"How many cars were on this train?"

The stonemason scratched his chin. "Well, that I don't
reckon I could rightly tell you. I recollect there was a coach
after the smoker, and I think the baggage and express car was
in front of the smoker. But I ain't shore to the number."

"Six?"

"Don't know."

"Four?"

Hamilton objected, saying the witness had answered once
that he couldn't remember, and Judge Goodman sustained.
Having made his point and anticipating the state's objection,

Johnson didn't mind. "A baggage car, smoker, three coaches and a Pullman sleeper, Mr. Penn," he said. "That's what made up the Chicago, Rock Island and Pacific Railroad Express that night."

"Reckon there was a locomotive, too," the witness answered, enjoying the laughter again, "and a tinder."

"Indeed." Johnson hadn't expected any wit from this oaf's mouth, but let the stonemason enjoy his performance for the moment. "Do you recall your statement during the coroner's inquest?"

"Not really."

"Well, let me refresh your memory. In July of eighty-one, just after the robbery, you couldn't recall hardly anything regarding Frank McMillan's death. How could your memory improve over two years?"

Penn hesitated, scratched his chin and at last explained that he had been "agitated" during the inquest, that he had seen two men brutally murdered and he was certain he had his facts straight now.

"How many robbers did you see?" Johnson asked.

"Just them three."

"Three. Other than the dusters, could you remember anything about them?"

"Not really."

"Why not? Your memory has been astounding so far this morning. Were they wearing masks?"

"Nope. But they had them slouch hats pulled way down over their faces and white bandanas round their necks, so I couldn't see no faces."

Johnson raised his voice. "So you cannot identify the defendant, Frank James, as one of the men committing this holdup, can you?"

"Nope."

Smiling, Johnson sat down and leaned back in his chair. "When Frank McMillan was killed, was the bandit in the smoker shooting to kill?"

"I don't reckon so. Frank was just unlucky, I reckon."

"Thank you, Mr. Penn." Johnson couldn't help but poke fun at the witness. "I reckon I'm finished, Your Honor."

"Redirect, Mr. Hamilton?" the judge asked.

"Just one question, to clear things up," Hamilton said, still sitting. "Mr. Penn, you could not identify the faces of the outlaws, but you can describe the man who shot McMillan, isn't that right?"

"Shore. He was the big fella."

"How big?"

"Gosh, I reckon seven, eight inches taller'n me."

"You saw the defendant when he walked in this morning. Would you say the killer was his height?"

"Yeah, that looks 'bout right."

In his itchy Sunday-go-to-meetings, Addison E. Wallcott took a seat and waited for solicitor William D. Hamilton to ask him questions, just the way they had rehearsed in the lawyer's little office over in the courthouse. Wallcott liked the opera house better than the courthouse, which smelled of tar and would probably burn like pitch pine if some fool dropped a match. He only wished it would rain. It was hotter here than the inside of the cab of his locomotive.

Hamilton spoke evenly, and Wallcott answered firmly, enunciating just the way his Sunday schoolteacher wife had told him to do. He was engineer on the Winston train. The train left the depot around nine thirty on the night of the robbery. They had gone maybe fifty feet when the bell rang to stop.

"What happened next?" Hamilton asked.

"I set the brakes and stopped. After stopping, a voice called out, 'All right, go ahead.' I gave her steam, and somebody called again, 'Go, you son of a bitch!' I looked around, and two men jumped off the coal into the cab, revolvers drawn, and told me to go ahead."

"Were you alone in the cab?"

"No, sir. My fireman, Tom Sugg, was with me."

"Did you obey the bandits?"

Nodding, he continued. "We went two thousand feet when the emergency brakes were set from the inside of the train. That excited those two men in the cab with me, and they said to get going or they'd shoot me. I got the engine going and one of the men told me to keep going till we got to the hollow near the water tank. He said he wouldn't hurt me if I did as I was told."

"Please go on, Mr. Wallcott."

"Well, sir, the outlaws started looking back toward the train, so Tom Sugg and I jumped out on the pilot, holding on and just praying. The bandits fired at us—one of the outlaws came out as far as the sand dome on the engine—but we let go and dropped to the ground."

Hamilton arched his eyebrows. "That means the train was a runaway?"

"I was afraid it might be, but someone knew how to stop it. That's how we caught up with the train later."

"Could you describe the men in the cab?"

"Common-size. It was dark, so I couldn't really describe them."

"Thank you. No further questions."

Wallcott shifted in his chair as Governor Johnson coughed slightly. He had not rehearsed any of his testimony with Johnson, and now he started sweating, but the lawyer smiled reassuringly and promised he only had a few questions.

"Did you see the conductor Westfall at any time during the robbery?"

"No, sir. I did not see him after we left Cameron."

"Did you or your fireman see any of the shooting in the smoking car?"

"No, sir. Sugg and I were in no position to see anything going on back there."

"Thank you."

Wallcott breathed easier, thanked the judge who had just dismissed him and left the opera house. So far, so good. He had done his duty, testified. Now if he could make it out of Gallatin without being killed by one of Frank James's friends, he'd feel all right.

Frank Stamper, who had been baggage man on the Winston train, and express agent Charles Murray of the U.S. Express Company, wrapped up their testimony under Hamilton's gentle probing. Stamper had a better memory than Penn, and Johnson couldn't shake him on cross-examination, plus the baggage man had been able to describe the outlaw who had pulled him out of the baggage and express car after the train had stopped the last time: a tall, slender man with a long beard, wearing a gray vest and white shirt. He couldn't identify the robber as the defendant, but that didn't matter. Murray was equally strong, detailing how he had been knocked unconscious by the bandits during the holdup and how one of the men said they had killed the conductor and were going to kill him, too. They had ordered him to his knees, then struck him from behind.

Coroner D. M. Claggett took the stand next, described the fatal wounds inflicted upon Westfall and McMillan, and a Winston doctor named Zeb Brooks followed to corroborate Claggett's testimony. Hamilton had just started his interrogation of Brooks, when the court reporter brought up the fact that Claggett had not been sworn in, an oversight that brought about much huffing from Judge Goodman. Claggett was recalled, sworn in, and requestioned for the record. Brooks testified after that, and court adjourned until one thirty.

"W. S. Earthman. I live about seven miles north of Nashville in Davidson County, Tennessee," the first afternoon witness said.

William Wallace had spent the morning half listening to the testimony while working on his examination of Dick Liddil tomorrow, but Tennessee witnesses would be taking the stand this afternoon, and Wallace felt ready. These were the people he had interviewed in and around Nashville, so he would do the questioning.

"What do you do, Mr. Earthman?"

"I am the back-tax collector, farmer and justice of the peace."

"Do you recognize the defendant?"

"Yes, sir. I saw him first in 1879, and we got well-acquainted at a horse race. I knew him as B. J. Woodson. He lived over on Smith's place, but left after a spell, and I don't know exactly where he lived after that."

"But he still lived around Nashville?"

"Certainly. I saw him about town up to the fall of 1880. I never saw him after that."

"Did you know Jesse James?"

Johnson's voice rang out. "Objection."

"Overruled." Judge Goodman's response had been just as loud and quick.

Wallace gestured at the witness to continue. "I knew Jesse," Earthman said. "He rode Frank James's horse at the same race that I entered my horse at. I wasn't as well-acquainted with Jesse as with Frank. Jesse went by the name of Howard."

"Did you see them together often?"

"Yes, sir. They were frequently together, at the fair and in town."

"Yesterday, did you not see Frank James while he was being escorted here from the jail?"

"I saw him, and he saw me."

"Did he speak to you?"

"Yes, sir. He asked me if I came up here to hang him."

Getting that answer in for the record surprised him. He expected Johnson or Philips to object. Relieved, he went on. "In Tennessee, did you also know a man named Tom Hill?"

This time Johnson objected. "There is no Tom Hill anywhere in the indictment."

"Your Honor," Wallace said, "the state will show that Tom Hill was in fact Bill Ryan, that his arrest caused the James Gang to leave Nashville. We will link all of these circumstances to lead to the Winston robbery."

Johnson shook his head. "This course is incompetent. The defendant is here to meet a specific charge, one of murder, accessory to murder and train robbery, and not an irrelevant charge that some band of robbers existed here or there."

Drawing a deep breath, Wallace suddenly wished he had spent more time predicting defense objections and not how to make a fiend like Dick Liddil sound believable. Goodman ordered the jury to retire, momentarily giving Wallace a reprieve—not enough, though—but Colonel Shanklin slowly rose from his seat beside Hamilton and addressed the court.

"May it please the court, any facts are admissible tending to sustain any hypothesis of the defendant's guilt or innocence. I cite Wharton's criminal evidence, section 23, and Bishop on criminal law, section 596. I can go on, too, but those should appease my distinguished colleague for the defense. If Frank James made damaging declarations to parties, these declarations are admissible."

Glory to God and John H. Shanklin. Wallace grinned at the old man with his always-present spit can. He walked back to the state's table, listening to Johnson and Philips argue over law points regarding conspiracy. Voices rose, and Goodman's gavel banged loudly to quiet the lawyers. In the end, thanks to Shanklin's citations, Goodman overruled the objection, and the jury returned.

So Earthman got to testify that he did know Tom Hill, who turned out to be Bill Ryan, a member of the James Gang. Wallace called James Moffat next, and the Louisville and Nashville Railroad depot master from Nashville confirmed more of the James Gang's stay in Tennessee. Pressman James B. May testified that Frank James and family had vacated the house at 814 Fatherland in Edgefield and disappeared. After Colonel Philips ended a brief cross-examination, Wallace called John Trimble Jr.

"You say you're in the real estate and fire insurance business in Nashville," Wallace said after the preliminary questions. "How long?"

"Ten years." Trimble spoke quickly, nervously, and Wallace couldn't understand why. It was a simple question. The man stared at his feet, at the floor, at his twiddling thumbs . . . anywhere but at the defense table.

"Do you remember the house you sold to James May, the house at 814 Fatherland Street in Edgefield?"

"I do."

"Before Mr. May bought the house, did you rent it?"

"Yes."

"Who was your last renter?"

"Woodson. B. J. Woodson. I rented it about February the fifth in eighty-one."

"And do you see Mr. Woodson in the courtroom today?" Wallace turned to watch the expressions on Frank James and his lawyers.

"No, sir."

Wallace whirled, eyes wide, stunned. Back in Tennessee,

Trimble had positively identified James from a photograph, swore that the James brothers had been the two renters on Fatherland Street. "What?" He caught himself, fought to remain in control and lowered his voice. "Are you certain?"

"I have not recognized the man since I have been here," Trimble said, still refusing to look up.

Wallace crossed the floor, his heels echoing in the surprisingly silent opera house, until he reached the witness. He wanted to slap the fool, figuring Trimble had supplemented his real estate and fire insurance business with a hefty bribe, but when the Tennessean finally looked up, Wallace knew the man had not been bribed. He was scared to death, and not of facing a perjury charge in Missouri. Frank James, or his friends, had gotten to the witness, but not with money.

"When did you sell the house?" Wallace said. His identification was shot, and a lot of attorneys would have surrendered after the witness's turnaround, but he could salvage something from this.

"Twenty-first or twenty-second of March," Trimble answered, his gaze falling to his shoes again.

"And did Mr. Woodson give any notice that he planned on leaving?"

"No. He just left."

Sarah Hite's blue-and-white-striped seersucker suit came complete with a knife-plaited skirt, ribbon bows, embroidered vest and lace-trimmed waist. It had cost a whole six dollars back in Nashville, and the seamstress guaranteed that it would cause a stir, so Sarah smiled when she heard the whispers and whistles as she walked to the witness chair.

She stared directly at that smug-looking Frank James, answering William Wallace's questions in a clear and calm voice. She wasn't afraid of Frank James and never had been, him and his holier-than-thou attitude, always showing off by spouting some nonsense from Shakespeare or some other writer. Now Jesse—she had been scared of him, but the Ford brothers took care of him.

"Did you know Wood Hite?" Wallace asked.

"I did. He is dead now. He died near Richmond, Missouri, so I was told. I think he was buried there."

"Describe Wood Hite, please."

"Wood was about five-foot-eight, had dark hair and light blue eyes. He had a light mustache, Roman nose, narrow shoulders, a little stooped. He was inclined to be quick in his actions."

"When did you last see him?"

"In November 1881. I had seen him before that in September. He said he was going west."

Two of Frank James's lawyers huddled together in some sort of lawyer palaver, and she wondered what they were talking about, but Wallace asked her if she recognized the defendant, so she had to look at him for a second, just to satisfy the jury and spectators.

"I have seen him. First time I saw him was on March 20, 1881. He came to my husband's house that morning. Dick Liddil came with him, and Jesse James came after him. Frank was riding. Jesse and Dick were walking."

"Did they tell you where they came from?"

"No, they didn't."

"Were they armed?"

"Goodness, yes. Frank had two pistols, and Dick had two pistols and a long gun. They stayed at our house a day or two. Clarence Hite and Wood and George Hite were there, too."

"Did you see them again?"

"Yes, on the twenty-sixth of April. That day, Dick, Jesse, Frank and Wood came back. They were still armed. Some men were pursuing them and came near the house. Jesse and Frank were excited and commenced preparing themselves."

"How do you mean?"

"Dick got near the front door, Jesse at the window and Frank was in the parlor. But the men just rode on by."

"Describe Clarence Hite if you would."

"He was twenty-one years old, tall and slender, had blue eyes, light hair, a big mouth, and one or two teeth out. He's dead. He died in Adairsville the tenth of last March. Clarence was then living in Adairsville, but he would come out when

Jesse and Frank and Dick were there. He left home in May of
eighty-one."

"Do you know where he went?"

"Missouri. He was in Missouri in the summer of 1881.
Wood Hite left home on May 27, 1881."

"When did you next see Clarence Hite?"

"I next saw him in September. He stayed there till November, and I never saw him again till he came home to die."

"And when did you last see Frank James?"

"April 27, 1881. I never saw him again till now."

"We have no questions of this witness, Your Honor," John
Philips said and turned back to his hushed discussion with
Charles Johnson while the state called Mrs. Hite's father, Silas
Norris. "Where can they be going with this?" he asked John-
son. "She doesn't know anything."

"She knows what the Hite brothers looked like," Johnson
said. "And she knows the brothers left Kentucky and could
have been in Missouri for the Winston robbery, and Frank and
Jesse left, too. Wallace is filling in a lot of blanks, hoping the
jury will read into this that Frank James had to be on that train,
and he looks nothing like the Hite brothers."

"Circumstantial," Philips said.

"I've seen men hanged on circumstantial evidence."

As soon as court was adjourned until Saturday morning,
Sheriff Crozier made a beeline to Wallace and handed him a
letter, saying Harfield Davis had received it in the afternoon
mail.

St. Louis, April 23d.
To Harfield Davis and Alex. Irving, Gallatin:

   *Your evidence against Frank James will be watched
   by tried and true friends of the hero. None but the writer
   and one other know how near Governor Crittenden
   came to biting the dust in April 1882, on the Sunday afternoon that he rode in the chair car from Jefferson City*

to St. Louis. The pistol was cocked twice and only policy prevented its use.

Frank James has hundreds of friends that will never see him sacrificed, and will come to his aid at the proper time. If you are wise you will be careful.

A.R.K.

The letter had been written in red ink, sent in an envelope from the Hotel Menfe in San Antonio, with a Wabash postal car postmark. Alec Irving had received a similar letter, Crozier said, written in black ink and stuffed in a plain envelope.

"Another crackpot?" Hamilton asked.

"I don't know," Wallace answered. "Likely."

"I got a couple of deputies guarding Davis and Irving." Crozier's voice was strained. The lawman remained angry at Wallace's allegations of impropriety, but he still did his job. That said something for the man.

Wallace watched the sheriff fall into the line of sweaty, excited people exiting the opera house. Hamilton said something, but Wallace didn't hear and slowly began stuffing papers into his satchel. The first day of testimony was over, and both the state and the defense had scored a few hits, drew a little blood, which he had expected. He stuck a cigar in his mouth started to leave, but saw Annie James sitting silently, eyes closed, in the upper balcony. Why hadn't she been behind her husband?

Colonel Shanklin cracked a joke and, smiling, Wallace looked at the lawyer who had saved the prosecution with his knowledge of the law. He didn't really listen as Shanklin and Hamilton discussed the precedents the old-timer had cited, and as the three men agreed to dine at Rottmann's, Wallace's eyes shot skyward to the balcony, but Annie James was gone.

Chapter 21

*There was a gang known as the James Gang; I belonged
to it at one time. . . .*

—Dick Liddil

August 25, 1883
Gallatin, Missouri

Waiting didn't come easy for John Philips, but timing was important in criminal cases, so he let Wallace call his witness, let the bailiff swear him in and almost let the prosecutor ask a question before he exploded from his chair, slammed his fist against the table and roared, "I object on the ground that the witness has been convicted of a felony!" Charles Johnson had earned his share of glory during the first day of testimony; now it was Philips's turn to shine.

The witness, Dick Liddil, stifled a yawn while Judge Goodman, sensing a protracted debate, asked the jury to retire. Philips nodded in approval at the judge's actions. This would be a regular round of Saturday-night fisticuffs. "Your Honor," Philips continued after the jury had left, "this man"—he pointed a finger at the outlaw, simply to give the press boys something to dramatize—"was convicted of grand larceny in Vernon County in November of 1877 and is not fit to testify. I introduce this evidence for the record." As Philips brought the papers to Goodman, Wallace rose from his seat and began his challenge, saying that James A. "Dick" Liddil had been pardoned and wished to introduce that into the record, but Philips and John Glover had prepared all night for this moment.

"That document is only a copy, Your Honor," Philips said, "and thus cannot be introduced as evidence."

"May it please the court," Wallace fired back, "I have in my hands a copy of the original pardon, with the seal of the secretary of state. And I read from this: 'Know ye that by virtue of the authority in me vested by law, and upon recommendation of the inspectors of the penitentiary, I, Henry C. Brockmeyer, acting lieutenant governor of the State of Missouri, do hereby release, discharge and forever set free James A. Liddil, who was, at the November term, A.D. 1877, by a judgment of the circuit court of Vernon County, sentenced to imprisonment in the penitentiary of this state for the term of three and one-half years. . . .'" He finished reading, triumphantly showed the pardon to Philips and gave it to Goodman.

Philips bowed slightly. He had underestimated his quarry, but if Wallace thought Philips would cower and retreat, he, too, had made a mistake in judgment. John Glover stood and began talking while Philips beamed. Two against one. See how the Jackson County prosecutor could handle this. Goodman had ruled only one attorney per witness but had said nothing about these fights over interpretation of the law.

"My esteemed colleague fails to point out, Your Honor," said Glover, his voice smooth as twelve-year-old Scotch, "that this so-called witness served a two-thirds term in the state penitentiary and thus did not receive a pardon in the true legal meaning of the word. The stain of Mr. Liddil's felony has not been washed away. He has only been restored to citizenship."

The response came not from Wallace, but Colonel John Shanklin, and once again Philips realized another miscalculation. "Gentlemen," Shanklin drawled, and Philips detected Wallace's smile, "you are objecting to points too technical for the court's consideration." He punctuated his argument by spitting into a tin can.

"I think not, Your Honor," Philips said with satisfaction as Wallace's grin flattened. "When a horse thief like Dick Liddil is discharged after a two-thirds sentence, it is simply the remission of the rest of his sentence, not a pardon." Again, he pointed angrily at Liddil, but this time he didn't care if the reporters wrote about him or not. He was mad, infuriated that the great State of Missouri would lower itself and put a rapscallion like Liddil on the stand. "This man wears a brand of infamy as a felon, and it would be wrong that any man, not just my client, but anyone, should have his life jeopardized by the testimony of a man who has been imprisoned. He has no regard for truth, no sense of honor, and I dare the state to cite any case in which a convicted felon has been allowed to testify with competency—except when a full pardon has been granted."

They went on, Philips and Glover for the defense, Wallace and Shanklin for the state, hammering over the finer points of law, arguing, debating, pointing fingers and raising voices, and citing precedents. *Black v. Rogers. People v. Bowen. State v. Foley. Houghtaling v. Kelderhouse. State v. Sloss.* Stimulating. Vigorous. This is what brought John Philips to the bar. It was more fun than a debate society and caused fewer headaches than chess. He continued his argument, far from finished, but Goodman's gavel shattered his train of thought. Philips stood, mouth agape, wondering what had happened as the judge pointed the gavel's handle in his direction. No, not at him, but behind him, at the defense table.

"Mr. Sanders, Governor Johnson," the judge said sternly, "newsboys will not circulate their papers in this courtroom. Do I make myself clear?"

Philips turned, trying to soak in what had happened. Charles Johnson sat with a folded newspaper in his hand, guilty as Dick Liddil. Apparently, Clifford Sanders of the *Post-Dispatch* had brought him a copy of the day's edition. Philips felt his stomach sour at the defense's first chair. That bastard had been so bored with the legal maneuvering he decided to do some reading. What did Frank James or John Edwards see in that man?

"Court will adjourn for dinner till two o'clock," Goodman said, "at which time I will announce my ruling."

Dinner? Philips checked his watch. Gosh, they had been arguing for two hours.

"I have weighed the arguments of both parties," Goodman said, "and discussed the matter with Judge R. A. DeBolt of

Trenton, who I asked to serve as an amicus curiae. In any case, Governor Brockmeyer did intend to pardon Mr. Liddil and so the witness has a right to testify."

Colonel Philips was on his feet again, objecting, saying the defense could prove Liddil had violated conditions of his pardon, but Goodman told the colonel to sit down. He had made his ruling, and the witness would testify, providing he could show he had indeed been pardoned.

Liddil was a thin man, about five-foot-ten with dark sideburns and mustache, his hair neatly parted on the left, with a prominent nose but not much of a chin, just the way Frank James had remembered him. Before prosecutor Wallace could begin his questioning, the judge himself asked that mealymouthed such-and-such a few questions. Liddil, the dumb oaf, said he tore up the pardon on the day he got it.

"You tore it up?" the judge said, blinking in stunned incomprehension.

"I thought it was of no use to me."

"Who gave it to you?" the judge continued.

"I disremember. He told me my time was up and turned me out."

Colonel Philips objected again, but the judge told him to be quiet, that this little farce had gone on long enough, that if Liddil got out of the Jefferson City pen before his sentence, if he had been given a paper, even if he did tear it up, it meant that he had indeed been pardoned, and that the witness's testimony as well as the paper produced by the state proved enough to satisfy this court. The judge told prosecutor Wallace to begin his questioning. Frank James leaned forward in his chair, anxious to hear what Liddil had to say.

He said he had known Frank James since 1870, said Frank, Jesse, Cole and John Younger and Thomas McCann used to ride together, and that he joined the gang in the fall of seventy-nine down in Jackson County. He rehashed a few dull adventures and described the various members of the gang, including the Hite boys and Jim Cummins, before telling the court that the James boys and Ed Miller departed for Tennessee, and Liddil joined them there in July of 1880. Bill Ryan and Jim Cummins also came to Tennessee, and they all lived around Nashville.

"When did you leave?" Wallace asked.

"In March 1881," Liddil said. "Frank, Jesse and myself, that is. We learned in the papers that Ryan had got captured, and we got scared and left. We went up to Old Man Hite's, stayed there for four of five days as officers from Tennessee were looking for us."

"Was Jim Cummins with you?"

"No. I don't know where Jim went after Nashville."

"Go on, Mr. Liddil."

"Well, myself, Frank and Jesse and Wood and Clarence Hite formed a band to rob express trains in Missouri. We shipped our guns from Tennessee, packed in a crate, and Frank had a sewing machine sent to General Jo Shelby for his wife to give to her mother. We split up and agreed to meet in Missouri later."

So this was how the James Gang took care of its own. Ten years back, no one who had ridden with Dingus, Frank and the Youngers would have considered testifying against another member of the gang, no matter what the state offered. By God, Cole and Dingus never got along, but neither would have turned yellow and told the law just to save his own neck. There was a credo among the guerrillas back then, but now? Frank James shook his head. You got shot in the back literally or stabbed in the back figuratively.

"I had my horse shod in Gallatin," Liddil was saying, "and we met a mile from Winston, dined at a little frame house on the road and rode to town. We hitched our horses and went to a saloon and got a glass of lemonade, then waited till the train came."

"What was your job?"

"Clarence and myself were to capture the engineer, and the others were to rob the baggage car."

"So it was your intention to rob the train."

"Yeah, we got on board to rob it."

"How were you armed?"

"Two pistols each."

"What happened?"

"When we got out a little ways, the train stopped and we heard shooting. We scared the engineer and made him move the train on. Then he pulled the throttle and him and the fireman sneaked out. We shot a couple of times to scare them, but they jumped off. We didn't know how to stop a train, but Frank come through and stopped it."

Wallace interrupted the testimony. "Frank James stopped the train?"

"Yes, sir. He did."

"Then what happened?"

"Wood and I got off the engine and went back to rob the baggage and express car."

"Who went inside that car?"

"Frank, Jesse and Wood Hite."

"How much money did you steal?"

"We each got about one hundred and thirty dollars."

"So it was successful?"

"Not really. We thought we'd get more. And Frank said he thought they had killed a couple of men. Jesse said he was pretty sure he had killed one, and Frank said a man had peeped in and he shot at the man and he fell off the train."

"Did Jesse say why he had killed the conductor?"

"Yeah. Frank was upset. He never wanted anybody to get hurt, but Jesse said he thought Westfall was reaching for a pistol. That's what he told Frank, but he later told me that Westfall had been on the train that took the Pinkertons to raid his ma's farm back in seventy-five. You recall, that's when Jesse's ma lost her arm and little Archie got killed. Jesse told Wood Hite that. Then Jesse and Wood just started shooting."

"But Frank James said he had killed the stonemason Frank McMillan."

"Well, we didn't know the gent's name, but, yeah, that's what happened. Frank didn't mean for it to happen. It just did."

Under the prosecutor's coaxing, Liddil discussed the getaway, and filled in a few blanks about the planning of the robbery, the shipping of the guns from Tennessee to the Fords, the clothes they had worn, every bit of it detailed, every bit of it damning, every bit of it true.

"When did you next see the defendant?"

"At Widow Bolton's in Ray County a while later. He said he, Charlie Ford and Clarence Hite were going to Kentucky."

Behind him, Frank's mother begin to sob. He clenched his fists at the anguish Dick Liddil had caused his family and didn't realize the prosecutor had finished his examination of the witness until Colonel Philips asked permission to bring forth a defense witness out of turn.

"This is highly irregular," the stiff-backed judge said.

"Yes, Your Honor, but we just subpoenaed the witness yesterday and he arrived today. We see no reason for Governor Crittenden"—that caused the audience to stir—"to wait so long when he has important duties in Jefferson City."

"Objections from the state?"

"None, Your Honor, but we do request a brief recess so we can prepare for any cross-examination."

"Granted."

Thomas T. Crittenden was royally pissed. He didn't like being served subpoenas, hated being put on the spot, made to testify for the damned defense. Then again, politically, it might be a better move than testifying for the prosecution, but he wasn't sure. Well, it would be over in a few minutes.

"Governor," John Philips said, "do you remember a conversation with Dick Liddil in which he stated that Frank James said he was angry over the deaths of the conductor and stonemason during the Winston train robbery?"

"Liddil did make such a statement. I think it was the second time he was at Jefferson City, before Frank James surrendered."

"What was the statement?"

"I asked Liddil why Jesse James had killed an innocent man engaged in his duties. By that, I refer to conductor Westfall, and not to McMillan."

"And how did Liddil answer?"

"He said it was his understanding that there was to be no bloodshed, and after the robbery Frank was upset, asking, 'Jesse, why did you shoot that man?' Frank went on to say that had he known or thought anything like that would have hap-

pened, he would have had no part in the robbery. Jesse answered, according to Liddil, that he thought the gang was
pulling away from him and that by committing a foul murder
he would make them all murderers and thus they'd have to
stick with him."

"Thank you, Governor. No further questions."

"We have no questions of this witness," Wallace said.

After checking his watch, Judge Goodman said since he was
certain the defense had quite a few questions for Dick Liddil,
court would adjourn until eight o'clock Monday morning.

August 26, 1883
Gallatin, Missouri

Wallace crossed the square from the courthouse, remembering
his conversation with William Hamilton a few minutes earlier.
"What I don't understand," Hamilton had said while pouring a
cordial of brandy, "is why they brought Crittenden in to testify.
The only person who had actually identified Frank James as
one of the robbers was Dick Liddil, a robber himself, and Crittenden confirmed that."

He had sipped his coffee before replying. "Crittenden was
just saying what Liddil told him, and making Jesse James out
to be the badman. It was for sympathy, nothing more."

"All right, but you have to admit, Liddil was a good witness. But I still can't believe that bastard Trimble turned yellow, refused to identify Frank James."

"He was scared," Wallace had corrected, "and we didn't
need him to identify Frank James. Others in Tennessee did that
for us. As far as Liddil is concerned, we'll see how he holds up
under cross tomorrow morning. The case isn't over yet,
William."

This case is far from over, Wallace said to himself and made
his way through the crowded boardwalk, listening to merchants, farmers and cowhands debate the first two days of testimony, the reasoning for letting a man like Liddil take the
stand. He received his key from the clerk and headed upstairs,

found his room, unlocked the door and had just pushed it open when he heard the voice.

"William?"

His hand was reaching for the Colt Thunderer in his shoulder holster when he recognized Annie James standing in the hall.

Chapter 22

The governor of Missouri simply said to Liddil, "You are released; you go free, but you go out into the world branded with an infamy which I do not pardon."
　　　　　　　—St. Joseph Daily Gazette, August 26, 1883

August 26, 1883
Gallatin, Missouri

"I really don't know why I even bother with this," Wallace told her as he dropped the heavy revolver atop a chest of drawers. "If someone wanted to kill me, they could get the job done long before I could stop them. Have a seat, Annie. Would you like something to drink?"

She heard herself answer no while looking around the spartan room and wondering what Wallace would have offered her had she asked. He didn't drink intoxicating spirits, so she doubted if he had a bottle stored somewhere. Her eyes fell on the unmade bed, and she turned away before she blushed. This was a compromising situation, a married woman and a bachelor, the state prosecutor and the defendant's wife. The entire hotel room needed a woman's touch, or at least a chambermaid's. Papers were strewn about the tops of furniture, and clothes had been draped over the backs of chairs or piled on the floor near the washbasin. She finally realized his bed was unmade because, like her own quarters down the hall, the room had not been cleaned. Service at the Alpine Palace Hotel had been lax the last few days. The entire town of Gallatin had become a circus act, and the staff at the town's best hotel continued to be run into a lather.

"Where's Robert?" he asked as he collected a pair of pants and shirt from the back of a chair, dumped his laundry on the building pile and offered her the seat. Her knees felt weak, and she was glad to get off her feet. Apologizing for the state of his hotel room, he sat on the edge of the bed and tried to grin.

"His grandmother took him to see his father," she said.

"Who's that?"

She stared at him in bewilderment, but he just blinked. "Robert," she said. "My son. You asked about him."

Shaking his head, Wallace laughed. "I'm sorry, Annie. My brain has wilted with the heat, the trial. What can I do for you?"

Annie locked her fingers and bit her lower lip. Why was she here, and what did she want? She really wasn't sure. Talking to the preacher the other night hadn't helped—she hadn't known what to say—and she couldn't very well discuss her feelings with Frank's mother. The way she doted on her son, if Zerelda Samuel knew what Annie had been thinking, she would probably have strangled her to death with her one powerful arm. Major Edwards, Colonel Philips, Governor Johnson or one of the other attorneys? The only one who had ever engaged her in conversation had been Edwards, and she found him to be a dolt and drunk. She liked Jo Shelby, but again, he was one of Frank's friends, not hers. Revealing her problems to her parents, she feared, would have resulted in I-told-you-so lectures, and she had never been close to her sisters and brothers after eloping with Frank. So when she had seen Wallace in the hallway, she had called out his name.

"Do you remember the time I jumped that four-rail fence?" she asked suddenly. "Over at Little Santa Fe?" It was a start at conversation.

"That was during one of those picnics," he said lightly. He had handsome eyes. "Whose horse was that? Jason Walsh's Morgan, if I remember correctly. He had been telling you ladies what a great equestrian he was, how no one could handle his horse except him."

"And I jumped up, pushed him down, leaped in the saddle

and took off, while he was screaming at me to stop before I killed myself. Then he just shut up."

"And ate crow," Wallace said, chuckling, and she joined in.

"Scandalous, he said, a woman riding like that. It was Jason Walsh, and he was mad." She wiped her eyes with a hanky.

"I thought I might have to defend you on a horse-theft charge."

"Balderdash. You weren't a lawyer back then."

They recalled other pleasant memories of her days in Independence and Little Santa Fe, and she realized maybe she needed this, to reach back and see the youthful, daring Annie Ralston, maybe discover what had become of that fun-loving girl. The woman she knew as Annie James had become a hermit like those blue-haired widows in Independence who never said good morning, kept their doors locked, curtains closed and had eyes as cold and hollow as the barrels of Frank's revolvers.

What was it Frank had told her the last time she had spoken to him? *Sometimes I feel I've trapped your spirit, Annie girl, turned you into a recluse like me.* He was right, too, although she had not conceded the point. All the hiding, the running, the lies—they had indeed turned her into someone she never thought she would become.

"Who am I, William?" she asked with a sigh after a pause. She could feel the tears beginning to well, and stared at the ceiling.

"You're Ann Ralston."

"No," she corrected him. "Ann James."

"You're still Ann Ralston to me." He stood behind her now, and she felt his hands on her tense shoulders, his fingers working magic, soothing, maybe trying to seduce her. Would he do that? Would she let him? Now she felt even more confused.

"I know this trial is hard on you, probably harder on you and Robert than Frank," he whispered, started to say something else, and drew his hands from her shoulders. "You really shouldn't be here, Annie."

She tried to stand, to face him, but her legs wouldn't work. Tasting salty tears, she blurted out, "He's a killer, William. I married a murderer." The logjam burst, and she was cursing her husband, shaking her head, clenching her fists, deriding the choices she had made. "I knew it," she said. "I knew it all along, but just told myself Frank was different. He was the witty, Shakespeare-quoting gentleman who swept me off my feet, a good father, good husband, good provider. I told myself that he never killed anyone except in self-defense, that the cashiers murdered in those robberies the law blamed on Jesse and Frank had been Jesse's doing, or some blackheart like Clell Miller or Bill Ryan, but not my husband. Damn him. Damn him! Damn him to hell. He killed that teller in North-field. He told me. Damn him!" Screaming now, but she couldn't control herself, not bothering to think what any neighbors would think. The hotel walls were thin.

She didn't remember standing, but realized she was pressed against Wallace, pounding his chest as if he were her lying husband, then looking up, reaching for him, pulling his face toward her and kissing him, the man, the good man, she should have married. He kissed back, hesitant at first, then hungrily, passionately, and she felt them moving toward his bed, felt the blood rushing, the longing, until both suddenly pulled away as if burned and simultaneously shot out:

"I *can't!*"

Silence.

She ran her fingers through her hair, wiped her face, apologized, heard him apologizing, as well. She caught her breath, muttered some lame excuse that, like him or not, she was married to Frank James and the vows she had said back in Omaha, the ones before God, did mean something to her, and he said that he understood, that he believed in those vows, too, and that he was prosecuting her husband and this would have been wrong.

"What I said . . ." she began.

"The law won't allow you to testify against your husband, Annie, and I don't care what Frank James did in Minnesota, just Missouri."

"Do you . . . ?" She stuffed a hanky that had fallen to the floor into her purse, and picked up after him like some homemaker, anything to keep busy. "Do you think he killed those two men on the train?"

"I don't think he killed the conductor." He righted the overturned chair she had been sitting in before exploding. She didn't remember knocking it over. "The stonemason," he said, "yes."

She had to leave now. She put her hand on the doorknob, realized she was blushing. "I'm sorry for . . ."

"It's all right." When she turned the knob, he called her name and she stopped but would not look at him, fearing that might be all it took for her to go to his arms once more.

"The Ann Ralston I know would never have married a pure scoundrel, a heartless cad. I don't think he killed that stonemason intentionally, but it happened, and it happened during a train robbery. Still, I've spent time with the man, and I know there is some good in Frank James, maybe a lot of good. Maybe . . . hell, I don't know what I'm saying. . . ."

"Thanks for trying, William," she said, and left.

August 27, 1883
Gallatin, Missouri

That fat, one-armed old witch gave Dick Liddil a look of pure hatred after she and a couple other witnesses were sworn in, and Liddil gave her a smirk as she went to sit behind her son. To hear Zerelda Samuel tell it, Frank and Jesse were the holiest men to walk the earth since Jesus Christ hisself and everyone else, especially Dick Liddil, was lower than dung-eating dogs. He looked forward to hearing the old bitch testify, what lies she could tell.

In a rare good mood, Judge Goodman didn't scold the two defense attorneys and one prosecutor who showed up a bit late for Monday's court session, seeing how they had been out of town for the Sabbath. As soon as things finally got settled in the opera house, Goodman reminded Liddil that he remained under oath and told the defense to begin the cross-examination. That diehard bluebelly John Philips rose. Liddil had hoped he would get to answer questions from a legend like

Henry Clay Dean, but all that old coot had done was just sit quietly at the end of the bench with a look on his face that said he was mightily provoked to get such shabby treatment from his colleagues.

"Where all have you lived in Missouri, Mr. Liddil?"

What a dumb-ass question. "I lived in Jackson County from 1870 to about 1875. Don't remember the exact year when I went to Vernon County, where I worked for my pa. That's about it."

"Sir, you lived in the state prison in Jefferson City, too, did you not?"

William Hamilton objected, but Goodman said the objection was overruled and that the witness had to answer.

"Yeah."

"What was the offense?"

"Horse stealing."

"Did not you have an associate in this crime?"

Philips, with his piss-up-a-rope grin and tomfool questions, had become about as irksome as a boil that needed lancing. "I don't think the name of my confederate in the stealing of horses has anything to do with the case."

"You will answer the question," Goodman said sternly, but at least he didn't bang away with that damned gavel.

"His name was Frakes."

"How long were you incarcerated at Jefferson City?"

"Thirty-one and a half months."

"So you did not meet Jesse James and the defendant until after you had served part of your sentence for horse theft?"

"That would be right. I first saw Jesse at Ben Morrow's back in seventy-nine. That's also when I first laid eyes on Ed Miller and Wood Hite. I think this was in the latter part of September. I saw Bill Ryan and Tuck Bassham at other places, but didn't meet Frank till later. That's when I joined the gang."

"And then you scattered?"

"I don't think that—"

This time, Goodman used his noisy gavel. "Answer the question!"

"Yeah. I went to Fort Scott in Kansas and stayed there about three months. We had been in some trouble and thought it best to scatter."

"What trouble?"

William Wallace objected this time, and started saying something that, under the Fifth Amendment, the witness had a right not to incriminate himself. Judge Goodman repeated the same damn thing as if Liddil was some simpleton, saying he didn't have to answer the question, but just as soon as he had finished, Philips was arguing that the Glendale robbery, to which he had alluded, had happened back in October 1879 and thus the witness was protected by the statute of limitations.

"Not for robbery, Your Honor," Wallace said. "I would think a counselor of Colonel Philips's standing would know his law better than that."

Rebuked, Philips still managed a grin. "I was not sure if the Glendale affair was robbery or larceny," he said.

"If Colonel Philips desires to bring up the Glendale matter, the state has no objections, Your Honor," said Wallace, beaming like someone had handed him a newborn son. "We can also take up the Blue Cut robbery."

Philips turned a shade red, stammered something, and stood there sweating, reminding Liddil of the time Frank had taken him to some play and the dumb fool thespian forgot the words he was supposed to say, called out for his lines, and Frank himself had stood up and told him what he was supposed to be saying. That had been in Nashville. Or was it up in Kentucky? Hell, who cared?

Philips finally regained his composure and resumed his interrogation, saying he wouldn't pursue the matter. Liddil figured the lawyer guessed anything linking Frank James to more crimes wouldn't look so good, the damn fool. He asked a bunch of stupid questions before asking him to detail their trip from Tennessee to Missouri before the Winston job.

"We left as soon as we heard of Ryan's arrest," Liddil answered. "That was March 26, and we went up to Old Man Hite's."

"How did you get there?"

"We borrowed horses. We didn't bother asking their owners'

permission, they being asleep and all." That got quite a few chuckles from the gallery, and Goodman, still feeling generous, let the laughter die naturally. Liddil continued telling how they had arranged things and moved throughout the country, refused to answer a few questions regarding other robberies but retold how the Winston job had gone.

"Do you recall seeing Jim Cummins during the summer of 1881?"

"No."

"In September of that year, while in the company of Jesse James, Wood Hite and Jim Cummins, isn't it true that you met Jo Shelby near Page City and the general asked about Frank James, to which Jesse replied that he his brother, in ill health, was down south? Isn't that the real truth, Mr. Liddil?"

"No, it ain't. No such conversation ever took place."

"In Kansas City, didn't you tell Joe B. Chiles that Frank James was not involved in the Winston train robbery?" Philips's face was flushed again, but not from embarrassment. He was riled up, shaking, waving his arms, preaching like some Old Testament–spouting, circuit-riding evangelist. "Isn't that the truth of the matter, Mr. Liddil?"

"Hell, no," he snapped. The judge admonished him for using profanity in his court, threatened him with contempt, and as soon as he had finished his scolding, Philips was at it again, asking wasn't it also true that he told Frank Tutt, a coal-oil inspector at Lexington, that he didn't know where Frank James was and had not for some time, as the two James brothers had been feuding. Liddil hadn't known lawyers could make up lies like that.

"That ain't true, either," Liddil said, and the judge said court would recess for dinner.

When they returned at one thirty, Philips's color had returned to normal and instead of asking about these thought-up conversations, he took another route.

"Prior to returning to Missouri for this case, where were you?"

"Alabama." Might as well spill the rest of it, he figured, since Philips would drag it out, anyway. "I was in jail in Alabama for eight months. I was turned out on April 28, 1883, stayed in Huntsville a week, went to Nashville and St. Louis, and came to Kansas City in June."

"Jail?" Philips looked perplexed and tugged on his beard. "Did you escape?"

"No. I was released."

"Someone must have posted your bail then. Who?"

"Mr. Craig and Mr. Timberlake."

"By that you mean Police Commissioner Henry Craig of Kansas City and Sheriff James Timberlake of Clay County?"

"I do."

"They paid your way?"

"No, sir. I paid my own way."

"How? You had been in jail for eight months!"

"Well, Bob and Charlie Ford sent me a hundred bucks."

Philips liked that answer. "You mean the murderers of Jesse James paid for you to come to Gallatin to testify against the assassinated hero's brother?"

"Objection!"

"Sustained. Restrain yourself, counselor."

"Have you worked since your release from the Alabama jail?"

"No, sir."

"How have you supported yourself?"

"I got some passes to travel on the railroad, and pawned my carpetbag and my pistols. And Mr. Wallace and Mr. Craig have given me some money since then."

"William Wallace, my distinguished colleague, the Jackson County solicitor? Is that the Wallace you mean?"

"Yes."

"By the way, Mr. Liddil, why were you in that Alabama jail?"

"I got convicted of robbing a federal paymaster. But that was a crock of—" The gavel drowned him out.

Philips's grin widened as the judge scolded Liddil, and when Goodman had finished, the attorney said, "So let me get this straight, Mr. Liddil. You are a convicted horse thief and robber. The chief police officers of Kansas City and Clay County posted your bail in Alabama, while the two brothers who murdered Jesse James helped pay your way here. You also have received stipends from Commissioner Craig and the lead prosecutor, plus railroad passes. You have not worked during the four months you have been free, and you admit to taking part in the train robbery of which Frank James is accused but refuse to implicate yourself in a slew of other crimes. Isn't that the truth of the matter?"

"I guess you could say that."

"One more question, sir. Why should we believe anything you have said under oath today?"

Chapter 23

It is leaked out that the defense will endeavor to prove an alibi, General Joe Shelby being their principal witness, and, further, that the Winston gang consisted of five men, but that Bill Cummings was the fifth man, not Frank James.

—*Elgin* (Illinois) *Advocate*, August 28, 1883

August 27, 1883
Gallatin, Missouri

He was glad that was over. Granted, Dick Liddil had stood his ground for much of the cross-examination, but William Wallace knew Philips's final point had resonated with the reporters, spectators and, quite probably, the jury, although he couldn't tell from the faces of those twelve somber men. He'd hate to play poker with that group. He kept his redirect short, basically having Liddil recall the train robbery and how Frank James had reloaded his revolver before they galloped away from the train, how Frank had said that he and Jesse had fired several shots during the affair. After that, he called Bob and Charlie Ford's father to the stand.

"Do you recognize the defendant?" Wallace asked after the cursory preliminary questions.

"I do," J. T. Ford answered. "My son Charles introduced me to him at my daughter's house in July of eighty-one."

"Where did your daughter live?"

"About a half-mile east of Richmond."

"Describe your first meeting with Frank James."

Ford shifted in his chair before answering. "Charles introduced him as Mr. Hall, but I knew then that it was Frank James, and I knew the law was looking for him."

"Do you remember the Winston robbery?"

"I do."

"And you're certain that you saw the defendant in Richmond, Missouri, just before that robbery?"

"It was between the first and tenth of July. I went down there and ate dinner with him at my daughter Maggie's. Her real name is Martha. She married a Bolton."

"And you are absolutely certain that the defendant is the man you saw at your daughter's house in July 1881 only a few days prior to the train robbery at Winston?"

"I am."

"No further questions."

John Philips handled the cross-examination, first asking Ford how he knew the man introduced to him as Mr. Hall was indeed Frank James.

"I had first seen the defendant in May. My son John told me who he really was."

"Did you tell anyone you recognized him as Frank James?"

"Just my wife. I didn't tell Charles or my other children."

"You did not report this to the local authorities?"

"No, I did not."

"Why not?"

"I always tried to keep from saying anything about them, because I thought it policy to do so."

"Policy? Whose policy?"

Ford coughed. "Anyone who wanted to stay alive."

Once the murmur prompted by the witness's answer quieted, Philips continued. "You say you saw Frank James in July of 1881. Are you certain?"

"Yeah. It was the tenth of July."

"Really? You told Mr. Wallace it was between the first and tenth. Has your memory improved that much over the past few minutes?"

Wallace began grinding his teeth as Ford said he was pretty sure it was the tenth. Philips hammered at the man's memory, asking for more details about the clothes "Mr. Hall" had been wearing, about other alleged members of the James Gang he had met during his life, before returning to the date in question. "So it was June tenth?"

"That's right."

With a wide grin, Philips leaned against the defense table. "Mr. Ford, you said it was July tenth. Now it's June. Which—"

"I meant July," he snapped.

"Of course you did. Do you know Jim Cummins?"

"Sure. He lived five or six miles from me."

"Did you see him around the time of the Winston robbery?"

"No, I think the last I saw of him was the year before. He stopped at my house."

"Really, are you good friends?"

"My brother married his sister."

"So you're family, and family will lie to protect family, right?"

"Objection!" Wallace shouted.

"Sustained."

"Do you know James C. Mason?"

"Sure. He's a neighbor of mine."

"Isn't it true that shortly after Jesse James was murdered you told Mr. Mason that Frank James was not in the Winston or Blue Cut robberies, and had not been in the county for a long time?" Ford was shaking his head emphatically as Philips went on. "And did not you also say that you never knew anything about the James Gang staying at your daughter's house?"

"No. I never said nothing like that."

"You also made a similar statement to William D. Rice. Isn't that so?"

"It ain't so."

The defense tactics had become predictable. J. T. Ford's son, Elias, and daughter, Martha Bolton, also testified that Frank James had stayed at the Bolton home in July 1881 shortly before the Winston train robbery, and no matter who handled the cross—Philips, Johnson or Glover—the questions regarded Jim Cummins and so-called statements to neighbors or friends in which the witnesses admitted they had not seen Frank

James during the entire summer of 1881. Philips and Johnson kept firing a sawed-off shotgun, hoping if the shot spread wide enough it might hit something. Each witness stuck with his or her original statement, refusing to be shaken by the defense attorneys, and when Glover tried to get Martha Bolton to discuss the killing of Wood Hite, suggesting that Dick Liddil had murdered the man, Wallace quickly objected and got that line of questioning squashed, at least temporarily. The defense had already shown that Dick Liddil was a thief, and Wallace wasn't about to let his star witness be accused of murder as well. Goodman adjourned for the day and said he would make a ruling in the morning.

August 28, 1883
Gallatin, Missouri

Frank James didn't look so good. His shoulders sagged as if he carried invisible saddlebags filled with lead, his face looked ashen, his hair thinner and grayer. Through her veil and from her seat way up on the balcony, Annie couldn't make out her husband's eyes. He was leaning in, whispering to Colonel Philips, who either nodded or shook his head in reply. At last, Frank sat up and asked one final question, and Annie could read his lips. *Where is my wife?* Or maybe it was *How.* Philips just shrugged and quickly rose with the rest of the crowd as the bailiff announced court was in session and Judge Goodman walked onto the stage.

"Colonel Philips," the judge said, "I will hear your argument now."

She scanned the makeshift courtroom as the colonel stroked his beard while talking about the defense's right to challenge Dick Liddil's credibility by showing him to be the murderer of Wood Hite and that he had killed Hite at Mrs. Bolton's home, that the witness and Elias Ford had both played roles in the brutal slaying of Hite and his indecent burial. William Wallace interrupted with his rebuttal, and Governor Johnson joined the argument. Annie only half listened.

Frank's mother sat behind him, dour as ever, and Annie spotted Charlie Ford in the back rows. The town had become even more crowded, and since Arizona Jack and his drunken troupe had been run out of Gallatin and the puppet show had performed its final act, the only entertainment in town had become the so-called trial of the century. Eastern newspapers had begun to send their own correspondents, and one had interviewed Annie's father last night. She couldn't find her father in the gallery, and wondered if he had been able to get a ticket from Sheriff Crozier. Her mother was in town as well, babysitting Robert this morning in her hotel room. There. She saw her father about three rows in front of Charlie Ford, leaning forward, gripping his cane, listening intently to the legal argument that seemed to bore everyone else. Next she found Major Edwards, his hands trembling, exiled by Frank's attorneys to the back pews. Johnson and Philips were trying to distance Frank James from a drunken fool like Edwards, as well as attorney Henry Clay Dean, who sat at the end of the bench, forbidden to talk, looking like a petulant child. Eventually, her gaze returned to her husband and stayed there, not moving away until Goodman's gavel caused her to jerk her head in his direction.

"Mrs. Bolton can be recalled," the judge said, "and examined as to her knowledge or participation in the killing or burial of Wood Hite." That caused a groan from the prosecution table. "The court will, however, apprise the witness of her rights."

She was a heavyset woman, prematurely gray hair in a bun, and dressed in a calico dress, wringing her hands like Pontius Pilate, as John Glover began asking her questions about Sunday, December 5, 1881.

"In what room of your house was Wood Hite killed?"

Wallace called the matter collateral, but Goodman overruled the objection and told the woman to answer.

"He was kilt in the dinin' room."

"How long did his body lay there?"

"I don't know." Her voice turned angry. "I had nothin' to do with the killin'. I don't remember how long the body remained in the dinin' room, who took it up upstairs or downstairs, or when it was carried out, you hear?"

"Your Honor," Glover said softly to Judge Goodman, "the defense concedes that the witness had nothing to do with the killing of Wood Hite but has knowledge of the crime." He faced Mrs. Bolton again, saying, "Isn't it true, ma'am, that you never went upstairs after the murder of Wood Hite?"

"That's a fact. Wood was kilt in December, and I left in January or February."

"Was he buried in a coffin?"

"No. He was covered with a sheet."

"Where was he buried?"

" 'Bout two hunnert yards from the house."

Annie looked at Frank again. She didn't know what the killing of Wood Hite had to do with this trial, or what Glover, Philips and the rest had in mind. Wood Hite had been killed, Frank once told her, by Bob Ford and Dick Liddil, but Liddil had been shot himself during the set-to, and knowing the temperament of the Hite brothers, the killing was likely done in self-defense.

On the other hand, she knew exactly why Frank's attorneys kept shouting questions about Jim Cummins to all of the witnesses, and why, on redirect, Wallace or Hamilton would ask for a description of Frank James at the time of the Winston robbery. Put the blame on Jim Cummins, accuse him of being the man who killed stonemason—what was his name? Heywood? No. Her stomach turned. That was the name of the cashier in Northfield.

Captain Elias Ford was recalled to testify about Wood Hite's killing, followed by the Bolton kids, two teenagers, both present when Bob Ford and Dick Liddil killed Wood Hite and buried him in the woods. Glover and Johnson pounced on the testimony that Hite had been given an unchristian burial, a fiendish act, they said. What no one seemed to grasp, or bring out in testimony, was why Hite had been buried without ceremony. He was Jesse James's cousin, a favorite, and blood being blood, Jesse would have tracked down the killers himself and cut their throats, probably would have brought Frank along to help in the crime. Liddil and Ford had buried the man and kept shut about it to save their own lives.

Yet Annie's heart pained for the Bolton children. Kids shouldn't have to grow up in households where men killed men. Maybe that was why Frank had worked so hard to keep Robert and her away from Missouri, even away from Jesse at times. Maybe he had cared more about them than his evil brother and callous friends. *Maybe.* She knew better. There was no *maybe* to it.

"State your name, occupation and place of residence?" William Hamilton told the next witness.

"George Hall. I'm station agent at Page City."

Her mouth turned into cotton. Although it had been years since she had seen the man with the sandy dundreary whiskers and thin wire spectacles—and had met him only once—she recognized him. "Dear Lord," she whispered.

"Mr. Hall, do you recall receiving an Acme High Arm sewing machine at the Page City station in March of 1881?"

"I do indeed. It was sent to General Shelby and put on consignment."

"To whom was it consigned?"

"A right handsome woman. That's one reason I remember her. I mean she was quite a looker."

"Her name?" Hamilton asked testily.

"She signed her name as Woodson."

"Have you seen the woman since?"

"Yes, sir. Here in town."

"By what name does she go by now?"

"She's the wife of the defendant. Mrs. Ann James."

The coffee and biscuits in her stomach rocked, and she lifted her hand to cover her mouth. Hall testified that he had mailed the sewing machine on to Independence and had not seen it since. The defense had no questions, and the witness was excused as Hamilton called Daniel Bullard to the stand. Bullard said he was station agent for the Missouri Pacific at Independence and that he had received the Acme sewing machine from Page City on April 28, 1881.

"Who picked it up?" Hamilton asked.

"Mrs. Ralston. Samuel Ralston's wife."

Annie had heard enough. For the past few days, she had told herself that she didn't care if Frank lived or died, but that was a lie. She bolted up the aisle, down the stairs, and forced her way through the crowd outside, still fearing that she might throw up at any second, and that her birthday gift, that damned Acme High Arm, might wind up hanging her husband.

Chapter 24

The true lawyer never takes the wrong side of a case,
knowing it to be the wrong side.

—William H. Wallace

August 28, 1883
Gallatin, Missouri

"I am Elder Jamin Matchett of the Presbyterian Church over in
Caldwell County."

He looked like a Presbyterian minister: black suit, stiff back,
white hair and bald on the top, with a nose straight out of a
Washington Irving story and fingers locked as in prayer as he
began his testimony.

"Sir," Wallace said, "do you remember visitors dropping by
your home on the day before the Winston train robbery?"

"I do. Two men stopped at my cottage beside the church and
asked for dinner. One rode a sorrel with two white hind legs.
The other had a bay mare. I remember one man—he called
himself Willard—because he said he hailed from the Shenan-
doah Valley, and being a Virginia man I started inquiring of his
life there, but he promptly changed the subject."

"What did he say?"

"He said that no man ever lived like William Shakespeare,
then immediately quoted a passage. *King Lear,* maybe. I'm not
sure. So we talked about literature awhile. They had their
meal, paid me—though I told them there was no need—and
left. I never saw them again."

"Do you see one of those men in the courtroom today?"

He answered by pointing a bony finger.

"Let the record show that the witness identified the defendant, Frank James, as the man called Willard." Wallace felt pleased as he returned to his seat. *Let's see how the defense negates the testimony of a man of God.*

Governor Johnson remained seated, didn't even look at Matchett as he said, "You said you live over in Caldwell County?"

"That is correct. Near Cameron."

"How did you get to Gallatin to testify?"

Wallace scratched his chin, wondering about the line of questioning.

"By train."

"How much was your fare?"

Hamilton stood up to object. "Your Honor, I see no purpose to these questions."

"If you will give me just a little latitude, Your Honor," Johnson said with a smile as he finally lifted his head, "my point will be made directly. A man's life is at stake."

"Very well, counselor. Answer the question, Reverend."

"There was no fee," Matchett said.

"Ah, because you're a minister?"

"No, sir. The prosecuting attorney of Daviess County arranged my transportation with the railroad. I am just a poor servant of the Lord."

"I see. So you turned Judas for thirty pieces of silver, sold your soul to join this nefarious plot against Frank James perpetrated by the district attorneys and railroad barons!"

"Objection!" Hamilton boomed.

"Sustained."

"I am finished, Your Honor," Johnson said in disgust.

Wallace glanced at the jury, but couldn't read anything, then huddled with Hamilton. "We talked about getting money budgeted for transportation of witnesses from *Tennessee,*" Wallace whispered.

"Yeah, but the railroad came to me, said they'd be happy to arrange travel for prosecution witnesses free of charge. They want to see Frank James convicted as much as anybody. You know what the budget is like for a county solicitor. . . ."

Wallace couldn't hide the grimace. "But he lived just down the road."

"He's a minister, for God's sake. I didn't—"

Goodman interrupted their debate, and Wallace apologized before calling another witness. Maybe Johnson's final statement, likening the Presbyterian to Judas would backfire with the jury. Maybe.

Annie dined in the hotel restaurant with her parents and son. It took twenty minutes—and two glasses of Irish whiskey for her father—before they could be seated, and they ordered quickly. Across the room sat Wallace and the other members of the state prosecution team. Occupied by their food, drink and animated debates, they didn't notice her.

"I've heard enough," said her father, the whiskey kicking in.

"Sam," her mother began, but he waved her off.

"What Colonel Philips suggests is a damned lie. Jim Cummins doesn't look a damn thing like Frank James—"

"Watch your language in front of Robert," her mother went on, but her father was in one of his moods.

"Frank was in that robbery." This he said to Annie, pointing his empty tumbler in her face. "Y'all were here in Missouri. He's guilty as sin. Hell, I've known that all along."

"Sam Ralston," her mother said, "you shut your mouth this instant."

Lowering his tumbler and his voice, he muttered, "Annie, we'll be taking our leave tomorrow, going home. You and Robert are welcome to join us. Stay with us. As long as you desire." He flagged the waiter and asked for another drink while her mother shook her head disapprovingly.

"I'm staying," Annie said firmly.

"By the saints, why?" he asked, astounded. He didn't bother pausing or even lowering his voice as the waiter freshened his Jameson. "You sent that sewing machine from Page City. That proves you were in Missouri, not Texas. The state has witnesses, and not just Dick Liddil, who say Frank was there. It's a hopeless cause, child. At best, your husband will spend twenty years, maybe his life in that hellhole outside Jefferson City. At worst, you're a widow, and Robert has no father."

Her mother started to scold her father again, but Annie spoke first. "For better or worse. Those were part of my vows, too." She was looking at William Wallace, passing out cigars to his colleagues, when she gave her reason. "I want my son to have a father." Her voice fell, and she dropped her gaze. "And I want a husband." She had searched her soul last night, understood that, in spite of Frank's shortcomings, she still loved him, no matter how many bank cashiers he had killed. Frank had been right in his confession. That hadn't been him, not the Frank James they both knew. That had been Jesse, and Jesse was dead. No longer could he reach for his older brother and pull him down.

Unless he was reaching now, laughing as he attempted to drag Frank to hell with him.

"I should go see Frank," she said, and started to rise.

"Annie," her mother said, "your supper isn't here yet."

She barely heard her mother. She had turned, recognizing the striking figure with shoulder-length hair, streaked with gray, entering the restaurant, holding the ugliest, deadliest-looking pistol she had ever seen in his right hand.

The little drummer sat in front of his scalloped oysters and tea, sweat dampening his pale face as if he had just taken a bath, still stirring the sugar into his drink, only now the pewter spoon slapped the edge of the china cup, spilling the tea and sounding like some badly tuned wind chime. The barrel of General Jo Shelby's LeMat revolver hovered less than an inch from the poor man's nose.

"You are a scoundrel and a disgrace to the people of Missouri," Shelby said, "the scourge of every decent man, woman and child who rose against the banner of Northern tyranny, and I shall enjoy doing my duty by ridding Gallatin of your stink."

The only stink William Wallace could smell was the rye on Shelby's breath. Well, *now* there was a new smell; the drummer had soiled himself. As soon as Wallace had seen Shelby's gun, he had begun moving toward the Confederate legend, trying not to startle Shelby or anyone else in the dining hall. Shelby's breath was ragged; the drummer wasn't breathing at all.

A dozen ideas raced through Wallace's brain. Shout. Run. Tackle Shelby. Draw his Thunderer and shoot him in the head . . . He liked none of those options, and closed in, aware of Annie James staring at him, hands over her mouth, aware of others watching him in silence, like the waiter holding a tray of plates on his shoulder, turned into a statue. An arm's length separated Wallace from the general, and he lifted his left hand slowly and pulled the unlit cigar from his mouth. He heard no sound except Shelby's breaths and the clattering of the drummer's spoon against the teacup.

"General." He swallowed and repeated it louder, although still a soft whisper. The only recognition came in the form of a series of blinks.

"General Shelby, sir," Wallace said, suddenly craving a drink of water. Shelby's gun hand never wavered, but he examined Wallace with bloodshot eyes and said, "I do not place your face."

"William Wallace, General, of Jackson County. Has this man insulted you?"

Shelby turned back to the drummer. "He has insulted scores of heroes, living and dead. Killing Dick Liddil will give me great pleasure."

Spotting movement to his right, Wallace chanced a glance, praying it wasn't Crozier or one of his deputies. The lawmen were so edgy they'd likely turn the dining room into another Lawrence massacre, and Wallace would be caught in the fusillade. It wasn't. Henry Clay Dean stood in the threshold separating the restaurant from the hotel lobby in front of a half dozen stunned, speechless patrons.

"General Shelby," Wallace said. "That isn't Dick Liddil."

"He looks like Dick Liddil to me," Shelby said, tightening his finger against the trigger. "He looks like vermin." There was a resemblance in the color of the drummer's hair, and his mustache, but Dick Liddil was taller, heavier and not as well-dressed.

Dean had managed to get his legs to work, and walked slowly toward the confrontation. Shelby considered him briefly, but when the portly lawyer held his hands away from his waist and smiled, revealing he meant no trouble and was not armed, Shelby dismissed the minister-lawyer.

"What's your name?" Wallace asked the drummer.

The man's mouth moved, only no audible words came out. He tried again. Still nothing. At last, he let go of the spoon and said dryly, "Thaddeus Whiting . . . of . . . Ann Arbor . . . Michigan."

"You are Dick Liddil—and must die," Shelby said.

"General Shelby." Dean spoke now, his voice rich, eyes bright. "It is an honor to see you again, Jo. You look well. We must talk of old times. You'll do me the honor of joining me in my hotel room. I have an excellent bottle of French brandy."

"I shall join you, sir, after I dispatch this louse."

When Dean spoke again, the nearest tables rattled. "You will do no such thing, Joseph Shelby! You will surrender your firearm immediately, or God will strike you dead where you stand. To this I swear, even if the Lord Almighty uses my own hand to do his work." Shelby spun, Wallace froze, and the heavy LeMat was trained on the old Methodist's gut, but Dean's hard eyes remained locked on the drunken Confederate.

"You once commanded the respect of not only the State of Missouri, sir, but the entire South," Dean's voice thundered. "I have heard you speak of loyalty, of chivalry, of Southern manners. You protected the fairer sex from the knaves of the world like Dick Liddil. You protected children. But this is my word, and my word, like the Lord's, is true. The Joseph Orville Shelby I know would not dare kill an unarmed man in front of women and children. Look around you, sir. You embarrass me. You stink of whiskey and you smell of Lucifer. Hand me your weapon, Shelby. Hand me your weapon or face God's wrath . . . and mine!"

Dean had kept walking during his sermon until the pistol barrel rested against a vest button.

"Job 21:17," Shelby said hoarsely. "'How oft is the candle of the wicked put out! And how oft cometh their destruction upon them! God distributeth sorrows in His anger.'"

"Deuteronomy 32:35," Dean replied. "'To me belongeth vengeance, and recompense; their foot shall slide in due time:

for the day of their calamity is at hand, and the things that shall come upon them make haste.' The gun, my friend. This is not Dick Liddil. This is . . . Thaddeus Whiting of Ann Arbor, Michigan. Dick Liddil is not man enough to show his face in public."

He reached up and gripped the LeMat. Shelby didn't resist as Dean took the revolver, lowered the hammer and stuck the gun in his waistband. Still, no one else in the restaurant spoke, not even a sigh or whisper. "Come," Dean said, placing an arm around Shelby's shoulders. He gave Wallace a quick nod and escorted the drunken Shelby into the lobby.

Dumbly, Wallace returned the cigar to his mouth and walked to his table. The drummer bolted out of the room, and men and women began talking excitedly. Wallace almost collapsed in his chair, and Hamilton struck a match and lighted Wallace's cigar.

"Well," Wallace heard John Shanklin say, "I guess the Reverend Dean finally got to make his speech."

August 29, 1883
Gallatin, Missouri

A forty-two-year-old farmer named Mallory said he had seen Frank James on the Thursday before the Winston robbery, and a blacksmith in Winston said he had shod the defendant's horses, a sorrel with a white blaze in June and a bay mare in July. A half dozen other witnesses, maybe more, also described the horses they had seen Frank James riding that summer. The state even called a man whose horse was stolen—a horse that looked a lot like the one Frank James was riding at the time of the Winston robbery—to the stand, plus a Gallatin doctor named William Black, who had examined Frank James at the Independence jail. All the doc said was that the two had discussed the acting merits of men like Keene, Ward and McCullough, all of whom Frank James had seen perform in Nashville (Frederick Ward's delineations were the best, James had said), and that the defendant could recite many passages from Shakespeare's sonnets and plays.

John Newman Edwards had sat in on many criminal cases during his journalism career, but never had he seen anything like this. Hamilton and Wallace must have called every farmer in Daviess County to the stand, and most of them just repeated each other. Some man who looked a lot like the defendant, or was the defendant, had been witnessed in the area in the summer of eighty-one riding a horse with two white feet that had been stolen in the area that summer. The affable man liked to recite Shakespeare. He carried a Remington revolver and Winchester rifle. He sported a mustache and burnside whiskers. The defense lawyers tried to get the witnesses to say, sure, some folks look the same, or prove that they had reason to lie under oath.

The highlight of today's testimony, Edwards figured as he flipped through the pages of his tablet, wasn't worth printing, either. Blacksmith Jonas Potts, who lived four miles east of Winston, testified that he had seen Frank James on a bay mare during the summer and thought, once while in his cups, that James and his friend, a fellow named Clarence, had tried to get some information out of him regarding the Winston train. That prompted attorney Glover, trying to discredit the witness as a drunk, to ask on cross, "Where do you get your liquor?" Answered Potts, "At Winston, I suppose, where you got yours." Even Judge Goodman had cracked a smile over that one.

Most of the testimony had been excruciating to sit through. Somnolent William D. Hamilton even asked Frank O'Neil of the *St. Louis Republican* to testify, but the stalwart, good-looking gent in the gray Prince Albert refused to break the sacred bond of confidentiality between a journalist and his source. Maybe the intent of the prosecution was to bore the defendant and jury to painful deaths.

A man needed the patience of an oyster to sit through this tedious play, or a stiff drink, and John Edwards had neither.

Frank James had stopped seeing visitors in his jail, except his mother, son and attorneys. Not even Major Edwards—the man who had negotiated the terms of Frank's surrender plus the glorious interview with the *Republican,* the man who had hired those damnable lawyers who now told Frank James what to do, what to wear and, the bastards, to whom he could see and speak—was allowed in the Gallatin jail. Johnson and Philips called Edwards a drunk, a reprobate, a man much like Henry Clay Dean who had outlived his usefulness.

Well, they couldn't keep him out of the makeshift courthouse. He still had a job to do, to file daily reports to his newspaper and to see Alexander Franklin James acquitted. He had not tasted a drop of scamper juice this day, not even during the recess for dinner.

James Timberlake had just finished his testimony. Edwards had expected the line of questioning to surround the activities of the James Gang. After all, two years ago Jimmy Timberlake had been the sheriff of Clay County, but Wallace maintained his dreary assault on the stolen horse. Yes, Timberlake remembered the bay mare. Yes, he recovered it shortly after the Winston train robbery, had kept her at Liberty for ten days or two weeks before the owner claimed her. Edwards defeated another yawn. Neither Philips nor anyone else on the defense team bothered to question the witness. Too bored, Edwards assumed.

"The state rests," Wallace announced.

Edwards straightened in his seat. "I'll be damned," he whispered.

"Governor Johnson?" Goodman asked.

The prissy fraud rose with a bow. "Your Honor, I think the attorneys for the defense have been necessarily so busy listening to evidence introduced by the state that we feel the need of time for consultation."

Goodman's head bobbed. "Owing to the fact that the attorneys in the case have occasioned no unnecessary delay, I will adjourn the case till tomorrow morning at eight o'clock."

Edwards was waiting in line to get through the crowded door, debating on having a drink before telegraphing his story, when someone placed a hand on his shoulder.

"Major Edwards," soft-spoken defense attorney Joshua Alexander said, "Governor Johnson desires a word with you in private. At the little shack behind the depot. Say, in two hours? Will that give you time to write your story?"

His eyes brightened. "Certainly," he said happily. "I shall be there forthwith." Well, now that the game of the Life of Frank

James had shifted to the defense, they needed him. Johnson likely wanted to discuss strategy, and Edwards had plenty of ideas. Mayhap his opinion of Lieutenant Governor Charles P. Johnson had been too harsh. This was cause for celebration. He was back with his friend, Frank James, back in need. One drink would not hurt him. Just one.

Chapter 25

Another day of the great trial draws to a close, and yet the feverish interest and excitement are more noticeable than on the opening day. Vast crowds throng the courtroom and crane their necks to catch every syllable of testimony that is to liberate or imprison the man on trial.

—*St. Joseph Daily Gazette*, August 31, 1883

August 29, 1883
Gallatin, Missouri

He studied the phlegm he had just coughed up as if it were a piece of gold. No blood, thank God. As bad as this hacking cough had become, Frank James had started to fear he had become a lunger. He turned from the slop bucket and sat in Annie's rocker.

"Are you all right?" Colonel Philips asked.

"Nothing an acquittal won't cure," he said with a weary smile, and added silently, *Or having my wife back.*

"I have a letter, Frank," Philips said, "from Henry Clay Dean. It's his resignation from the case. He gave it to me before leaving this afternoon to speak at a convention of coal miners in Colchester, Illinois. He says he hopes for your acquittal. Would you care for me to read the letter?"

"No, thanks, Colonel, and don't play me for a fool. Dean didn't resign. You and the governor ran him off."

"Frank—"

"Don't *Frank* me, Colonel. And where's Major Edwards? I

haven't seen him in a coon's age. I—" Only another coughing spell allowed Philips to interrupt his tirade.

"The major has his own demons to fight, Frank. Governor Johnson thinks it best to keep him clear of you. His notorious drinking binges cannot help our cause."

"*Cause*. You lawyers are bigger thieves than Dingus, Cole and me ever dreamed of being."

"We're trying to guarantee your acquittal, Frank. So you can live the rest of your days a free man."

He spat at the bucket, missed and didn't care. A minute ago he had joked about being found innocent, but the anger had been boiling inside him for several days exploded. "Acquittal. Why should I care if I live or die? Hell, as sick as I feel, I'll likely die in this cell before the damned trial ends. What good is my freedom if Annie isn't there to share it with me?"

"You have your son . . . your mother."

He shook his head, crossed his legs, picked up a book of Balzac. "We need to discuss your alibi, Frank," Philips said softly. "We need to get everything down to the last detail. Texas. You'll have to take the stand. Frank, will you listen to me?" He refused to look up. "Listen, I don't agree with all of Governor Johnson's tactics, but he's smart." When that failed, Philips said, "Annie loves you, son. She'll be there for you in the end. Trust me."

Frank wished he were deaf, tapped his foot, turned page after page—anything to make noise, anything to drown out John Philips's words. The counselor tried a few more tactics, but nothing worked, though the colonel kept talking. Lucky him. Nineteen years ago, Frank James would have killed Philips just to shut up his banter. Nineteen? Hell, maybe only seven.

"Upper balcony," Philips said after a heavy sigh, and waited.

He looked up from his book, curious.

"Annie's been in court every day, Frank," Philips said. "She sits in the upper balcony, wearing a black veil to hide her face. I warrant she'll be there tomorrow as well."

* * *

Vomit and blood. His own. He could smell, taste both, but couldn't see anything except a blazing orange light. His lungs also refused to work. John Newman Edwards felt himself being lifted, heard the voice, opened his eyes. The room spun out of control, and he felt another wave of nausea, tried to swallow down the bile, couldn't and heaved.

"You son of a bitch!" the voice screamed, and Edwards fell to the floor. A boot slammed into his groin, and he gagged, groaned, pulled himself into a ball. When he heard the man curse again, he covered his face with his hands and arms and began sobbing, begging. "Look what you did to my suit, you walkin' whiskey vat," the voice said. "You ruint it."

"I'm sorry." Every syllable hurt.

He tried to remember. Where was he? Who was his tormentor? He knew the voice, the Southern accent. "Get up," the man ordered, and Edwards wanted to obey, anything to avoid another punch or kick. He managed to get on his hands and knees, but the sickness returned, yet he had nothing left in his stomach to purge, and could only dry heave. When that finally passed, his attacker jerked him to his feet, swearing that if he vomited on him again, he would die here.

Raymond B. Sloan, defense counselor from Nashville, Tennessee. He could make out his face, remembered meeting him near the Gallatin depot, only it wasn't Sloan he was supposed to see, but Charles Johnson. Despite the blur from pain, nausea and inebriation, he knew he had been duped. Major John Newman Edwards, the Victor Hugo of the West, was no fool. The lawyer opened Edwards's coat and stuffed an envelope inside a pocket.

"Your ticket to Sedalia. The train leaves in two hours. That gives you time to clean up, pack up and skedaddle. Savvy?"

"Why?"

The answer came with several stinging slaps that opened his busted lips wider. God, how he really needed a drink.

"You've been paintin' your tonsils too long, Edwards. You embarrass us, you embarrass Frank James." Sloan slapped him again, pressed forefinger and thumb into his cheeks, forcing open his mouth. "Frank James is your friend, isn't he?"

"Un-huh."

"You don't wanna see him hung, do you?"

"Uh-uh."

"So you light a shuck out of here. We'll take care of Frank James, Gov'nor Johnson and the rest of us. The defense begins tomorrow morn, Edwards, and the gov'nor and me are riddin' Gallatin of certain undesirables. You fill that bill."

"But—"

"You want to die, Major?" He released Edwards, began brushing off his suit, cursing him again for ruining his clothes with his drunken disgorge.

"My paper. I have . . . stories . . . to write. It's the trial . . . of the . . . century."

"Write 'em from Sedalia. I'll say it once more. Savvy?"

Edwards nodded. Like the men who wore the gray, the fallen guerrilla heroes like Quantrill and Anderson, he had lost the war. Like Jesse James, he had been defeated, betrayed by his own kind.

August 30, 1883
Gallatin, Missouri

"This is one of the gravest and greatest cases ever tried in this country," William Rush said to begin the defense's opening statement. "I ask you to consider the defense in the light of the facts produced in the court."

It had been a smart move, William Wallace conceded, for the defense to postpone its opening statement until after the state had rested, but Wallace would have bet money John Philips or Charles Johnson would have made the defense argument, not William Rush. The man had always been a capable lawyer, even if Wallace found his integrity sorely lacking, but Wallace thought Henry Clay Dean would have made a much better speech had Johnson let him. Of course, Dean wasn't here, had resigned and left Gallatin. Resting his chin against his left hand, Wallace listened.

"Mr. Wallace attempts to show that a conspiracy existed in Tennessee, but he has failed utterly to prove this except by Dick Liddil, who is unworthy of belief. The defense will show that Frank James was not at Winston. We propose to show the moral sensibilities of those Ray County people who buried Wood Hite are such as to render them unworthy of belief. We propose to prove by a man who was on that train that Frank James was not at Winston.

"When Dick Liddil went to the governor he contracted to prove the defendant guilty of murder in the first degree, but the contract was more than he could fill. The Fords corroborate Dick Liddil because they are in the same boat with him. They must not allow Frank James to be acquitted because he would avenge the death of his brother.

"We expect to prove, beyond even the shadow of a doubt, by witnesses far above those Ray County witnesses of the prosecution, in point of moral responsibility, that Elder Matchett, Ezra Soule, Frank Wolfenberger, Squire Mallory and Mrs. Lindsay saw a man who bears some resemblance to Frank James, but that he was not Frank James."

Maybe Wallace had underrated Rush. Attack Dick Liddil and the other witnesses, bring up the Ford brothers, and say a man who looked like Frank James had taken part in the robbery. Not a bad plan, but the defense had played its cards, and Wallace felt confident he could shatter any evidence that Jim Cummins had been that fifth man.

"The motive which actuates the Kansas City officials is one of revenge, because the defendant did not allow himself to be captured by them or surrender to them, thus depriving them of the rewards. Hence the conspiracy between these officials and the Fords and Liddil.

"We shall show that Frank James was seen in Nashville every week, while Bill Ryan and others were committing depredations.

"Frank James has not willingly been an outlaw. Long ago he would have surrendered if he had any assurance of a fair trial, but he very naturally feared the civilization that threw a hand grenade into his old mother's house, shattering her arm and killing his innocent little brother. We shall show that defendant is persecuted as a man never was before, the prosecution having money and railroads at its back."

He hadn't expected that. A conspiracy involving Liddil, the

Fords, the law and the railroads. Wallace tried to read the jury as Rush took his seat. Most farmers didn't care much for railroads at all, which was one reason the James Gang had been so successful at evading capture for so many years. They had declared war on the railroads, so bully for Frank and Jesse James. Wallace even marveled at Rush's introduction of the botched Pinkerton raid on the James family farm, always good for sympathy.

The state had called fifty-two witnesses. Now the defense would make things interesting.

Sandy-haired Samuel Brosius looked relaxed as he took a seat and began answering questions put to him by John Philips. A thirty-six-year-old Gallatin attorney, he knew how to handle himself in a court of law. William Wallace scratched a few notes during Philips's direct.

"Were you on the train the night of the Winston robbery?"

"I was. I was in the smoking car."

"Tell the jury what happened."

"We left Cameron on time, and shortly after departing Winston, two men entered the car and commenced firing."

Wallace looked up. *Two* men. Putting his pencil aside, he listened closely.

"They said, 'Hold up your hands,' and we obeyed."

"Where was the conductor?"

"He was standing about one-fourth down the length of the car, from the front end. One of the robbers was a large man, with whiskers all over his face, and he devoted himself to the conductor while the smaller man kept his eyes trained on the passengers. I was afraid he might shoot me. I looked at him steadily the whole time as he was shooting in the car."

"Did the larger man shoot conductor Westfall?"

"He did."

"Were these men wearing masks?"

"Not at all. Neither had on a mask."

"You see the defendant, Frank James. Was he one of the two robbers in the smoking car?"

"He was not."

"Are you certain?"

"He was not there."

Philips sat down with a smile. After a final glance at his notes, Wallace stood and walked directly to the witness chair before beginning his cross-examination.

"How long did you stare at the bandits?"

"I'd say a full minute."

"In your seat the entire time?"

"Yes, sir."

"While bullets were being fired?"

"Well, the bullets were hitting the ceiling."

"Did either of the bandits wear dusters?"

"I'm not sure."

"How were they dressed?"

"To be honest, I couldn't swear to a stitch of clothing that either of the two men had on."

"That's understandable. You must have been scared."

"I guess so."

"Well, sir, you testified that you thought one of the men might shoot you."

"Sure, I was scared."

"Only two robbers? Other witnesses say three men entered the smoking car at first."

"They're mistaken. I saw only two."

"You're certain of that?"

"Indeed."

"Other witnesses also say the passengers hid under their seats during the shooting. You didn't duck underneath your seat?"

"No, sir. If any citizen says I was under the seat, he is a liar."

"You admit you were scared," Wallace said sharply. "You thought you might be killed. The train's being robbed. Bullets are flying through the smoker, two men are murdered, and you remained in your seat the entire time?"

"As I said, the bullets were hitting the ceiling."

"Not all of them. Two killed conductor Westfall and another killed Frank McMillan. Could you recognize the bandits if you saw them again?"

"I don't think so."

"You couldn't recognize them, but you swear that the defendant isn't one of them. How is that possible?"

"He wasn't the man."

With a mirthless laugh, Wallace said he was finished with the witness for now, but might call him later during rebuttals, and returned to his seat. Hamilton leaned over and whispered, "What's this two-man theory? I thought they were trying to prove that Jim Cummins was the fifth man?"

"We've been duped," Wallace answered. "They realize that they can't link Cummins to the robbery, so they're changing their defense. Four men committed the Winston robbery, not five."

"That won't hold up," Hamilton said, straightening as Colonel Philips called a Nashville detective named Fletcher Horn to the stand.

"We shall see," Wallace replied.

Fletcher Horn testified that Frank James, known to him in Tennessee as B. J. Woodson, had been a hardworking gentleman who, as far as Horn could tell, never associated with the likes of Dick Liddil, Jesse James (alias J. B. Howard) and Jim Cummins. Defense attorney Raymond Sloan pretty much said the same thing when Colonel Philips called him to the stand. After that, John Glover took over the questioning of Elizabeth Montgomery and her daughter, both of whom said strangers stopped at their house near Winston on the night of the train robbery, but neither could say for sure whether Frank James had been one of the riders.

Every time the judge dismissed a witness, Frank James would shift in his seat and crane his neck toward the balcony. He couldn't find Annie up there, but he believed she was somewhere behind all the paper fans and hankies being waved to fight off the oppressive heat and humidity. Colonel Philips would not have lied to him about Annie's presence.

"Who you lookin' for?" Sloan asked him.

Frank James did not care much for Raymond Sloan. In fact, of all the lawyers sitting beside him, he considered the Tennessean the worst of the lot. The man certainly didn't act like any attorney he had ever known, and his plaid coat was stained with something that smelled god-awful. He didn't bother an-swering.

"If it's that wife of yours, don't you worry, *amigo*," Sloan said. "I'd bet good money that she'll be sittin' by your side, purrin' like a kitten, come the morrow. Yes, sir, I'd surely would make that bet."

He despised Sloan's cackle and the look in his eyes, too, and wanted to grab the man's thick throat, strangle him, but Colonel Philips had called an important witness, and Frank James felt his heart jump as the woman behind him rose and made her way toward the aisle, mumbling apologies, walking slowly in ovenlike temperatures. His mother, her hair turned completely white, still wore a black armband for Dingus—and likely always would.

"State your name and place of residence for the record, please, ma'am."

"I'm Mrs. Zerelda Samuel. I have lived for forty years in Clay County, three miles from Kearney. I am the mother of Jesse and Frank James." With her one arm, she pulled a hand-kerchief from her tiny black purse and dabbed her eyes.

Chapter 26

*During the examination of Mrs. Samuels the defendant
who, during the entire trial, has looked each witness in
the face, dropped his head and seemed very much
affected by the presence of his mother in the court room.*
—*St. Joseph Daily Gazette,* September 1, 1883

August 30, 1883
Gallatin, Missouri

"Do you have any other children, Mrs. Samuel?" Philips
asked.

"I do. Three girls, all married, and my son, John T. Samuel.
I had another boy, Archie, my baby, but he was murdered by
those Pinkertons on the twenty-sixth of January, 1875."

"And when did Jesse die?"

"He was kilt two years ago next April," she blurted out, and
broke down, sobbing uncontrollably, muttering over and over,
"My poor boy. My poor, poor boy."

How maudlin would this become? William Wallace already
heard quite a few sniffles from the women in the gallery while
tears crawled through the crags in the old woman's face and
John F. Philips, ever the thespian, shook his head sadly at all
the right moments. Wallace considered objecting—what rele-
vance did the Pinkerton raid on the Samuel farm or the murder
of Jesse James have on this case?—but knew better. Object,
and the newspaper reporters, crowd and jury would consider
the state prosecutors a callous, coldhearted bunch with no regard for a poor mother, twice a widow, who had been crippled

by agents of the law and seen two sons killed: one shot in the back for reward money and the other, only eight years old, killed by what many assumed had been a hand grenade, although Allan Pinkerton denied that rumor vociferously.

"Did you see Jesse during the summer of 1881?" Philips asked.

"I did. He come to my house, either in May or June—May, I think—first time he'd come home in a coon's age."

"Was your son Frank with him?"

"No. The first time my Jesse come, Jim Cummins and Dick Liddil was with him—no, that first time it was only Dick Liddil. Jim come later that summer. I remember askin' Jesse where Buck was—Buck's what I call my Frank." Her eyes found her son and she smiled, but Frank James stared at his boots, wringing his hands, maybe praying. For all Wallace could tell, the outlaw might have been crying. "Jesse," Mrs. Samuel continued, "he told me that he had left Frank in Kentucky, said he was in bad health."

The tap opened, and tears, previously a mere trickle, cascaded down her face, and more sobs sounded in the gallery. She barely choked out the next few words. "I said . . . I said . . . 'Son . . . you know he . . . is dead, and you might as well . . . tell me.'" Philips handed her a fresh handkerchief, and Judge Goodman asked if she could continue. Hamilton muttered something about the old woman's performance, but Wallace shook his head. Zerelda Samuel was not playacting. She had always loved her boys. Everyone in Missouri knew this to be gospel, and Philips and Johnson had been smart to put her on the stand.

With a polite nod, she thanked the judge for his Christian kindness and said the Good Lord would see her through this ordeal, the dredging up of bad memories. "Dick Liddil told me the same thing, but God as my witness, I was a-feared they was a-lyin' to an old woman as not to break her heart. I thought Frank was dead, but glory to God, he weren't."

After she caught her breath, Philips continued. "When did Jesse leave your farm?"

"After the Winston robbery. Don't know the exact time."

"And during his stay at your home, did he have other visitors?"

"Yeah. Charlie Ford, Dick Liddil, the Hite boys met there, and I saw Jim Cummins that summer. His relations live three or four miles from my house."

"But you never saw Frank that summer?"

"Frank wasn't there that summer. Fact is, I had not laid eyes on my Buck for seven years, back in seventy-six, till I saw him at Independence last October." She dabbed her eyes again. "The last time I saw Buck a-fore that was when the sheriff come to my house with some killers and shot at him." Her words and eyes had turned icy.

"Did you know where Frank was?"

"No. Like I told you, I figured he was dead."

"Who visited Jesse the most during his stay during the summer of eighty-one?"

"Dick Liddil and the Hites."

"Thank you, Mrs. Samuel. I know this was painful for you. Your witness, Mr. Wallace."

The sniffles and sobs in the gallery had ceased, the handkerchiefs replaced by the paper fans, as Wallace walked toward Zerelda Elizabeth Cole James Simms Samuel. He remembered her sermon in his office when she had arrived with Annie James and tried to broker Frank James's surrender terms, and the old woman hadn't softened any. Wallace had seen friendlier faces on rattlesnakes and hydrophobic dogs. He'd keep his cross-examination short and would not rile the witness.

"Thank you for your patience, ma'am," he said with a bow, "on such a hot day. I'll keep you only a few minutes. How did Jesse leave your farm after the robbery?"

"By wagon." There was no friendliness in her voice.

"Was he alone?"

"No. Charlie Ford, the Hites and Dick Liddil was in it with 'em. They took food and clothin', and I give 'em a dress, apron and bonnet so one of them gentlemen could pass for a lady, so you couldn't catch 'em."

"Was Jim Cummins there?"

"No. I didn't see him but that once, one night in June, but Johnny—that's my boy, Johnny Samuel, John Thomas is his given name—he said he seen Jim once standin' outside a window."

He stared at Charles Johnson during her answer, trying to read the counselor's face. Nothing. Like the twelve jurors, the former lieutenant governor should have followed a career on the gambling circuit. John Philips buried his face in his notes, and Frank James had lifted his gaze, but instead of watching his mother, he seemed to be trying to recognize a face in the balcony.

He knew who the outlaw sought, knew Annie James was somewhere up there. He wanted to look himself but would not. He had to concentrate on his cross-examination.

Zerelda Samuel had put Charles Ford on the family farm, suggesting he had been the fifth bandit in the Winston robbery, and had cleared Jim Cummins. Samuel Brosius, however, had testified that only four men had taken part in the robbery. Wallace couldn't figure out the defense strategy. Would they change mounts again, going from the Jim Cummins theory to the four-bandit theory to the Charles Ford theory? The state had subpoenaed Cummins, but nobody could find the vagabond, and he dared not put Charles Ford on the stand. That boy was so shaken, morose and drunk, a smart attorney like Philips would gut him like a perch on cross-examination, and berate the Fords as cowards who killed Jesse James from behind.

He could do nothing but wait and see how Philips and Johnson decided to play their hand.

"Thank you, Mrs. Samuel. I have no more questions of this witness."

"Redirect?" Goodman asked.

"No, Your Honor."

"Very well. Court will adjourn for dinner. We shall reconvene at one thirty."

That afternoon, Philips and Johnson paraded G. W. Trigg, James L. Farris, Arthur B. Elliott, John Millstead, Thomas D. Woodson, James Duval, John Warrenstaff and a few other men and women who pointed out that state witnesses such as the Fords and Boltons were, in their opinion, liars. You couldn't believe a word they said under oath. They swore they never saw Frank James in the summer of 1881, but Jim Cummins, who looked a lot like the defendant, was around then. They contradicted denials made by prosecution witnesses and swore that J. T. and Elias Ford and Maggie Bolton had told them they hadn't seen Frank James that summer and had invented their pack of lies to convict a man they loathed and feared.

"It's a wash," William Hamilton said after opening a desk drawer in his office. He found a bottle and emptied the last of his whiskey into a dirty tumbler.

"We knew that going in," Wallace agreed while loosening his tie. "It depends on if the jury believes our witnesses or theirs. Dick Liddil still put Frank James at the scene."

"If they believe him." Hamilton killed his drink in one swallow, stifled a cough and sat down. "I wish we knew where Jim Cummins was. He can't look that much like Frank James. If we had him on the stand—"

"*If.* A big *if.* We don't have Cummins, and we aren't going to find him unless he wants to be found. And you remember what Brosius said on the stand. If we had Cummins, they would argue that only four men took part in the robbery."

"We can disprove that easy enough, if we have to attach every passenger in the smoking car." He hefted the empty whiskey bottle, tossed it into an overflowing trash can and shrugged. "Allen Parmer and Dave Poole arrived this afternoon from Texas. Parmer's Frank James's brother-in-law, and Poole rode with Quantrill, now has a big ranch down there. If and when they take the stand, they'll be saying Frank was in Texas that summer. We can impugn their testimony easy enough. They have reason to lie for the defendant. Who do you think they'll call tomorrow?"

"More of the same, and at some point Jo Shelby. Would you like to handle cross on him?"

Hamilton answered with a smile and slight shake of his head.

"You found the sewing machine connection," Wallace said. "We'll have to bring that up on cross, likely treat him as a hostile witness. You'll get your name in papers across the country. I thought that's what you wanted."

He shook his head again. "Yeah, I can see those headlines. 'Confederate General Shelby Shoots Prosecutor Dead in Courtroom.' You cross-examine the good general, and if he kills you, I promise to indict him for your murder, though I can't promise you a conviction. You want to grab some supper?"

"Cafés will be packed right now. How about if I meet you in a couple of hours at the hotel?"

"Good enough."

As soon as she stepped out of her room, Annie James noticed one of her son's shoestrings had become undone and, sighing, closed the door and knelt to retie it.

"We goin' to me-maw's?" he asked.

"No, Robert, not this evening." She had been dumping her son in her mother-in-law's lap for too long now. Her parents had returned to Independence, and she had made up her mind to be the woman she had been before Frank James. Proud, brave, determined, the girl with a sense of adventure and humor, the one the blue-haired widows back home would call scandalous, brazen or a shameless hussy. The Annie Reynolds Ralston of 1873 would not have hidden behind a veil and forgotten her vows and responsibilities as a mother.

The time had come to see Frank, talk to him, sort out this mess.

A shadow fell over her as she brushed off Robert's pants. When she looked up, the large man with a mirthless smile and dull eyes mumbled a good evening and tousled her son's hair, which she had spent five minutes combing neatly.

"Peanut," he said in a thick Tennessee accent, "you don't mind if I have a word with your mommy, do you? 'Course not. Why don't you trot downstairs and wait for us." He fished out a coin and placed it in the boy's hand. "Treat yourself to a sarsaparilla. Your mommy don't mind."

Annie took the coin, flipped it back at him, and rose, saying, "His mother does mind. What do you want?"

While the smile vanished, those dead eyes began to show life, anger, and Raymond Sloan lowered his voice. "Gov'nor Johnson and me figger things would look a mite better for your husband if you'd sit beside him durin' the trial, ma'am. I think it's time you remembered you were his wife."

Robert asked something, and Sloan said coldly, "Put the boy in your room so we can talk freely." He punctuated the sentence by cracking his knuckles.

"Robert," she called out, but sensing something, the boy turned, bolted down the hallway and disappeared on the stairs. She screamed his name, but Sloan shoved her against the door and said, "He'll be all right. You will, too, ma'am, if you listen to reason." She matched his glare and he released his hold, the smile returning, and glanced over his shoulder to make sure Robert had not returned with an army. He tilted his square head toward the door that led to the alley.

"It's 'bout time you went to see Frank. He misses you, ma'am." An urgency sounded in his voice. Scared, likely, that Robert would bring someone to his mother's rescue.

"I'll go when I'm good and ready." She didn't dare admit to this brute that she had planned on going to the jail to see Frank when he stupidly interrupted her. She cursed Charles Johnson underneath her breath, if this were indeed his idea. It wasn't Frank's. She knew her husband better than that, and neither John Philips nor Major Edwards would have tolerated such treatment. She hadn't seen Edwards all day and wondered what had happened to him.

"You'll go now, lady," Sloan said, shoving her toward the back doorway. "One way or t'other, you'll be goin'." He pushed back his coat, revealing a small, nickel-plated revolver stuck in his waistband.

She slapped him, tried to, anyway, but for a big man he was surprisingly quick and caught her wrist in a viselike grip, spun her around and forced her toward the door. "Let go of me," she said through the pain, "or so help me God, I'll scream."

Sloan relented, and she faced him again, rubbing her aching wrist. Apparently, the oaf had not considered her screaming. He twisted the ends of his mustache while staring at her blankly before glancing down the empty hallway. In a town like Gallatin, a man caught mistreating the wife of Frank James would likely be lynched.

"You'd best leave," she said. "I'll see my husband on my own volition."

"You'll see him now," he said, and drew the pistol, cocking it, and placing the barrel against her throat. If Robert had not returned with a posse by now, he likely was cowering in the crowded lobby, his sobs going unnoticed by hungry or hurried patrons. "And you'll be a dutiful wife from now on. 'Cause if you don't, and if you even think about screamin', I'll wallpaper this hallway with them golden locks of yourn and your brains. That might be cause for a mistrial, don't you think?" He laughed, and she realized that he wasn't entirely stupid. "That's why I was hired," Sloan added. "To get your husband off, and a mistrial is a damned good start."

"You'd best pull the trigger now," she said, closing her eyes.

The pistol barrel pushed harder against her throat. She tried to swallow but found her mouth too dry. Annie heard the revolver cock, then remembered Sloan had already thumbed back the hammer, and no longer felt the coldness of the Smith & Wesson. The next things she heard were metallic clicks—sounds she had grown familiar with during her marriage—and a heavy thud.

Forcing open her eyes, she saw Raymond Sloan stepping back, hands raised, a wicked revolver barrel pressed behind his left ear. William Wallace held his Thunderer, and behind him stood her white-faced son. She comprehended the noises she had heard. Wallace had cocked his own weapon, even though it was double-action and could be fired without thumbing back the hammer, and Sloan had lowered the hammer of his tiny popgun and let it fall to the floor. Annie felt it at her feet and kicked it away.

"Step outside," Wallace said in a hoarse whisper, and Sloan opened the door that led to the outside stairwell. Sloan looked resolved, but anger clouded Wallace's face, a look that scared her more than the burly man's threats.

The two men moved passed her and slammed the door. "It's all right, Robert," she said. "Wait here for one minute." She spun, jerked open the door just in time to see Sloan tumbling down the stairwell, Wallace bounding after him, kicking Sloan in the face in the alley below, then dropping on top of him and shoving the Colt's barrel under his busted, bleeding nose.

"Don't!" Annie screamed. Nearby, the courthouse's heavy bells sounding six o'clock drowned out everything else, prevented any passerby from hearing the commotion.

Wallace's shoulders relaxed, and he pulled away his Thunderer, gently lowered the hammer, then swiftly slammed the steel frame against Sloan's head. The giant man shuddered, stained the fly of his trousers and lay still.

"What?" Colonel John Philips's clenched fingers whitened while his face turned the shade of a ripe beet. "Where is the son of a bitch?" he asked Wallace. They sat in the crowded Alpine Palace's dining room, and Philips didn't give a damn how many people heard him swear.

"Shackled in my hotel room."

Philips's eyes darted from Wallace to Hamilton to Annie James to Robert, finally settled back on the Jackson County prosecutor, who was doing most of the talking, although Annie James filled in a few details. Raymond Sloan had threatened her, was forcing her to go see her husband, when Wallace had intervened, knocked the lout unconscious and, after he came to, prodded him to the lawyer's room upstairs, where he was interrogated and, courtesy of manacles purloined by William Hamilton, left chained to a bedpost.

"Annie." Philips turned back to his client's wife. "Annie, I swear I had no part in this, nor did Frank."

"I know that, Colonel," she said kindly. "He says it was Governor Johnson's idea, that they have—in Sloan's words— been ridding Gallatin of certain undesirables."

Philips swore again, softly this time, and pushed away from his table. "That explains why Major Edwards left town on such short notice. Johnson had been complaining about his drinking binges—well, so did I—but I don't . . . I can't believe Governor Johnson would have any part in this."

"Sloan could be lying," Hamilton suggested.

Johnson would certainly deny it. No matter. "What do you propose?" Philips asked, calmer now, but worried about how

Sloan's stupidity could affect the trial. "Going to Judge Good-man and asking for a mistrial?"

Wallace shook his head. "As far as we know, Sloan didn't try to intimidate any witnesses. No state witnesses that I know of. I suggest we do like Sloan wants, and rid Gallatin of one more undesirable."

What a relief. Philips relaxed his fingers. He didn't want a mistrial; he needed an outright acquittal. He liked William H. Wallace and wished they were on the same team. The man had wit, a certain style, integrity beyond reproach. "I think the de-fense can supply a one-way ticket for Mr. Sloan to Tennessee," Philips said, "if the state can escort him to the depot tonight."

Wallace and Hamilton answered with smiles.

Chapter 27

Drunkenness is nothing but voluntary madness.
　　　　　　　　　—Seneca, *Epistulae ad Lucilium*

August 31, 1883
Gallatin, Missouri

She brought Robert to the opera house that morning. She no longer hid behind a veil, although she still sat in the upper balcony, and if anyone recognized her, they remained respectfully silent. Thanks to Raymond Sloan, Annie James had delayed visiting her husband. Sloan's threats made her wary of Frank again. Sure, Colonel Philips had sworn that neither Frank nor anyone else on the defense team had known of Sloan's activities, but she wanted to study her husband today, make sure that this was the Frank James she had loved and married.

Annie James could care less about the morning testimony. More train witnesses said they couldn't identify Frank James as one of the bandits, and a handful of others talked about stolen horses, Jim Cummins, Charlie Ford and swore that Frank James had been in Texas during the summer of 1881, although Annie knew better. Frank had taken part in the Winston robbery, but she didn't know if he had killed Frank McMillan or William Westfall. Until her husband had admitted he cold-bloodedly murdered the cashier at Northfield, she never once considered him capable of such cruelty.

Yesterday evening, however, she had seen a side of soft-spoken William Wallace that caused her to gasp. He had turned into some deranged animal when he attacked Raymond Sloan, and had not Annie screamed at him, Wallace might have killed the Tennessean. "I wouldn't want to sit through another murder trial," she had told him later, to which he had answered, still taut, "It might have given me great pleasure."

She stared at Frank that entire morning, grimaced at his coughs. He looked haggard, almost a corpse, and she wondered how long a man could live like that. For almost a year, he had been imprisoned. That seemed like a death sentence for a man like him, one who loved the outdoors, loved going to fairs and racetracks, loved playing with his son or taking his wife or friends to the theater. His resolve fading, Frank James looked like a man with a broken heart, and Annie felt her own heart sink. She had broken it.

"There's Daddy," Robert said softly, pointing as the deputies led him away after the judge called for a dinner recess. "I miss Daddy. When can he come home?"

"I don't know, Robert," she said, feeling a lone tear roll down her cheek. "I miss him, too."

He carried a shimmer in his eyes and swagger in his gait that afternoon. The gallery sat quietly until General Joseph Orville Shelby, hero of Westport and countless other Confederate campaigns, swayed, whirled in confusion and roared, "Where the hell do I sit?"

The chair sat three feet in front of him, and a nervous Sheriff Crozier swallowed hard, gently called out Shelby's name and guided him to his place. Shelby crossed his legs after sitting, combed his long hair with his fingers and nodded contentedly. A second later, however, his mood flashed angrily, and he shot out, "Where's the judge? I want to see the judge."

"I'm right here," Judge Goodman said—no humor in his voice, either—and Shelby greeted the jurist as if tipping his hat, said something else unintelligible and recrossed his legs.

One forty in the afternoon, and Jo Shelby was in his cups.

"Your Honor," Charles Johnson said meekly, "if we may have a short recess, I think—"

"There will be no recess, Governor." Goodman turned his anger on the defense team. "If you want to question this witness, get on with it."

As Johnson sank in his chair, John Philips muttered, "There are two more undesirables you should have evicted from Gallatin: General Shelby and yourself." He stood angrily, shook his head, and approached Missouri's greatest hero of the Lost Cause. He liked Jo Shelby, actually respected the man as a warrior, but there was no excuse for his condition. Johnson had seen what Shelby was capable of when they interviewed him at his estate, and should have made arrangements to keep him sober—especially today—but the great former lieutenant governor had been too consumed with his own affairs, or maybe his nefarious plots with Raymond Sloan.

"General, would you state your name and place of residence for the court?"

"I am Joseph Orville Shelby, General Jo Shelby, and have for thirty-four years resided in Lafayette County. I live nine miles from Lexington and nearer Page City."

"Did you know any of the following men: Jesse James, Dick Liddil, Bill Ryan and/or Jim Cummins?"

"Indeed." Shelby thwarted a belch and shifted his legs once more as if his kidneys were about to rupture. "I remember those four men comin' to my place in November of 1880. I was spreadin' hemp at the time, workin' some twelve or fifteen men, and when I returned home that evenin' I found four men with horses in my yard. Jesse James was there. Young Cummins I knowed before, and this man Liddil passed as Mr. Black at that time. They spent the night, bein' good ol' rebel soldiers, and the next morn I had a conversation with Jesse James, in the presence of Dick Liddil, in which I said that a couple of young men had been arrested for supposed complicity with the alleged bank robbery at Concordia, and that I didn't think they had nothin' to do with it. So I told Jesse if he knew anything about that affair to tell me, and he said, said while he was pointin' at Dick Liddil, 'There is the man that hit the Dutch cashier over his head.'"

Philips let out a sigh. Drunk or not, Shelby was doing fine. He had implicated Dick Liddil in the Concordia robbery, although hearsay, and suggested that the state's star witness was nothing more than a brute, not a man to be trusted. If Shelby could keep it up . . .

"Was that your only meeting with Jesse James and Dick Liddil?"

"Not at all, suh. The followin' fall I remember meetin' Jesse and Liddil in my lane, and saw two more riders ahead of 'em whom I could not quite make out, so when I asked Jesse who was ahead of them, he replied, Jim Cummins and Hite. Wood or Clarence, I disremember."

"Was that after the Winston train robbery?"

"Yes, suh."

"Was Frank James with his brother?"

"No, suh. I recollect askin' Jesse about Frank, and he announced that Frank's health was such that he had been south for years, and when I asked Liddil the same question, he said he had not seen Frank for two years."

"How well do you know Jim Cummins?"

The legs crossed again. "I reckon I know Cummins better than any man except the Fords and his own people. I knew him in the army—the Confederate Army—and since the war. He has been at my house a dozen times."

"And when was the last time you saw Frank James?"

"I have not seen Frank since 1872, but I believe he sits right there now." Turning toward Goodman, Shelby asked, "With the permission of the court, can I be tolerated to shake hands with an old soldier?"

"No, sir," Goodman barked, and slammed his gavel to silence the infectious laughter spreading throughout the opera house. "Not now."

Philips tried not to groan and, as soon as quiet returned to the proceedings, asked, "Are you sure you have not seen him, before today, since 1872, General? I mean, the state has brought about witnesses who say he was in Missouri in the summer of 1881. Can you be absolutely certain that the men you saw in 1881 were Jesse James, Jim Cummins, Dick Liddil and one of the Hite brothers?"

"I have not seen him since seventy-two. I am correct about it, suh, when I say that the four parties to whom I have alluded by name did not include Frank James, who was not with 'em."

Shelby belched, but, thankfully, no one heard him but

Philips. "And what about your seeing Mrs. Frank James that spring?"

"Well, it seems a lady arrived at Page City. Now I can't talk about dates, like any other farmer. But that spring, Mrs. Scott, a widow woman whose husband was captain of the Third Louisiana and who died at Wilson's Creek, well, she sent her son over to see me, and he stated there was a lady who wanted to see me. Well, suh, I went at once, and Mrs. James said to me, 'I am in distress. This mad Liddil and others are committin' depredations in the South, and they are holdin' my husband amenable for it, as he has been charged with being connected with 'em. I have come over on purpose to ask you to intercede with the gov'nor.'

"I told her there was no necessity for that, and no hope of success. She wanted me to interfere on her husband's behalf with the gov'nor, but I told her it was folly to do so, and advised her to go home to her father. I think I remained half an hour talkin' to her. She remained at Mrs. Scott's all night, and she didn't stop at my house although she could have stopped there if she had desired."

The man held up pretty well, Philips thought, and at least no one in the jury or gallery could smell Shelby's potent breath, although after the earlier outbursts, everyone in the opera house had to realize that Jo Shelby was roostered. "General," Philips continued, "we have heard much testimony from the state's witnesses about some scwing machine that, for some reason I can't comprehend, my esteemed colleagues prosecuting Frank James believe links my client to the Winston train robbery. Could you provide us with any insight regarding this sewing machine?"

Shelby nodded, moved his legs again and said, "I don't know what time the sewin' machine arrived there. She simply gave the agent at the depot directions for shippin' it. I don't know where she directed it to be shipped at all." He shifted, pulled himself forward in the chair, and Philips spotted the anger flaming in his eyes. "I was only assistin' a woman in distress." He launched into some nonsensical, profanity-laced tirade until Goodman's gavel sounded like a pistol shot, and

Philips backed away as the judge told Shelby he would behave himself or face a fine for contempt of court.

Shelby mumbled an apology and continued in a softer voice. "Mrs. James left orders with the agent for the shipment of the sewin' machine. She was a lone woman, with a little child, and cryin', and any man who would have faltered in givin' suggestion or aid ought to be ashamed of himself."

"No Missourian has every faulted your chivalry, General. She was alone with only her son? Is that right, sir? Her husband was not with her?"

"No, suh. Frank James wasn't there."

"How long have you known Frank?"

"Since 1862, suh. I know him now, the first time I have seen him in twelve years. I got acquainted with him in our army."

"Thank you, General. I have no more questions."

Philips returned to his seat, feeling pretty good considering what he had to work with, but he feared how easily Shelby could be massacred by William Wallace.

Wallace tried not to laugh as he passed Shelby on his way to the witness chair. He politely asked the drunken fool if he would mind returning to his seat for a few more questions. Shelby answered with a grin, spun on his bootheels and marched back to a few snickers from the newspapermen.

"This sewing machine," Wallace began, "you didn't see it at all?"

"Nobody knows better than yourself that I didn't see it." Shelby had turned defensive, fists clenched, eyes hard, no longer fidgeting in his seat.

Judge Goodman had tired of Shelby's inebriation. "Answer the question in a straightforward manner," he said, and Shelby obliged.

"You didn't have anything to do with it at all?" Wallace asked.

"Nothin' in the world."

"Sir, you are just as sure of that as you are sure of anything else?" That was a slap at Shelby's intoxication, although the general was far too inebriated to catch the insult.

"Yes, and I am just as sure of anything else." Locating

Goodman again, Shelby pleaded, "I'd like to know if you is gonna permit a lawyer to insult an unarmed man, a witness in this case?"

"Every witness comes in here unarmed, sir," Goodman said wearily and motioned for Wallace to continue.

"What are your initials?"

Shelby scoffed. "If you are desirous of knowin', go to a bank here and you'll find out."

The gavel hammered. "Answer his question."

"Joseph O. Shelby is my name," he said petulantly.

"Then your initials would be J.O.S."

"Go to the banks."

Wallace handed the witness a piece of paper he had been carrying during his examination. "Look at this waybill, General, and see if that has 'J.O.S.' as the consignor of that sewing machine." He took the paper from the uncooperative Shelby, introduced it as evidence and handed it to the nearest juror. "There may be a great many J.O.S.'s," he said facetiously. "Who in that area has those initials beside you?"

"You had better go and inquire," Shelby said hoarsely.

It was Goodman's time to explode. "I won't have any more nonsense of that kind, General Shelby. You will have to answer questions as they are put."

"You ain't protectin' me a'tall," Shelby whined, and Colonel Philips quickly rose and requested a recess, but Shelby shook his head. "Not a'tall, not a'tall. Better let it go on." Philips, looking like he was about to lose his dinner, sat down in defeat while Goodman continued his lecture.

"General Shelby," the judge said, and the reporters' pencils scratched vigorously, "you are a man that I respect and a man with a statewide reputation as a gentleman. We did not expect such demeanor in this courtroom, and I must admonish you that I cannot permit this to go on any further."

Shelby pulled himself from his chair, fluttered a bit on his bootheels and lashed out at Goodman while jabbing his finger in Wallace's direction, muttering more nonsense that had Wallace shaking his head in disbelief and the newspaper reporters grinning as they filled pages with Shelby's sloshed babble.

When Shelby finally slumped back in his chair, Wallace picked up where he had left off.

"I ask you, sir, if when Mrs. Frank James came there with a sewing machine to be shipped, you did not yourself become the consignor and ship it thence to Independence for the purpose of keeping anyone else from getting track of it."

"No, suh! I did not."

"Then I ask you if this 'J.O.S.'"—he picked up the bill from the last juror and handed it to the bailiff—"does not indicate that?"

"Not at all," Shelby said testily. "She arrived there as I related." He began another diatribe, berating Dick Liddil and William Wallace, until Goodman's gavel cannonaded, and for a moment, Wallace thought the judge himself might be incited to curse or clobber the witness.

"All right, Judge," Shelby said, waving his hand at Goodman and sneering at Wallace. "He's forced it on me. If I am guilty of a misdemeanor, correct me or punish me for it."

"I shall do it," Goodman snapped.

"When did you last see Dick Liddil?" Wallace asked.

"That viper! I don't recall."

"Didn't you see him at the hotel the other night," Wallace said with a smile, "or was that a drummer that you took for him?"

"No, suh. By no means."

Having caught Shelby in a lie, and one easy to prove, Wallace raised his voice. "Were you not about to kill the drummer, thinking he was Dick Liddil?"

"I have lived thirty-four years in this state and never killed anybody," Shelby fired back, eyes locked on Wallace, "*yet.*"

"Answer the question!" Goodman thundered.

"I was not!"

Wallace continued his assault. "This gentleman was seated in the Alpine Palace Hotel's dining hall while I was there. I have his card in my pocket. He is a Michigan man, and I can bring him forth if needed, not to mention several witnesses of this shameful incident. Now, General, did you get your pistol?"

"No, suh!"

"And what of the witnesses, myself included, you say who saw you aim your pistol at this Michigan drummer because you thought him to be Dick Liddil, a traitor to your friend Frank James?"

"They are nothin' but damned liars, as you are, you damnyankee son of a bitch."

Goodman's gavel slammed again. "General, I want no more remarks such as that or I will fine you fifty dollars."

Wallace waited for the murmur in the gallery to die. "I'm a Southerner, General, Kentucky-born and Missouri-bred," he said softly, then lifted his voice to continue his assault. "Isn't it true, sir, that you in fact did see Frank James in 1881?"

"No, it ain't. The last time I saw Frank was in 1872. He was bleedin' at the lungs then and stayed with me two or three months."

"You protected him, as you protected Jesse James, even though you knew they were wanted by authorities."

"I would shelter and protect anyone, suh, even a federal soldier, providin' they was Christian gentlemen."

"You know Jim Cummins well?"

"Indeed."

"He doesn't look a thing like Frank James, does he?"

"I reckon it depends on your point of view, suh. I'd say a cur dog like Bill Ryan looks a lot like you." He smiled and hiccuped.

Shaking his head, Wallace walked away. "I'm finished, Your Honor," he said.

"Judge," Shelby said from his seat, "would it be all right, now that I'm done, if I walked over yonder and shook hands with Frank James, my comrade?"

"Call on him some other time," Goodman said icily, "and remove yourself from this courtroom."

Shelby hiccuped again, pulled himself out of the chair and weaved a path that took him near Frank James, where he whispered, "God bless you, ol' fella," before stumbling out of the opera house.

Chapter 28

*If I admitted that these stories were true, people would
say, "There is the greatest scoundrel unhung!" And if I
denied 'em, they'd say, "There's the greatest liar on
earth!" So I just say nothing.*

—Frank James

September 1, 1883
Gallatin, Missouri

Criminal cases would be a hell of a lot easier if it weren't for
witnesses. At times, they were as unpredictable and unreliable
as attorneys. William Wallace had no idea what strategy the
defense really thought the jury would believe. Every time he
became convinced that Philips and Johnson had committed to
the Jim Cummins theory, they brought forth a witness who
said only two men entered the smoking car on the night of July
15, 1881.

The bandit sported a beard. The bandit had only a mustache.
Mustache and whiskers. A fake beard. The outlaws wore
dusters. No, they didn't. For that matter, the state witnesses
had not been overconsistent. The defendant killed both men.
The defendant only shot McMillan. Jesse James murdered
Westfall to force his gang to stay on the owlhoot trail. Jesse
James murdered Westfall because the conductor carried the
Pinkertons on their assassination raid in 1875. Or because he
thought the conductor was drawing a gun.

What was the jury supposed to believe?

It didn't matter, really. Not today. Frank James's sister,

Susan Parmer, and her husband swore that the outlaw had spent much of the summer of 1881 in Texas and couldn't have committed the crime at Winston, and stuck to their story during Wallace's heated cross, although he scored a major point. When Allen Parmer said Frank James had worked on his ranch some, Wallace introduced the stockman's ledger books for 1881 into evidence and found no Frank James, nor any of his known aliases, on the payroll. Now none of that meant a damn. For all of the state witnesses, including Dick Liddil, and all of the defense witnesses, including the whiskey-soaked Jo Shelby, every previous bit of testimony had been forgotten. Everything would depend on the witness taking the stand this afternoon.

"Are you the defendant in this case?" Colonel Philips asked.

"Yes," Frank James answered.

"Begin your statement of the history of this case, where the prosecution began, with the time of your departure from Missouri for Tennessee some years back. When was that?"

"That was in the winter of 1876, if I remember it correctly."

"Where did you go and stay?"

"Well, sir, it is quite a route to follow it all around. I ranged across southeast Missouri directly into Tennessee, crossing the Mississippi River, I think, perhaps about between the first and fifth of January, if I am not mistaken."

"When did you arrive in Nashville?"

"I didn't get there till July 1876." He went on, detailing where he rented and worked, his testimony interrupted only by his coughing spells, amplified in the starkly quiet opera house. No one in the audience spoke, not even whispered, and Wallace doubted if anyone would dare blink while Frank James talked. Even the newspaper reporters' pencils worked quietly.

"When and where did you meet your brother and Bill Ryan for the first time in Tennessee?"

"My first meeting with Dingus, uh, Jesse, was entirely accidental." Frank James spoke easily, like a trained actor, his friendly eyes addressing Philips, various jury members, the judge or his mother. Johnson and Philips might have coached him a little, but this man was a natural entertainer, and Wallace would have a hard time chiseling through the outlaw's facade during his cross. "I was farming on the Walton place and had gone to the B. S. Rhea & Son store. While I was sampling oats and talking to one of the clerks, Jesse walked out of the office, came up to me and says, 'Why, how do you do?' I spoke to him—didn't call him any name, of course—and told him I was living in Humphreys County, which, if I am not mistaken, is one hundred miles west of Nashville. That was in the spring of seventy-eight, in late February or the first of March."

"And Ryan?"

"That was in the fall or winter of seventy-nine, I think. I am not positive to that date."

"Where did you meet him?"

"At my house. He had returned there with Jesse. Dick Liddil was there, too, on and off. I was a little apprehensive when they were together."

"Why was that?"

"Well, they were making trips to and fro, and knowing their temperament, I thought it might bode ill for my plans to live in peace with my family. That's why I lied to my brother about where I lived, but he found me out eventually, as you see."

"Your concerns were well-founded as you learned upon Bill Ryan's arrest."

"Yes, sir. I left after the arrest. My first purpose was to protect my life so as to be able to support my family, and secondly to get shut of those parties who were around me. I could not prevent it. Of course, I had no control of things, and that was the reason I left there and went to Logan County, Kentucky, to George B. Hite's, who had married a sister of my father's for his first wife. I don't recall the date we arrived there, nor how long we stayed. I think, however, we arrived in the latter part of March, or the first of April."

He went on with his testimony, and Philips eased back to the defense table, which he leaned against while listening. This was Frank James's show, and he did most of the talking. He left his brother and the other outlaws in May and began his journey, alone, to Texas by horse, buggy and train, arriving at his sister Susie Parmer's place in early June. He stayed there five or six weeks, then took a ride into the Indian nations for ten or fifteen days and wound up in Denison, Texas, where he learned of the Winston robbery.

"How did you hear of the Winston train robbery?"

"I cannot state whether I read of it in a newspaper or whether somebody told me." He coughed again, apologized to the jury, wiped his mouth with a handkerchief and continued. "After that, I went back to my sister's in Clay County, stayed there through August and part of September. I'm sure I left my sister's between the tenth and fifteenth of September 1881. I know as I returned on that trip I heard of the Blue Cut robbery."

"Where were your wife and son during this time?"

Frank James hesitated, searched the upper balcony briefly, and forced a smile when his gaze returned to Colonel Philips. "When I left Tennessee, I gave my wife directions to go see General Shelby and see if there could be any arrangements with the governor for my surrender." He now turned to the jury box. "If I could have a fair and impartial trial accorded me, I felt perfectly satisfied I could be cleared beyond a doubt. I told her if anything could be done in this behalf to communicate with me in North Texas, otherwise go to her brother in California. She went there."

"What did you do while in Texas?"

"Not much. I needed rest, for the three and a half years of hard work in Tennessee had told on my health. I would sit and read and lounge, not really engaged in anything while I was there. When I left my sister's that September, I went up again to Denison and to the Chickasaw Nation, stayed there, oh, two or three weeks, then went to Kentucky. My wife met me there some time in the latter part of October."

"You never received any word regarding your petition to surrender?"

"No, sir, else my wife would not have gone on to California and I would not have remained in hiding."

"After your wife and son joined you, what did you do?"

"We took the Cincinnati Southern to Chattanooga, Tennessee, stayed at the Stanton House. From there we went over the E.T.V. & G. Railway to Bristol, changed cars there for the Norfolk and Northwestern, which carried us to Lynchburg."

His testimony ended like that, full of tiresome details that, upon closer inspection, really weren't that detailed at all. He concluded with his surrender to Governor Crittenden, denied ever shipping any arms to Missouri and said, in fact, that he had only been in the state once since 1876, and that was while passing through on his way to Kentucky in the fall of eighty-one—well after the Winston robbery.

Frank James had cited a lot of names and places, not too many dates, though, yet most of his testimony had been rather vague. Wallace grasped that thought when he stood up to begin his interrogation, but opted for a different beginning.

"'If thou speak'st false,'" he said, hoping he could remember just enough to get by, "'upon the next tree shalt thou hang alive till famine cling thee.'" The light in the defendant's eyes almost made Wallace smile, but he remained in character. "'If thy speech be sooth, I care not if thou dost for me as much. I . . .'"

When Wallace shrugged, Frank James cleared his throat and continued:

> "'I pull in resolution, and begin
> To doubt th' equivocation of the fiend,
> That lies like truth: "Fear not, till Birnam Wood
> Do come to Dunsinane!" And now a wood
> Comes toward Dunsinane. Arm, arm, and out!
> If this which he avouches does appear
> There is nor flying hence nor tarrying here.
> I 'gin to be aweary of the sun,
> And wish th' estate o' th' world were now undone.
> Ring the alarum bell! Blow wind, come wrack!
> At least we'll die with harness on our back.'"

"You have a fine memory for the classics," Wallace said.

James bowed graciously from the witness chair. "*Macbeth* is one of my favorites."

"Did Jim Cummins or Jesse James enjoy Shakespeare, too?"

"I wouldn't call Cummins a lettered man," he said smugly. "My brother favored the Bible."

"When did you last see your brother Jesse?"

"We separated in southeast Missouri when I went to Tennessee in 1876."

"Where did he go?"

"I don't know."

"How did you travel to Tennessee?"

"In a wagon."

"Studebaker? Phaeton?"

"I don't recall."

"Did you enjoy your stay in Texas?"

"It was relaxing."

"You did a lot of traveling."

"I rode to and fro, like I told Colonel Philips."

"You said you went from Denison back to your sister's place?"

"That's right."

"Tell us about the trip."

He blinked, and his cocksure look vanished. "Not much to tell," he said and coughed slightly.

"What was the country like?"

"Hot. Like it is here."

"Really?"

"Well, maybe not so hot."

"Green like Missouri in the summer? What kind of trees? What were the roads like?"

"I really couldn't tell you. Guess I wasn't paying much attention."

"But your testimony revealed lots of information about railroads you took and towns you visited, places you stayed. Surely, you must remember something about a horseback ride from Denison to your sister's house."

He opened his mouth, but never said a word, and closed it after a moment and just shrugged.

"Did you meet anyone?"

"No."

"Oh, come on, Mr. James. You had to meet several people in Denison, and I'm sure you weren't the only traveler on the road from that fair city to your brother-in-law's ranch. Certainly you met somebody."

"Well, yeah, maybe. I guess so. Just nobody I'd met before."

"Such as?"

"Well, I think I met this cowboy—"

"What was his name?"

"Gosh, it's been a while—"

"Details, Mr. James. You can tell us exactly what train you took from this point to that point and which boardinghouse you spent the night. You can quote Shakespeare as well as any actor, so I am sure you can remember the names of any cowboys you met in Texas. Can't you remember one name?"

"Objection!" Charles Johnson shouted.

"Overruled."

"But he's badgering the witness!"

"I don't think so. Answer the question, sir."

Frank James wiped his face with a handkerchief, stared toward the balcony and finally said, "Haynes. I think his name was Haynes."

"Where did you meet him?"

"Clay County, Texas, I think. He worked for J. H. Stone & Company, a big outfit down yonder."

"Your brother-in-law, Allen Parmer, has a substantial spread himself, does he not?"

"He's done well for Susie and himself. I'm proud of him."

"You worked for him while in Texas, you say."

"Not much. Just some odds and ends to help earn my keep. That's why I wasn't on his payroll. See, I was plumb tuckered out from working so hard in Tennessee. I mostly read and relaxed to get my health back."

"How many people did Allen Parmer employ?"

"Oh, I couldn't tell you. Depends on the time of year."

"You met some of them I assume."

"I . . . no. I didn't meet any of them hands. Don't recall any names."

He had gotten wiser, remembered the ledger book was already admitted into evidence. Wallace smiled and asked, "Even when you did some of those odds and ends?"

"I worked alone. I had to be careful back then."

"Sure. I understand. Who was the county sheriff?"

"I don't recall."

"But certainly a careful man like you would know the local authorities. Who was the sheriff?"

"Asked and answered," Philips said. "The witness said he does not remember."

The judge agreed, and told Wallace to move on.

It was time to throw down the gauntlet. Wallace leaned forward, close enough to Frank James that he could see the sweat coming out of his pores. "You were in Missouri in the summer of 1881, Mr. James. Isn't that the truth of the matter? You were with Jesse, Dick Liddil and the Hite brothers. Isn't that the real truth?"

"No, sir."

"You stole horses for the train robbery!"

"I did not."

"You were seen, sir. You were seen with Clarence Hite in Indianapolis in 1881. You were seen at Georgetown as well. You worked with your brother. You went into the smoking car after the train left Winston with your Remington revolver drawn, and you fired. You fired constantly, sir, and it was you who killed Frank McMillan. Isn't that the truth?"

"None of it. I was in Texas at that time."

"Sure, but the only proof you have of that is testimony from your sister and brother-in-law, family, blood as you call it, with every reason to lie. You were in Texas, but no one else saw you except some cowboy named Haynes? How could anyone believe that, sir? You killed Frank McMillan. You shot him dead. Admit it."

"No, sir. I am innocent."

Wallace whirled around and marched back to his seat. "I'm finished with this witness," he said bitterly and sat down. He hadn't expected to shake Frank James. A man who had ridden through countless guerrilla raids with villains like Quantrill, Anderson and Todd, an outlaw who had been committing depredations since the War, Frank James wasn't one to be intimidated in a court of law. Wallace had done some damage, though, and would do more with his rebuttal witnesses. The jury had to see that Frank James was guilty. They had to.

"Redirect, counselor?" Goodman asked.

"No, Your Honor," Charles Johnson answered. "At this time, the defense rests."

"Very well," the judge said. "If that is all, then we will begin rebuttals on Monday at eight thirty."

John Philips rose quickly and told Goodman that there was a request from a gentlemen waiting outside. Jo Shelby, he said, wanted permission to address the court.

"Is he armed?" John Shanklin quipped from the state's bench, but Goodman found no humor in the remark. For that matter, neither did William Wallace.

Chapter 29

*Well, the only apology I desire to make is that every man
reserves the right to make a damn fool of himself now
and then.*

—General Joseph Shelby

September 1, 1883
Gallatin, Missouri

Gone were the cock-of-the-walk attitude and drunken sway.
He walked down the aisle, head bowed, chagrined, looking
more like a scolded hound dog than the great Confederate
general. Jo Shelby didn't look up until he stood in front of
Goodman, muttered something no one could understand and,
hands clasped at his waist, cleared his throat and said
meekly, "If anything that I may have said or done yesterday
offended the dignity of the court, I regret it exceedingly."
Turning to the crowd, he continued to look apologetic as his
eyes crossed the defense table, but as soon as he saw William
Wallace, his voice turned bitter. "As to other parties, I have
no regrets."

Which brought Judge Goodman to his feet, his face masked
by anger as he pointed the gavel at the sober, though likely
hungover, Shelby.

"General Shelby," Goodman barked, "your conduct in ap-
pearing before the court in an unfit condition and showing an
insubordinate spirit was reprehensible in the extreme, as it was
not only in defiance of the dignity of the court, but calculated
to prejudice the interest of the defendant. You are a man of na-

tional reputation and enjoy the respect and confidence of a large number of people of Missouri." The gavel's hammer shook at each point, and Wallace would not have been surprised to see the judge hurl the wooden instrument like a tomahawk. "I can only say that I was much astonished at your actions. The court is amply satisfied with your apology to it, but your attitude toward the attorneys for the state in answering in a threatening and offensive manner and your talk of calling them to a personal account cannot be overlooked." Goodman's gavel slammed—almost broke. "You are fined ten dollars, sir."

After opening a small purse, Shelby handed the judge a greenback and left the courtroom, whispering to Wallace as he passed. "This ain't over."

September 2, 1883
Gallatin, Missouri

"You have a letter," the hotel desk clerk told Wallace. "I meant to tell you about it yesterday evenin', but truthfully, I've just been swamped. All these people . . ." He glanced around the crowded lobby and shrugged.

"Won't be long till we're all out of your hair," Wallace said as the carrot-topped teenager handed him the envelope and his key. After crushing out his cigar in an ashtray, Wallace slipped the key into his coat pocket, tore open the envelope and pulled out the letter.

Us tru & sworn frends of our hero hav ben watchin the evidens & we mean bisnes, the sloppy scrawl began, and Wallace checked the postmark—Independence—before finding a chair to finish reading the threat.

> *U dam sonsobitchs wil be in Hades befor the new year The days r numberd for that cowrd Liddil & them dam Ford boys as me & my pals Will be in Galatin 2day*
> *Dam ur ignorant hid frank James was not at them robres Jesse don the Kilin & By God u know it If frank is*

convictd we shal aveng this purjre by kilin more of u
dam sonsobitchs than ther r hairs on franks heaD so u
must watch what u say in ur finl statment r els u r 1
DED man

A Frend

"Letter from home?"

Wallace found William Hamilton, satchel in hand, shook his head and handed his colleague the note. The two had planned to meet at Wallace's hotel room to make final preparations for rebuttal testimony. "As soon as I'm back in Jackson County," Wallace said, "I think I'll try to get a law that prohibits idiots from access to ink, paper and stamps."

Hamilton didn't seem amused when he returned the letter. "It might be wise to take something like this seriously."

"It's not Jo Shelby's handwriting."

"I'm not kidding, William. Crozier's deputies have collected forty-some-odd pistols and knives from people with tickets to the trial, trying to get inside with weapons. No telling how many men have actually got inside with a gun. They could kill you, me or Judge Goodman easily."

He didn't really hear what else Hamilton had to say as his attention turned to the handsome woman coming down the stairs. Annie James didn't see him, however, and he lost her in the crowd as she made her way outside. He hadn't seen her since the Sloan incident, wondered if he would talk to her again before the trial ended, or ever see her again no matter the verdict. Hamilton's timbre caused him to look back at the county solicitor.

"What?"

"I said you haven't heard a damn thing I've said." Hamilton shook his head pityingly.

"I'm not going to let some simpleton's threats break my concentration," Wallace replied, "and as soon as I cower to intimidation, I might as well resign and go back to teaching the three R's. We have rebuttal witnesses to call and a closing argument to prepare. Let's get to it."

*　　*　　*

The hinges squeaked as one of George Crozier's deputies opened the door separating the sheriff's office from the jail cells, but Frank James, immersed in Alexandre Dumas, didn't bother looking up. Dinnertime meant more corn mush, coffee and bacon, or maybe only a bowl of broken cornbread covered with milk, hardly stimulating to anyone's appetite, and he wasn't hungry these days, just sick.

His health might be failing, but his ears remained as alert as they had been during his guerrilla days. He detected two sets of footfalls, and knew one immediately, yet couldn't bring himself to look up from the pages of *The Black Tulip* lest he be mistaken. Heavy keys rattled on the deputy's key ring, metal clanged, and the door to his home opened. "Visitor," the deputy muttered, closed and locked the door behind him and left. He could smell the lilac scent, still feared his eyes would betray him, but forced himself to close the novel and lift his gaze.

Annie James looked striking, as always, wearing the navy gingham dress trimmed with turkey red embroidery that he had bought her back in Chattanooga. "You'll need a new dress for our new life," he remembered telling her that fall afternoon in southeastern Tennessee. "I promise you, girl, this time I'm done with Dingus forever." He hadn't been sure if she believed him, but he had kept his word that time, and they had enjoyed their life together after settling down in Virginia.

Was she wearing this dress because she remembered? He couldn't tell anything from her face. She could be coming back to him, but just as easily could be here to ask him for a divorce. Annie hadn't brought Robert, which meant she was here to talk. She also hadn't brought anything to knit, lace or embroider.

He sat up, tossed his book aside, and tried to think of something to say. Open his heart, slice his veins, plead with her? Rush to her, embrace her? At last, he simply pointed his chin at her rocking chair and asked her to have a seat. She considered the chair for a moment, glanced his way one more time and accepted the invitation.

They just stared at each other.

"I've missed you," he said. Her mouth moved. She started to respond, but couldn't find any words. Perhaps she didn't know why she had finally come to see him.

"Colonel Philips says the state will call a few rebuttal witnesses Monday, then start closing arguments. He figures that'll take a day or two, and then the judge will charge the jury, and we . . . I'll have to wait. No telling how long it'll take to reach a verdict." He coughed and changed the subject. "Ma's been bringing Robert over a lot. I been reading to him some, Shakespeare—guess he don't understand anything, but he sits through it, anyhow. He's growing like a weed, be reading himself before too long I expect."

"He misses you," she said. "Wishes you were home." He loved her voice, had longed to hear it, and now the sound made his heart sink.

He felt the tears begin to well and stared at his scuffed boots. "Yeah, well, I miss y'all something fierce. We'll see what happens with the jury." He stared at her again, wanting to say more, but . . .

Silence and stares followed, broken by Annie's sudden: "Have you been faithful to me, Frank?"

He blinked in surprise. He never expected that. "Yeah," he said, flabbergasted, wondering what had brought that out. What he wanted to do was to rush to her, pledge his love, kiss her all over, but not yet. Small steps, he told himself. "Shoot yeah," he said more emphatically. "I can't say I never looked at another woman but, my Lord, Annie, I've never seen a gal that could light a candle compared to you." He considered reciting a sonnet but, no, Annie didn't come here to hear Shakespeare. "Now certainly we spent some time in houses of ill repute, especially in Minnesota that time, but that was for guys like Charley Pitts, Bob Younger, them boys still sowing their oats, and it was a good hideout. Law never looked once for us in a cathouse, but all those times, I'd stay in the parlor, reading, or outside keeping an eye out for the law. That's the gospel truth, Annie. I never was tempted by no whore, nor any woman. I've always been true to you."

"I have, too," she said, and quickly looked away.

"I never doubted it," he said, but wondered why. Leaving

her alone, breaking his promises to live within the law, riding
out with Dingus to rob . . . he couldn't blame her if she had.
He studied his boots again. "Annie," he said softly. "I told
you this before, but I mean it. I'm not blind. I know you'll be
looked after if things don't turn out like we had hoped." He
let out a short, mirthless chuckle. "All these folks have been
predicting how I'll go gunning for the Ford brothers if I'm
acquitted, avenge Dingus's death, but I've never had that notion. Jesse was my brother, and I loved him, but I can't
rightly say I liked him—not in the end, not after Northfield. I
can't abide with what Bob Ford done, and I'll hate the son of
a bitch forever for breaking Ma's heart like that, but I won't
go after him. Hell, somebody will do that for me—I'll likely
get blamed for it, too." He laughed again, shook his head and
raised his eyes. "I guess what I'm trying to say, Annie, is that
if . . . well . . . you got no cause to fear me, no matter what
you decide."

"Frank . . ." she said, and began sobbing.

He moved now, crossed the room, knelt beside her and felt
her head against his shoulder. He stroked her pretty hair, knew
he was crying himself. Annie pulled herself up, tears streaming, and choked out, "I want you, Frank. I want to be with you.
I want Robert to have a father." She shook her head angrily.
"God, Frank, I'm afraid that sewing machine I wanted for
Mama will be our undoing, will mean you'll spend the rest of
your life in prison or. . . ." She couldn't finish.

He kissed her hand, then patted it. "Colonel Philips doesn't
think the sewing machine will have much weight with the jury.
To him and Governor Johnson, everything comes down to
Dick Liddil's testimony, if they believe him or not."

"I shouldn't have come to Missouri," she said. "We never
should have sent that sewing machine."

"I couldn't leave you and Robert back in Tennessee, Annie.
I just couldn't." He could hear his brother's haunting laughter
again. "I never should have listened to Dingus. We just got
scared after Bill Ryan got arrested. I had to support you and
my son and, damn me, robbing banks and trains was just about
all I knew. I figured we'd have to start a new life together, but
we needed money. That's why . . ."

They embraced, and he held her tight against his chest, thanking Jesus Christ for answering his prayers, asking him for just one more favor.

"Frank," she whispered, "I have to know. What happened that night?"

Chapter 30

There has been much in my life that I don't want to think of—would to God I could forget it. Years before I quit the old life I was as tired of it as the other people.
—Frank James

July 15, 1881
Winston, Missouri

We'd been trying to rob the Express since June, but something always stopped us. Got there too late one night and missed the damned train, and Dingus come down with a toothache the next chance we got and called it off. Maybe that was the Good Lord trying to tell me not to go through with the robbery. I don't know.

Anyway, early that evening, Dingus, Liddil and me stopped off at a farmhouse for a bite of supper before meeting up with the Hite brothers at this thicket southeast of Cameron. The Hites had taken our mounts—ones we stole—and hobbled them at the point not far from the tracks where we planned on stopping the train. Hot as blazes it was. I'd hoped it would cool off a mite once the sun went down, but it didn't. Not that night. By the time we rode to Winston, it was still a regular furnace, and even the fireflies didn't have any energy. We rode in and tethered our horses to the hitching rack in front of the saloon and went over the plan one more time.

We never did believe in wearing masks. Don't know if that was our vanity or because, as Cole used to say, only a coward hides behind a mask. We'd pull down our slouch hats real low, and turn up the collars on our dusters, none of us had shaved, as you recollect, so we sported a fair amount of whiskers. In case things got hot with gunplay, all of us wore white bandanas so we wouldn't shoot each other accidentally if we got separated. We'd been hanging around Winston and Cameron off and on, getting a feel for things, and knew the Express should be carrying a right smart of money, four thousand or maybe as much as eight thousand on its run from Kansas City.

"Clarence, you and Dick get on the platform outside the baggage car," Dingus said, "then make your way to the locomotive. Don't let 'em stop the damned train. Keep it a-runnin' till we get to the hollow near the second tank."

"Nobody gets killed," I said. Wonder how many times I said that over the years before we did a job? Dingus just give one of his smirks. Looking back, I think he planned on murdering that conductor all along. So we checked the loads in our pistols, holstered them and went inside the saloon. Didn't drink any whiskey or beer, just lemonade. Couldn't afford any mistakes, thus we all stayed sober.

Once we heard the whistle, we moseyed out toward the depot. It was Friday night, but none of us had taken that into consideration, and the depot was packed solid with passengers waiting to board. That might have been the Lord's third and final sign for me, but I paid no heed. We'd been tarrying about for too long, and I had a hankering to get you and Robert out of Missouri so we could start over.

Dick Liddil and Clarence Hite went their way, and Dingus, Wood Hite and me stepped onto the platform in front of the smoking car, waiting for the conductor to wave that lantern of his and get us moving. Once the wheels started squeaking, we pulled up our collars. I reached for my plug and bit off a mouthful.

"Let's go," I said, but Dingus shook his head.

"Not yet," he said, and held out his hand for my tobaccy. I passed that to him, watched him take off a bite and start working it, then slip my tobaccy into his own pocket. He give me a wink, and I just shook my head and spit.

That's when the conductor walked past us on his way to the smoker. "Evenin' gents," he said. "Mighty warm night."

"I'm a-thinkin' it'll get even hotter," Dingus says, but there ain't no humor in his eyes. The conductor just smiled pleasantly and went inside. Damnedest thing is, he didn't ask for our tickets. Maybe he figured on getting us on his return. Maybe he was scared of us. Dingus give Wood a look, and I should have known what was coming. He nodded at Wood, gestured at the conductor and drew one of his pistols.

See, Annie, that's why I think he planned on murdering that poor man the whole time, like some folks say, and he told Wood Hite what he aimed to do. Dingus told Wood everything, more than he ever confided in me, so I think he told Wood that conductor Westfall had carried them damned Pinkertons to Ma's place back in seventy-five when they killed Archie and crippled Ma. Had I known what he was planning, I never would have boarded that train, but it was too late now.

"'For he is the minister of God to thee for good,'" Dingus said, quoting from Romans as he cocked Baby. "'But if thou do that which is evil, be afraid; for he beareth not the sword in vain: for he is the minister of God, a revenger to execute wrath upon him that doeth evil!'" I could see his eyes darkening, and he busted one of the panes of glass with his bootheel and smashed through the door.

Wood and I followed him, guns cocked and ready, and I yelled, "Hands up!"

I stayed by the door, like we had planned, and Dingus and Wood started walking down the aisle. They were just supposed to disarm anybody and toss the guns out the window, but Dingus fired a shot at the conductor, and he and Wood ran after the man, shooting and running, bouncing off the seats because the train was really picking up speed, and it was hard to stay on your feet. I was sick, madder than hell, at what they did to the poor man, but in for a penny, in for a pound, I guess, and I couldn't do a thing about it now. They threw the man off the back platform, and I pulled out my pocketknife with my left hand, braced it against the Remington till I got the blade open, and cut the emergency cord. That was part of the plan, too, to keep the passengers from signaling the engineer to hit his brakes, but I reckon I pulled too hard on the cord, because the train stopped.

That scared us for a second, but we heard the engine groan and start moving. Dick Liddil had smashed a chunk of coal against the engineer's head, convinced him to get rolling again, and it got going in a hurry, and me, Dingus and Wood stepped outside again.

"What the hell was that about?" I snapped, and had to restrain myself from grabbing Dingus by his throat and tossing him off the train. Him and Wood Hite both, the bastards. "I said nobody was to get killed!"

"I thought he was a-pullin' a gun on me, Buck," Dingus shot back, but I could see in his eyes that he was lying. He was enjoying this.

"Bullshit!" I said, but my attention turned to something else, and I looked toward the engine. I thought I heard some gunshots from there, only couldn't be sure, though one thing was certain. "We're moving too fast."

Dingus blinked, then started cursing Liddil and Clarence Hite. "Damned fools can't do nothin' right. You best get up there, Buck, and get us stopped a-fore this locomotive carries us all straight to the gallows."

I holstered my Remington, climbed on top of the baggage car and moved through the night, swaying, trying to keep my balance, forgetting everything that had happened so far, just picturing you and Robert, telling myself I had to do this for y'all. Smoke and cinder stung my eyes, and I slipped once and almost fell. I crawled the rest of the way, cussing Dingus and his black heart the whole time, jumped into the tinder and called out for Dick and Clarence—didn't want me scaring them and catching a bullet—before I dropped into the cab, saw Clarence and Dick, but no engineer or fireman.

"They jumped off the train!" Clarence yelled at me, and he was whiter than his bandana. "How the hell do we stop this thing, Frank?"

I slowed her down, and we pulled to a halt just a little past where we had planned on stopping. That's right, Annie. I might have made a fair hand as an engineer if I had put my mind to it. Wouldn't that be something if by God's mercy I get freed and become a locomotive man? Ha. Anyway, we jumped off and headed for the baggage and express car.

"How did things go back there?" Liddil asked me.

"Not worth spit," I said, and we met up with Dingus and Wood about the time the fool baggage master opened the door and stuck his head out, waving his lantern and asking, "What the hell's goin' on?"

I grabbed him by his leg and jerked him down. The lantern crashed in the dirt and exploded, but Clarence took off his duster and beat out the fire. Dingus and Wood fired a couple of rounds into the car, and the express agent hollered at us not to shoot no more, that he wasn't armed, so Wood, Dingus and me jumped inside and saw the little man stand up from behind some trucks, hands stretched high.

"Open the damned safe, you son of a bitch," Dingus tells the man, pressing the Schofield's barrel against the gent's nose. "We done kilt us two other sumbitches on this here train, and if you don't do just like we tells you, you'll be number three."

"Two?" I bit off another curse, and screamed at the agent to get moving.

He followed orders, but when we peered in the safe, the pickings looked mighty slim. Wood tossed cash and coin into a wheat sack, while Dingus slammed the barrel of his pistol against the agent's head.

"Where's the rest of the money, mister?" he screamed, but the gent just shook his head.

"That's it," he said, tears and blood streaming down his face. "On my poor mother's grave, that's all we're carryin'?"

"Horseshit!" Dingus hit the guy again, while I looked around for more money, but the guy wasn't lying to us. Clarence Hite called out that we'd best stop lollygagging around, and Dingus shoved the agent against the wall and cocked Baby.

"The conductor's a-rottin' in hell," he's telling the guy, "and so is some other sumbitch. We're a-gonna kill you, too, you worthless piece of dung, so get down on your knees and pray to God and make it quick."

"No." The agent's sand surprised me. I mean, he was crying, probably soiling his pants and shaking like he was freezing to death, but he wouldn't make it easier on my brother. Dingus just pistol-whipped the poor guy, and was about to kill him—

shoot him dead while he lay there unconscious—but I pushed him aside, told him there wouldn't be any more killing, not this night, and we left, got our horses, and skedaddled.

We rode hard, back toward Winston, figured the posse wouldn't look for us there, and counted the money at this old shack a mile from town.

"Six hundred thirty dollars and change!" Dingus tossed a handful of greenbacks atop an Arbuckles coffee crate, and kicked a hole in a rotting baseboard. "Son of a bitch."

"What happened, Dingus?" Wood asked. "We had this all planned."

"They musta switched trains on us, put the big money on the Wabash run," he said.

He wasn't the only one of us mad. Dick Liddil cursed and said, "Two men dead for this? Hell, Dingus, now I'm facin' a rope if we get caught."

"So am I," Clarence Hite said. "We all is."

"That's right, you yellow sons of bitches," Dingus said, hands on his guns, daring anyone to try his patience. "You'll hang like Judas, so don't even a-think 'bout crossin' me or Buck."

"Dingus," Wood said, always the peacekeeper, "you know us better than that. We ain't never once thunk 'bout crossin' you an' Frank."

"We'd best ride," I suggested, but Dingus shook his head. "Let's go back to town, see if maybe that money's still there, waitin' for the next train."

"Hell's bells!" I argued, but Dingus was already walking outside and swinging into the saddle. Clarence and Wood stuffed the money back in the sack, and we rode off. Dingus figured it smart if we split up, so the Hites rode south while Dingus, me and Liddil went back to Winston, a crazy idea for sure.

We stopped at the post office, and Dingus walked to the door, was just about to open it, when we heard horses. I guess the law had found our trail after all. Liddil swore—we knew it was the posse—so Dingus flew into the saddle and we raked our spurs, lit a shuck out of there before more shooting commenced.

We met up with the Hites again just before daybreak along the Crooked River, divided up the loot—what little there was—and parted company. Dingus and me went back to Ma's, hid in the woods, Ma bringing us food. Dingus was already planning to rob the train at Blue Cut as soon as things cooled off, but I told him then and there that I wanted no part of it.

"You a-plannin' on startin' a new life with Annie and that boy of yourn with a hundred twenty-six dollars, Buck?" He grinned at me like he was prone to do.

"It's a start," I answered, and started stuffing my possibles in my warbag. "I'm getting Annie and Robert, and we're going east, soon as I tell Ma good-bye."

"Buck, you ain't a-pullin' away from me and the boys just 'cause Wood and me kilt them two jackasses on that train?"

"You ain't the same, Jesse," I said, about the first time I'd called him by his Christian name in a coon's age. "Ain't nothing been the same since Northfield."

"But we're blood," he tells me.

"Yeah," I fired back, "and this time I'm washing the blood off my hands."

He didn't say nothing to that, and the emptiness returned to them cold eyes of his. Hell, he might have even been crying. I don't know. I just left him in the woods, and never saw him again, never even wanted to.

No, Annie, I didn't kill Frank McMillan, but I might have had I been in that smoker instead of going to the engine. I never asked Dingus who killed the stonemason, him or Wood. I think it was an accident, but he's dead, and I can't help thinking that had I told Dingus no—hell, I had plenty of chances—had I pulled away from them, they wouldn't have gone through with the robbery. Them two men would still be alive, and I wouldn't be facing a rope.

Chapter 31

The evidence declares that from early morning of
Monday to nightfall on Saturday, week after week, year
after year, he delved, drove teams, hauled logs, for $1.50
per day; and for five years he was no further from his
little home than the nearest trading village or town.
Respected and much liked by his neighbors, he ate his
bread in peace.

—John F. Philips, on Frank James

September 3, 1883
Gallatin, Missouri

Heavy thunderstorms Sunday night had broken the heat wave
and turned the streets of Gallatin into a quagmire. By Monday
morning, the worst of the storms had moved east while the pit-
ter-patter of raindrops on the opera house's roof sounded
pleasantly as the bailiff called court to order.

Annie James sat on the defendant's right, ever the dutiful
wife now, holding little Robert on her lap. Even brooding
Zerelda Samuel seemed to smile, glad to see the couple together again. So Annie had gone back to him, forgotten about
Northfield. Maybe not forgotten, just accepted it. *Well,* Wallace thought, *what did you expect? She's his wife, and you
knew she loved him even when . . .* He shook away his
thoughts and recalled Gallatin attorney Samuel Brosius to the
stand.

After Judge Goodman reminded the witness that he remained under oath, Wallace asked, "Who is your law partner?"

"W. C. Gillian."

"Didn't you tell him, on the day after the train robbery, that you were so scared you could not recognize any of the robbers?"

"No, sir."

"Really. Well, R. L. Tomlin, Boyd Dudley and T. B. Yates say you told them that you were so frightened during the affair that one man seemed fifteen feet tall. Are they lying, sir?"

"I doubt if they would lie, Mr. Wallace, but if I said that, it was just to introduce some levity to the situation. I do recall telling Mr. Bostaph, the druggist, that I couldn't describe the men and didn't recognize the bandits."

"I see. But you're certain Frank James wasn't there? I don't see how that's possible."

"It wasn't him, as I told you the other day."

"Thank you, sir. I am done."

Charles Johnson had just one question on cross, and Brosius reiterated that anything Dudley, Yates and Tomlin heard the day after the robbery had been an attempt at pleasantries, a simple joke. Wallace called Boyd Dudley, W. M. Bostaph, A. M. Irving, Eli Dennis, T. B. Yates, R. L. Tomlin, George Tuggle and W. C. Gillian, Brosius's partner and brother-in-law, to testify that the attorney had said he had been scared witless during the robbery and didn't know any of the bandits, nor could he ever identify them.

The newspapermen might write that he was beating a dead horse, but Wallace wanted to make sure Brosius's testimony had been impugned. Neither Johnson nor Philips bothered much with cross-examinations, although they did bring up the fact that Boyd Dudley worked in William Hamilton's office although Dudley swore that his job had nothing to do with his testimony.

Sarah E. Hite next took the stand, called to refute testimony that Wood Hite or Jim Cummins could have been mistaken for Frank James. She said that Wood Hite was untidy, never read any books, and was a typical oaf, while Frank James was neat, fond of quoting Shakespeare and didn't look a thing like either of the Hite brothers, or Cummins for that matter. Her father,

Silas Norris, followed to corroborate everything his daughter had said.

The rebuttals satisfied Wallace. Let the defense try to argue that Jim Cummins had been the fifth man, or Wood Hite had killed McMillan. Enough evidence had been introduced that one of the robbers, often identified by witnesses as the defendant, had been a well-dressed man, quite literate, fond of the classics and quick with a quotation. The Hite brothers could barely read, and Cummins talked so slow it would have taken him a week to recite a passage from *Macbeth*.

"Your Honor," Wallace announced, "the state calls United States marshal Major J. H. McGee."

Philips, Johnson and Frank James promptly huddled together, whispering excitedly as the tall man with thin sandy hair and a well-groomed mustache entered the opera house in muddy boots, swore the oath and took a seat. Having pulled a surprise of his own, Wallace felt pleased. Philips bit his lower lip, while Johnson leaned forward anxiously, both staring at the witness. The defendant reached back and gripped his wife's hand.

"Do you remember the Winston robbery, Major McGee?" Wallace asked.

"I do, because I was on the train that was robbed."

Philips leaped out of his seat. "Your Honor, I must object to the introduction of this testimony. It is ambuscade. It is not rebuttal, and the repetition of what occurred in the car is at this time out of place."

He had expected a fight—would have done the same thing had he been on the other side—and told the judge, "The state has had no witness who was in the car, while the defense introduced Mr. Brosius to detail the transactions in the car on that night."

Philips shook his head vehemently. "The state had Mr. Penn for that purpose. He talked of what occurred in the car."

This would be a free-for-all. "Major McGee is here in rebuttal as a coolheaded man who had as good opportunities to observe as Mr. Brosius," Wallace said. "Mr. Penn, Your Honor will recall, witnessed much of the robbery from the platform outside the smoking car. Major McGee was inside."

"I object!" Philips looked as if he might suffer a stroke. "The law is opposed to accumulative evidence."

Wallace stepped back, staring pleadingly at Judge Goodman, who tugged on his beard. Ever the legal mastermind, Colonel Shanklin coughed slightly before rising and telling the judge, "It is within the discretion of the court to admit an omitted witness."

"Perhaps," Goodman said, "but I cannot conceive that this testimony is in rebuttal."

"It is in the interest of justice the witness ought to be admitted," Wallace said, but he could see in Goodman's eyes that he had lost the argument even before Philips argued that the witness had been available for almost two weeks.

"He's right, gentlemen," Goodman said. "The marshal hasn't been called in rebuttal, so I will not admit his testimony."

"Your Honor," Shanklin said angrily, "I insist that the testimony should be admitted. The state should not be deprived of this testimony simply because it had been overlooked. The witness would tell nothing but the truth, and that could hurt no one but the defendant. He should not fear the truth."

William Hamilton joined the assault. "It may be stated by way of explaining the omission that Major McGee had to attend the United States court."

The judge leaned back and again stroked his beard, his eyes falling on the witness, the defendant and finally at his gavel. "All right," he said, leaning forward, "the witness will be allowed to testify in the interest of justice."

"Your Honor!" Philips shouted, but Goodman's gavel silenced him.

"I've made my ruling, counselor. Now sit down. Proceed, Mr. Wallace."

They had not called McGee earlier because he couldn't identify Frank James as one of the bandits, but Wallace and Hamilton had decided they needed him now to refute Brosius's claims that only two men entered the smoking car. Neither had been certain Goodman would allow the testimony, but the rains and cooler temperatures must have brought good fortune. Wallace returned to his table to recheck his notes, and when he looked up he saw General Jo Shelby sitting in a back row, his eyes blazing with anger.

"Major, how many bandits entered the smoking car that night?" Wallace asked, still staring at Shelby.

"Three," McGee answered, and the general leaped from his seat, spun around and stormed outside.

"Where were you sitting at the time?" Wallace looked at the marshal and leaned against the table.

"In the middle of the car."

"Scared?"

"Nervous, perhaps, but not scared. I've been in shooting scrapes before. I was unarmed at the time, so I could not put up a fight, but I thought to observe everything carefully so that the law might eventually bring these culprits to justice."

"You heard Samuel Brosius testify that only two outlaws boarded the smoking car. Is he mistaken?"

"Indeed. Three men got on with guns drawn. I am certain of that."

"Thank you, Marshal. No further questions."

"Could you identify the bandits?" Philips asked from his seat.

"No, sir. I could only tell the size or height of them."

"Why is that, sir? You are the trained observer, and we have heard testimony that these men were not donning masks."

"When the bandits entered the car, they immediately yelled for everyone to get down, and we all obeyed them, except conductor Westfall."

"I see. Can you say in all certainty that Frank James was one of the robbers?"

"No, sir. I cannot."

That answer made Philips happy.

When the last of the rebuttal witnesses had finished testifying, court adjourned at noon for the day. Nothing left but closing arguments and jury instructions, and those would begin in the morning. Overall, Wallace felt content with everything that had happened in the courtroom. Getting Marshal McGee's testimony admitted had been a pleasant victory, a surprising one at that. Dick Liddil had fared well on the stand, but so had

Frank James. Wallace's rebuttals shot down almost all of the
defense's testimony, no matter what theory they elected to
pitch. Certainly, he had tried stronger cases, but the evidence
was there. Maybe no one could identify Frank James—or
rather had the courage to identify him—as one of the bandits,
but the state had made a compelling case that linked the defendant to the crime. He was guilty of murdering Frank McMillan.

"We'll go point by point on everything during our close,"
Wallace said as he weaved a path along the wet boardwalks,
dodging men, women and children, moving like a locomotive
pulling his assistants toward the hotel. Shanklin and Hamilton
tossed out suggestions, and Wallace nodded at most of their
ideas. He carried his rain slicker tucked underneath his arm,
heavy satchel in his right hand, mind working, listening, wishing he were already at the hotel so they could start on the
speech. Even the aroma of fresh-baked bread at Rottmann's
failed to stab his stomach.

The rain had stopped, but the heavily traveled streets resembled a pigpen and smelled of horse manure and thick Missouri
mud. An omnibus churned its way through the sludge heading
to the depot, a crowd waited two dozen deep outside the café,
and two cowboys rolled their smokes while rehashing the
day's testimony and trying to decide who had the upper hand.
Listening to the myriad singsong voices, Wallace had to wonder how many more people would descend upon Gallatin to
hear the closing statements and wait for the jury's verdict.

Shanklin made a joke and punctuated it by emptying his spit
can into the muddy street. Hamilton made another suggestion,
which prompted an enthusiastic debate among Joshua Hicklin
and Marcus Low. Wallace paid little attention. Finally clear of
the crowd, he dropped his head and tried to think if he had
missed something during the trial, some point he should have
hammered home, some statement a witness had made that he
should have noticed and either trashed or praised.

One fleeting thought caused his heart to quiver. *The only
thing you missed was Annie.*

Civic-minded deputies had laid two-by-eight planks across

the filthy streets to connect the boardwalks, and Wallace, still looking down, put his right foot on the makeshift bridge.

"Dear Jesus Christ in heaven," Hamilton said suddenly, and Wallace stopped, realized the city block had suddenly turned quiet. He looked up and almost dropped his satchel and slicker into the filth.

Standing across the street, about to step on the plank himself, stood Joseph Orville Shelby.

Their eyes locked. Shelby's hands were hidden inside the black India rubber poncho he wore over his suit, and could easily have gripped a gun. Wallace's coat was buttoned, slicker pressed between his right arm and side, satchel in his right hand, and it would take him a lifetime to reach the Colt in his shoulder holster.

He was a dead man.

Waiting. Wallace didn't know how long they stood there, probably just ten or fifteen seconds, although it seemed much longer. Shelby stepped away from the plank as his right hand appeared—empty—and swept off the black hat.

With a dramatic bow, Jo Shelby called out, "You pass first, Mr. Wallace."

Voices again. Excited chatter. Laughter. The tension had passed. Wallace pulled the train of prosecutors across the trestle without incident, each man paying respects to the smiling Shelby, and made a beeline for the second-story room at the Alpine Palace Hotel, where, had someone offered him a whiskey, William H. Wallace gladly would have accepted.

Chapter 32

It is plain that the attempt to prove an alibi has been a
most miserable failure, and if the jury is governed by
law and evidence it must bring in a verdict of guilty. It
will be a sad day for Missouri when such a robber and
murderer is set free. We hope we may be mistaken, but
certainly things look suspicious about Gallatin.
> —Kansas City Journal, September 3, 1883

September 4, 1883
Gallatin, Missouri

He loved making speeches. That was one thing John F. Philips
had in common with Henry Clay Dean, or Frank James for
that matter. Everyone in the opera house probably expected
Governor Johnson to make the closing argument for the defense, but Philips took the stage late that morning after the attorneys had filed their instructions and listened to Judge
Goodman's rules for the final statements.

The truth of the matter was that Johnson had started working on his speech, had planned to make the case himself, but
Philips had had enough of Johnson's hell-with-everyone men-
tality hidden by his holier-than-thou facade. So had Frank
James.

The two attorneys had met the day before in the guerrilla's
jail cell, and as soon as Johnson began outlining his final statement, Frank James had cleared his throat and said, "Begging
your pardon, Governor, but if it's just the same to you, my
druthers are for Colonel Philips to make the speech."

It was the only time Philips had ever seen Johnson speechless.

"You see, Governor, Annie told me what happened with that Raymond Sloan fella—"

"I had nothing to do with that, Frank!"

"That's fine with me, Governor, and I appreciate all you did for me, how you and Mr. Rush picked the jury, your brilliant legal mind, all that. I'm not even upset, now, about how you run off Mr. Dean and Major Edwards. But I've been watching and listening to the two of you palaver in court, and, well, the colonel here is a damn fine lawyer, and if anyone has to plead my case one last time, it needs to be him. That is, sir, providing I have a say in the matter—which I didn't have regarding Dean, Edwards and Sloan—considering that I'm paying your fees."

"You can't . . ." Johnson began, but Frank James had silenced him with a wintry stare. "Guilty or innocent, I'll be having to talk to those newspaper reporters once the verdict comes in. It's your call, right now, as to how I'll speak of you and your deals, Governor."

Philips considered the jury briefly before beginning, hoping Frank James had made the right decision, praying that he wouldn't let his client down. "May it please the court," he said, nervously at first, but he knew that would pass, "and you gentlemen of the jury.

"Common fame has invested this defendant with unmerited notoriety—given to his life of romance," he said, pacing, his voice building with strength. "How much of truth and how much of fiction there is in it all, you and I know not in this trial. Under the broad shield of the constitution of the state, he stands before you in this courtroom as any other citizen. The bond of your oath is that you know him only as the evidence shows him to be. You are to take him where the evidence finds him and leave him where it places him."

He made sure to speak directly to the jurors, to maintain eye contact, to look secure. He talked briefly about the rumors regarding Frank James, gesturing two or three times at the defendant, who sat upright, wife and son at his side, mother behind him.

"What does the state's own testimony disclose?" Philips said. "In 1876 he left this state, with all his earthly possessions, a two-horse wagon and his young wife, and went to Tennessee. Everything about that movement indicated what? To my mind this is impressively significant. The miseries and ghosts of the war hung around his footsteps in Missouri. Weary and heartsick of it all, he determined to turn his back upon it, and seek a new home, under an assumed name, in the hope that he might find a new life of peace in humble, honest industry. He had just taken to his bosom and confidence a young, trusting, sweet woman. That of itself was highest proof that he was no longer seeking adventure, but that pleasure and happiness which come surest from domestic life and retirement."

Annie James didn't look happy at all. She sat wringing her hands, agony and anxiety stamped on her face. Philips couldn't blame her. The trial had exacted a heavy toll on the young woman, and the pressure would only build until the jury announced its verdict.

He went on singing the praises of Frank James before blasting the appearance of Dick Liddil, asking why Liddil's story should be believed and not the defendant's, then moved to the sewing machine.

"Mr. Wallace has discovered a real Trojan horse in this much-traveled sewing machine," he said, smirking at the prosecutor. "All that was left to the fugitive, panting, little wife of Frank James was her babe and the family sewing machine. Wallace has run that machine down with the whole detective force of two railroads, and all the express companies between Kentucky and Kansas. There is nothing in history or fiction comparable to this discovery of the efficient prosecuting attorney of Jackson County.

"I am now satisfied that the extraordinary effect put forth by Mr. Wallace to run down this sewing machine was to use this remarkable piece of evidence as a substitute for Dick Liddil's testimony, in the event the court should exclude Dick as an incompetent witness, he being a convicted thief."

Another swipe at Liddil. He liked that.

"It is unchivalrous to assail the character of a woman. When a woman falls, she goes lower than any other object of nature. As the rock which falls from the highest elevation sinks deepest into the earth, so the fallen woman sinks lowest. So with

Mrs. Bolton. She was a bad woman. After the death of poor Wood Hite a singular affinity sprang into existence between Dick Liddil and Mrs. Bolton. They were like two roses on the same stem. Ben Jonson says the last refuge of a scoundrel is turning patriot—hence Dick Liddil turned patriot.

"The men who swore to the identity of this man were sincere enough, but when Frank James surrendered, a great many men wanted it to appear that they had seen him before. I venture that there are at least a dozen men in Missouri who might have been identified as the bandit."

He continued, point by point, illustrating the flaws of the state's case while showing the logic of the defense. He wasn't sure how long he spoke, but no one seemed bored by the time he wrapped his package.

"Free men of Daviess County, let it not be said of your verdict that law and personal freedom have, in their march across the centuries, lost one atom of their vigor or virtue by being transplanted in American soil. Be brave and manly. If you err, let it be on the side of mercy. It is Godlike to be merciful; it is hellish to be revengeful. 'I will have mercy and not sacrifice,' said the Savior when on earth. Let your verdict be a loyal response to the evidence and the spirit of the law; and as true manhood ever wins tribute, when the passion of the day is past, and Reason has asserted her dominion, you will be honored and crowned."

Philips bowed at the jury box and returned to the defense table, discretely checking his pocket watch. He had been talking for three hours.

Judge Goodman's gavel popped. "We'll pick things up tomorrow morning with the state's closing argument," he announced.

September 5, 1883
Gallatin, Missouri

"You have quite a turnout," Hamilton whispered. "Senator Ingalls from Kansas, Senator Kenna of West Virginia, and those are just the ones I know about."

Wallace craned his neck, trying to be discreet, and examined the crowd. Although the temperature had dropped, the opera house felt like an oven, and hundreds of paper fans moved hypnotically back and forth, back and forth. He could recognize neither Ingalls nor Kenna, but his eyes stopped on one person in a calico dress sitting at the end of a middle row: a curly-haired, freckle-faced Missouri teen he had first seen in his Kansas City office back in January of eighty-one. Lizzie Wymore, whose brother had been murdered during the Liberty bank robbery in sixty-six. His hand dropped to his pants pocket, but the button she had given him wasn't there. The reminder must be somewhere in his hotel room, resting with spare change and matches in a pocket on another dirty pair of pants.

That was all right. He didn't need a button to remind him of his duty, of what he had to do this morning.

"All rise."

Wallace and Hamilton were already standing. He looked across the aisle at Annie James, holding her husband's hand tightly, nervous. Little Robert stood next to his surly-as-ever grandmother. Newspaper reporters were packed together so tightly, he didn't see how they'd be able to take notes.

"Mr. Wallace, are you ready?" Goodman asked.

Wallace answered and nodded his head, took a deep breath and slowly exhaled before stepping around the table. "May it please the court, and you gentlemen of the jury," he said, and started his delivery, pacing in front of the jury members, explaining the evidence, studying Frank James and his wife. Annie's lips trembled, and tears welled in her eyes, so he turned away. That was a mistake. Concentrate on the jury.

"You gentlemen," he said, "are the twelve pillars upon whose shoulders, for the present at least, Missouri's temple of justice is made to rest, and you could not help but notice how these men in the final argument, like blind Samsons groping in the dark, reached out to find you, threw their brawny arms about you and, to secure a firmer hold, thrust their fingers into every niche and scar left upon you by the bullets of a cruel war. Stand firm in your places as they press against you, lest

ou and they, the fair name of our state, and all that is nearest
nd dearest to her people, perish in the ruin that ensues.

"Who are the parties to be considered in this most important
rial? To come to an impartial and intelligent verdict it is well
o hear them all in memory. The first one that presents himself
o an unprejudiced mind is Frank McMillan, but it has been so
ong since you have heard his name that I almost feel like
pologizing for its mention. But it can do no harm—nor
;ood."

He wished he had a tintype or photograph of the dead stonemason to pass around the jury box. Since the defense phase of
he trial began, Frank McMillan had been pushed aside.

"For two years has his voice been hushed in death," Wallace
aid, "and even if I so desired, I could not now catch up the
aintest echo of his dying shriek and sound it in your ears,
leading for pity from your hearts, or justice at your hands."
Maybe that was too much, but Missouri farmers liked a big
peech, full of drama, and these twelve men filled that bill.
He was a poor, innocent, insignificant stonemason, who, in
he summer of 1881, with the pale blood oozing from his
rain, was laid away to rest." He raised his voice, pointing an-
rily at the defense attorneys. "For days have gifted attorneys
f his *gallant* slayer trod above his ashes, with scarcely a
vhisper of his fameless name. The evidence shows that he,
oo, had a wife—plain, humble woman no doubt, dependent
pon his daily toil for the food she ate and the raiment she
vore. Even now while I speak, with tattered garments and
treaming eyes she may sit upon his tomb, trying to fathom
hat mysterious providence by which her stay in life lies slum-
ering in the grave, while his murderer sits at his trial—'the
bserved of all observers,' 'the most remarkable man of the
ge.'" Facing the jury again. "Let her sit there, gentlemen. We
ave not brought her here as is oft times done, in piteous dis-
onsolate widowhood, to crave your sympathy. Let her sit
here."

He went on, chronicling the fifteen-year career of the James
jang, then moved to a subject he didn't want to bring up, but
new he had to.

"A third party, who though not a party to the record, is

touchingly presented to your view by opposing counsel."
Hamilton and Shanklin had made a pretty good case that
Annie James would be a sympathetic figure to the jury, and
thus Wallace needed to discredit her, somehow, some way.
Well, Hamilton and Shanklin might not agree with his meth-
ods, but they couldn't stop him now.

"I may run contrary to the wishes of my associates and to
the will of the good people of Daviess County," he said, "even
should I run the risk of losing the case by so doing, I want to
say that I have in my heart the profoundest sympathy for the
defendant's wife." Honest enough. He stared at her and
smiled, saw a lone tear roll down her left cheek. "I am glad she
is here, standing by her husband in this trial, and I am as willing that you should extend to her your sympathies as any attorney in the case. When the welcome day shall come and I shall
cease to be a public prosecutor, I shall at least have learned
what I might never have learned in purer spheres of life—and
that is that the truest, grandest, most unchanging thing beneath
the stars is a woman's love."

Again he faced the jurors. "Let a man once reign as king in
the heart of a true woman, and she is blind to all his faults, or
all his crimes. He may pillage, plunder, burn, rob—he may
shed blood until he sits at his trial as a red-plumed murderer—
but she sees it not."

He moved on now, distancing the prosecution from the railroads, saying that this was not a "railroad" prosecution, that
the railroad officials, unanimously despised by Missouri farmers, had no bearing in bringing Frank James to justice. Next he
discussed aspects of the law, and pointing out how and why
they must find the defendant guilty.

"The supremacy of the laws of Missouri and the strength
and dignity of her courts are at stake," he said. "Not only the
life of a human being, but the very life of the law itself is put
in issue in the eyes of the world. For fifteen years, it is
boasted, has Frank James successfully contended with the officers, the exponents of the law, and now with bold and uplifted
front he comes of his own accord into a court of justice,
throws down the gauntlet and proposes to grapple with the law
itself.

"And the question you are to decide is: Which is the stronger n Missouri, the arm of the bandit or the arm of the law?"

He let that sink in while crossing the room to the prosecution table, where he filled a tumbler with water and slaked his thirst. Step by step, he detailed the crime that had been committed on July 15, 1881, the robbery and the heartless killings of McMillan and Westfall. He pointed out every bit of testimony that had linked Frank James to the crime, and how nothing the defense had put forth discredited the state's case.

"You have it in your power, on overwhelming testimony, to proclaim justice for this horrible crime." He stopped in front of the defense table, and locked eyes with John F. Philips.

"Colonel Philips talked much about popular clamor, whose mighty storm he seemed so much to regret and fear, and he implored your bravery to stand against it." He looked at the jury again, walking to the twelve men. "So no matter who the defendant is, or was, or who his friends may be, we ask and implore you to stand bravely by your duty and your oaths given to your country and your God.

"Gentlemen, my task is ended." So was his voice. He had been talking for hours, and the pitcher of water on the state's table was empty. "May the 'God who ruleth in the armies of heaven, and doeth His pleasure amongst all the inhabitants of the earth' . . . 'who holdeth the hearts of all men in His hands, and turneth them as the rivers of water are turned' . . . may the God of the widow and the fatherless'—of McMillan's wife and child—come into your hearts, and guide you to a righteous verdict in this case. I thank you for your kind attention."

The applause surprised him. People began standing, clapping loudly, cheering, on both levels of the opera house. Goodman's gavel hammered repeatedly and he called for order, and Sheriff Crozier kept shouting, "Folks, all this noise must stop! I say all this noise must stop! You're in court!" It was no use. Nothing would halt the outburst.

Exhausted, Wallace collapsed in his chair.

"What time is it?" Hamilton asked.

No one answered. Only ten minutes had passed since Hamilton had asked the same question. They sat in the

cramped quarters of the prosecutor's courthouse office, waiting. Dinnertime had long passed, and the courthouse clock, as
in answer to Hamilton's question, chimed four times. John
Shanklin fingered out the remnants of snuff from his mouth,
screwed open a tin and placed a fresh pinch inside his gums.
Wallace stared outside at the crowded streets below.

Waiting.

He would never be able to enjoy, or even accept, this part of
the criminal justice system. It upset his stomach, made him
sweat, made him long to be teaching school or writing a boring newspaper story about the new hotel arrivals in Independence.

Waiting.

Shanklin was the first to hear the footsteps coming up the
stairs and down the hall. The old man gripped his spit can
tightly and stared at the door. Hamilton clenched his fists and
sat on the edge of his seat. Marcus Low burned his fingers
with the match he had just struck to light his cigar. Hicklin and
McDougal braced themselves against the wall as if facing a
firing squad. Wallace refused to look at the door, just kept
watching the people crowd the streets.

Two hours ago, the six prosecutors had almost wet their
pants at the sound of footsteps, but it had just been the county
clerk returning from dinner.

Waiting.

The footsteps stopped, and someone rapped slightly on the
door. Wallace's stomach and heart danced a jig.

"Come in," Hamilton said in a squeaky voice.

The door opened, and Sheriff Crozier's head appeared.
"Jury's back," he said.

No one responded.

Chapter 33

We have a criminal jury system which is superior to any in the world; and its efficiency is only marred by the difficulty of finding twelve men every day who don't know anything and can't read.

—Mark Twain

September 5, 1883
Gallatin, Missouri

That afternoon scene reminded Annie James of a gold rush, or at least how she pictured one. As soon as word spread that the jury had reached a verdict, men raced across the quagmire that once resembled city streets, shouting, slipping, sinking, charging toward the opera house as if chasing free whiskey. Children joined the men in the dash, while most—though certainly not all—of Gallatin's ladies acted a little more dignified and kept to the boardwalks and planks crossing the worst of the muddy streets.

She didn't see how the sheriff's deputies would be able to keep the crowd in control, but that wasn't her concern. She turned down an alley, slipped inside the side door Colonel Philips had told her about, and found a seat at the defense table. The colonel and Governor Johnson huddled in front of the makeshift judge's bench, talking excitedly, while the prosecutors sat silently, looking more dignified, or perhaps just nervous. As the front doors opened, men and women trickled in, racing to get the best seats, but soon the dam burst and a flood of men and boys, who apparently had seen Annie's route, stormed through the unlocked side door. Deputies standing near the jury box leaped down, shouting orders and hurrying to block the open door. A few tried to round up the unticketed crowd, but soon gave up as the dam burst at the front door and the opera house turned into bedlam.

Years had passed since she had vomited—back when she had morning sickness while pregnant with Robert—but the way her stomach felt, Annie would not bet against her having to run to that side door at any moment. She bowed her head and began reciting the Lord's Prayer, wringing her hands, trying to block out the din surrounding her and keep the bile a respectful distance down her throat.

"Mommy?"

She opened her eyes to find Robert and Mrs. Samuel beside her, and pulled her son closer, unable to hold back the tears, and opened her right arm to embrace her mother-in-law, as well. "It'll be all right," she whispered. "Everything will be all right." Little Robert sobbed, too, although he couldn't comprehend why his mother and grandmother cried.

"Four hours. Is that good or bad?" Hamilton asked.

Wallace answered with a shake of his head, followed by a shrug. Considering all the testimony the jury had to sort through, he had not expected a verdict this soon. No one had. Stunned reporters crammed into the press area. Annie James sat in tears with her son and Zerelda Samuel. The sheriff's deputies had finally brought the courtroom into some semblance of control by the time Judge Goodman took his seat, told the sheriff to bring in the prisoner and hammered his gavel to stop the rising noise.

He looked drained of emotion, but Frank James still sported a confident air, and his presence did more to silence the crowd than Goodman's gavel. Two deputies escorted him to his seat at the defense table, and he gripped Annie's hand after sitting down.

The opera house had turned deathly silent. "Bring in the jury, Mr. Sheriff," Goodman ordered.

The twelve men filed silently inside, looking straight ahead, not at the judge, not at the defendant, not at the attorneys.

Their faces remained as blank as they had been throughout the trial. Hell, Wallace thought, they hadn't even broken a sweat during the hottest of days.

"Gentlemen of the jury," Goodman said with quiet dignity, "have you arrived at a verdict?"

"We have," answered Foreman William Richardson. He had close-cropped gray hair, dark mustache, thick salt-and-pepper chin whiskers and elephantine ears. Holding out a slip of paper, he looked directly at the judge.

"Hand up your verdict," Goodman ordered.

Wallace's eyes followed the paper as it passed from Richardson's hand to Crozier's to Goodman's. The judge unfolded it, glanced at it briefly, his face as expressionless as any member of the jury, and looked directly at Frank James. "The defendant will rise."

The only noise came from the shuffling of feet and the scraping of chair legs.

"State of Missouri versus Frank James—murder," Goodman read. Wallace felt his heart thumping. He couldn't remember the last time he had been this nervous. "We, the jury in the above entitled cause, find the defendant not guilty as charged in the indictment."

Frank heard Annie's gasp and turned to her, saw the color returning to her face as if by magic, and embraced his wife. She pulled away, beaming, looking like the old Annie Ralston, happy-go-lucky, not afraid of the devil himself. She bowed graciously at the jury and swooped up Robert in her arms. Her nervous tears had become tears of joy.

No one spoke immediately. Too stunned, Frank James figured, and Colonel Philips slowly turned and offered his hand. Someone in the upper balcony began clapping, and the applause spread, growing louder and louder. A few hours ago, the cheers had been for prosecutor William Wallace's speech, but now they were directed at the man of the hour. Men were so fickle. Unable to control his grin, he said, "'O heaven! were man but constant, he were perfect.'"

"What's that?" asked Colonel Philips, pumping his hand, shouting to be heard above the cacophony.

"Thank you!" Frank shouted back. "I can never repay you for all you have done!"

Philips winked. "Take your wife and little boy and acquit yourself as I believe you can, and I'll have my reward!"

"I shall do it, sir," he said, and turned back to kiss Annie and his mother. Across the room, Wallace, Hamilton and the other stone-faced prosecutors, struck dumb, stared blankly ahead, probably not seeing a damned thing.

The echoes of the gavel faded with the cheers and applause. Order restored, Judge Goodman thanked and dismissed the jury and asked that any more business of the court be brought forward at this time. No one spoke until Frank James and his attorneys finished their handshakes and settled into their chairs.

Not guilty? Frank James was guilty as hell. How could twelve decent men have reached a verdict of innocence? John Shanklin simply spit tobacco juice into his peaches can while William Wallace just sat there, shoulders sagged, drained. Not guilty.

"Mr. Hamilton?" Goodman asked.

Hamilton forced down whatever it was that had been stuck in his throat and pushed himself to his feet, not really knowing what he would say, dreading having to meet with all the reporters later, wondering what repercussions the verdict would have on his aspiring political career. Well, he could always blame the outcome on Wallace. He had been the lead prosecutor. No, not now. Maybe the old William Decatur Hamilton would have done that, but not after all they had been through. Together they had tried a hell of a case, maybe not perfect, but certainly one that should have resulted in a guilty verdict.

"Your Honor," Hamilton said, surprised at the strength of his voice. "May it please the court, the defendant, though acquitted of the charge today, still faces other indictments in Daviess County." He could hear the rumblings behind him from those so-called friends of Frank James. "He has been charged as an accessory to the murder of conductor William Westfall and for the murder of Captain Sheets. He also faces indictments elsewhere in Missouri, Minnesota, Alabama, and must be considered a flight risk. The people ask that he be returned to custody at this time."

Goodman's gavel banged away as the judge and sheriff called for order. This time, the reaction seemed mixed: a smattering of applause, a few cheers, boos, curses, hurrahs, groans.

"So noted," Goodman said. "The charges shall be carried over to the October term of this court. Sheriff, before you escort the prisoner back to jail, I am ordering the saloon closed for the remainder of the day, not to reopen until five o'clock tomorrow afternoon."

Crozier cleared his throat. "Do that include the liquor they serve at the Alpine Palace restaurant, yer honor?"

"Yes, sir, it does. No intoxicating spirits are to be served at any public establishment! This court is adjourned!"

This time, Goodman's gavel couldn't silence the hisses and heckles.

September 6, 1883
Gallatin, Missouri

The good people of Gallatin, Missouri, presented him with a gold watch, but Wallace politely declined, saying as a public servant, he couldn't accept such a generous gift. He did take a cigar from William Hamilton, and the two attorneys shook hands. Bags packed—Colt Thunderer and shoulder rig resting among his dirty clothes—Wallace checked out of the Alpine Palace Hotel and walked outside.

Normalcy had returned to Gallatin. The muddy streets were empty except for a few riders on horseback, a family in a wagon and one empty omnibus. "Need a ride to the depot?" the driver asked.

"No, thanks," Wallace answered and lit the cigar. "I'll walk. Got some errands to run first."

He crossed the street for the courthouse, where he met one diligent reporter, writing tablet and pencil at the ready.

"Will you dismiss the other charges facing Frank James?" he asked.

"No," he answered, walking as he talked. "I'm certain about one thing, and that is Frank James will stand trial again. I sent Bill Ryan to prison with nowhere near the evidence I had against Frank James."

"Upset at the jury?"

"You don't get upset in this business. Nothing's personal. The jury must live with its decision."

"They all checked out of the hotels in a hurry," the reporter said with a smile. "Probably figured they'd be lynched."

Or voted mayor, Wallace thought.

"Can I get your reaction to some comments, sir?" He didn't wait for an answer, simply flipped back a few pages and read, "This is from Frank James himself. 'The prosecuting attorney has no malice for me. He ought to enter a nolle prosequi in the other cases. He admits that they have tried their strongest case and I have convinced twelve good honest men that I am innocent of the crime charged, and I am prepared to convince the people of Missouri that I was not in any of the robberies charged to me.' Do you agree with Mr. James, sir? Can the state win the other cases against him? Are you wasting taxpayers' money pursuing a living legend?"

"As long as I think I have a case against Frank James, I'll take him to court."

He scribbled the answer, flipped another page and said, "This comes from Robert Ford. He found out at some theater in Indianapolis where he's performing in a play. 'I never believed that it was possible for the jury to acquit, knowing as I did that he was guilty.' He goes on to say he had wagered a thousand dollars that very afternoon that Frank James would have been found guilty. No, he offered to make the wager, didn't actually bet it."

"Lucky him," Wallace said, and left the reporter outside as he entered the sheriff's office.

"You gave a good speech there at the end, Mr. Wallace," Frank James said from his jail cell. "Almost applauded myself. I particularly liked the part where you said, 'When the welcome day shall come and I shall cease to be a public prosecutor,' because I will welcome that day as well." He stuck his hand through the iron bars, and Wallace considered shaking the proffered hand, but couldn't. He had to concede the prisoner had an affable nature, but they were separated by more than just bars.

"I will prosecute you, sir," he said, "to the fullest extent of the law. That's my job. It's not personal."

"No?"

"It has nothing to do with . . ." He stopped himself, regained his focus and said, "I plan to pursue a case against you and Charlie Ford for the Blue Cut robbery."

The outlaw winked. "Well, sir," he said, "when I beat that one, too, you are welcome to come join Annie and me for supper sometime. I reckon she'd like to see you."

Wallace had reached the door that led to the sheriff's office when the bushwhacker called out without a trace of malice in his voice, "I'll tell Annie you dropped by to say hello."

February 12, 1884
Kansas City, Missouri

His coffee had turned cold, but Wallace really didn't care. He wasn't in the mood to drink, eat, or even work. He still felt sick from yesterday's proceedings when he had stood on the doorsteps of the Jackson County Courthouse in Independence and announced, with regret, that the State of Missouri was dismissing charges against Frank James and Charles Ford for the Blue Cut train robbery of 1881.

Everyone knew that had been coming. In November, William Hamilton had been forced to drop the charge against James for the Westfall killing. The man had been acquitted of murdering Frank McMillan during the same robbery, so another trial would waste taxpayers' money, and the Daviess County solicitor had been granted a continuance in the Sheets murder case, but that would never come to trial. Then in December, the Missouri Supreme Court ruled that a witness convicted of a felony could not competently testify for the prosecution. Dick Liddil had never received a full pardon for his 1874 horse-stealing conviction, and he had been Wallace's star witness for the Blue Cut trial. For the next two months, Wallace had tried to come up with more evidence, but it was hopeless, so the case was scrapped.

Frank James, at least temporarily, had won again.

The door opened, without a knock, and Wallace blinked in recognition at the carrot-topped, curly-haired, freckle-faced teen in bonnet, coat and over-gaiters who he had first met in this very office and later seen briefly on the last day of the Frank James trial in Gallatin.

"Hello," Lizzie Wymore said.

He fished the black button from his vest pocket, studied it a moment and offered it to the girl. "I let you down, Lizzie," he said, his voice barely audible. "I guess you want this back."

She shook her head. "You done your best, I warrant. Ain't your fault that high court said your witness can't testify. Ain't your fault that the jury didn't do its job in Gallatin last fall." She wiped away a tear, pursed her lips, and the two just sat in silence.

"Arm of the bandit," she eventually said, rising to leave.

"How's that?" Wallace asked.

"It's like you said when you was speechifyin' in September. You said somethin' 'bout which be stronger in Missouri, the arm of the law or the arm of the bandit. Well, now we know."

He had to tell her something, had to make her feel better, so he cleared his throat. "Lizzie, the U.S. marshal plans to arrest Frank James next week and take him to Alabama. He'll stand trial there for the robbery of that federal paymaster."

She shook her head as she opened the door. "I reckon it don't matter, Mr. Wallace. He'll get off scot-free on that charge, too. The James boys was always bigger'n the law. An' it don't make no nevermind to me no more. Ma died day after Christmas. Heartache, the preacher man said. I dunno. Law can't bring her back. Can't bring Jolly back, neither. Frank James'll pay his debt one day . . . to God. That's all that matters. So long, Mr. Wallace. Thanks for tryin'."

He stared at the button, remembering the first rule he had learned as an attorney: never take cases personally. Lizzie Wymore was right. The people of Missouri had spoken, had chosen Frank James over the law. Well, so be it. There were other criminals in Jackson County he had to try, and if he wanted to keep his job, he had to stop moping around. He pulled open a drawer, dropped the button inside and headed for the door, whirled around and fetched his mug.

His coffee needed warming up.

Epilogue

Frank James, today, is the biggest man in Missouri. The Missouri Democracy should now unite in presenting his name as a candidate for president in the next Democratic National Convention.
     —*Salina* (Kansas) *County Journal,* September 13, 1883

February 20, 1915
Kearney, Missouri

His wife gripped his hand as he limped past the coffin, saw the old man with a waxlike face lying inside, rose pinned to the lapel of his black Prince Albert. The deceased looked at peace, and Judge William H. Wallace nodded a polite good-bye before heading down the aisle to find a seat in the old James family home. On the front row of chairs were Cole Younger, who looked ready for a coffin himself, white-haired John Philips and a handful of state dignitaries. Across the aisle sat the family: Annie James; her son, approaching middle age now, and his wife; and behind them Jesse's two kids and others Wallace didn't recognize, maybe because he concentrated on Annie James. Her black veil reminded him of the time she had come to his office thirty-three years earlier, looking to see what kind of terms she could get for the surrender of her husband. She had been a dazzling young woman then, the envy of many a man—William Wallace included—but now, shoulders sagging, white handkerchief clenched tightly in her right hand, she looked like the recluse she had become, a heartbroken woman whose best friend had been called to Glory at last.

"You all right?" his wife, Elizabeth, asked as he dropped heavily onto an empty folding chair.

"Yeah," he said, patting her hand. They had been married . . . what was it now? . . . why, twenty-eight years come June, had a daughter and a son, both grown although still at home, looking after, they said, their aging parents. A good marriage, a great wife. He had truly been blessed with a loving woman. In that regard, he and Frank James had much in common.

John F. Philips used a cane to stand up, cross the aisle to say a few kind whispers to Annie and Robert, then stepped onto the makeshift podium to begin his eulogy. The last time Wallace had seen Colonel Philips—and Frank and Annie James, for that matter—had been at General Jo Shelby's funeral eighteen years ago. That long? He shook his head.

"About a year ago," Philips began, "at the Hotel Baltimore in Kansas City, Frank James took me to one side and said, 'You and I are getting old and soon both of us will go. I know no other man I prefer to speak such words as your heart will prompt at my death.'" The colonel's voice trembled, and he had to pause before continuing. "'I want you to promise to make my oration.' That is why I am here."

This was how Frank James would have wanted his funeral. No press, no church, just family and friends, and Wallace couldn't deny that somehow over the years he had grown to like and admire some qualities in Alexander Franklin James. He had befriended the old bushwhacker, and not just because of Annie.

Wallace only half listened as Philips told how he had first met Frank James. He knew that story well, and he thought about all the events that had passed since the Gallatin trial of 1883.

He had lost touch with William Hamilton, although he heard his colleague had married and was involved in politics but had never made it to the governor's mansion as he had once hoped. Likewise with Charles P. Johnson. John Shanklin and the other prosecuting attorneys had either died, moved or just been forgotten. John Newman Edwards fell dead of a heart attack in Jefferson City in 1889, and the state mourned the loss as if the old major were royalty. Bill Ryan was paroled after ten years in the state prison and disappeared. Not many who had been involved in the great trial of the previous century were still around.

After leaving the governor's office in 1885, Thomas Theodore Crittenden served as consul general in Mexico City from 1893 to 1897, returned to Missouri and was serving as referee of bankruptcy in Kansas City when he fell dead at age seventy-seven in 1909.

Dick Liddil had gone east and done well for himself running horses, his own, and died in the summer of 1901 while watching the thoroughbreds race. The Ford boys, on the other hand, had not fared as well. Ever morose, Charlie took to morphine in addition to John Barleycorn, contracted consumption, and killed himself in the spring of eighty-four. Brother Robert joined him on June 8, 1892, when a man named Ed O'Kelly gave the killer of Jesse James two loads of buckshot from a scattergun at point-blank range in some hellhole in Creede, Colorado. "I don't pull off women's toenails with pincers," O'Kelly said, "but I can kill such men as Bob Ford." Imprisoned briefly, O'Kelly was gunned down a few years later in Oklahoma.

And what of Frank James? He had been acquitted of the Alabama robbery in April of 1884 only to be indicted for the 1876 Boonville, Missouri, robbery, but the following February, the Cooper County solicitor dismissed the charge after his star witness died of cerebral apoplexy. Outgoing Governor Crittenden refused to extradite James until all of Missouri cases had been settled, and the Minnesota lawmen got tired of waiting, dropped the case, and Frank James became a free man.

He lived a quiet life with Annie and Robert in Missouri, Texas and Oklahoma but, to support his wife and son, toured with the recently paroled Cole Younger in 1903 and took to acting in plays for a spell after leaving the Frank James & Cole Younger Wild West Show. After Zerelda Cole James Simms Samuel's death in 1911, Frank and Annie moved back to the Kearney farm, where Frank greeted visitors, posed for an occasional Kodak, although cameras were barred on the farm, and charged four bits' admission to hear his stories and our the old house where the James boys grew up and hid out. Annie never cared for the constant traffic, so Frank had ordered one of those do-it-yourself house additions from some catalog and put up two new rooms, one where Annie could sew and keep away from prying tourists. Two days ago, Frank James had collapsed in his bedroom and had been pronounced dead at two fifty that afternoon from a heart attack, maybe a stroke. He was seventy-two.

The outlaw remembered what souvenir seekers had done to his brother's grave, chipping away at the headstone till nothing remained, and so had asked Annie to cremate his body, store his ashes in a vault, and maybe, after the Good Lord called Annie away, they could be buried together somewhere. By then, he figured, most folks would have forgotten about Frank and Jesse James.

"He has endured the scoff of the world and, by fortitude and courage, has succeeded at the end of a tragic life," Philips concluded. "As I look on his inanimate face I think of what Shakespeare said: 'He that died, pays all debts.'" The old colonel bowed toward Annie and hobbled back to his seat. An organ began playing, and mourners filed outside. Wallace stood to leave as well, but Robert James tugged his coat sleeve and said, "Mr. Wallace, sir, Mom desires a few words with you."

He shook her small hand, gestured to Elizabeth and said, "I'm not sure you remember my wife, Elizabeth, you recall Annie . . . Ralston."

"Annie James," she corrected, and he smiled.

"You'll always be Annie Ralston to me."

She lifted a veil, wiped away a few tears and said, her voice soft but strong, "I thank you for that, William. Thank you both for coming."

Elizabeth spoke up. "William talked of you and Frank often. Your husband truly loved you."

"No finer husband lived," Annie said with a nod. "You have a good man, yourself."

"I do, indeed."

Automobile engines began sputtering to life in the cold outside, causing a few nervous horses and mules to snort and stamp their hooves. "We should be getting along, Annie," Wallace said. "I'm truly sorry for your loss."

"Thanks again for seeing an old friend, William. God bless you."

They hugged briefly. Annie sat back down as Cole Younger came to pay his respects. Wallace and his wife walked away, but halfway down the aisle he turned around, asked her to wait and went to the casket before the lid was closed and taken to the railroad to be shipped to a St. Louis crematorium. He stared at the pale face of Frank James.

No one would ever know for sure if Frank James had been aboard that train at Winston, if he indeed had killed the stonemason. The jury said he was innocent, and Annie admitted years ago that Frank had told her Wood Hite or Jesse had killed McMillan, but William Wallace could never be certain. Nor could anyone testify truthfully that Frank James had murdered Captain Sheets in Gallatin. The only people alive who knew Frank James had killed the cashier in Northfield were Cole Younger, Annie and himself, and none would ever talk, especially Judge William Hockaday Wallace. He owed Annie that much. Besides, it was hearsay and no longer mattered.

Frank James was dead. For three decades, he had lived a peaceful life. That had to mean something. It was like Lizzie Wymore had told him back in eighty-four. *Frank James'll pay his debt one day . . . to God.* Colonel Philips had reiterated that remark in his eulogy, quoting the bushwhacker's favorite author. *He that died, pays all debts.* "The case is closed," he said in a hoarse whisper. "May God have mercy on your soul."

Not really knowing why, Wallace fished out the two pieces of a broken black button and slipped them into the outlaw's coat pocket. He glanced once more at the outlaw's face before limping toward Elizabeth, waiting for him at the door.

Author's Note

Although I have used actual quotes and letters whenever possible and followed the documented course of the surrender and trial of Frank James (with a few minor changes for the purpose of narrative structure), *Arm of the Bandit* is a work of fiction. Almost every person in this novel existed in history, but all characterizations are my own inventions. As far is history is concerned, there was no love interest between William Wallace and Ann Ralston James, although the two did know each other, at least in passing, before she married Frank James. Likewise, the rivalries between prosecutors Wallace and Hamilton, and defense counselors Philips and Johnson, come from my imagination. History labels John Newman Edwards and Jo Shelby alcoholics, but lawyer Raymond Sloan probably was no thug. Whether Daviess County sheriff George Crozier and defense attorney William Rush conspired to seat a jury sympathetic to Frank James has been pondered for more than a century, but Wallace did witness the sheriff consulting a list while summoning the venire facias and threatened to quit after Judge Goodman's ruling, much as described in the preceding pages.

I have also expanded the defense phase of the trial and contacted the closing arguments. Defense witnesses actually testified on August 30 and 31, 1883, while closing arguments began September 1 and continued September 3–5, after which the jury was charged and reached its verdict in less than four hours. Although all attorneys were allowed to speak, I limited final statements to two days and let only Wallace and Philips make their final cases.

Annie James, by the way, survived her husband almost thirty years, dying at age ninety-one in an Excelsior Springs,

Missouri, sanitarium in 1944. Her ashes were mixed with her husband's, and their remains were buried at Hill Park, not far from her childhood home in Independence. John F. Philips, Charles P. Johnson and William H. Wallace died in 1919, 1920 and 1937, respectively.

The biggest obstacle in writing a novel about this trial is that transcripts, as with a myriad criminal cases during the 1800s, have been lost. Many records and newspaper accounts in Gallatin, Missouri, were also destroyed by fire. Luckily, two books cover the Gallatin trial and proved invaluable in my research. *The Trial of Frank James for Murder* was published in 1898 by George Miller Jr. A century later, Texas Tech University Press published *Judgment at Gallatin: The Trial of Frank James* by Gerard S. Petrone. Those are fine starting points for anyone wishing to read more about this trial.

Other helpful works included *Speeches and Writings of Wm. H. Wallace with Autobiography,* published in 1914; *Frank and Jesse James: The Story Behind the Legend* by Ted P. Yeatman (Cumberland House, 2000); *Jesse James: The Man and the Myth* by Marley Brant (Berkley, 1998); *Jesse and Frank James: The Family History* by Phillip W. Steele (Pelican, 1987); and the September 28, 1883, edition of The Wide Awake Library, *The Life and Trial of Frank James.* Period newspapers, particularly the *St. Joseph Daily Gazette* and *Topeka Daily Capital,* were equally invaluable.

The folks at the Jesse James Home, Liberty Bank and Jesse James Farm museums proved friendly and a tremendous help as well as the archival staffs at several public libraries, most prominently Boise, Kansas City, River Bluffs Regional, St. Louis, Salina, and Topeka and Shawnee County.

As always, my wife, Lisa Smith, was my first copy editor and sounding board. I'd also be remiss without praising my editor, Dan Slater, who—though I cursed him, threatened him and considered hanging him in effigy during the writing process—is a great editor and a good friend. He turned this novel into a much better book.

Johnny D. Boggs
Santa Fe, New Mexico
December 27, 2001

JUDSON GRAY

RANSOM RIDERS   20418-2

When Penn and McCutcheon are ambushed on
their way to rescue a millionaire's kidnapped
niece, they start to fear that the kidnapping was an
inside job.

DOWN TO MARROWBONE   20158-2

Jim McCutcheon had squandered his Southern
family's fortune and had to find a way to rebuild it
among the boomtowns.
Jake Penn had escaped the bonds of slavery and
had to find his long-lost sister...
Together, they're an unlikely team—but with
danger down every trail, nothing's worth more
than a friend you can count on...

S308

JASON MANNING

Mountain Passage   0-451-19569-8

Leaving Ireland for the shores of America, a young man loses his parents en route—one to death, one to insanity—and falls victim to the sadistic captain on the ship. Luckily, he is befriended by a legendary Scottish adventurer, whom he accompanies to the wild American frontier. But along the way, new troubles await...

Mountain Massacre   0-451-19689-9

Receiving word that his mother has passed away, mountain man Gordon Hawkes reluctantly returns home to Missouri to pick up the package she left for him. Upon arrival, he is attacked by a posse looking to collect the bounty on his head. In order to escape, Hawkes decides to hide out among the Mormons and guide them to their own promised land. But the trek turns deadly when the religious order splits into two factions...with Hawkes caught in the middle!

Mountain Courage   0-451-19870-0

Gordon Hawkes's hard-won peace and prosperity are about to be threatened by the bloody clouds of war. While Hawkes is escorting the Crow tribe's yearly annuity from the U. S. government, the Sioux ambush the shipment. Captured, Hawkes must decide whether to live as a slave, die as a prisoner, or renounce his life and join the Sioux tribe. His only hope is his son Cameron, who must fight his father's captors and bring Hawkes back alive.

To Order Call: 1-800-788-6262

S575